IGUIN

Summer Fever

Summer Fever

KATE RIORDAN

PENGUIN BOOKS

PENGUIN BOOKS

UK | USA | Canada | Ireland | Australia
India | New Zealand | South Africa

Penguin Books is part of the Penguin Random House group of companies
whose addresses can be found at global.penguinrandomhouse.com.

First published 2022
001

Copyright © Kate Riordan, 2022

The moral right of the author has been asserted

Set in 12.5/14.75pt Garamond MT Std
Typeset by Jouve (UK), Milton Keynes
Printed and bound in Great Britain by Clays Ltd, Elcograf S.p.A.

The authorized representative in the EEA is Penguin Random House Ireland,
Morrison Chambers, 32 Nassau Street, Dublin D02 YH68

A CIP catalogue record for this book is available from the British Library

ISBN: 978-1-405-94998-9

www.greenpenguin.co.uk

For all the excellent women in my life

Day 12

When it's over, you pick yourself up, ears ringing, and look around. You shed dust as you do, like you're made of it. To your surprise, the world is still there. Behind you, the outbuildings remain standing, more or less. As the earth settles and the moonlight begins to filter through again, their silhouettes still approximate buildings, though one is lost, reduced to rubble.

'Come on,' you say, putting out your hand. 'Get up. It's over.'

The two of you stumble uphill towards the villa. You expect to see it collapsed, or at least mortally wounded: a foot-wide crack fissuring straight through the stucco. There is fallen masonry and the line of the roof looks wrong, like an old mouth without its false teeth, but it's basically OK. Luna Rossa is still standing.

PART ONE

The Previous October

They have been searching for two tense hours. Laura blames Nick for this. He probably blames her. She has lost count of their false turns: wild tracks of pale rubble that narrow to nothing. She has a headache from squinting at the map that bears no relation to the landscape around them.

The afternoon is overcast. Bottom-heavy clouds bear down on them as they skirt the hills in their little rented Fiat. It's late October and the night swoops down fast here in autumn. Tomorrow they fly home, back to London.

She's worried that none of this augurs well for their grand plan, that this house they're trying to find – which the agent has assured them is *molto bella*, The One, a rare treasure no one else has even seen yet – will be another disappointment: either dark and forbidding, without floors or running water, or becoming wildly expensive as soon as they register any proper interest. Signor Ricci's manner, languid as a Sunday afternoon, has begun to grate. She doubts he has the English to comprehend it, and she certainly doesn't have the Italian, but she wants to say to him, *Do you know how important this is? We're not looking for a holiday home. We need a new life.*

They turn off the road and start bumping down yet another *strada bianca*. It's crowded with misshapen olive trees, whose arthritic fingers reach out to scratch the Fiat's paintwork. That they're probably a thousand years old, that the rough road beneath the wheels was probably laid down before the birth of Christ, no longer feels romantic.

She rests a hand on her stomach and Nick, glancing over, slows down slightly. It's flat but it would be, at eight weeks. That's the thing about IVF. One of the many *things*. You know virtually from the second you're pregnant. Last night, at the guesthouse they're staying in, run by a smiling octogenarian who insists they call her Nonna, she had been kept awake by strange stretching pains in her abdomen. Was this good? A sign of healthy growth? Or would it herald her third miscarriage? In the dark room, she picked up her phone.

'Don't do it,' Nick mumbled, still half asleep, as the screen lit up. 'Don't go in those chatrooms.'

Then he'd pulled her in to his warm body and she had let the phone drop silently onto the soft rug beside the bed.

The lane goes on and she's just about to say they should give up when the trees abruptly part. They are in a clearing that ends in a tumbled wall, beyond which is a sheer drop to a valley, vast and green-swathed. Nick brakes so hard that the car shunts them forward in their seat belts. His arm goes out to hold her back. The whole thing is so unexpected that it feels like a bribe, offered up just as they were losing patience. As if Italy herself had spoken: *Aspettate, Signore!, Signora! Wait!*

They get out, blinking. While they've been driving, eyes sore from looking out for fallen signposts and speeding drivers on the wrong side of the road, the sun has broken through, sinking low enough to light the undersides of the clouds, burnishing them gold in a way that looks celestial.

'Jesus,' says Nick, 'it's like a bloody fresco. All we're missing is a couple of angels.'

'Do you think someone went over that?' She points to the ruined wall, the car's-width gap in the stones.

'Some *capo* getting whacked for turning informer, probably,' says Nick. 'Had his brake cables cut.' He scissors his fingers and she laughs.

The house is just visible beyond a large cypress at the far edge of the clearing. The land falls away so steeply beneath it that the front façade appears to float over the valley. As they approach, the house's stucco blushes rose-gold. In places it has cracked and fallen, revealing the stone beneath, but this decay only contrives to make the place lovelier. Black iron balconies curl and twist beneath the upstairs windows. The largest pair, centrally placed, must lead to the master bedroom, or perhaps even a suite. She imagines a claw-foot bath from which she could watch summer showers move across the valley, shadowing the green velvet draped so artfully over ancient rock. At that moment, a hill-top village in the distance is spot-lit by the sun, grey walls and terracotta roofs dialled up to ochre and carmine.

For years, she had browsed Italian property online, sending Nick links, fantasizing about a new life in a new country; a rambling old house of a size they could never afford in England made beautiful and rented out to guests. But it had been little more than a game until the second miscarriage. After that, relocating became Laura's alternative, an actual plan B. She knew Nick wasn't sure, but they struck a deal: if the third round of IVF didn't work, he would seriously consider it.

Her heart has begun to beat fast. She feels a sort of

7

desperation that Nick won't see what she's seeing, that he won't get that this place is *it*. I'll die if I lose this house as well, she thinks, in all seriousness. *As well*. She already feels certain she will miscarry again. It's just a matter of when. She glances at her husband, who is already at the front door, fitting the enormous iron key Ricci gave them into the lock.

You owe me this, Nick, she thinks, one of those hard little thoughts that come unbidden now, but then the door swings in and he turns back to her with a smile. She can see her own excitement reflected in his face. It's still a beloved face. Softening, she goes towards him, and towards Villa Luna Rossa.

The Following May

Luna Rossa is theirs. They live here in Italy now. Whenever Laura thinks about this fact, she gets a jolt, a tiny electric shock that they have so thoroughly abandoned their old lives for this new one. The audacity of it makes her like herself more than she has in years. Perhaps ever.

It was two weeks after finding the villa that a sonographer told her the pregnancy had failed. There hadn't been any bleeding: it was a *missed miscarriage*. In its eagerness to prepare for pregnancy, her body had failed to realize that the embryo had stopped developing. Distracted by the hum of its own industry, it hadn't noticed the tiny heart slowing and finally stopping.

She has thought a lot about that last beat. Judging by the measurements, the heart had stopped when they were in Italy. Probably it was just in the night, when she was fathoms deep in sleep, but maybe it was as she climbed the metal steps to board the plane at Ancona airport, nervous because she never liked flying but pleasantly taken up by thoughts of the villa which had already entranced her.

She had expected the pregnancy to go wrong, like the others. Of course she had. Simultaneously, she had also believed this one would stick. Partly because she'd felt more nauseous and exhausted than the other times, but also – absurdly – because *third time lucky*. Instead, and because she hadn't miscarried in the proper way – the kind Nonna's beautiful white sheets spared – she would have to take pills to make her uterus contract so hard that what the nurses called the *pregnancy material* would *come away*. Such tidy euphemisms. It was either the pills or a D&C under general anaesthetic and she'd decided she'd rather be at home.

'Do you want a picture?' the sonographer said after that final scan, while Laura got dressed. 'Some do. But you don't have to.'

She had never said yes before. She only nodded this time because it was the end of the road. The sonographer pressed a button and a glossy monochrome square, like a Polaroid, was spat out. There, in the dark and strange terrain of her womb, was something small and white. She couldn't remember when an embryo officially became a foetus. Whatever it was called, it wasn't a baby, not yet. Lots of women thought of it like that, of course, and she totally got it. She just couldn't do it herself. The heartbeats, though. They were difficult to get past. The associations with a beating heart and life, a stopped heart and death, were very difficult to sever.

As she tucked the photograph into the inside pocket of her bag, it occurred to her that she alone knew she wouldn't be a mother – she and this kind sonographer whose badge said Mila. No one else in the world.

'Your name,' she'd said vaguely, as she zipped up her boots and reached for her coat. 'It's pretty.' And Mila had smiled sadly.

Nick knew soon enough, of course. She'd rung him once she left the windowless room of pale plastic and scuffed walls. But even then her body hadn't known, not as she got into an Uber and was taken home by a blessedly silent driver, and not when she discovered what was on Nick's iPad while she waited for him to come back from work. And perhaps that was the strangest thing of all. She felt obscurely sorry for her body as it continued to prepare for the pregnancy: the hormones ramping up, the uterus walls thickening. That all of it was continuing, entirely pointlessly, seemed pathetic in the gentler sense of the word no one really used any more: *to be pitied*.

She and Nick haven't talked about any of this since they took possession of Luna Rossa. In truth, she doesn't even allow herself to think about it, or at least not in the house. She goes outside, if she needs to: there's a quiet corner by the linden trees, which you can't see from the villa. Sometimes, she takes the scan picture with her, only bringing it out when she's sure she's not being observed.

A superstitious little voice in her head likes to tell her that falling in love with the idea of another life abroad made it happen – that her and Nick's deal somehow signalled to the gods that she wanted Italy more than she wanted a child. She's getting better and better at silencing it, though. As the days get hotter, the awful winter before they left London more distant, she hardly lets it speak at all.

It's her favourite time of day now, mellow, soul-soothing dusk, the garden cooling fast because it's still chilly once the sun has gone. This is when the voice is quietest, and also when she and Nick get on best: the never-ending list of jobs that need doing on the villa abandoned, a bottle of wine opened, plans for dinner vaguely coming together.

She tucks the picture into the back pocket of her shorts and sets off towards the kitchen.

Tonight they can't be bothered to cook properly. Laura rubs garlic into long slices of toasted ciabatta and douses them in the olive oil they buy down the road, in big tins like petrol canisters. Even the precious first press, a delicate pale green but tasting of peppered sunshine, is a ridiculous bargain here in the Marche region. Squeezed between the knobbled spine of the Apennines and the Adriatic, no one at home had ever heard of it. 'It's east of Tuscany but cheaper,' she'd ended up saying, as short-hand. She piles the burnt-edged bread with tomatoes chopped up with tiny black olives, anchovies and basil. Her shoulder muscles ache from decorating the smallest guest room, but in a good way.

They sit at the inherited kitchen table, too big to remove, the wood pale and silken from decades of scrubbing, and remind each other of what they would be doing if they were still in London – what their friends are still doing in this very instant, trapped on the tube in the tunnels beneath the city, breathing in the stale heat of strangers, teeth gritted against wheel-shriek on the bends. What she would be doing: sitting through an overrunning staff meeting, maybe, or wading through a pile of year-ten essays on *Macbeth*.

Laura doesn't miss much about their old life, but it's at the end of a day of physical work on the villa – cleaning paintbrushes, switching off the sewing-machine – when she feels most exultant, most certain they've done the right thing. These enchanted hours are when it's possible to banish all her doubts, even if it's just for a little while.

'We're buying a villa!' they'd said to friends invited round for dinner at their poky Balham maisonette, as the purchase inched painfully through Italy's predictably arcane system. It wasn't all showing-off. Both of them had been half fearful, half hopeful the other would bottle it; repeating it aloud in public was a kind of test. 'Four hundred grand,' Nick could never help adding, though Laura thought it was a bit crass. 'Seven acres, outbuildings and a bloody olive grove, and it was less than our two-bed. We've basically bought a hamlet.'

None of their friends, to their eternal credit, asked if they were going to keep trying for a baby. They must have gathered that three failed rounds of IVF were enough for anyone. Still, she had wanted to make clear that Italy wasn't about running away. Laura viewed it as the very opposite, actually: a massive *fuck-you* to the whole fertility 'journey'. *No, we can't have kids but look what we get to do instead.*

'That little store at the back of Giuseppe's House is full of scorpions,' Nick is saying now, mouth full of bruschetta. 'I just smack them, these days. I couldn't give a shit. Remember the first one?'

She laughs. They don't mention the scorpions in their email updates to family. She hadn't even known Italy had scorpions. They don't mention the earth tremors either, though they've experienced a few small ones now. The region is prone to them. They knew this before they bought. In 2016, the town of Amatrice – just over an hour to the south-west – was more or less flattened. They'd seen the footage on the news in London when moving to Italy was still an idle dream: medieval rubble and survivors being pulled out from under it. The mayor said, 'The town no longer exists,' and was quoted everywhere. Laura tells herself she'll eventually get used to the idea that this could happen again, anytime.

Giuseppe's House is a one-up, one-down that is part of their parcel of property. 'Part of the estate,' says Nick, only half joking. Unlike the two dwellings adjacent to it, which are missing their roofs, Giuseppe's is in surprisingly good condition.

Giuseppe isn't a real person. Laura invented him when they opened the door and discovered a 1970s time capsule, as though someone had simply walked out forty-odd years earlier without a backward glance. It was all Formica, deeply varnished wood and swirly wallpaper in yellow and brown. Even the crucifix above the bed was a lurid burnt-orange. There were rusting tins of plum tomatoes in the cupboards, and a cutthroat razor on the bathroom sink, tiny black hairs still clinging to the blade, like iron filings. She pictured Giuseppe shaving there in the morning light, white vest stretching over a paunch and braces holding up his trousers.

'Maybe Giuseppe broke the Mafia code of silence,' Nick had said, pulling his fingers across his throat. 'You know . . . What's it called?' He taps his head, frustrated, before his face clears. '*Omertà.*'

Now, she watches as he takes another enormous bite of ciabatta, garlicky oil running down his chin. He's hunched over his plate with both elbows on the table.

'You eat like a peasant these days,' she says.

'I am a bloody peasant, that's why.' He holds up his free hand, which is calloused and paint-flecked. Two of the knuckles are freshly skinned. 'All this hard labour makes me starving.'

'Well, you're not the only worker. I finished the Nun's Cell. The ceiling is deep blue now, like Heaven. I'm going to paint some gold stars on it.'

They have names for all six bedrooms. That they are so numerous they need to distinguish between them still seems incredible. In London it was just the main bed-room, the box-room they used as a study and the loft conversion they had never managed to finish.

They're in bed by ten, the lazy supper eaten and night draped softly around the house. She's propped up with the iPad, while he's lying on his back looking at the ceiling, apparently stupefied by tiredness.

'Oh my God, I've found her Instagram account.'

'Who?'

'Madison, obviously.'

Last week they'd had their first booking since getting the keys to the villa. Madison is the name of the American woman who wants to come with her husband to stay in their most expensive room. The relief of it is profound. Within twenty-four hours of receiving the email enquiry, Laura felt as though she'd lost two stone off her shoulders.

There are plenty of things she and Nick don't discuss here. Along with the miscarriages, money is one of the most strenuously avoided. She's had to come to terms with it: the various ways the move to Italy hasn't fundamentally changed things between them. Perhaps she had been naive to think it would. But the booking – three whole weeks at the high-season tariff – has saved them. This is no exaggeration: they are down to their last fifteen thousand euros, all the spare cash from the sale of the London flat simply absorbed into the villa's refurbishment. Now they'll be able to pay six months' worth of bills, if they're careful. It means they aren't going to fail. Not at this. Not yet, anyway.

She turns round the iPad so Nick can see the screen. Madison's posts reveal a self-consciously covetable life at home in California.

'She's, like, *todally* perfect,' Laura says, in her best Valley Girl accent, as she scrolls down.

Madison's Instagram is as irritating as it is envy-making: a chequerboard of yoga, hiking, plates of clean food and a rescue pit-bull that balances pretzels on his nose. At least half the squares are blue: dark ocean, bright chlorine and faded denim cutoffs. She and her 'hubby' (Nick snorts at the endearment) live in one of the canyons, forty minutes from downtown LA when the freeway is clear. Madison imparted these exotic-sounding details in her second email.

It doesn't take much sleuthing on Laura's part to find out what Madison and the hubby do. She is on every platform going.

She nudges an almost-asleep Nick. 'You'll love this. She's a wellness coach and he works in film production. Fancy that, in LA. What a shocker.'

Without opening his eyes, Nick raises an eyebrow. 'Do you think they're making them somewhere, in Silicon Valley? These perfect Californian specimens?'

Most of the posts feature Madison pulling the same expression and pose, her head tilted down, her hips twisted slightly. She prefers her right side, clearly. She is good-looking in a generic kind of way, with the glossy, streaky mermaid hair and long bones privileged American women always seem to have. Both Nick and Laura have put on a little bit of weight in Italy, despite the relentless chores. Too much pasta and bread and cheese. Way too much wine.

'How do you think we should play it, when they come?' She turns to look at him.

'What do you mean, play it?'

'Like, with meals and stuff. The website goes on about guests feeling as though they've found their second home, but what does it actually mean? We eat with them or we serve them? Do they think they're getting full-board or what?'

Nick yawns. 'I thought you'd figured this out already.'

'Well, I wrote some enticing copy. It was pretty vague.'

'I think the home-from-home thing is good. It means it doesn't have to be hotel-tidy all the time. I reckon they eat with us.'

'Like friends.'

He kicks off the sheet so his feet are poking out. 'Yeah, exactly. Nice and laid-back.'

'But they're not friends. They're total strangers. It's a really weird concept when you think about it. They could be anyone.'

Nick laughs. 'Like inviting vampires over the threshold. Anyway, it's a bit late to freak out now. How old, do you think?' He's squinting at the screen again.

'God knows. Mid-thirties? Early forties if she's had work? Or is handy with the filters.'

'No kids?'

'No. Unless they're too un-photogenic to be seen.'

'Where's he, then? They're all of her and the dog. I'm thinking someone in Wayfarers and white T-shirts. *Top Gun* but with tattoos.'

'He's probably the one taking the photos. This is clearly The Madison Show.'

'Well, I don't care who he is. Him and the blessed Madison have saved the day.' Nick turns his head to grin up at her, mouth still purpled from the evening's wine, though he's brushed his teeth. 'What a fucking relief. We have this amazing place and now we'll earn some money off it too. I'm so glad we did this, Laur. I know I was resistant at first but you were right. You're always bloody right.' He stretches his arms above his head, sighing contentedly. 'How sorted are we?' he says. The emphasis is on the 'we'.

Instead of replying, she nudges him affectionately with her elbow. Now that the enchanted hours have slipped away the question becomes literal in her head, the stress moving to 'are'. How sorted *are* we?

She scrolls on as Nick begins to snore lightly, his arms flung over his head like a child. She turns off the bedside lamp. The shutters are open and, outside, the stars have come on. The night sky here is of a different order from anything she's ever seen in the built-up south-east of England. You can see actual galaxies here, milky eddies and swirls that make her dizzy.

Carefully, so she doesn't wake him, she gets out of bed, the iPad tucked under her arm. She wishes she could go outside with it, do what she's planning under those ancient flickering lights, but it'll be too chilly by now. She creeps downstairs and, still in the dark, curls up in the armchair she bought at a roadside sale and reupholstered herself.

Clicking off Madison's Instagram, she opens a new window. A memory of London comes then, rain thrumming on a glass skylight. She'd just got back from the clinic for the last time. The recollection stops her. She reaches for her laptop instead. She and Nick have taken to sharing his iPad here. The laptop is hers alone.

LinkedIn makes her paranoid. She's barely ever used it before – it's always seemed so clunky and corporate. Yesterday she'd set it up to search privately, but hadn't quite trusted it. She'd emailed Lou, her best friend, the person she misses most acutely in Italy.

I went on your LinkedIn profile just now. Have a look and let me know if it comes up anonymously or not.

Shit, was that you? came the reply. *I was hoping it was that bloke from Bumble. I think he's ghosting me. God, what a life.*

So the privacy settings worked, but she was still worried. If he sees it's her, she'll die. Or will she? Isn't it just flattering for him rather than embarrassing for her? He'd looked her up once on Facebook, years ago, when she was still content enough with Nick, and though it had thrown her, made her dream about him that night even, she hadn't done anything about it. It was enough to know he'd thought of her, then searched for her. She'd carried that little ego-stroke around, a hot flutter inside her, until it receded into nothing again.

Nerves stir within her now, making her restless. She goes through to the kitchen to get the wine from earlier and pours herself a glass, finishing the bottle. Tomorrow she'll try to have a day off the booze. She can feel the alcohol swimming inside her almost immediately, mingling with her blood, thinning and corrupting it. She feels hyper-aware of everything: the fridge's off-key hum, every grain of grit pressing into the soles of her feet. The cool eye of the moon regards her through the window as she drinks.

She and Nick are getting on better, now that they have a booking. They'd always pitied couples who bickered and sniped as a matter of course; they had always believed themselves above this, much too respectful of the other to point-score like irritable siblings. And then suddenly they were doing just that, and once they'd fallen into the miserable rhythm of it, it seemed impossible to stop.

She'd watch him abandon one job on the villa to start yet another, and wonder how she'd got through the last twenty years with him when everything he did annoyed her so profoundly. She believed she was totally justified in this, while simultaneously hating her own pettiness – the way she would snatch up his sweaty socks and T-shirts and hurl them into the drum of the washing-machine. She suddenly understood why resentful women took scissors to their husbands' suits.

So she's perfectly aware that it seems perverse to do what she's about to do, when things are looking brighter. But perhaps that's exactly why she's doing it now, the lift in spirits from the booking giving her a taste for more, another hit of life. Though she's been playing with the idea of sending *him* a message for a while, she's not sure when it tipped into a real possibility. Her old diaries haven't helped. Some days, sequestered in this beautiful place where she knows no one, where she feels like she's living in a painting, the past trapped between their scuffed covers feels more real than the present.

She sits down at the laptop again, the room shrinking to the rectangle of the lit-up screen. She goes to Settings, turns off privacy mode and types in his name, clicking on it before she can change her mind, the wine egging her on. Quick as a flash, as though it's burnt her, she clicks into a different window. It's BBC weather, set for Urbino, the nearest city. She stares at the row of yellow sun symbols without seeing them. Her heart thumps.

She glances at the clock in the corner of the screen. Ten minutes and then she'll check. She'll go back up to bed after that. Nick will have slept through her absence. Sometimes, when he's out of it beside her, exhausted by the kind of manual work he's never done before, she touches herself. Her movements are slight so she doesn't wake him, her breathing kept silent and shallow. It isn't forbidden, of course – Nick would probably love it if he caught her – but it feels like it. That makes it stronger when she gets there, back arching and eyelids fluttering in the dark. Sometimes, afterwards, her heart still racing, she cries, and she does that silently too.

She glances at the clock again. Only four minutes have passed. At that moment, twin beams of light swing across the dark room. Still unused to the villa's isolation after years in London, it takes her a second to remember they're not near enough the road to see any lights from passing traffic. Someone must be coming down the drive. She stands, her first instinct to run upstairs and wake Nick. Instead she unbolts the heavy front door and tiptoes barefoot to the cypress tree that guards the gate. She can't hear the engine over the rasp and saw of the cicadas. The head-lights, veined by olive tree branches, begin to grow smaller and she realizes they're reversing. Just a wrong turn, then.

She remembers the waiting laptop and rushes back in. Eight minutes, but she can't wait any longer. And there it is: a new view. There's also a message waiting.

Hello stranger x

She slams the screen down. Then she opens it again, to check that the prompt for the password comes up.

As she tiptoes silently upstairs, the stone steps chill underfoot, she tells herself she won't touch herself tonight: punishment for her tiny infidelity, and the possibilities she's lifted the latch on. Still, she can't help thinking about him as Nick slumbers on beside her, his body turned to hers while she faces away, his breath between her bare shoulder-blades making her skin goose-pimple. Too abruptly alive to switch off, she doesn't sleep until pale grey dawn outlines the shutters.

The next morning she lurches into consciousness, eyes snapping open when she remembers the message. She usually takes a long time to wake up properly but not today. She doesn't want to hang back from today.

Hello stranger.

She hugs her knees to herself, thoughts tumbling over each other. The bed beside her is empty, Nick already up. It's late, maybe ten. She can tell by the light behind the shutters, white with mid-morning intensity. Suddenly hot, she kicks off the sheets. Her legs in pale blue chambray shorts look brown and smooth. She eases the shorts down over her hips, pulls off the matching top and inspects her naked self: the thighs that are a little fleshier than she'd like, but still quite toned; the stomach that's always pretty flat, even when she puts on weight elsewhere. She stretches out T-shaped across the expanse of the bed, arms spread wide enough to touch the sides, toes pointed, and runs her hands down the mounds and dips of her body. She closes her eyes, just for a moment. *Hello stranger.* Her heart beats hard in her chest.

She finds Nick in his usual spot at the kitchen table, head bent over the iPad, reading the news. She loves him more today, in spite of the message. Because of it. There's no lasting guilt. Not yet. She's not sure there will be. Not after what he'd done to them in December.

'Morning,' he says, without looking up.

She kisses the top of his head and begins to massage his shoulders.

'That's nice.' He can't keep the surprise from his voice.

He reaches round to squeeze her hand. It's one of those suspended moments when she could tip it into more or walk away without offending him. She pictures herself leaning over him, pressing her breasts into his shoulder-blades, hair falling like a sheet in front of his face. He would pull her into his lap and they would start to kiss. He would taste of slightly stale coffee.

She straightens instead, walking over to the counter to pour herself a cup. The door to the garden is wide open and the air is already warm enough to prickle the skin. The sun falls in a broad stripe across her bare feet, which look pretty against the old terracotta tiles, toenails glossy because she only painted them yesterday, the exact shade of pistachio ice-cream.

'Do you want some breakfast? There's leftover pastries.'

She shakes her head. 'Not hungry.'

And she does feel full, the word *replete* arriving in her mind. Lou's voice echoes in her head, as it often does here, now she doesn't get to see her in real life. *You always get thinner when you're into someone*, she says in her wry tones. *You're getting down to your hunting weight.*

'What are you smiling at?' Nick has turned to watch her flexing her feet in the doorway, his expression half quizzical, half affectionate. He stands and opens his arms. 'Come here.'

She burrows into his embrace, her nose tucking into the cleft between his arm and chest, glad to hide her face. He smells more familiar than anything else she can imagine, of toast and sleep and, somehow, his parents' house. A surge of emotion eddies up through her body to swell behind her eyes. She waits until the tears have retreated, then takes his face in her hands, kissing him quickly and chastely on the mouth before stepping away.

'Love you,' she says.

'Yeah, cheers.'

They both smile at the old joke. When they were first together he'd found conversations about feelings as embarrassing as she'd found them stimulating. She never minded, though – it was touching. Besides, it was so obvious he loved her that she didn't really need him to say it. From the very start, even in this difficult last year, she had never, not for a second, doubted that he loved her.

It was she who had asked him out the first time, though admittedly in the knowledge that he already liked her. It was the summer she'd graduated and they were both working at a pub in the Warwickshire town where they'd grown up. He worked behind the bar and she was a waitress. They'd gone to different schools and had never crossed paths before. Like her, he'd just finished university, though he'd stayed at home to save money on accommodation. Both of them were on the cusp of proper adulthood. Neither felt entirely ready for it.

Every time they coincided in the pub's kitchen, the chef would tease them about when they were going to get together. He did it with the barely contained aggression he showed to the food he cooked, and to the customers who didn't like his hunter's chicken or pie and mash.

Nick had the sort of skin that flushed easily. He wasn't really her physical type. But then, after a while, she found herself hoping they would be working the same shift. Whether it was him she liked, or how much he liked her, she wasn't sure.

One Saturday night, they had a lock-in to celebrate a week of high takings and excellent tips. After a few drinks, Nick began to reveal a different side. He was quick and funny; he could run verbal rings round Danny the chef. She observed him across the table and thought, *Oh, why not?*

It was she who had kissed him after their first date, she who had led him to bed with a smile after the second. Oh, and the power that conferred on her, a total self-assurance that only made him want her more. Love like a warm bath in a safe house, door locked against dark night. Such a relief after what had come before, during her final term at university.

Hello stranger.

As she swims laps in the new pool that's only just become usable, the butter-coloured stones around it still waiting to be cemented into position, she thinks about what she's going to write in her reply. She has already brushed away the possibility of not replying.

For the first time, she forgets to admire the view towards the hills that change colour throughout the day but are richly green now, the air so clear that she could pick out every curving line of the millennia-old terraces if she bothered to look. Instead, her thoughts are turned inward. She gives up the lengths and floats on her back, hands circling slowly. High above is her favourite pine, the one with the cloud-shaped canopy that perfectly frames any photograph taken of the view. Beyond it the sky is turning a deep, hard blue.

She doesn't register those, either. She is thinking about his hands, strong and square rather than elegant. Large enough to encircle both of her wrists and hold them fast. She dives underwater and away from the memory that makes her insides contract, kicking hard to the bottom. Letting out her breath, she sinks. When her knees bump the tiles, she opens her eyes. They hate chlorine but she keeps them open, even when they start to sting.

She waits until the men who are finishing off the pool arrive before she opens the laptop. She doesn't know these two: they're not Massimo's usual men. Nick has joined them outside, ostensibly helping, though they would probably rather he didn't. She's noticed that when he inevitably leaves any of the builders to it, once the sun gets too fierce, they resume talking easily, the staccato rhythm of the language she still can't penetrate curling in through the open windows, like the heat.

All that signing and gesticulating with the locals, the linguistic long-way-round you have to go when you know only a few dozen words, she finds it exhausting. She hasn't said so to Nick but she doesn't think she will ever be good enough to convey or understand any nuance here. She misses being quick and finding the perfect word to describe something; she misses silly puns. In Italy, she feels slow and stupid much of the time. She suspects it's the same for Nick and that's why she doesn't want to bring it up. If they start admitting to these little failures, where will it end?

She'd wanted to live in Italy for so many years that she had long ceased to unpick the urge and examine the component parts. Whenever it came up in conversation she always sighed dreamily and said, 'One day I'm going to live there.' A fortnight's holiday never felt enough. As soon as she'd settled into the rhythms of it, it was time to return to London, which always seemed so colourless and chaotic by comparison.

But if she could actually *live* in Italy, it would be totally different. She imagined herself speaking the language fluently, and striking up awkward but meaningful friendships with eccentric local characters. She would get up in the rosy dawn to walk to market, a basket on her arm, her body brown and lean. *But you hate getting up early*, Nick would say. *Basically you're expecting Italy to turn you into a completely different person.*

But then came the miscarriages, and the rest of it, and suddenly Italy was going to happen. She knew Nick was privately worried she was pinning too much on it but what could he say in the circumstances? Nothing.

She doesn't know what she's expecting, but when there is nothing new in her inbox, an obscure disappointment washes over her. She clicks on the message that followed her through the night, then goes to email Lou about it. But she finds she doesn't want to. She tells Lou everything but she doesn't want to tell her this. She wants to keep it close. She doesn't know what she thinks about it yet, and doesn't want Lou's opinion to darken the outline of it, to colour it in before she's had the chance.

She starts typing him a reply but she's so nervous she's going to hit the send button by accident that she opens up a Word document instead, starts again in that. The liberation of that blank, unconnected page turns it from a cool, witty little rejoinder into something much closer to the truth.

I thought of you all night after your message. I thought about how it was when we slept together the first time. Do you remember? You were only my second but I was your fifth. I thought it would be awkward – I thought it was always going to be awkward – but it wasn't. It was late morning in your room, rain loud in the gutter above your window, and we were both hung-over from the night before. Your housemates were in and playing Goldeneye in the living room below and you didn't have a lock on your door but we did it anyway. I think I can even remember what I was wearing: a short denim skirt that rode around as I walked so that I was always twisting it to get the zip at the front. You hooked my knickers off with one hand, the other in my hair at the back of my neck, but I kept the skirt on and it was so tight that the hem made marks around the tops of my thighs from where you pushed them open.

She deletes the words, the cursor speeding up as she holds down the key. Outside, she can hear Nick laughing slightly too heartily, probably at some painfully mimed joke because his Italian is even worse than hers.

Hello you, she types. *It's been a while. Is it normal to miss someone you haven't seen in so many years?* She deletes the last sentence, writing instead *How's life treating you?*

She copies and pastes it into the box and presses send before the inner debate can start up. She realizes almost immediately that she forgot to put a kiss to match his, but then decides that's better. It seems cooler, more aloof. It's such an old game, the advance and retreat of who's keenest, who's chasing hardest. In and out like those German weather clocks, the wooden figure of the man coming out, then backing away as soon as the woman approaches. In and out. Back and forth.

She's fast approaching forty now and he has just turned forty-one but she knows, even from the few sentences that have joined them, like a narrow rope across the ether, that it would be exactly the same. She would never quite know where she stood or what he was thinking – she never had. Except for those times when he'd muttered her name over and over into her ear, into the tender nook between her neck and collarbone, into the gap where the bottom rungs of her ribcage met, and she'd known that right now she had him.

Outside, louder and higher-pitched than the rumble of the builders' tones, Nick laughs again. Perhaps all that bickering they do about the house is just a distraction from the bigger stuff. It fills up the silences so that there's no space left for her to say what she's really thinking now that she's got time to, now that there's no teaching or commuting or friends to meet for dinner. *Is this marriage it? Is this all we get, for ever, until we're dead?*

Lately, she's been rereading her old university diaries and there's one entry she found the other night that she vividly remembers writing on the little flat roof of the kitchen extension in her third-year house. They weren't supposed to use it, not least because it involved a precarious climb out of the bathroom window to get to it, but did anyway. Three nights earlier, she had kissed *him* for the first time.

'What are you writing today?' Lou had said. '"The beautiful young woman sniffed the evening air. It was pregnant with possibility. All of life was before her."'

She laughed. 'Yes, I always refer to myself in the third person. Lends the whole thing some gravitas. What's the word for this smell again? You know, after it's rained.'

'Petrichor,' said Lou. She pulled her sleeve down over her hand to twist the cap off a bottle of supermarket lager.

'I can never think of it.'

'My ex I met doing Duke of Edinburgh was in a band called Petrichor.' She took a swig of the lager. 'He was such a pompous twat.' She started laughing, choking on the fizzy beer she'd just swallowed.

Laura took the bottle while she recovered, drank some herself. 'I can't imagine you orienteering.'

'I didn't even get my bronze, to be honest. The

expedition went spectacularly wrong. We ended up trying to cross the M1 and a lorry driver called the police.'

They were both laughing now.

'So,' said Lou, when they'd calmed down, 'would you say you're making an accurate record of our supposedly halcyon days? Or are you doing your usual romanticizing?'

'It ends up being a bit of both, like a slightly shit *Brideshead*.'

'I'd just write down everything as I hoped it would be, regardless of how it actually was, so that when I found it again, aged eighty, I'd be pleased to see I'd had such a bloody great time being so popular and funny and sexy.'

Laura had felt so happy and hopeful that early autumn night, like she was brimming over with it. There really had been a sense that everything was ahead: endless doors ajar, each one inviting her to push it open.

'Remember this,' she'd said to Lou. 'This is where it all begins.'

When she'd lifted her head from the diary and remembered she was almost forty, that the night on the roof was literally half a lifetime ago, the realization was so jarring that it had made her catch her breath.

Now she studies the profile photo of the man she hasn't known for twenty years, who was still a boy when she was up on that roof, just as she was still a girl. She reads again the words he typed to her last night. Something lithe and dark swoops inside her.

1999

You've seen him four times on campus now, twice today. You first locked eyes on the steps outside Devonshire House, and again in the library last week. Then at lunchtime he'd been behind you in the refectory queue. You had been about to pick up a clingfilmed turkey salad, but knowing he might see and think it unsexy, perhaps even neurotic, you asked for a burger and chips instead. Boys love girls who eat.

'Eight and a half,' you had muttered to Lou, as you passed him an hour later. The two of you were on your way to the campus bar for a pre-presentation vodka – you always paired up in seminars for these, and always did them half cut. It had become one of your traditions. Of course it was a fine balance, that sweet spot between lucid confidence and pissed rambling: two vodkas for you, three for Lou. Just like being good at pool.

'Nine,' Lou replied loudly, so he'd hear. 'Though I think he might know it.'

This game is a recent invention. You rate every boy you see out of ten. A bloke called Dave compiled a list of the fittest girls in halls in the first year, so it seems fair enough. You had made the top ten for your 'eyes and tits' and were secretly delighted, which you know is pathetic. It doesn't make you any less pleased. You have taken on a different persona at university, quite by accident. You hadn't felt particularly pretty at school. Not ugly at all – but maybe just the plainest of the prettiest girls. Here, though, where they hadn't known you in those awkward years when almost everyone looks half cooked and oddly proportioned, you are considered good-looking. *Fit*.

In the sixth form, everyone had talked about university as somewhere you could reinvent yourself, and you'd thought about this in literal terms. Like you could randomly call yourself by your middle name, or stop listening to the R&B you knew was a bit questionable if you also claimed to be a feminist – the songs by Blackstreet and Jodeci that Lou called 'that shit shagging music' – and listen instead to Radiohead and Skunk Anansie. You hadn't done this, though you still liked the idea of being someone who listened to indie music, going to the Cavern club on Fridays with the working-class kids from the valleys and up north, instead of the Home Counties public-school types who owned Wednesdays, which was AU night, as in Athletic Union. It was all hockey, rugby and lacrosse there, and they liked R&B too.

You still feel like an idiot for having had so little clue of what you were getting into at this particular university. You're reading English and the course is reputed to be one of the best, with loads of film and American literature, and very little Chaucer or Beowulf. It had really high grade requirements – your offer had been two As and a B – and that was all you'd thought about. That, and the fact it was near the sea. You'd fondly thought it would be sunny in the summer and that some boy you hadn't met yet would take you to the beach in his convertible Golf. You'd have sex there, and he'd take you home to meet his parents, and the house would be Georgian, with a big lawn. You'd play games after dinner. *Supper.*

Despite these vaguely aspirational fantasies, you hadn't known how posh it would be. The ratio of private- to state-school kids was ridiculous. It was something like forty per cent when nationally it was more like one in ten. And, of course, forty felt more like eighty, thanks to the Teflon-coated confidence that was what their parents had really shelled out for. Thirty grand a year was the cost of their offspring being able to strut into the campus bar and somehow take up twice the space everyone from a comprehensive did. They aren't cool – when was posh ever really cool? – but they think they are, and eventually that conviction, that armoured self-assurance, works on you, like a sly kind of con. You think you despise them and then you find yourself watching them, coveting the same clothes, speaking like them when you're drunk, mouth almost closed.

And, God, they're easy to imitate. Ralph Lauren button-down shirts, the collars turned up, preferably in candy pink. Gilets from Gap. Tan leather deck shoes. Marlboro Lights. A fucking pager – surely the most convoluted piece of technology ever. The girls wear pearl earrings with baseball caps, luxuriant ponytails threaded through the strap at the back. It is, by any standards, a ridiculous uniform, but you still find yourself asking your mum to take you to the Ralph Lauren factory outlet in the holidays to shop for your birthday present.

'Well, if you can't beat 'em, join 'em,' says Lou, who, like Laura, is considered a northerner because she comes from the Midlands.

'At least you haven't got a fucking Brummie accent,' a boy had drawled at her last week. He said he meant it as a compliment. He'd bought her three drinks by then so she let it go.

The second the seminar ends, the presentation just about blagged, your mind slides away from Mary Wollstonecraft and straight back to him.

'Let's go and have more vodka, to celebrate,' you say.

'You're hoping he'll be in there, aren't you? Mr Nine?'

You sit at a rickety round table on black varnished stools. Someone has put 'Mr Jones' on the jukebox again. Every time a group of boys sidles in, you brace, in case he's among them. You don't know when you went from vaguely fancying him to feeling ill in his vicinity.

'At least he's not one of *them*,' you say, because you want to talk about him all the time and know Lou will humour you.

The boys who have come in couldn't be more archetypal Sloane. Collars up, voices loud.

'He's mates with them, though,' Lou points out. 'I've seen him with that lot.' She tilts her head towards the group, who are now at the bar, ordering gin and tonics and pints of Guinness. 'They must think he lends them an air of urban sophistication.'

In freshers' week, everyone had been obsessed with this statistic, probably made-up, that 70 per cent of students meet the person they'll marry at university. You'd loved this idea: that the man you would end up with was probably out there on campus right now, just out of sight. It had felt safe and tantalizing at once. You'd thought about all those times when you decided to go to this club over that one, while your future husband had chosen the other. Sliding doors. It had kept you going, the idea that one day the stars would align. But then the first and second years had passed unremarkably and still you waited, wondering when you'd ever find him.

And then the third and final year began and, out of nowhere, new on campus, there he was.

Day 1

June

The Americans are an hour early. Of course they are. Everyone in the expat chatrooms says guests always turn up early, when their hosts are still rushing around checking light-bulbs and vacuuming in the unforgiving afternoon heat.

Laura is so hot she's stripped down to her underwear. Loose strands of hair are stuck to her face, and her lower back aches from making the bed without allowing the white-white linen to wilt against her damp skin.

'Shit, they're here!' she shouts, in the vague direction of the stairs, though Nick probably isn't even in the house. He's always in one of the bloody outbuildings when she needs him. Every morning she writes a list of jobs for him to do that day: put up a shelf in the green bathroom, rewire the chandelier they found at the antiques market last week, investigate the smell coming from the cellar, make sure there's enough ice – aren't Americans obsessed with ice? – tasks she could reel off endlessly that, if she didn't write them down, he would never think of doing.

She approaches the window carefully, not wanting to be seen yet. She should go down immediately but if she hangs on there's a chance Nick will get there first, and then it will be down to him to welcome them, get them their first drinks, generate the kind of bonhomie she has to work herself up to, even with friends. Nick has always been good at that stuff, better than her. Socializing invigorates him where it exhausts her.

On the gravel outside, the Americans have pulled up in their huge hire car. She already knows what Madison looks like, of course. Laura pulls on the T-shirt dress she'd dropped to the floor and creeps closer to the window. Hubby – it can only be him – is admiring the view of the valley, baseball cap on, hands behind his head, elbows out in a stretch. His arms are pumped-up with muscle, his skin a deep brown. Madison gets out of the passenger side as Laura watches, bending to check her reflection in the side mirror before turning to look up at the house. Laura ducks further down, grasping the windowsill to keep her balance. Annoyed that she's being so ridiculous, she presses her fingertips hard into the new paintwork, which starts to give, the wood beneath it spongy and presumably rotten. But she hasn't time to worry about that now. A bead of sweat runs down her temple.

'Where are you, Nick, you bastard?' she says, under her breath.

Now they're no longer jointly pitted against the grind of London, there are moments when being irritated with her husband veers towards actual dislike. The force of these, while they last, unnerves her. It's not so much the red mist as white-hot contempt. And, actually, if she's absolutely honest, there's something thrilling about it.

Maybe some of it is hormones. Women seem to spend their lives stoically suppressing the extremes of them, not just the fury but the tears, the soul-crushing blues, the feeling like a barrage balloon for half the month. She digs her fingers even harder into the wood, feeling the paint finally crack, like eggshell. She or Nick will have to touch it up but she doesn't care. It seems worth it. A tiny act of destruction. A tiny pressure valve opened.

'Hey, there! Anybody home?' She freezes. It's her: Madison, her voice lower-pitched than Laura had imagined. Then the rumble of Hubby's voice, too low to make out the words. She'll have to watch she and Nick don't actually call him Hubby. She knows she needs to go down to say hello. Any longer and they'll look rude. English eccentricity only takes you so far on Tripadvisor. Madison will be the type to report back on everything.

She creeps over to the full-length mirror propped against one wall. It's one of her best finds: seven feet tall, gilt-framed and authentically but not unusably foxed. She looks like shit in it, despite the soft patina of the old glass. There's toothpaste down her front and the cheap dress, bought at the market for ten euros, pulls uncomfortably across her stomach. She's due on in two days. Her whole body feels swollen with water retention, like a cheap chicken breast.

'Guys, welcome. Welcome!'

She closes her eyes in relief. It's Nick, doing his jovial bit. For the time being, she loves him again.

Five minutes later, she hurries down the stairs, pride and vanity warring with her fear of looking ill-mannered. She's tried to sort out her hair but it's frizzy from her exertions. It's something that she looks flushed in a healthy way now, rather than just sweaty. She had planned to wear a pale green linen dress for the grand arrival – it's ironed and waiting on the back of a chair in the bedroom – but she can't bear to put it on before showering and there isn't time for that now.

The alfresco dining table is further into the garden, in deep shade under the vine-wrapped pergola but, as agreed beforehand, Nick has seated the Americans on the low-slung L-shaped sofa Laura has festooned with throws and cushions. It's a good vantage point from which to show off the terraces and a tantalizing glimpse of deep blue pool water. She peers through the kitchen window, carefully in case anyone is looking her way.

She has almost steeled herself to go out when Madison shifts her position, allowing Laura to see her face properly. She's uncharitably heartened to see that the other woman is definitely in her late thirties or early forties. She obviously uses filters for her Instagram shots, though that would hardly be revolutionary. Either way, the realization is fortifying. Laura is both dreading her fortieth and disbelieving that she's already there. Nick had got his out of the way: they'd made his February birthday into a joint leaving party. This had suited them both: neither was yet ready to face their fifth decade. She feels twenty in her head. She suspects she always will.

Madison obviously takes care of herself – her make-up, despite the journey, is immaculate – but she has the tanned, freckly skin that lines and thins early. She's over-dieted, too, her bare upper arms toned to an almost sinewy degree. A bit of extra flesh would make her look younger. Laura's hand goes to her stomach again.

The husband is still only visible from behind. His arm is slung casually along the back of the sofa. Poking out from the neck of his T-shirt is a small tendril of black. A tattoo. She wonders what it is and how far it extends under his clothes, and the thought makes her blush. If Italy has switched her on, the messages she exchanges most nights have turned her up to eleven. She smiles at the Spinal Tap reference, which Lou and she once used all the time.

Nick appears at the door. 'There you are,' he whispers. 'What the hell have you been doing? Didn't you hear them arrive?'

'I was making the bed and I looked a state. I couldn't meet them like that.'

'Well, come out now. It's beginning to look weird that you haven't. I've just come in to get some nuts and crisps and things.'

'No, I told you, I made stuff.' She wrenches open the fridge and pulls out a covered platter of crostini she'd made earlier: toasted rounds of bread with tapenade on half of them, and a kind of improvised broad-bean pesto on the rest. 'You should have given them these. I did them specially. What are they drinking?' A wasp buzzes close to her head and she bats it away. She's suddenly boiling hot again. The atmosphere of Luna Rossa, now that they're no longer alone, has sharpened and intensified.

'Wine. White wine. Gavi, I think.'

'That was supposed to be for the first course tonight. Fuck's sake, Nick, I said all this earlier. You never listen.'

'If you're so particular, you should have come down to greet them yourself, instead of hiding.' He stalks back outside clutching the crostini plate, leaving her standing with the bottle of Aperol she'd meant him to mix with Prosecco.

Is this how it's going to be? she thinks, as she pours herself a glass of water, still putting off the inevitable as though she's paralysed in the wings with stage-fright. Sniping at each other behind the guests' backs and pretending everything's under control when, really, they don't know what the hell they're doing?

Three heads turn expectantly towards her as she finally steps outside.

'I'm so sorry,' she begins, as her gaze is naturally pulled towards the other woman, who looks back at her with shrewd blue eyes. 'I was upstairs and didn't hear you arrive.'

She and Madison smile at each other. Then Laura moves her gaze to the husband, dimly taking in that, just as Nick predicted, he's wearing Ray-Bans, which he now removes. Their eyes meet just as she opens her mouth to ask them if they want a cocktail.

'I thought you might like an Ap–' she is already saying, but she's suddenly so dizzy that she sways where she stands. 'I . . . Sorry, I . . .'

She somehow gets herself back to the kitchen and clunks down the Aperol bottle she's still clutching. Her clothes are soaked through and sticking to her. She turns on the tap again and, though water is precious here, lets it gush out of the tap and down the plughole while she leans over the sink, saliva filling her mouth as though she's about to be sick.

'Laura, what are you . . . Are you OK?' Nick is suddenly there, the flat of his hand between her shoulder-blades. 'God, you're drenched.'

'I feel like I'm going to pass out.' Her voice sounds a long way off.

He fills a glass with water and turns off the tap. 'Drink this, you must have got overheated rushing around. You didn't have any lunch, did you? I told you to but you wouldn't stop.'

She sips the water, still afraid that she'll be sick or simply slump to the floor. Glancing towards the window, she is overwhelmingly relieved to see that the Americans are still seated. Nick pushes her down into a chair.

'You've gone a really funny colour. Like, white with blotches. Put your head between your legs so you don't faint.'

She does as she's told.

'Stay there. I'll go and tell them you're feeling off. Explain you'll be out later.'

She nods without looking up, but as soon as he's gone, she gets to her feet and stumbles out of the kitchen, then up the stairs. Closing the bedroom door behind her, she lies down without even taking off her flip-flops. The light has moved round the house by this time and the room is blessedly dim. She closes her eyes and tries not to listen to her heart speeding and skipping in her chest.

A couple of hours later she forces herself to get up. Miraculously, given her banging heart, she has managed to doze a little, and though she wakes with a jolt, the nap has made what happened earlier seem like a surreal dream.

As she had wanted to before, she showers, then takes her time dressing and applying make-up. Perhaps if she'd been similarly armoured earlier, her body wouldn't have betrayed her so badly.

It's almost seven now. From the hall, she can hear the Americans – even now they're here she can't shake the habit of thinking of them like this – getting ready, the shower in their en-suite going full-pelt, the clean, astringent smell of male shower gel curling under the door. She makes herself go down to the kitchen to help Nick.

It's less than ten minutes later that a sweet and cloying perfume wafts in from the hall and she realizes that the guests are on their way down. It's a surprisingly synthetic scent, way too heavy on the vanilla and peach. *Tacky* is the word that steals nastily into Laura's head.

'Hubby's name is Bastian, by the way,' Nick mutters, one eyebrow raised, just as the Americans appear in the doorway.

'Hey, guys, can we do anything to help?' Bastian's voice is low, assured.

As Nick demurs and offers drinks, Bastian comes forward and briefly rests his hand on Laura's shoulder.

'How are you feeling now?'

She's so aware of the heat of his hand that she can't think of anything to say.

Madison rescues her, coming over and taking up Laura's hands, leaning in to kiss the air near her face.

'Oh, honey, you still look a little peaky. You mustn't worry if you need to go lie down again. Nick's been taking real good care of us.'

Laura isn't quite sure if the assurance not to worry is genuine or a very slight reproof. She smiles, unable to look either American in the eye.

46

'It was so strange. Maybe I had too much sun this morning. I feel fine now. I'm sorry to be so late to say hello properly, though. Is your room OK?' She is relieved to hear her voice sounds perfectly normal. Nick hands round the Aperol spritzes they were supposed to have had on arrival. He's made her one too, and she takes it gratefully.

'The room is great, thank you. So, obviously, I'm Madison.' She lets out an effervescent little giggle. 'And this is Bastian.'

Laura holds out her hand to shake at the same moment Bastian leans in to kiss her. He smells like the shower steam, menthol and something fragrantly woody, like rosemary. As their faces cross for a second kiss, she sees that his deep brown eyes are slightly open. They glint behind the fringe of his lashes.

'You're doing it like a Continental already,' she manages to say, when they pull back.

He smiles, teeth white and even, but she's already turning away, towards the open door to the garden.

'Why don't we go outside?' she says, gesturing. 'Leave the chef to his work.'

'He does all the cooking too?' says Madison. 'Wow. Do you want to swap?'

Nick laughs, gratified, but Bastian doesn't smile. He's still looking at Laura – she can feel it. Outside, the air is blessedly cool and the light has waned, the valley greens turning the colour of smoke. It's such a relief after the spot-lit kitchen that she gulps at the air.

When the Aperols are finished, Nick opens a bottle of decent white. Verdicchio, it's called. She'd never heard of it before but Nick had spent days researching local specialities online, then driving round trying to find a good deal while Laura had carried on working on the house. 'I'm painting actual rooms while he drives around like the Del Monte man,' she'd said to Lou, on Skype. 'We haven't got a finished kitchen but we've got shit-loads of wine.'

Lou had shrugged. 'Sounds all right to me.'

In the end, Nick had returned triumphant with a couple of cases from a vineyard just outside Cupramontana. To be fair, it's very good: smooth and dry and tasting of lemons and almonds. In some lights, it looks almost green. Because she's still feeling slightly strange, off-balance, she recites the full name of the wine in her head: Verdicchio dei Castelli di Jesi. So gorgeously over the top. Nick pushes a full glass towards her.

'Bastian was saying earlier that he's Italian,' he says, raising an eyebrow again.

Bastian shrugs, takes out a vape and switches it on. 'My paternal grandfather was from here. So I guess only a quarter.'

'Still,' says Nick, 'that counts, doesn't it? Do you speak the language?' His voice is a shade too hearty.

'He's really good, actually,' says Madison. 'My man of many talents.'

'I can get by,' says Bastian.

'So, have you been to this region before?' says Nick.

'Weirdly, never,' says Madison. 'We always talked about it, you know, but never quite managed to.'

'We could never quite find the excuse,' says Bastian. 'Till now.'

'Have you guys seen *Eat Pray Love*?' says Madison,

brightly. She's hardly touched her wine. Laura watches a bead of condensation run down the glass. She's half finished hers already.

'Oh, yes – Elizabeth Gilbert,' says Laura. 'She's great.'

Madison's smile turns blank. 'Oh. No. The one with Julia Roberts? I watched it three times last week. I've been *so* excited.'

'And does it live up to the dream so far?' says Nick. 'We're a long way from Rome. The Marche is kind of off the beaten track. Looks like Tuscany but with fewer tourists and more earthquakes.'

Laura shoots him a warning look.

'Oh my gosh, *yes* it lives up to the dream,' says Madison. 'It's just perfect here. I love that it's so undiscovered. I told this woman at the gym about it and, you know, she goes everywhere, and she'd never even heard of it. Then Lonely Planet ran this piece on the best places to discover this year and I was, like, *that*'s where me and Bast are headed.' She sighs. 'You're so lucky. We're *so* jealous, aren't we, hon?' She turns to Bastian and reaches out to lay her hand on his.

'Oh, sure,' he says languidly. 'The whole place is unreal. Like a movie set. I can't believe I'm here.'

'No, nor me,' says Laura, and then, noticing Nick's panicked look, grasps how rude it might sound. 'We've been so looking forward to it.' She smiles and catches Bastian's eye, daring to hold his gaze for a beat too long. He blows out a cloud of vapour without breaking eye contact. It curls and twists into nothing in the darkening air over them. She turns to Nick and holds out her glass for more wine.

*

Laura and Nick have retreated to their bedroom, though it's only nine thirty. The shutters are open and insects are finding their way in, drawn by the light neither of them can be bothered to get up and switch off. They had come up to give the Americans some time to themselves on the terrace but the master suite's door had creaked open and closed within minutes. They're probably tired after their journey.

'That went pretty well, don't you think?' Nick rolls onto his side and presses his lips to her bare shoulder. Though she's lying flat, she feels completely alert. She is so aware of her body that she can feel the blood tingling in her fingertips and toes.

'Well, they ate everything,' she says. 'Or he did, at least.'

'Two hours for that beef and it was gone in twenty minutes.'

'And we've got to do it all again tomorrow.'

'It's full-on, isn't it?' He massages his temples. 'Three weeks they're here, Jesus.'

She closes her eyes and concentrates on the sensation of her sore muscles sinking into the mattress. A whisper of breeze brushes her skin and an image surfaces in her mind: the black tendril of a tattoo. She hadn't thought she liked tattoos much, before.

'It's our job now, though, isn't it?' she says, to banish it. 'Doing this. We're going to have to get used to it.'

'It's so weird. Thinking about them being here, on the other side of the house. It's just been us for ages.'

'It's not that weird,' she replies contrarily – because she'd said exactly the same thing when the booking first came in.

'They're under our roof, no one else within a mile, and they're basically complete strangers. You said it yourself. How is that not weird?'

She pictures their guests then, in the suite she'd once dreamt of sleeping and bathing in, lying between the sheets she'd washed and ironed so carefully. The bed in there is old and high, a four-poster made of ornately carved oak. You have to clamber up to get onto it. She wonders if Madison has noticed how threadbare the canopy is, and whether, if she has, she will judge it as scruffy or charming. She wonders if they'll have the energy for sex before they pass out. The thought sends a flicker of heat through her.

She and Nick haven't had much sex in Italy. It's one of the things they don't talk about but the shared knowledge of it follows them around the house, getting between them, inching them further and further apart as the days pile up. Each night, she knows she should put down her book, turn towards him, initiate things. *But it's still early*, she always tells herself. *We probably will in a minute.*

But Nick has always been an early bird to her night owl so she knows that if she keeps reading a bit longer he'll fall asleep and then she'll be off the hook. Every morning she wishes she hadn't been so lazy or resistant, or whatever it is that stops her when it's so much easier between them when they do, and though she actually enjoys it when they bother. And yet, in the moment, she's always relieved to hear his breathing slow and deepen. It's perverse, she knows that. How do someone else's expectations – someone she still loves more than

51

anyone, despite all they've been through – make something so good seem like work?

She'd hoped Italy would solve what has been a problem for some years now. But they're just the same couple in a different place. The worst thing is that in many ways Italy has worked on her, just as she hoped it might. Everything about the place is ludicrously sensuous. In April, with the first soft green stirrings of spring, all that time in her own head had nearly got her into trouble, spilling over into real life in a way that the messages, existing only in the ether, couldn't. She'd had what she could only call an *encounter*.

He was a mechanic in their nearest town, about twenty minutes down the winding hill road towards the coast. Nick was supposed to take the car in but she'd offered at the last minute, suddenly desperate to escape the half-renovated villa – to drive away from it with the windows down, a cloud of red earth rising in the rear-view mirror. To be in the world again for an hour or two. To be visible to people other than Nick, and herself in the mirror. She'd washed the cobwebs from her hair, worn a dress that swung around her thighs, even put on some perfume and lipstick.

She'd messaged Lou afterwards, deliberately crafting an amusing anecdote from it. *He was wearing an actual blue boiler-suit. With a zip. Nothing underneath, as far as I could tell. He said, 'Ciao, bella,' when I left.* Lou had emailed back from her Uxbridge office in about four minutes: *Oh, my God, this has made my fucking day. So old-school porn. You should have. I totally would have. In fact, when I come out to visit, I'm GOING to.*

Laura had known Lou would say exactly that. She pre-dated Nick and had no real loyalty to him. Laura wasn't convinced her other friends, all of them married like her, or as good as, wouldn't have disapproved or been a bit too shocked. Lou just thought it was hilarious. And it was, and it wasn't, because it hadn't been funny at the time. It had been terrifying, and not just because she was stone-cold sober, but because she had almost gone with it. Because she regretted *not* going with it afterwards.

The workshop had been dark and so much cooler than the forecourt outside. He had fixed her with eyes that were startlingly blue against his dark skin and she knew, as you did sometimes, that she could sleep with him – that it would require her only to half smile, and it would happen, there and then. The thought made her dizzy, actually dizzy. She'd stepped back to steady herself, and knocked against something metal, which had screeched across the oil-stained concrete. A jack or some sort of *tool*. She had choked with laughter as she emailed this detail to Lou, even as the excitement of it still pulsed low down inside her.

He'd deliberately brushed her hand as he took the keys from her. In her head afterwards, this had been the suspended moment: when it had teetered on the brink of something else. Flustered, she had held on to the keys and they almost tussled for them, but then he had them and she had regained her balance. In under a minute, he had written down her details and she was back out in the blinding sunshine.

It wasn't until she was in bed that night, safe in the dark, Nick fast asleep, that she changed the ending, allowing the mechanic to back her against the counter, his other hand already pushing up the hem of her dress, dirt-rimmed nails spread on her bare thigh.

53

It was only a few weeks later that she had looked *him* up. He had virtually no social-media presence so it had taken her a while to find him – on LinkedIn, of all things. His name was slightly altered, but his education was the same, and that was how she'd tracked him down. *Hello stranger.*

Next to her, Nick turns onto his back, letting out a long sigh. She tiptoes to the door and thinks about all the nights she's crept downstairs to check her messages, to write *him* a new one, setting down the words she's rehearsed in her head all day.

She waits but there's no sound from the other side of the house. The hallway is pitch-black but she knows its dimensions now, and which boards creak. She hovers a few feet from the Americans' closed bedroom door. It's already theirs.

From within is total silence but then, just as she's turning to go, she hears a deep murmur followed by a laugh, or perhaps it's a gasp. She freezes, expecting more, but there's nothing. After a while, she goes downstairs to her waiting laptop. She has no idea what she's going to write tonight, but she expects something will come to her in the dark, her face blue-lit by the screen, and it does.

By the time she gets back to him, Nick hasn't stirred. He's still wearing the smart shorts he'd worn for dinner but his chest is bare. It's much whiter than his tanned arms because there hasn't been much time for sunbathing.

She closes the door and takes off her clothes, letting them drop to the floor. She snaps off the light and goes round to Nick's side of the bed. Undoing his shorts, she begins to ease them off.

'Hey,' he says, voice thick with sleep. 'What's this?'

She places a finger over his lips as she gets onto the bed and straddles him. His hands go to her hips and she feels him tense, waking fully as he discovers she's naked. He reaches out to turn on the bedside lamp but she stops him.

'No, I want the dark,' she whispers, letting her hair fall around them as she begins to kiss him.

Day 2

On the Americans' first morning at Luna Rossa, Nick rises in the pearled dawn to prepare the complicated breakfast he'd planned yesterday. He kisses her before he leaves the bedroom, strokes her hair. Even though she keeps her eyes closed, she can tell he's looking down at her fondly. They've had sex and she can almost smell the relief on him.

Apart from a brief good morning, she doesn't see their guests until Madison appears in the kitchen doorway, dressed in a cornflower blue dress that deepens her tan. She smiles the smile that is already becoming familiar to Laura, bright and brittle. She doesn't know if anything about it is real yet.

'Nick said you might be going to the market this morning.'

Laura puts down the bowl she's been drying.

'Oh. Yes. I always get the vegetables there because they're local. There's this seafood stall, too, and . . .' She tails off.

Madison puts her head on one side, oddly coquettish. 'Would it be a pain in the ass if I came with you? Bastian isn't interested in shopping and he's got a work call anyway. I'd take our car but I don't know if I dare.' She raises her narrow eyebrows. 'They were *crazy* on the *autostrada* yesterday. I thought LA was bad.'

Laura finds herself nodding, though in truth she could do without the company. She has a lot to do around the house and the trip to Castelfranco will take much longer with Madison tagging along. Plus there's all the extra energy required to be chatty and polite in the car during the journeys there and back. She'd been hoping for some time alone with her thoughts. She's grown accustomed to living a lot of the time in her head.

'I could help you pick out the vegetables,' Madison is saying. 'I wanted to ask if you could get some stuff for my juices anyway. You could show me around the town a little too. It'll be fun. Girls together.' That smile again: full-wattage-white that practically glows in the dim kitchen. 'And it isn't just food, right? There are, like, gifts and clothes and stuff?'

Laura feels weary already. 'It's mainly food. It's for locals rather than tourists really. That's the thing about round here, like Nick was saying yesterday. It's not touristy at all – that's why we love it so much.' Even as she says it she isn't sure it's true. It might have been easier in Tuscany, in *Chiantishire*, with more expats around.

Madison waves her hand. 'It doesn't matter if it's basic. I get restless if I'm in one place. Bastian always says I turn antsy if I have to sit still for more than two minutes in a row.'

Laura resists the urge to ask why they had booked a holiday in rural Italy if that were the case.

'OK, great, so I'll ride along with you, then,' Madison continues. She reaches out to straighten a row of spice jars. 'Let's meet in the hall in fifteen minutes, yeah?'

Laura nods mutely for the second time.

*

'I'm taking Madison with me to the market,' she says to Nick. She'd found him in the extraordinary vaulted cellar, which seems to bear no relation to the house above it in either shape or size. He's going through some boxes from London that are yet to be unpacked. There's nothing urgent about this task. She knows he's avoiding having to make small-talk with their guests, presumably feeling hosted-out after breakfast and the previous night's efforts. It's exactly how she feels about Madison, so she can't be too irritated.

'That's my fault, isn't it?' He pulls a sympathetic face.

She sighs. 'It's fine. She's going to tell me what she likes to put in her smoothies or juice cleanses or whatever.' She starts back up the stairs.

'Hey, Laur,' he calls after her.

She turns.

'Last night. It was . . . I thought I'd dreamt it for a minute this morning.' His smile is so grateful that she has to look away. He reaches for her and she holds out her hand. He kisses her fingers. 'It was amazing.'

'Yes.' She smiles, still not meeting his eye. 'Look, I'd better go.'

'Have fun now!' he calls after her, mock-hearty, as she goes up the rickety wooden stairs.

She continues straight up the main stairs to get changed. Distracted, she almost collides with Bastian at the top.

'Laura,' he says. He smiles at her. He's one of those people who is comfortable with a loaded silence. She is not.

'Did you sleep well?' she blurts.

He tips his head on one side, regards her as she shifts about. 'Kind of.'

'Oh, is it the bed? Were the pillows not . . .?'

'The bed's great. I felt like a king in it. I was a little restless, that's all. My brain wouldn't shut down. I went out into the garden to look at the moon for a while.' He drops his eyes in a show of embarrassment at such a fanciful urge, but they're soon seeking hers again.

She thinks about how she had padded about in the night, how she'd listened out for sounds in the dark. She could have bumped into him. The idea of it makes her swallow.

'So, do you like it then, the villa? Does it live up to expectations?'

'Oh, more than. It's just how I imagined it would be.'

He is smiling his slow smile again. It does something peculiar to her. She has hardly ever felt drawn like this, a physical force pulling her in. It can only be chemical, surely. Pheromones and complementary DNA. Opposite DNA. Half-known details from magazine articles about sex flit through her head as he continues to drink her in, quite unabashed.

'I must get on,' she says ridiculously. 'I need to change. I'm taking your . . . I'm taking Madison with me to the market.' She wishes she hadn't mentioned Madison.

She walks away before she can say anything else. Closing the bedroom door behind her, she is hugely relieved to be out from under his spotlight even as she's wondering when it might shine on her again.

Madison is already waiting for her in the hall by the time she's changed into a sundress, not wishing to look dowdy in her usual shorts and vest top. But in fact Madison has apparently used the intervening minutes to smarten herself up even more, and is now wearing lots of delicate gold jewellery and a pair of Grecian-style sandals, complete with narrow laces that criss-cross up her leanly muscled calves. Her perfume – so sugary-sweet that it clashes with the quiet old beeswax and almond scents of the hall – fills Laura's nose as she descends the stairs.

'Hey, you,' Madison cries, when she notices her. 'I was just starting to think you'd forgotten me.'

'Oh, sorry,' she says reflexively, Britishly, because according to her watch it's exactly a quarter of an hour since their exchange in the kitchen. 'Have you been waiting long? I thought we said fifteen.'

'It's fine, honestly.' Madison waves her hand, the stones in her rings bouncing light around the walls. 'You're here now.'

The drive is an arresting one, the narrow road twisting and turning down the hillside towards the small town of Castelfranco, the startling blue of the Adriatic a thick marker line at the horizon. The burnt-out Alfa Romeo, which hangs suspended in branches above one vertiginous drop, is still there. Massimo had told Nick that the driver had been forced off the road – at least, that's what his gestures and sound effects seemed to be trying to convey. There are vendettas here more complex and labyrinthine than any incomer could ever hope to untangle, 'vendetta' meaning 'blood feud', from the Latin *vindicta*.

The heart of the old town is chaotic with the usual market crowds. The women are at the stalls, squeezing fruit and haggling in tones that still sound hostile to Laura's ears. The men are almost exclusively on the margins, most of them smoking and drinking espresso at the outside tables of the café that overlooks the main piazza. The old ones debate and gesticulate while the younger ones remain watchful, expressions sullen.

'Oh, my God, what a perfect place to people-watch,' says Madison. She actually claps her hands and Laura has the sense that she's watching someone play a part, and not entirely convincingly either: an actress in a TV movie.

'Shall we have a coffee before we start?' Madison turns to her excitedly. 'I shouldn't, but when in Rome, right?'

'Why shouldn't you?' says Laura, as though she'd like to be even more irritated than she already is at having company she doesn't much want, by this woman she has already half dismissed as vapid and high-maintenance.

'I try to eat clean,' Madison says, with a little shrug, as Laura knew she would. 'No caffeine, no dairy, no sugar, as little alcohol as possible.' She counts them off on her fingers. The diamond on her wedding finger is arrestingly large. 'Of course the good thing about doing that most of the time,' she leans closer, her buffed nails brushing Laura's forearm, 'is that when you do have something forbidden, it's so much better.' She smiles and this time it reaches her eyes, the skin around them creasing. It makes her look older but more attractive. 'Who needs hard drugs when a real Italian espresso is going to blow your mind?'

Laura finds herself smiling back, her irritation slinking away traitorously. She doesn't want to like Madison but it strikes her she might yet be disarmed. She hadn't expected that.

A radio blares from an unseen kitchen at the back of the café, the aromas of frying garlic and onions already emanating from it. Except for a couple of old ladies made sexless by their vast age and shapeless black dresses, every customer is male. They watch closely as the two obviously foreign women thread their way through the tables to claim the last, right in the thick of it. In northern Europe, probably the States too, this scrutiny would be undertaken far less frankly, especially in the kind of establishment where men drink espresso in the mid-morning. To Laura, this feels more like walking past a building site, or going into a greasy spoon. 'God, talk about feeling like an object,' she says sottovoce.

Madison shakes back her ponytail. 'Oh, I like it. I always have. No man in LA dares do it now. They're too scared they're going to be called out, or end up on some list. But we're animals, aren't we? We want men to look at us, don't we, if it's men we like? That's why we dress up to look pretty. That's why we hate getting old, turning invisible. Isn't it?'

She sits down and pats the other seat. 'You should see how horrified you look, Laura.'

'I'm not,' she protests. 'It's just that no one ever says that.'

Madison shrugs, tosses her hair again. 'I like men look-ing at me. So shoot me. I don't bother to look like this for myself. I don't ban bread for myself. Well, maybe a little. I get anxious if I go over a hundred and twenty pounds. But it all comes back to men in the end. I want to look good for them.'

'Them plural – not just for Bastian?'

Madison raises an eyebrow, then laughs. 'No, not just for him. Tell me,' she leans forward, 'you dressed up a little yesterday, didn't you? Before you came down to meet us. I saw you at the window but you didn't appear for another ten minutes.'

'Oh, I . . . I'd been making the beds and . . .'

Madison waves her hand. 'No, I get it. We were early too. I bet you were cursing us. But my point is, you made an effort. And then, after you . . . well, for dinner you dressed up properly: washed your hair, put on heels.'

'I wanted to look presentable for our new guests. For you.'

'Some neat flats would have done that.'

'Together, then. I wanted to look together. Like I imagine you always do.'

'Did you look us up before?'

Laura blinks, wrong-footed by the abrupt turn in the conversation, and feels herself beginning to blush. Madison reaches out to take her wrist, circling it lightly between her thumb and middle finger. It fits perfectly, like it would between her own fingers.

'Oh, don't be embarrassed,' Madison says, amused. 'Who wouldn't do a bit of digging nowadays? It's just prudent, isn't it, if you're going to let people you've never met come stay in your house for weeks on end?'

Laura takes a breath. 'I honestly think I made myself look better for both of you. Maybe subconsciously because there was a new man I was about to meet, but also because of you. Women are usually the ones you want to approve of you, I think. Men are far less fussy.'

Madison laughs and it isn't the breathless, tinkling giggle she'd employed in front of the men last night. This is earthy, sexy. It makes her think of Lou.

'Maybe you're right,' she says. 'Maybe I do dress up and stay thin so women think I look good. Or maybe I'm just competing with them. Do you have lots of girlfriends?

Back home, I mean? None of the women round here seem to be under seventy.'

Laura nods. 'Lou. She's my best friend. There are others, but she's the one I tell everything. We met at university.'

'You majored in literature, right?' When Laura stares, she laughs the new laugh again. 'I looked you up too.'

Their coffees arrive, and before Laura really knows how it's happened, Madison has begged a cigarette off the men on the table next to them and is turning back with it already lit. She exhales expertly.

'Don't tell my husband. Now he vapes he won't allow cigarettes in the house.'

Laura can't remember ever meeting anyone she feels so undecided about. She had pigeonholed her wrongly and now doesn't have an inkling who Madison really is, how many layers there might be to peel. She'd had her down as a humourless Goop type, without the innate taste or Waspy breeding, perhaps, but that wasn't right. She's brighter than she'd first appeared too. Not just sharper – she'd obviously been sharp – but more articulate, and much more self-aware. Lou would either love her or hate her. Laura isn't sure about that either.

'So, tell me about Lou,' said Madison, making Laura start, the question running so close to her thoughts. 'Were you roommates?'

Laura leans back in her chair because Madison is slightly too close. She can smell her sweet perfume again, mingling with the cigarette smoke. It seems not to fit her any more, too ingénue-like. The sun strikes Laura's face from behind the church opposite and she raises a hand to shield her eyes. The coffee is waking her up already.

'We lived together, yes. In a house-share with two others. We were on the top floor together, up in the eaves.' A memory, then: Lou sitting on her bed and picking at the old-fashioned woodchip on the walls, Laura swatting her hand away, saying, 'Oi, that'll come out of your damage deposit, not mine.'

She looks back at Madison. 'I think women concentrate on their romantic relationship as though it's the only important one in their life,' she says. 'It's all husbands – and, of course, kids and parents and siblings too. But what about friends?' She pauses, embarrassed because she's speaking so intensely. 'Sometimes I think a friend can be one of the great loves in your life. Maybe *the* love of your life.'

Madison is still watching her, the cigarette between her fingers burning down, forgotten. 'I love that,' she breathes. 'I totally love it and yet I've never had it. Wow, I'm jealous. All that trust and closeness and you don't even have to sleep with them.'

'Yes, it's not sexual,' Laura says, emboldened. 'But it is like a crush in some ways. It's just an adult version of how you feel at school when a new girl starts and you know you'll be best friends. You want them to yourself, to be *yours*.'

'And there's definitely no sexual element to it? When you're an adult?'

Laura shakes her head. 'Not for me. It's purer than that. Like a kind of recognition. It's sort of . . . joyful. Lou and I always say we wish we were gay and then we could forget men and just be together for ever. But we aren't.' She pulls a face. 'Irredeemably straight, the pair of us.'

Madison cocks her head to the side, as she had done in the

66

kitchen, and Laura realizes why it seemed odd earlier, slightly off. It's because it's flirtatious – the sort of female body language you might use on a man. She doesn't know exactly what its evolutionary origins might be – maybe exposing your neck releases pheromones, or signals a willingness to offer yourself up to someone more powerful, like a dog rolling on its back to expose its vulnerable belly. But then Madison reaches for Laura's wrist again, this time pinning it lightly to the table. Her ring glitters, fracturing the sunlight.

'So you and Nick,' she says, after a silence, which Laura is surprised to find is not awkward. She knows she needs to go and buy the items on her list – some of the stalls are beginning to pack up already – but she can't quite muster the willingness to move.

'Me and Nick . . .' She swallows the last gritty dregs of her coffee and stops a passing waiter, asking shyly in Italian for a Diet Coke, which actually only requires one foreign word: the ever-useful *prego*. She wants something cold and clinking with ice now. It's almost eleven and the air is beginning to sear.

'Oh, I want one too,' cries Madison, as the waiter turns on his heel. He inclines his head and smiles. 'Jeez, this is turning into the best day. I'll be eating *gelato* next. But don't avoid the question.' She trains her blue eyes back on Laura. 'You and Nick.'

'What about us?'

'Where did you meet? When did you meet? Was it romantic? Did you just *know*?'

'Oh, God, we've been together for ever. We met in our early twenties.'

'So at college, then? Like Lou? Did you meet in the first week and that was it? There was a couple like that where I went.' She gives Laura a wry look. 'Yes, I actually did go to college.'

Something in Laura's expression must have betrayed her because, it's true, she wouldn't have had Madison down as the academic type.

'Oh, no one thought I'd go, but anything to get away from the town I grew up in. You know those coming-of-age movies set in some deadbeat town where the kids have nothing to do but sit in the back of a flatbed, drinking beer and dreaming of the big city? That was my actual high-school experience. I was even a cheerleader.

'It wasn't a very good college. It was about as far from the Ivy Leagues as you can get. Bastian is the brains in this outfit.' She centres her wedding diamond, which is slightly loose. 'But, you know, it was something. No one else in my family had done it. Anyway, there was this girl in my dorm who met this guy, and they kind of looked like twins from the start, weirdly, and that was just it for them. They were very Christian so they weren't doing anything – well, they weren't doing *that*, anyway – but they stuck together the whole way through.'

'Maybe that was why,' says Laura. 'All that anticipation.'

Madison laughs. 'Yeah, maybe. They did marry straight after apparently. We're lucky, me and Bastian. It's still exciting. It's pretty unusual for that to last beyond the first few years. I know that.'

Laura feels herself souring minutely, her growing sense of kinship with Madison draining away a little.

'But I think that's more me, if I'm brutally honest with

myself,' Madison continues, as if she's sensed Laura's slight cooling off. 'I'm the keener one. I'm the adorer.' She shrugs her broad, yoga-honed shoulders. 'I'm OK with that. It works for us.'

'The adorer,' Laura repeats softly. She thinks about Madison looking at Bastian last night, and Bastian looking at her, Laura.

'Yeah, I think people are one or the other and you need one of each to be a balanced couple. You seek out your opposite without knowing it. Obviously the power balance being equal is held up as the ideal, but I don't think it's like that for almost anyone, do you? Honestly? Maybe it shifts about between some people, but everyone I know seems to be stuck in their roles. In some ways, I've ended up like my mom, God help me. She did everything for my dad. She brought me up with all this bullshit about how to keep your man happy, like it was a job you never got a vacation from. You know, I never thought of it, but she didn't have a single close girlfriend. Not a one. I used to fight with her about how small her life was, say she was the original Stepford wife, but without the nice suburban house. I get it more now. He made sure he was all she had. The crazy thing is that I find myself doing some of the same crap. I mean, it's not like I run to put on red lipstick when I hear Bast's key in the door, but almost. I check the mirror, you know. I go down on him without being asked.' She smiles slyly at Laura's startled expression. 'I wouldn't let him go without a fight.'

Laura's impression of Madison shifts again. For all her talk of being a little woman, she has teeth and claws. But she's not quite a man's woman either. She looks up and realizes Madison is waiting for a response.

'I actually think me and Nick are pretty equal,' she says carefully. 'I hope we are anyway.'

Madison begins to laugh, then claps her hand over her mouth. 'Oh, shit, you're serious, aren't you? I'm sorry. But it's, like, so obvious to me that Nick is the adorer. He's me, honey. All the way.'

Laura laughs too. There's no edge to Madison's words and all the knowingness has gone from her face, if it was ever there. Besides, she's probably right. Laura knows really that she is. She'd been thinking about it only the other day, hadn't she? How she'd picked him out and he'd simply gone with it. *You*, she'd thought across the table in the pub. *You won't ever make me feel so bad I want to die. Not like he did.*

'You're wrong about set types, though,' she says, as the waiter reappears with their Cokes: silver cans matte with condensation, two tall glasses full of ice, thick wedges of lime on top. She drinks and fine droplets of fizz moisten her face. Madison waits expectantly, elbows on the table between them. 'I was an adorer too, once,' she says and a strange urge to confess more steals over her, though the pain of what happened can still make her wince in an empty room. 'Never again.'

'I'm so intrigued right now,' says Madison.

Laura paints on an enigmatic smile, shakes her head. If she was drinking wine she'd tell. And then tomorrow she would wake with that sinking feeling, the sense that she'd given too much away, too cheaply, and probably without the reciprocated confidences that would have made it an equal baring of souls. One of the reasons she'd loved Lou when they first met was that she was just the same. They had developed a signal to rescue the other when they were over-sharing in public, a mime of someone reeling in a fishing line.

'Hey, there a guy staring at you.' Madison's mouth is suddenly close to her ear, her breath cold from her drink. 'You don't know him, do you?'

It's the mechanic, though Laura might not have noticed him in his off-duty clothes: jeans and a black T-shirt, both tightly fitting. He doesn't smile but one eye closes in a wink, so quick she almost misses it. Heat flares immediately in her cheeks, as much from embarrassment for him being so cheesy as from her own English reserve.

'Holy shit, you do know him,' exclaims Madison. 'You have to tell.'

Laura silently reminds herself again that Madison is not Lou. 'Oh, Christ, barely. He works in a garage. I had to take the car in the other week and he was a bit flirty. The men are often like that here.' She forces herself to laugh. 'It takes a bit of getting used to but it doesn't mean anything.'

Madison raises an eyebrow. 'Seriously, that's all? I was hoping you were having a torrid affair. I wouldn't tell Nick, you know. Or Bastian.' Laura glances quickly at her before she can help it. 'You don't betray the sisterhood, right?'

She risks another glance across the piazza but he's gone, absorbed into the throng of housewives. Her shoulders drop. She doesn't know now why she'd thought about him so . . . vividly. He seems completely obvious, even a little oily. She notes the unfortunate choice of adjective, and imagines emailing Lou an update about the *oily mechanic*.

'What are you smiling about? Tell me.' Madison pokes her in the ribs with a sharp finger.

And Laura decides that she will – at least, a watered-down version – partly because she has the urge to, and partly because she finds herself wanting to keep on-side this woman she can't quite get the measure of. Anyway, the mechanic is nothing compared to what she had felt this morning on the stairs with Bastian. Recalling it makes her breath hitch a little in her chest. She mentally tests herself for sisterly guilt as they drive away from Castelfranco, with only half the items on her shopping list, like pressing down on a new bruise. Now she thinks she might like Madison after all, she should feel bad, and she does, a bit. The trouble is, there's a stronger impulse. She believes, if she's honest, that she deserves this ... connection. The messages with someone she hadn't seen for years were one thing, but this – so unexpected, and under her own roof – is real life, happening right now. She's been going through the motions of life for so long, stuck in a kind of permanent power-saving mode. Energy, electricity, courses through her. She feels like she could spark and crackle with it.

Dusk has thickened and spread so that it's almost completely dark under the pergola by the time she lights the candles. The dinner table looks perfect. Magazine-worthy. She can't help the little rush of pride that she has created all this. Nick has too, in a practical sense, but it's *her* style and *her* eye that have turned somewhere tatty and dated into something special.

The tablecloth is old with scalloped edges, the cotton washed fine and soft over decades by Italian housewives she'll never know. She's placed sprigs of foliage in narrow glass vases along the length of the table – sage, lavender, eucalyptus and something she doesn't know the name of. Everything is white and eau de Nil, warm light flickering from tall tapers and tea-lights and the strings of small white globes Nick was instructed to thread through the vines that twist around the slats of the pergola.

When the four of them are seated she sees that they're all dressed in white or cream. Their skin is smooth and sun-kissed in the flattering light. Even Nick's pinkish skin is rendered golden.

'Look,' she says, gesturing round the table, 'we match.' She catches Bastian's eye and glances down as if he's singed her. Sensing that he continues to watch, she picks self-consciously at the globules of soft wax that have gathered at the bottom of the candlestick nearest to her. She also, without conscious intention, sits up straighter, pushes out her chest, tucks her hair behind her ear. She licks her lips. Her body does all this before she can help it.

She had drunk two or perhaps it was three glasses of wine while she dressed the table. There's a new box of dry white in the fridge – an attempt to economize when it's just them – which she finds hard to resist. She always has good intentions – to have just half a glass – but is then drawn back, pushing the button of the little plastic tap for a couple more perfectly cold inches.

'You've sure got yourselves a magical place here,' Bastian says, raising his glass. They clink, Laura having to get to her feet to reach Madison's. 'Was it like this when you moved in?'

'God, no,' says Nick. 'It looked amazing on first glance

but the stucco was falling off, there were two enormous satellite dishes round the back, and the weeds were something else. I had to hire a blow-torch.'

'And I'm guessing it's you who's responsible for all this?' says Bastian to Laura, gesturing at the table, the whole tableau in general.

She glows, nods.

'It was a joint effort,' says Nick, as she opens her mouth to reply.

'Well, the decor wasn't,' she says sharply. She smiles to soften it.

Nick opens his hands. 'Apparently I'm just the weeds bloke.'

'And a talented chef, don't forget,' says Madison, pointing with her fork at her food. 'You're gonna make me fat.'

The night is closing in fast around them now, the gaudy sunset cooled to a deep electric blue. It feels like they're inside a room under the pergola, but then, somewhere across the valley, music starts up, the sound travelling easily through the inert air. They all notice it at the same time, the bass not regular but with a trip in it.

'Someone is having a party,' says Madison, gleefully. 'We should crash it later.' She reaches across the table and runs her nails lightly down Bastian's forearm. 'Do you remember how we used to do that all the time?'

She turns to Laura. She seems to address Laura more than she does Nick. It's another unexpected thing about her.

'It's just like this in the canyon back at home. You can hear everything for miles. We just follow the sound. No one ever cares if you're supposed to be there or not. If

74

you act like you belong, people think you do. And, anyway, people in LA are terrified of offending the wrong person. I'd just walk up to the host and say, *Hi, how are you? You look amazing!* And then we'd be in.'

'My wife has no shame,' says Bastian.

My wife. Laura ignores the odd little kick those words give her. She smiles at Madison. 'I can imagine you'd have fitted right in anyway.'

Madison blows her a kiss.

Bastian reaches over for the corkscrew and pulls an unopened bottle from the ice bucket. 'So, Nick, you were a journalist back in England?'

Laura sees Nick's slight stiffening, his eyes on the wine as Bastian turns the corkscrew. His wine.

'Yeah, well, a sub,' he says. 'Headlines, pull quotes, sorting out other people's shitty copy. That kind of thing.'

'So you don't write yourself?'

'Not really. Once in a blue moon.'

Laura twists her glass round. 'Well, that's not quite true, is it?'

Nick shrugs, making her feel slightly weary. In fact, before Italy, he had managed to get a decent-sized feature in every couple of months and Laura doesn't know why he won't just say so. Why he doesn't boast a little bit. It's hard to see his expression in the next seat but pride always makes him petulant and brittle. Underneath it, she knows, is something deeper: a low-level resentment born of years of being overlooked, a piece of the office furniture without even the security of being on permanent staff. It's another reason he gave in to the Italy plan, though this, like so much else, also goes unsaid. To discuss it would

75

acknowledge that nothing would ever get better at the paper, that at some unmarked point in the road Nick had gone from being on the way up at a national to being stuck. *Don't ask any more*, she pleads silently, but Bastian is already speaking.

'If you're a creative yourself, it must be extra galling, making some famous columnist's writing better. They still get their name at the top, right?'

Nick's smile is tight. 'That's the way it works.'

'Tell Madison and Bastian about that investigative piece you did,' Laura prompts.

'What – the one they hacked down to fifteen hundred words after three months' research?'

She resists rolling her eyes. *Why don't you want to impress them?* she thinks but doesn't say. He always does this when he's not comfortable – and always with other men. 'He's not an alpha, your Nick, bless him,' Lou said once. They'd been at a dinner party and Nick had almost got into an argument with a mutual friend's self-assured barrister boyfriend. 'I reckon he's got PTSD from all those public-school dickheads at the paper.'

He's shrugging now, shoulders slumped. He picks up his glass and goes to drink but it's empty. Bastian tops him up.

'The trouble with journalism is it's still a bit of an old-boys network.'

Don't get into this, she thinks. She's heard it a million times. The Americans won't get it either.

'But isn't it really liberal at that place?' Bastian refills Laura's glass before Madison's and looks at Nick expectantly.

'Supposedly,' says Nick. 'I went in thinking I'd find my

people, but they all knew each other from these posh London day schools.' He slightly slurs the word 'London' and Laura cringes.

'And you're in film production, Bastian, is that right?' she says. 'What side do you work in?'

Bastian considers. Unlike Nick he is apparently entirely at ease. Madison smiles proudly. *Look at my man. Isn't he something?* Laura can hear the words as if Madison had spoken them aloud.

'I guess my work is all about connecting,' he says eventually. 'I put different people together, create synergies, you know?'

'Lots of schmoozing, then,' says Nick. His tone is light, but Laura knows him well enough to detect the barb. He's taken the bottle back now.

Bastian shrugs, looks down. 'I'm not pretending I'm saving lives. It's Hollywood. I guess my job is just to keep all the cogs greased and moving, whether it's show-runners and scouts or development guys with casting directors.' His body is still loose, comfortable.

'LA is nothing but connecting people,' breaks in Madison. 'It's one big networking event.' She strokes Bastian's arm. 'And he's, like, the *best* at that. He knows exactly who to put together.' She leans over to kiss his cheek. He doesn't look at her or acknowledge the kiss but Laura sees his hand disappear under the table and knows he must have laid it on her thigh.

He meets her gaze then and, for a split second, she thinks he won't say anything, just keep on looking at her. Then he smiles and she can't help glancing sideways to see if Nick's seen it because it's too much, too knowing, somehow. But Nick is occupied pouring himself more wine and she allows herself a glance at Bastian.

'So, Laura,' he says. 'What about you? What were you running away from?'

Nick looks up at that, making her hurry to answer.

'I was a teacher. Nothing exciting. At a secondary school – like a high school.'

'Oh, I can totally see that,' says Madison.

Laura doesn't know how to take this.

'I bet the boys loved you,' Madison continues.

She looks down, embarrassed but pleased. 'Oh, I'm not so sure about that.'

'What did you teach?' Bastian shifts in his seat and his foot knocks against hers, which she pulls away as if it's burnt.

'English and some drama,' she says, too fast. She's being ridiculous. She takes a breath. 'The drama wasn't my thing at all, but they needed someone who could cover both. The older kids who'd chosen it were fine but teaching drama to thirty fourteen-year-olds is no joke. The boys basically saw it as an extension of break.'

'I'd have been the worst teacher,' says Madison. 'I'd have wanted them all to love me.'

'Laura was a bit like that, too, weren't you, darling?' Nick picks up his glass. 'It's a nightmare for discipline if you are. They're like wild animals, kids. They can smell it.'

In reply, she puts down her knife and fork, Nick's main course only half eaten. She's got no appetite anyway.

'Actually, my discipline was fine. I just found it demoralizing how little most of them cared. It wasn't so bad with English because it's a core subject – they all needed to pass it. But my timetable ended up being fifty, sixty per cent drama. It was . . . wearing.'

'I can imagine you being a great teacher,' says Bastian. 'It's one of those professions that is so under-appreciated but, to me, it's as important as being a doctor. Much more important than the average lawyer, though you'd never know that in the States. Those kids would have known you cared, even if they were playing it too cool to ever say so. The good ones would have known. They'll remember you years from now.'

Her cheeks flush with pleasure. She wants to ask him why he thinks that, but it would sound like she was just fishing for compliments. She almost certainly is. 'Actually, I'd just started applying for a job at a different school when we finally decided to move here.'

'She was about to sell her soul,' says Nick. 'Go over to the dark side.'

'What Nick's getting at is that it was a public school,' says Laura. 'Well, a private school. He didn't approve.'

'I never get this,' says Madison, laughing. 'Which is it?'

'What you call public schools are known as state schools in the UK,' says Nick. 'Fee-paying schools are referred to as private but also public. But I suppose "public" schools tend to be the big old famous ones, like Eton. Where our Tory prime ministers cut their teeth.'

'And this is the dark side?' says Bastian. 'I went to private school.'

There's a beat of silence, which Madison rushes in to break.

'I'm guessing no one but me watched *Gossip Girl* but Bast's school was straight out of that. Or *Cruel Intentions* maybe.'

'I loved that film,' says Laura. '*Dangerous Liaisons* in a New York private school. That Buffy actress was in it, doing coke in the girls' loos.'

She smiles at Madison, who is nodding. She has the sense of the two of them smoothing over the fissures the men have created, like women always do.

They work their way through the rest of the meal, the main course followed by something alcoholic with figs and mascarpone – and again it's gone too quickly. Laura vaguely understands that the pudding is very good without really registering each mouthful. While they eat, the bassline of the music across the valley thuds on, like a heartbeat. It changes the atmosphere, somehow, like a hint that something might happen imminently: a slow-motion drumroll. Their own slightly off-kilter soundtrack.

'Where do you think it's coming from?' says Madison, as though she's overheard Laura's thoughts. She keeps doing this. 'What are the neighbours like?'

'The neighbours are miles away,' says Nick. 'I'm not sure they even count as neighbours.'

'You haven't met any of them yet?'

Laura shakes her head. 'We keep saying we should go and introduce ourselves but everyone is tucked away down these long drives and our Italian is so limited.'

She stops herself: it might reflect badly on them to admit to being the amateurs they are. She wishes she'd reminded Nick not to let slip to the Americans that they're the first guests. The truth is that they've made little real effort to get to know anyone around here. She had such good intentions – mastering the language, making friends – but they all trickled away. The one time she'd really tried, at the market, with the stallholders and the women who haggle with them, she'd been received with bemusement. Actually, it had felt more like resentment. *What do you want with us here? Are we supposed to make allowances for you?*

'I still think we should crash,' says Madison. She's re-applying lip gloss, blind. It gleams stickily. 'Drive around with the windows down until we figure out where the music's coming from.'

'There's this path actually,' says Nick. His eyes glitter in the light from the candles.

He's part-way to being properly drunk, Laura realizes. Not that she's much better, now at the stage when she has to think about where she's placing her wine glass so she doesn't clash it against her plate. 'What path?' she says. 'You haven't told me.'

'I found it one morning when I went for one of my early walks.' He lowers his voice conspiratorially. 'Laura is not a morning person. While she's still asleep, I get up to all sorts.'

As Madison laughs, he realizes what he's said and glances across at Laura. Bastian is also watching her again, his chin dipped so he's peering up at her through his dark lashes, surprisingly long and boyish for such a masculine man. It makes him look softer.

'I think it's probably an old Roman road,' Nick continues. 'There are a lot of them round here. Although aren't Roman roads always straight? Anyway, it curves round the hill, and if you keep going, you come to this incredible garden with fountains and statues and God knows what. There's this series of pools that go down the hill. Three of them, each bigger than the last. Black-tiled with granite slabs round them. And all the plants are spiky, like sculptures. It's a bit much, actually. It doesn't really look right in the landscape.'

'Sounds very Tom Ford,' says Madison.

'More ostentatious than that. Much further along the spectrum towards oligarch.'

'Didn't it make you want to find out who lives there?' says Bastian.

'Well, I was going to explore but then these dogs started barking. They sounded huge so I had to leg it. Serious money, though, whoever it is.'

'I can't believe you didn't tell me about this,' Laura says.

'I bet that's where the party is,' Madison cuts in, widening her eyes at Laura. 'You're in, aren't you? Hey, Nick, I wasn't going to say anything, but I think your wife is a bit of a dark horse. She told me a couple of her own secrets when we were at the market.'

Laura colours again and is glad of the low, flickering candlelight.

'What's all this?' says Nick. His hearty tone is back. 'Don't tell me you bumped into one of her Italian lover-boys?'

'Oh, just the one,' says Madison, winking at Laura, who wonders if Madison caught Bastian looking at her, and is now asserting her status as wife. But then Madison reaches across the table to brush her fingers. Her smile seems genuine. 'What do you say, Laura? Why don't we try out this path, find the party? We can take our bikinis and check out these black pools.'

Laura has already started to shake her head when Nick lays a hot, slightly damp hand on her bare arm. 'It sounds really fun but it's already half past ten and we need to clear up. You and Bastian should go though, Madison. You can report back to us in the morning.'

'Actually, I think I will go,' Laura interrupts, shifting so that Nick's hand falls. 'We can leave the clearing up till the morning, can't we?'

Madison claps her hands. 'That's my girl.'

'You mean *I* can clear up in the morning,' says Nick.

'Later then.' She's already getting to her feet. 'We'll do it later. Or I'll do it, seeing as you cooked.'

'Come on, Nick,' says Madison. 'I want our clever chef to come too. Anyway, we need you to show us the path.'

'I'm sure we can figure it out,' says Bastian, standing. He cracks his knuckles. 'If Nick doesn't want to come, he can just point us in the right direction.'

Nick blinks a couple of times, then stands too, his napkin falling to the grass. 'No, it's OK, I'll come. It'll be a laugh.' He starts blowing out the candles.

'Yay!' Madison rushes round the table and takes Laura's hand. 'Come on, let's go get our swimmers. We should probably change into something else too.'

'Something else?' Laura smooths down her white cotton dress, which flares at the waist.

'Oh, it's gorgeous,' says Madison, 'but if we're going to be mixing with oligarchs we need to glam up more. LBDs and heels, a ton more make-up.'

Laura feels a flare of anticipation that takes her straight back to being nineteen or twenty, the excitement of a night when you don't already know the outcome.

Madison holds out a hand. 'Come on. Let me do your eyes. I've got a dress you'll look poured into, too.' She sees Laura's face. 'Oh, don't take it the wrong way, sweetheart. I would kill for your curves, that teeny little waist. I'm all angles. Isn't she sexy, Bast?'

He appraises her frankly. 'Sure she is,' he says, and her self-consciousness cuts straight through the wine.

It's dark away from the carefully curated lights of the dining table. Gauzy cloud, or perhaps it's the dispersing heat of the day, has blinded the stars. The only thing she can see is the pale stone of the path underfoot, another forgotten Roman road. Trees crowd in on either side and a fallen branch – so brittle it cracks like gunshot as she treads on it – makes her stumble and turn her ankle. Someone catches her before she hits the ground, the grip around her arm so strong that she knows it'll leave bruises. She doesn't need any light to know it's Bastian. She hadn't realized he was so close.

'Careful,' calls Madison, from somewhere behind her and suddenly Nick is there, his hand lighter on her arm than Bastian's had been. She can still feel where each of his fingers had held her.

'You OK? We should have brought the torch.'

'I couldn't find it,' she says, slightly breathless.

'Not far now, anyway.'

It's true that the music is getting louder, the heavy, stretched-out bass the lure that's got them this far. She pulls at the hem of her dress, which is actually Madison's. It's skin-tight – *body-con*, as Madison put it – and that's entirely apt because she is hyper-aware of her body in it, even in the dark. With every step, it rubs and rides up her thighs.

She's expecting a wall or a fence, some sort of solid boundary encircling this grand and mysterious property, but there's nothing. The clots of trees and vegetation gradually give way to something more manicured until the stone path softens into grass. It's as though the whole valley belongs to this one house: a wild extension to the garden.

They round a bend and there it is: a modern approximation of a villa floating above them, lit up like a liner crossing the Atlantic. The pools Nick had mentioned shine like onyx. The three of them, stacked diagonally up the hill, are connected by a narrow channel down which water moves as silently and viscously as oil. Guests cluster around the largest, at the top, which is sunk into the villa's jutting terrace. The music reveals itself now: not just the simple solar-plexus thud that has guided them here, but a woozily melodic hip-hop.

'See what I mean?' says Nick, softly. 'Not quite what you'd expect.'

'No,' she breathes.

Madison fluffs out her hair. 'I feel like someone's teleported us back to LA.'

They split up, Madison taking Laura's hand and pulling her up the twisting steps towards the terrace. She glances back towards Nick, who shrugs. Bastian stands off to the side, also watching them go.

'Less conspicuous if it's just us girls,' says Madison. In the light of the house, which is dazzling after the walk, her eyes shine. People, the buzz of them, is oxygen to

Madison, Laura thinks. Fuel. Maybe it is to her, too, more than she knows. She wonders how lonely she's actually been in Italy, hungry for other people for months, her diaries and laptop her only company. She glances back again. She can't make out Bastian's expression in the gloom, but he hasn't moved. It's only as she turns to catch up with Madison that she realizes she didn't check to see if Nick was still there too.

They station themselves at the edge of the pool on the upper terrace and when a waiter passes with a tray of drinks, Madison neatly swipes two.

'You really are an old hand at this, aren't you?' says Laura, admiringly, and drinks half of hers in one gulp. It's some kind of martini with a floral twist she can't identify. Her throat burns. She never drinks spirits, these days. She knocks back the other half and Madison laughs, delighted.

'Attagirl.' She finishes her own and nods towards the waiter, who is about to circulate again. 'Now, your turn.' They grin at each other, and it makes her gleeful that Madison is here, her new friend.

Signalling for the waiter draws wider attention. A man in a black, open-necked shirt, his sharply cut hair not so much blond as colourless, glances over and then again, more closely this time. Separating himself from the people he's standing with, he moves purposefully towards them.

'Oh, shit, here we go,' mutters Laura.

Madison tosses back her hair. 'I've got this.'

'*Buona sera*,' he says smoothly, beckoning the waiter over and gesturing for them to swap their empty glasses for fresh ones. 'I find I don't mind gatecrashers when they are lovely ones.' His accent is hard to place: Slavic, maybe, like his cheekbones. It's only faint, his intonation of English almost flawless.

'We just followed the music,' says Madison, with a sly smile. 'We couldn't help ourselves.'

'Like the Pied Piper. I'm Ivan. And you're American.' He kisses Madison's hand, then Laura's.

'Madison is American,' she says. 'I'm English. And actually I'm your neighbour. Madison is staying with us, our first paying customer at the guesthouse we came here to run, and just in the nick of time, too.' She cringes at the slip-up she'd thought Nick would be the one to make.

Madison gives her a questioning look, then smiles. 'Well, we're just thrilled to be your first. And don't you worry – with the review we're gonna leave, trust me, you'll be booked out in no time.'

Laura looks down, still embarrassed but touched now, too. 'Thank you,' she says quietly.

'I'm afraid our husbands have also gatecrashed,' Madison continues easily. 'They're around here somewhere.'

'We hope you don't mind,' says Laura.

Ivan tilts his head and smiles at them both, his teeth so perfect they must be veneers. When he lights a slim cigarette, gold-tipped, she sees that his hands, like his garden, are recently manicured. He shrugs. 'Why would I mind some new blood? I get tired of seeing the same faces. But you must promise you'll come back later this week, spend a whole day here so I can give you my full attention. Will you?'

He should be creepy but he isn't at all: too polished, too entirely un-predatory. They nod at him, like eager schoolgirls. He gifts them a last smile before moving on.

'Wow,' says Madison. 'You live next door to Jay Gatsby.'

Laura laughs. She feels fizzy with their success. The second cocktail is beginning to hit her now. She's not sleepy like she gets with just wine. Her senses feel heightened, elevating the evening into something that she knows will feel hyper-real in retrospect.

'Are you going to be Daisy or shall I?' she says.

'I think if anyone's gonna be Daisy it'll be Nick or Bastian, don't you?' Madison raises her eyebrows.

'Oh!' Laura searches for Ivan in the throng, as if another look might confirm it, though it suddenly makes perfect sense. 'Do you think?'

'I do. He's too well put-together not to be.'

Time passes in fits and starts, as it always does when she gets like this. *I'm in my cups*, she keeps thinking, wondering where in her memory she's dredged up the archaic phrase. *I feel happy right now*, she thinks. *I feel alive again. I'll remember this night for ever.*

She's on her own now. Madison went off to find a loo some time ago and hasn't returned. She drifts through different layers of the garden. Sculptures, mostly made of metal, are dotted around. Sharp-edged and artfully rusted, there's nothing organic about them. They look like they've been dropped from the sky by aliens. She perches on one, cold against her legs. Behind the music, and the insect chorus that hums like a power line, the air is utterly still. It must be almost exactly body temperature.

'It's like being inside, isn't it?' It's Ivan.

He's so close she can smell him. It's a scent that's hard to describe, and doesn't quite match his decorative taste: much more subtle, almost severe. 'You smell like a rich person,' she says aloud, and claps her hand over her mouth.

He laughs. 'I am rich.'

Encouraged because she's amused him, she tips her head, considering, on one side. 'Yes, but in a different way from the house. Less . . .'

'Less ostentatious?'

'Exactly.' She stops. 'Oh, sorry, that's so rude. I think I'm drunk.'

'Don't be sorry. My partner – my ex-partner – was more flamboyant. He chose everything. One day I'll have changed it all back. Make it mine again. Make it Italy's again.'

'I'm sorry. That he's an ex, I mean.'

'I'm not. He was a leech.' Ivan leads her back towards the terrace. 'Would you like to see inside? I've started stripping back the worst of Raoul's excesses but it's something of a work in progress.'

It's impossible to gauge how old the bones of the villa are. Everything has been hollowed out and extended and knocked-through. The living space has even lost its ceiling, soaring to double-height with a glassed-in gallery. Through an open door that leads to some sort of library or study, she spots Bastian deep in conversation with a man she's never seen before, his bald brown head shining like a conker in the lamplight. She stops.

'Is that your husband?' says Ivan.

'No, not mine. Madison's. That's Bastian.'

'Lucky Madison. He's Italian?'

'Well, a quarter. American, really.'

'His Italian must be decent. Angelo's English is terrible.'

They watch for a little longer and Bastian must sense it

because he looks up. It would be normal for him to smile in recognition but he doesn't. He holds her gaze, then lifts his chin. A summons. The intimacy of the gesture thrills her, making her face burn even as her eyes skitter away, finding Ivan's instead.

He's regarding her with interest. 'I think I would be blushing too. Take care, won't you?' He touches her shoulder lightly and leaves her with another smile, expensive teeth white in the low light.

Knowing she should find Nick, or Madison, she goes towards the men instead. Bastian pours her a whisky from a selection on a lacquered tray and hands it to her without a word. She doesn't even like whisky but she likes the way he did it without asking her. Another casual intimacy between them, as though he's been making her drinks for years. The whisky sears her throat just like the cocktails outside. She catches sight of herself in the mirrored back of the shelves behind Bastian. Her eyes are huge.

'This is Laura,' Bastian says to the man, who is appraising her candidly. '*Lei è Laura.*'

'Angelo,' the man replies. He brings her hand to his thin, dry lips and, instinctively, the urge cutting through her euphoric mood, she has to fight not to recoil.

'Angelo runs a construction company,' says Bastian.

'You live . . .' Angelo fixes her with his black eyes and gestures in the vague direction of the garden. Laura isn't sure if it's a question or a statement. His accent is heavy. 'Live' becomes *leev*. Perhaps it's the language barrier that makes him seem hostile. He doesn't smile, like most people do when they are meeting someone at a party.

'I live at Villa Luna Rossa,' she enunciates carefully.

'*Sì, sì,*' he says impatiently. 'I know this.' *Thees.* Then a burst of Italian.

She shakes her head. 'I'm sorry. My Italian –'

'He says he's met your husband,' Bastian cuts in.

'Oh.' She can't work out how this can be, her brain fogged by alcohol. She catches her reflection again, the frown line between her brows 'You know *Nick*?'

She realizes with a lurch that she's pronounced it 'Neek', but Angelo is nodding. There's a lull and then he says something in an undertone, obviously for Bastian's benefit, making himself laugh. Bastian doesn't react, just keeps on looking at her. She's glad he's here.

'What's he saying?'

Bastian smiles lazily. Angelo regards her down the beak of his nose. *Take care*, she hears Ivan say again, and it forces her to put down her half-drunk whisky. She can't get her head round this strange man knowing Nick. He's not the sort of person you would forget to mention.

'I should find my husband,' she says. Despite the presence of Bastian, she feels an urge to get away. Lou would say Angelo had a dodgy aura, only half joking. She moves away from the two men, half hoping Bastian will follow but, when she turns, unable to resist checking, Angelo is leaning in to mutter something in Bastian's ear. The Italian's laugh follows her out. 'Prick,' she says under her breath.

Bastian catches up with her in the garden.

'What did he say to you?' she says. 'When I was walking away? I didn't like him.'

'Yeah, he cornered me when I was having a look around.

He seemed to know where I was staying without asking. Wanted to know why we came to this part of Italy, if it was becoming *alla moda* in LA circles.'

She looks at him. He gives her an inscrutable smile. 'I guess he's *the* guy in this town.'

'What do you mean?'

'The guy who runs everything behind the scenes.'

'Well, Luna Rossa is none of his business.'

'Hey, relax.' As he says it, he reaches out to tuck a loose strand of hair behind her ear. The touch is only brief but its easy intimacy banishes all thoughts of Angelo. Her ear where he brushed it tingles.

'There's something about you,' he says. 'I feel like I've known you for ever.' He laughs softly.

She swallows, automatically looks around to check for the others, for Madison. There's no one but the shadows of other guests, thrown long by the lights from the house. She can hear the cicadas better here, out of time with the bass from the sound system.

'I should find Mads,' he says eventually, puncturing the spell.

'Yes,' she says. 'Yes, you should.' But she's the one to walk away, quickly, before he can, before she can change her mind.

She finds Nick in the lower reaches of the garden, close to where they came in off the path. He's sitting on the grass, knees bent, head lowered between them. When she hears her and looks up, his face is moon-pale and clammy. Irritation blooms inside her, and she glances around to check no one else is nearby. Then it strikes her that he seems more than just drunk.

'What's wrong?' She leans down to put her hand to his forehead nonsensically. He's not a child with a fever.

'Had a bit of a smoke,' he mutters. He spits to the side and she smells the vomit then. He wipes his mouth with the back of his hand.

'God, Nick. You know you always do this with weed.' She slaps the air near her head as a mosquito whines in her ear.

'You didn't even want me to come, did you?' His voice is petulant. 'I was just trying to have a good time. You'd gone off somewhere with the Americans.' He sounds about fifteen and she fights the temptation to say so. No one else at the party is in this state.

'Well, with Madison actually,' she says. 'Listen, I just met someone who knows you. Some intense builder bloke called Angelo. He made my skin crawl actually.'

Nick's expression as he takes this in is peculiar. It's not a face she knows and she knows all Nick's faces. So suddenly that it makes her rear away from him, he turns and retches.

1999

You aren't expecting him to be out tonight. He's never out on a Monday. You feel relaxed getting ready, knowing you can just spend a night with your friends, like in the days before him. Less memorable and less intense, but less exhausting too.

You and your housemates drink three bottles of cheap Soave – not quite cold enough to mask its roughness – before the taxi even arrives. You walk to the town's bars and clubs in summer, to save money, but it's winter-proper now, late in the Michaelmas term, roads slick and shiny with rain, damp making your hair frizz as soon as you step outside.

The club's interior is black and seems comprised almost entirely of Escher-like staircases, corridors and fire exits. Small fuggy rooms lead off them like afterthoughts, each one playing a slightly different sub-genre of dance music, but all decked out with the same UV lights that make everything white glow, not just teeth but pale bras under dark tops and dandruff on shoulders.

Coming in from the cold on a night like this, the air hits you like a hot, damp wall. Cigarette smoke immediately makes your clean hair reek. It mingles headily with the sharp-sweetness of alcohol, unlabelled spirits and cheap deodorant. The cloakroom is a pound and so are the drinks. In fact, it's only 75p for a shot of vodka and 25p for the mixer: Coke or lemonade. It's more if you want Red Bull, which is suddenly everywhere and apparently pretty toxic. You don't really like the taste of it but that's hardly the point.

The wine at home has made you dozy-drunk so you order double vodkas with Red Bull for you and Lou once you've fought your way to the bar, then make it two each because it's such an arse to queue. You down the first one so you've got a free hand to smoke with, and it's then, as you turn to get a light from some rugby boy, that you see him.

Your stomach drops, and it feels more like dread than anything good. The shock of it hits instantly, like a dozen Red Bulls, everything around you suddenly turned up – the music louder, the faces around you sharpening. Your skin tightens with it. For a split second, you have the clear thought that you wish he wasn't here. You don't feel equal to it, not tonight, when you haven't prepared for it mentally, when you're on the heaviest day of your period, when you haven't bothered shaving your legs.

You crush the ungrateful thought because he is so often elusive. You go every day to the same places on campus where you've glimpsed him previously, hoping he might be there again. Unlike you and your friends, he doesn't live in the streets of Victorian terraces that skirt the sprawling green hill the campus perches on. He has a car, like all of his group, and they live somewhere further out of the city. A lot of the rich kids do, some of them even out in the actual countryside. If they're too drunk to drive, they just get cabs, even though the meter will easily tick up to twenty-five or thirty quid.

It's almost a fortnight since you last saw him and the accumulation of the days without a sighting are beginning to make you feel desperate. Sometimes it's enough to day-dream about him, to invent scenarios in which you coincide in the library looking poised and polished. He might suggest a coffee break or, if it's later in the day – and you like this better: the library emptied, the windows turning to dark mirrors – he will ask if you need a lift home.

But now he's here you want to postpone it. You turn to see that Lou is watching you.

'What is it?' she says. 'You look like you've seen a ghost. Is it him?' She cranes to see.

'Stop being so obvious.'

'He never comes here – none of that lot do. Too gritty. He must have come to see you.'

The possibility of this swirls in your head, though you're already dismissing it as implausible. He's kissed you once, nothing more. He's probably not given you a second thought since. That's why most of your fantasies take place in a sober context, enabling him to see you in a different light from those drunken nights when everyone is on the pull and none of it means much.

Really, you want to be courted, asked out for dinner, but that doesn't seem to happen much. People pull multiple times and it either turns by careful, unacknowledged degrees into a relationship or it falls away. You don't want either, even if the first would mean being his girlfriend eventually. You want the two of you to burn brightly or nothing at all.

You tip up your glass but there's nothing left except ice-water. Inside your chest, your heart revs. You turn to tell

Lou you'll wait before you risk another drink, but she has already been absorbed into the crowd pushing towards the bar. When the drinks come – another two doubles – you decide to just go with it. It feels easier to do that than stop.

The new hit of alcohol works through you fast. You know you're drinking much too quickly but your sense of self-preservation has clicked off. You don't care. You're too busy watching him to care.

Actually, you're not watching him. You'd rather die than do anything so blatant. You don't need to, anyway. You always know where he is, as though his every move-ment tugs on a rope looped around your waist, like a diver invisible below the sea. You think you would like to tell him this one day, your lips pressed against his ear as his heft pushes you down into the bed. 'I always know where you are in the room without looking.' You would breathe the words right into him. 'I just know.'

Now he's talking to a girl you haven't seen before. She is tall and athletic-looking with the thick, swingy hair all the public-school girls have. Her stance is open and she's smiling, while his arms are crossed, which is the only thing keeping you on the spot, when your every instinct is to flee to the loos in case something happens. Your leg mus-cles twitch with the desire to do this.

While this is going on, you are actually mid-conversation with a boy on your course. He – Rob – is a rarity as a male English literature student and he's just like the other six: clever, sweet and ultimately unfanciable. His face is shiny and eager in the sickly green light from the fire-exit sign above him, and you nod and smile and make him laugh, even as you continue your surveillance, even as you internally convulse with terror that *he* is going to lean over and start kissing the rich girl in the expensive pink shirt and pearl studs.

Eventually Rob moves on with a chaste peck on your cheek and you're simultaneously glad because you can concentrate better and flooded with renewed dread now there's nothing else to distract you.

He's been talking to that girl for twenty minutes now. It's just the two of them and, oddly, in a room so overcrowded, a ring of space has formed around them. You are scared that this lacuna – a new word learnt this week – is an effect of the chemistry between them, that the kiss you dread so much is imminent. You wonder if it was like that when he kissed you that time, when he swooped down so suddenly that you'd actually said, 'Oh,' into his open mouth. You wouldn't have noticed if there had been, if the whole club had been evacuated around you.

Another girl appears and paws at his arm. This one you do recognize. Lou is instantly at your side.

'She can't ever leave him alone, can she? She's so pathetic.'

You twist Lou round because she is looking so obviously again, her glare towards the girl he'd been seeing a few weeks back so hostile that it causes her to look over before turning back, her expression briefly confused. But now she takes his hand and pulls him towards the dancefloor. He resists slightly, forcing her to stop and shake her head at him, mock-frowning and protesting, the last few words stridently audible over the music. *Stop being so dull.*

'Oh, for God's sake,' says Lou, emphatically. 'Look, fuck them. Let's go and dance ourselves. We always dance to this.'

You allow yourself to be led right past him, so that he can't fail to notice you. You don't look his way. You make yourself smile, and when Lou turns back to check on you, you press your body against hers, hugging ostentatiously, then jumping up and down to the music, still clasped together.

'I love you!' you shout, and of course you do, so much, but you're also acting for him, in case he's watching, as you're pretty sure he is now, the rope tugging hard, watching you be popular and nonchalant and fun. When a male friend you and Lou both know from halls joins in, prising the two of you apart so he can be hugged too, kissing you both, the one for you slightly too close to your mouth, his eyes scanning across your chest a shade too long, you feel giddy with gratitude for him.

It's a long song, this one, six or seven minutes, but the DJ doesn't cut it short because the whole point of it is the build-up, the anticipation of the bassline kicking in again. Everyone knows all the words, too, those humdrum words injected with weird menace by the beat that thumps and vibrates in your ribcage. Bread and jam. Tights and teeth.

The panic from the alcohol and caffeine, and whatever else they put in Red Bull, ebbs as you dance. You can feel it burning off, burning out. Another boy you don't really know turns you round and pushes up against you, his knee edging between your legs, but you spin away from him without losing your footing. You dance back to Lou, who holds out her arms. You kiss her on the lips, your beloved accomplice: a thank-you for the performance she is putting on out of solidarity, even as you perform for *him*.

He's watching you openly from the edge of the dance-floor now, his only movement the beer bottle he lifts to his mouth. His *mouth*. It was cold from beer last time, just for a second before the kiss heated it up. The bass of the song, which had paused, restarts and the room seems to lift as one. He starts to walk towards you.

Day 3

She wakes with a lurch. Her mouth feels odd, fizzy almost. She remembers the floral cocktails, the whisky, but she can't remember anything about getting to bed, and it's been a long time since she was that drunk. Those blank patches were completely normal at university – you woke, inspected yourself for damage, inside and out, and then got on with your day. Now she feels jittery, paranoid. Anything could have happened.

She turns towards Nick and then away again because he's breathing through his mouth and it's sour. His body smells odd, too – not like his usual scent. This is a meaty odour, almost high. An image comes to her then, the inky darkness of a fast stumble home, her breathing loud in the silence of deep night, the music finally stopped, even the cicadas muted.

She concentrates, trying to grasp more of the memory before it slips away, like a dream. She thinks she was alone. She remembers stopping at one point, her hackles up, some instinct in her lizard brain managing to penetrate the drunken fog. There had been a rustling off to her right, in the thick of the trees. A fox? It would be a fox at home, but in Italy? Perhaps it was a wolf. There are wolves up in the mountains, she knows. The thought of being so close to one makes her shudder, though she has no idea if they ever venture this far. She's never quite sure of anything here. It feels like she'll be guessing for ever.

She'd feel better if she got some more sleep, but even as she's thinking it, she's getting up and opening the door quietly so she doesn't wake Nick. He'll be useless with the guests today: he's always suffered badly with hangovers, his own brand of man-flu. The thought of preparing breakfast and then lunch and then dinner while he suffers makes her want to get into the car and drive away.

She doesn't bother getting dressed: she isn't expecting to see anyone. The old clock in the hall downstairs confirms her instinct that it's early: not yet seven. The house feels peaceful, undisturbed, not yet awake itself. It's only as she walks into the kitchen that she understands this second instinct was off. Bastian turns, a spoon in his hand.

'Oh!' she says, at exactly the same moment he says, 'Hey.'

She is immediately conscious of how little she's wearing: a tiny pair of shorts and a vest. The morning heat is more noticeable today than it's been since they moved here, an intimation of the intensity summer will bring. Or perhaps it's just the alcohol in her system making her sweat slightly. The only cool parts of her are the soles of her feet on the terracotta tiles. Glancing down, she sees they're filthy, nail varnish chipped. Another memory strikes her, a clear recollection of sitting on a step in Ivan's garden to take off her shoes, of dancing in bare feet, and finally the discomfort of forcing the heels back on when she set off for Luna Rossa.

As she's thinking all this, slower than usual, eyes still cast down to her feet, she's still with it enough to sense Bastian looking her up and down. Men do that, often brazenly. Obviously there are men who do it to intimidate but she also thinks they can't help it sometimes. Because she is not all there yet, because she's probably still drunk, she lets him without embarrassment. And while it goes against her feminist instincts to stand there so passively while his eyes rove all over her, another part of her likes it. Maybe Madison is right about this. Just as it objectifies, maybe it also bestows power.

When she looks up, it's as though he's been waiting for her.

'Last night was fun,' he says. He reaches into a cupboard for a cup and she notices the pot of coffee on the hob. She doesn't care at all that he's taken it upon himself to do this and wonders if she'd feel the same about Madison rooting through their things.

'It's all a bit hazy, to be honest,' she says, voice hoarse from shouting over music for hours. 'You know, when you can remember the odd thing but none of it hangs together?'

'Big gaps?' he says, with a smile, and hands her a coffee. 'I remember the bare feet.'

Her grubby toes automatically curl with embarrassment. 'Perhaps you can enlighten me, then. I think . . . I think I was dancing.' She laughs.

'Yeah, dancing. And dangling your feet in the pool.'

She remembers then. The lowest of the pools, which was also the smallest. Swinging her legs in dark water so smooth and warm that she could barely feel it. Like brushing through layers of silk. Bastian next to her, the heavy silhouette of him against the light of the party suspended above them.

'Was that you, then?' She knows it was. 'I *think* I remember.'

'Yes, that was me.' He holds her gaze until she looks away. It's always her who looks away.

It's not that they did anything. She's hazy on the details of the night after a certain point but there's no way she'd forget that. And yet . . . She wonders if his hand brushed her thigh where that ridiculous dress of Madison's had ridden up. She thinks she can recall the shivery heat of his touch spreading across her flesh, like sunburn by evening. But maybe it's got all mixed up with her daydreams.

And then they come back to her in a dizzying rush: a few seconds perfectly recalled. It must have been at the very end of the party, the crowd's hum abruptly loud as the dance music was switched off, the night's soundtrack ceded to the insects. Hot chlorine bleached the night air. She and Bastian were sitting together on a lounger watching Madison, who was acting out some anecdote. While they laughed at her performance, his thumb traced a hard line up and down Laura's lower spine. She shifted away slightly, not because of Madison, but because it almost hurt. He had moved his hand, started doing it again.

She jolts back into the present to see that he's leaving the kitchen with two cups. The other is for Madison, of course. He raises them in a goodbye.

After he's gone, she drifts aimlessly around the kitchen, walking one foot in front of the other as though a slanting bar of sunlight is a high wire. She picks off a grape each time she treads her way back to the fruit bowl on the side – it's the sort of thing a child does: purposeless, nothing more than itself, with no adult guilt. She is still restless and jittery from the hangover, her mind muddled, but there is one clear thought in it.

Something is going to happen soon.

She crosses to the hall and into the makeshift snug. Her laptop has only got twenty per cent battery left but she doesn't plug it in. She'll watch it tick away to five, which is when it starts threatening imperiously that she really must connect to power. Her fingers itch for it suddenly, for a return to the university days she'd thought about on waking.

She has been saving the messages all these weeks. She started after the third or fourth, when they started to take on the shape of a proper story, rather than a random couple of episodes that would come to nothing. She also wanted them saved in one place, offline, safe as houses. A Word document with the whole exchange copied and pasted in order has been given a title Nick would never click on: 'IVF stuff'. Still, to be sure, she's made up a list of dates and appointments and medications given so that it looks, on opening, to be genuine. It's only if you bother to scroll down that the truth is revealed.

Hello stranger.

To Laura, jangly as she is with hangover, the emails seem almost like a refuge this morning. Compared to how she felt just now in the kitchen, the neat document is contained and safe. She's in control of it, just like a diary. She needs that right now.

Upstairs, above her head, she hears a creak. It's the Americans' bathroom. She wonders who's having a shower: him or her? Is Madison in bed, drinking her coffee, while Bastian showers, naked, above Laura's head? The oddness of sharing her home with people who are giving them money strikes her again. Why would anyone choose this invasion of someone's private house over the easy anonymity of a hotel? There's something voyeuristic about it. But what about her and Nick? What are they, to have a website that entreats people to come? It suddenly seems so needy. *Please come and stay with us so we don't have to be alone together!*

She reads through the whole exchange, some 150 messages or so, from start to finish. When she looks up, jumping because she thought Nick was coming down the stairs, the room in front of her looks alien, altered somehow, and less solid than the document on her laptop. She clicks into her email and begins to type.

> Coffee is not doing much for my hangover this morning. Do you remember how hangovers always made me? 'Most people would be throwing up but you go all nympho,' you said once. Do you remember? I seem to remember everything. No, that's not quite right. They haven't all come at once. Each memory hands me the keys to a couple more.

She presses send before she can think too much about it. In her weird, slightly dissociative state, she doesn't even care that it's his turn to message, or that he'll probably think she's peculiar. She suspects he always thought that about her anyway, and liked it. The girls he'd known from home were always so uptight, or so he said. They never let themselves go enough to be weird.

Upstairs, back in their bedroom, Nick hasn't moved. His snoring seems to have got louder. Despite the open window behind the closed shutters, the air in the room is

108

stale. She goes over to open them, then changes her mind, tiptoeing out instead.

She wonders if she should knock on the Americans' door to give them extra towels, to see if they would like breakfast soon. She can't hear the water running: Bastian must have had his shower by now. Perhaps she should just leave it: go downstairs, chop up some fruit, wait.

The linen cupboard door is slightly ajar – the small catch, which Nick has fixed twice, is hanging loose again. She pulls out two towels and goes towards the Americans' door, also slightly open. She can't quite see the bed through the gap, though as she taps lightly and waits, she's absolutely certain the scene will be as she pictured it downstairs: Madison, more dishevelled than she's seen her and prettier for it, in bed with her coffee, gazing out over the valley. Or, more likely, scrolling on her phone. Bastian will be dressed and ready to head out to the pool. When no one answers, she pushes the door wider.

The room is apparently empty. She walks in but stops dead when she catches movement in the huge foxed mirror. For a moment she thinks to inspect herself, see how rough she looks, and therefore looked downstairs to Bastian. But the angle is wrong. The movement in the mirror is not her.

It's them. The bathroom door is open and they are in the shower together, the water turned off. Madison's hands are raised to the tiles either side of her head, fingers splayed. She's facing away, cheek flat against the small blue majolica squares Laura grouted into place herself. She's spent hours in that very spot. Bastian is right up behind Madison, his hands on her hips, lifting her slightly.

Though Laura hasn't moved, Bastian looks round, as if sensing her presence. He seems entirely unsurprised to see her there, watching him as he fucks his wife. She supposes there's no reason he would be surprised. After all, it was he who'd asked for the towels as he left the kitchen. 'Give it twenty minutes so I can rouse her,' he'd said. 'Thanks, Laura.'

The sound of tyres on the loose stones of the drive cracks open the still morning. Laura goes to the window of the snug. She has been pacing in here since the incident in the shower, nerve-endings tingling.

Outside, a van has pulled up. Actually it's a flatbed, with cherry-red paintwork and black windows, shining like it's just been waxed. It looks absurd against the muted colours of the valley. Also shining is the driver's head as he gets out and slams the door.

He doesn't look towards the house, but turns instead to the view. Everyone does this because it's spectacular, but there's something about the man's stance that riles Laura, observing from the snug window. It's that he's so comfortable, proprietorial. It annoys her that she so often hovers at her own windows, ready to crouch and hide, while people like this stranger are entirely at ease.

When he turns and, inevitably, she draws back, she sees that it's the man from Ivan's party, who had been drinking whisky with Bastian. Angelo. There's something else, too, some other association, but she can't think of it. She takes in more details now: his extreme leanness, the leather of his skin, his small skull. He makes her think of a bog man, preserved beneath layers of peat for thousands of years.

He approaches the front door, and because it's next to the snug, it feels as though he's gaining not just on the house but directly on her. A large gold watch, loose on his wrist, flashes as he lifts his arm to knock.

Surprised by how quickly she pulls back the door, his smile is slightly delayed. In the instant before he summons it, his eyes are empty, his expression flat.

'*Ah, signora*,' he cries, the tone in sharp contrast. '*Buon giorno*.' He is so suddenly animated that she instinctively steps back. He flings out an arm to gesture at the view.

'*Bella vista*,' he says, and she almost laughs because even she can understand this, though it makes her think of English seaside bungalows.

But then he carries on talking, the Italian ratcheting up, and she has to shake her head, repeating the words of last night. 'My Italian. *Mi scusi*. I'm trying to learn.'

The *thunk* of another door closing makes her start. A younger man, perhaps thirty, has emerged from the passenger seat. He is built to the same specifications as Angelo except he has hair, shaved to a fine, centimetre-long pelt all over.

He walks unhurriedly towards them, still speaking into a mobile phone. Again, she catches a shuttered expression before he ends the call and gifts her a boyish smile, self-consciously cheeky. She imagines female relatives pinching his cheeks when he was little, declaring that they wanted to eat him up. He has probably contrived to evoke this reaction from women ever since.

Angelo throws out his arm again. 'My son, Tommaso,' he says, accent as heavy as it was the previous night, 'son' not like 'un' but like 'on'.

Tommaso performs a small bow. '*Signora*. I speak English more than my father. You can talk to me.'

Without quite intending to, she stands aside to let them in. In the kitchen, they refuse anything to drink but simply stand there expectantly.

'I'm sorry,' she says, wondering why she does nothing but apologize to people here, 'have you come to see Bastian?' Something is plucking at her memory but she can't get hold of it.

This is translated and relayed to Angelo, who shakes his head in apparent confusion.

'He say, "Who is Bastian?"'

She looks at Angelo. 'But you were talking . . . At Ivan's?' She tails off. 'I will get my husband. *Un momento.*'

She rushes out of the kitchen, cross now. *I will get my husband.* She doesn't think she's ever said that in her life.

She finds Nick sitting on the loo, reading. It never fails to irritate her that he takes a book to the toilet. It feels like a habit he's cultivated to seem contentedly eccentric: a man utterly at ease with himself. It's not endearing, though. To her it seems like another opportunity he's lit upon to waste time. The Americans are out, have gone to pick up something unspecified from the chemist in Castelfranco – and there are many tasks that could be got on with while the villa is returned to her and Nick, without the pretence that everything gets done by magic.

'This guy Angelo is here,' she says. 'With his son. I don't know what to say to them.'

Nick blinks a couple of times but says nothing.

'He's a builder. He was at the party last night. I thought

he must be here to see Bastian but apparently not. Do you know anything about it?'

'Oh. But I . . .' Nick pulls up his shorts. Slowly, so slowly, he places his book on top of the cistern. It's her book, she sees now, its pages splayed and its spine cracked. She snatches it up and sticks an emery board in it to keep his place – more to maintain the moral high ground than out of consideration.

'You didn't tell him to come here, did you?'

'Well, not as such . . .' He starts to soap his hands.

She has to be bossy with Nick when he's like this. It's not how she ever wants to be or how she sees herself. 'You must have met him last night.' She suddenly remembers. 'Yes, he knew your name. We talked about it when you were sick. Look, come on, they're waiting.'

'I didn't ask him.'

She turns. She can't read his expression in the mirror over the sink.

'Not that I can remember, anyway.'

She can't believe how slow he's being. 'Well, *I* didn't bloody ask him. Go.' She chivvies him out into the hall and down the stairs.

She doesn't intend to join them, but curiosity gets the better of her after a couple of minutes.

'So, have you worked out what this is all about, then?' she says, as she walks into the kitchen. They all turn.

'It looks as though it was me.' Nick smiles bashfully at her, eyes not quite meeting hers. 'Apparently Angelo and I were discussing the water situation.'

'What water situation?'

'On the land. Our land. The way the well runs low when we fill the pool.'

'This gets bad in summer,' says Tommaso. 'So bad. By July,' he flattens his hand, 'nothing.'

There's a strange dynamic between the men. It's both tense and complicit. Instead of two pairs she feels like she's the odd one out.

She forces a smile. 'Did you tell them about the little well by the linden trees, that we've got that too? Don't you remember Massimo said that would be more than enough for this house? That it had always been enough? He said that the way we're positioned means the water never runs dry.' The smile is growing fixed.

Nick shrugs. 'Well, according to . . .'

'Your husband wants us to come, find a new well, a new . . .' Tommaso mutters and confers with his father. 'A new source? Is right word? It's different, do you see, *signora*, when you have pool.'

Nick nods. He's taller by a head than both Italians and clearly finds this awkward, his shoulders stooped.

'So we go look now?' says Tommaso, jerking his head towards the garden.

They're almost at the back door when Angelo turns back and takes Laura's hands in his. His skin feels like leather, too: dry and smooth. He speaks in fast Italian, squeezing her fingers so that they almost hurt.

Embarrassed, she tries to smile, though what she really wants to do is shake him off. 'What's he saying?'

Tommaso grins, his eyes raking fast over her body, down and back up. 'He ask when you have babies. Every house need a *bambino*, *sì*?'

Nick steps forward, interposing himself between her and Angelo. 'Shall we?' Straight-backed now, he steers the men outside.

Laura watches the three of them cross the garden, swiping away a single, furious tear with the back of her hand. 'Fuck you, Angelo,' she mutters, and it helps, a little.

'A good place will be by the small buildings,' she hears Tommaso saying, as they drift out of earshot. 'It must be done correctly, you understand. For the earthquakes. There are regulations now. So many regulations.' Angelo is nodding.

She lets them go and thinks about their bank balance, the precious euros the Americans have paid them. She wants to buy things – pretty, elegant things. Not a well. They already have two wells. Massimo had said that was more than enough.

She trusted Massimo, who had done all the building work at the start, back in the tail-end of winter. He had brought his food in a small, half-rusted pail and, even when it was raining refused to eat inside, sitting instead on a tree stump under the dense canopy of the hazel trees. His wife made his *pranzo* for him every morning, he told her. My angel, he called her, showing her a small creased photo of a large, raw-boned woman who was handsome rather than pretty. *Amore mio*. My darling. My treasure.

Angelo and Tommaso leave half an hour later, a cloud of pale dust rising in the wake of the flatbed. The son is driving this time, she notes from where she is stationed again, at the snug window.

'I hope you didn't agree to anything,' she says to Nick in the kitchen. He's standing at the sink, halfway down a glass of water. His T-shirt is patched and dark with sweat.

He doesn't reply.

'Nick?'

'I don't think so,' he says irritably, 'but who knows here?'

'Can you really not remember asking him to come?'

'I didn't ask him. Just because I was pissed . . .'

'Stoned.'

'Whatever. But I wouldn't have forgotten that.'

'Well, he can't have made it all up.' She sighs. 'I don't want to blow a load of money on a sodding well.'

'They said we'd run dry in summer if we didn't. Not just the pool. The taps, the loos, everything.'

'That's not what Massimo said.'

'Tommaso says Massimo is an old man who doesn't know what he's doing any more.'

'I liked him.'

'Yeah, me too. Those two . . .'

'What?'

Nick blows out his breath, tips away the rest of his water and goes to the fridge. He hesitates, then reaches inside for a beer. 'I dunno.'

'Well, I don't like them.'

'That thing they said, about babies –'

'It's not that,' she cuts across him. 'They scare me.' She only realizes it's true as she says it.

'They're going to come again in the week, with a few more men. Just to have a proper look.'

'You literally just said you hadn't agreed to anything.'

'I haven't!' His voice breaks, shrill and boyish. He puts the cold bottle to his forehead. 'Sorry.'

She sighs. 'As long as they're not expecting any money for that.'

'No, they're not. I mean, I don't think so.' He hands her the beer and gets another.

She needs a day off from the booze but she can't resist. It's cold and deliciously dry. It makes her care less almost instantly.

'Well, you can deal with them. I don't want anything to do with it. And ring Massimo. See what he says.' A thought occurs and she tries to bite back the words, then says them anyway. 'Why can you never be assertive? Why do I always have to sort this stuff out, like I'm your mother?'

He slams out of the kitchen. She watches him cross the garden, retracing the steps he'd not long taken with the two Italians. She knows he'll be going to the barn behind Giuseppe's House, where he keeps his tools and all the little projects he's got on the go, none of them ever quite finished unless she nags and nags.

His shoulders as he moves out of sight are slumped again. He reaches up to rub at the nape of his neck where it's recently been shaved at the barber's in Castelfranco, the exposed skin still white and vulnerable. Her heart clutches traitorously. That she can't even be angry with him without feeling guilty only makes her more furious. When the men come back, she'll make sure Bastian is around. It's not just his grasp of the language, it's his physical solidity, too. She didn't think those things would appeal to her but, in him, they do. Men like him . . . Women don't mother that kind of man.

*

The Americans don't return for dinner. She and Nick wait until half past eight, the food Nick has prepared keeping warm at the bottom of the oven.

'It's drying out,' he says. 'We'll just have to have it cold tomorrow. Are you sure they didn't say anything?'

She shakes her head, too irritable to answer the same question he's asked her twice already. It's not just Nick, though: she had been looking forward to dinner. There's something about the decorum of the ritual – dressing up a little, laying the table formally – coupled with the intense beam of Bastian's attention from across the table that heats her blood, causes it to run faster. The whole thing makes her feel alive in a way that turns the previous years grey and flat in retrospect. The messages were one thing, but having someone to flirt with in real life is something quite different. She feels she deserves a bit more of that after what has turned out to be a pretty shitty day. It doesn't help that it's a perfect evening, the air balmy and subtly perfumed in a way she hasn't noticed before. Some flower or plant that has been waiting for a secret signal – another notch on the thermometer, an extra minute of sunlight – must have opened.

She finally hears their car out on the drive just after nine, anticipation swelling inside her so powerfully that she has to stand. Nick looks up from his almost-finished meal. They'd given in and eaten some odds and ends so they could save the expensive lamb for lunch tomorrow, not that she'd eaten much of anything.

'Don't be off with them, will you?' Nick says, as she heads towards the hall. 'Remember they're on holiday.'

She doesn't say anything. Apart from that moment in

the kitchen when Nick stepped in about the *bambino*s comment, she hasn't really liked him all day. She expects he feels the same.

'Hey you,' says Madison, when she catches sight of Laura framed in the doorway. 'Oh no, are you pissed? Bastian said we should have called.'

Laura knows her face always gives her away and makes a mammoth effort to smile properly. She wonders what Madison read or misread there. Impatience that's actually eagerness? All different kinds of frustration?

'Don't be silly, you're on holiday,' she says, with careful lightness. She's glad Nick isn't there to hear her parroting his words. 'I'm just tired. Hormonal. You know.'

She doesn't know why she's said it but it's actually true. She wouldn't have if Bastian wasn't still removing packages and bags from the boot of the car, though. It's so ingrained in women not to embarrass men with talk like that, not to put them off.

'Tell me about it,' Madison is saying. 'I've been ready to strangle someone all day. The waiter at dinner was so rude I felt like knocking him out. We should have come back. The food wasn't a patch on Nick's. Was it, honey?'

She turns and relieves Bastian of some of the shopping bags.

'Hey, Laura,' he says, 'good to see you.'

She smiles and it's easy to summon this time.

'Shoes,' says Madison, holding up the bags and doing an excited little dance on the spot. 'And maybe a couple of purses. Well, it's Italy, right?'

It's a relief for Laura to perform with her, to shake off her mood in a way she couldn't have done if it was only her and Nick. 'I'll make us all drinks,' she says, to Nick, as the Americans go out to the garden.

He hesitates, then leans in to kiss her cheek, so briefly that he almost misses. She knows it's done out of relief because she's playing the game, being a good host. He's nervous of her moods in a way he never used to be. Maybe the really harmonious marriages are just about pretending more: being so scrupulously polite that there are no gaps for contempt to sidle into.

Soon, so soon, they are on their third drinks: some rum, lime and mint concoction – she'd bookmarked the recipe on her phone. They're strong, but taste deceptively healthy because of all the mint. She knows they're drinking too much. It's one thing for Madison and Bastian – they're on holiday – but she and Nick can't keep this up all summer or they'll be alcoholics. The loosening that it brings is so seductive, though. She's about to go and get some grissini to soak up the rum when Madison says it.

'You know what this set-up would be perfect for, don't you?' She laughs, tosses her hair back over her shoulders. Bastian is looking off into the distance. Madison has been doing most of the talking and Laura doesn't think he's been listening properly for a while.

Nick smiles. 'Er, a guesthouse? I thought that's what we were doing.'

'No, silly,' says Madison, leaning forward to slap his knee, which she misjudges slightly, the slap too sharp, making him flinch. 'I mean, you'd probably need a few more guests to make it really interesting.'

'Oh.' Nick's eyes widen comically as he rubs his knee. 'You mean keys in the bowl and all that?'

'All that.' Madison winks. 'I'll tell you a secret. Bast's parents were into it, once they'd moved out of the city to the 'burbs. You wouldn't have thought you could beat New York City for life experiences but that place, my God, flags on the front lawn and keys in the bowl.'

Laura tenses. Madison has got Bastian's attention now. He's had only one of the cocktails, switching to beer at some point she hadn't noticed.

Madison finishes off her drink and puts the glass down by her feet. It overbalances but she doesn't notice. She's downed all three drinks so fast that Laura thinks she must have let herself get seriously dehydrated. Apparently they'd had wine with dinner and were in the sun all day. The same sun has long slipped below the hill-line now, but even in the low light Madison looks much more undone than Laura has yet seen her: mascara smudges under one eye, a grease stain on her vest top and the label at the back sticking out.

'They moved out there when Bast was, like, thirteen. His sisters were already at college so he was the only one left. Mommy's happy accident. It was her who wanted them to leave the city. She thought it might stop Bast's dad working his way through the bored wives of the Upper East Side. But then they got out to Westchester and it was even worse.' She laughs again and reaches to retrieve her fallen glass, only to put it down again when she sees it's empty.

'Let me get you another,' says Nick, already on his feet, patently relieved to leave the conversation.

'Water or soda. Thanks, Nick.' Bastian's voice is low and controlled.

Madison looks up at Bastian, waiting. For what, Laura isn't sure. Details to add colour to the anecdote? Maybe it's one they've told before at dinner parties, a double-hander that amused their friends. Laura doubts it, though, and she cringes for Madison, whose inebriation is making her slow, her smile beginning to falter now.

'Hey, are you mad at me?' she says, in a baby voice so intimate that Laura thinks her own presence must have been forgotten.

Bastian doesn't reply and something about his silence and stillness makes Laura go cold. She gets up and heads for the kitchen, for Nick, whom she suddenly wants to be near for the first time all day.

Behind her, Madison continues to wheedle in her cutesy voice. Before she goes inside, Laura glances back in time to see Madison lift herself effortfully onto Bastian's lap, straddling him. She looks away so fast that she cricks her neck, the hot pain of it making her blind for a second.

A muffled cry makes it impossible for her not to look again. Madison is in a heap on the ground, Bastian standing and looking down at her impassively. Laura realizes he must simply have got up, letting Madison slide off his lap to the ground. Transfixed at the kitchen door, revulsion, sympathy and something horribly like triumph whip through Laura, one by one.

Day 4

At breakfast under the pergola the next morning, Madison has the idea of them all going to Urbino for the day. Laura suspects that it isn't spontaneous: Madison's enthusiasm feels forced. She has a frenetic edge this morning, her eyes so bright they look glassy. Some of it is probably hangover but she's also overcompensating for Bastian, who is quiet. *Dangerously quiet*, is the phrase that comes to Laura.

Last night, after Madison had talked about Bastian's childhood, the atmosphere had soured irretrievably. Within a few minutes, Bastian had thanked Laura and Nick for the drinks, apologized again for missing dinner and gone up to bed – all this without a word to or even a glance at Madison. She'd followed him soon after, looking stricken.

And then, in the thick of deepest night, Laura had woken with the certainty that something had just broken the quiet. Not her own dreams, or something to do with Nick, still unconscious beside her, but something else. She crept out to the landing and the window whose shutters were never closed. She was already expecting to see those car lights again, retreating into the tangle of trees until the darkness swallowed them. But it was silent outside. Even the cicadas had paused.

Then she heard a sound, only it was from down the

landing, a soft, barely audible susurration that could only have been a woman crying softly. Madison. She waited, straining so hard to hear that white noise boomed and hissed in her ears. She realized she was waiting to hear the low rumble of Bastian's voice, reassuring and comforting, telling Madison to stop. But there was nothing and it was so hard not to imagine the American woman in there by herself that Laura had to fight the instinct to go to her.

Eventually, the weeping stopped, or became too muted for her to hear, and she crept back to bed. For a long time, she lay wide-eyed but unseeing in the dark room. She wasn't just thinking about Madison. In fact, she was thinking about herself, her past. A memory of something similar had come to her from nowhere: crying without being given comfort, the settling around her of a terrible bleakness made so much worse by night. She'd left that out of her university diary. She'd checked as soon as Nick got into the shower that morning.

'So, what do you guys say? Are you in?' Madison smiles her thousand-watt smile. She hasn't eaten anything yet.

Laura has a hundred jobs to be getting on with today, the most important of which is to ring Massimo. She knows Nick won't. But she finds herself nodding, wanting to help the woman whose husband has still not looked at or spoken to her today at all, as far as Laura can tell. Also as penance for the shaming surge of victory last night, when Madison had fallen unceremoniously to the ground.

'Why not?' she says. 'We've only been to Urbino once, haven't we?' She raises her eyebrows at Nick, who is looking mystified by her enthusiasm. 'It was gorgeous, even in the rain. But today, in this light, it'll look spectacular. Shall we go?'

Nick shrugs and smiles. 'You're the boss. I've got a list of jobs you said I had to do but if I can have a holiday-day, I'm all over it.'

She laughs. She and Nick are easier with each other in the face of the other couple's obvious tension. Because of it, probably.

'When we moved here,' she says to Madison, 'we promised ourselves we'd have holiday-days – you know, where we did proper tourist stuff. So it never just became about work. How many have we had, do you think?' She looks at Nick.

'Two?' he says. 'Maybe three? In how many months?'

'Great!' Madison is twisting a long lock of her hair round and round. A single strand gets tangled in her ring and she tugs it away, breaking it. It must be a nervous tic, the twirling: she's been doing it all morning. 'Let's all go together then. It'll be fun, won't it, Bast?'

It's a risk putting him on the spot like this and they all know it. The moment stretches and Laura feels a disproportionate horror that he's going to blank her. But then he smiles, briefly at Nick and then, more lingeringly, at Laura.

'It'd be great if you came,' he says. 'A holiday-day.'

'This is so exciting!' cries Madison. 'I thought I'd have to do so much persuading to get y'all to say yes. Let's go in our car. There's no point taking both and it'll be fun to talk on the way. What is it – an hour from here?'

'I'm happy to drive,' says Nick. 'I know the roads – we've been that way a few times.'

'You sure?' says Bastian. 'More room in ours.'

125

'It's fine,' says Nick, standing. 'I'll get more coffee.' He's gone before Bastian can say anything else.

When he returns, Laura and Madison are looking slightly nervously from one man to the other, ready to head off any horn-locking over the cars, but Bastian has apparently decided to let it go. All the energy women expend to make sure men's egos are not ruffled, Laura thinks. Always smoothing, smoothing.

When the Americans have gone inside to get ready, Nick off to do something to the pool chemicals, she stacks their breakfast plates onto a tray. Her mind goes again to the strange disturbance in the night. She replays it a couple more times until she's almost sure that what she heard was more than a voice. Something was thrown or dropped first, she's sure of it.

As she straightens up, Bastian is suddenly there, his fingertip pressing into her spine at the small of her back. He does it so fleetingly she might have imagined it, only she hasn't. She knows instantly that it's designed to remind her of the party. She starts to turn towards him but he moves so he's behind her and she's pinned between him and the table. His hands come down over hers on the handles of the tray and, flustered, she grips it harder. He peels her fingers off, one by one. His breath moves her hair.

'What time are we heading off, then?' It's Nick calling as he approaches from the pool, the vines that twist around the pergola only partially shielding her and Bastian. She freezes but he's already moved away, the space behind her abruptly cool without him in it.

'Let me take that,' he's saying, and the tray is borne away, so easily. She looks over at Nick, who has stepped back to let Bastian pass. She watches her husband watch Bastian as he walks towards and then into the villa, their villa, without looking back.

They're on the road by eleven, Nick driving, though there'd been another debate about that before they set off. It was her doing: some devilment making her suggest the hire car might be better because it so obviously *was*, and it was only Nick's irritating pride that was inconveniencing all of them. She was also embarrassed by how filthy their car was. She insisted on going through it, collecting sweet wrappers and old receipts, napkins from the *gelateria*, before letting anyone get in.

A contrary part of her wants to remain cross but as the journey gets under way it's impossible, her irritation simply falling away. Every time she leaves the house she thinks she should do it more, but then she forgets, or the jobs in the house become too pressing. Besides, Luna Rossa is her dream home and there's only a certain amount of dissension towards this notion she can allow, even from herself.

Today, the sense of liberation is joined by excitement. Bastian sits behind her, Madison insisting Laura go in the front next to Nick, and she can sense his eyes on her. She piles her hair on top of her head and secures it with a clip. She knows her neck is visible through the gap between the seat and the headrest.

It's a perfect day, hot without being oppressive, the sky above the road a brilliant, startling blue. There's no air-conditioning – another embarrassment – and, as usual, Nick has wound down his window all the way. Madison, behind him, is getting the full effects. As they accelerate up to the speed limit on the fast road, Madison has to hold her hair back so it doesn't whip her cheeks.

Laura taps Nick's hand, nods in Madison's direction. 'For God's sake, put your window up.'

She thinks for a second he's going to put it right up to the top, in the infuriatingly literal way he has when he's criticized, but when he doesn't, she wonders if the escape from the house has had a positive effect on him too.

Urbino looks like an entirely different place in the sun. She'd thought it beautiful when they visited before, but it had been deserted then, the students who attended the historic university not yet back for a new term, and a persistent soaking drizzle keeping everyone else indoors. The city had felt like an abandoned film set, melancholy and forlorn, and they hadn't stayed more than a couple of hours. Even lunch in a trattoria their guidebook had raved about had been underwhelming, though neither of them said so. Places like that are made for the sun, for sitting outside. The interiors are almost always disappointing: shiny tiles underfoot – the same as those in the toilet – bad prints on the wall, silk flower displays stiff with dust.

But now, seeing Urbino in sunshine, she understands. A festival must be taking place soon, or has just finished, long tongues of scarlet and gold festooning the buildings, and banners strung high across the streets leading off the main squares, each one a different contrada or district: *duomo, lavagine, monte*. There is a glut of these medieval festivals from spring into early autumn; Castelfranco is due to hold its moderately famous one next week. Though it's only a Tuesday, the streets are busy, everyone apparently at their leisure: children eating ice-cream, couples strolling arm in arm, stopping to look idly in every shop window.

The four join the throng. Nick is still smiling because he managed to manoeuvre the car deftly into a tight space on a shady side-street, so that they didn't have to pay.

Madison has taken Bastian's arm, as though she saw the other couples and wanted to be like them. Suddenly she turns and pulls Laura towards her. For a moment, she thinks Madison is going to kiss her. Instead, the American woman cups her cheek, fingers hot.

'This place is so gorgeous,' she says breathily. 'Thank you for showing it to us.'

Laura smiles back and lets the last of her tension melt away. It's so good to be out among the crowds, like the world has opened up to her again. She's pleased with the dress she's wearing, boat-necked and black with a skirt that brushes her legs as she walks. She's worn her huge Gucci sunglasses with the gold on the arms, bought at Heathrow as an OTT gift to herself when they flew out for the big move, and she feels glamorous. She's even remembered to wear her flat sandals, though she feels self-consciously short compared to Madison. The roads are cobbled in fan patterns – Florentine Arches, they're called, like the vaulted ceilings of churches flattened into roads – and hard to walk on in heels. Up ahead, she can see that Madison, in unforgivably rigid-soled wedges, is struggling.

'I know we should see some sights,' says Madison, spinning round again, and only just saving her ankle from turning, 'but it's after twelve now. Can't we find somewhere for lunch? Have some cold wine? It's getting hot.'

It's true. The sun is high over them, as high as it will be. The biscuit-coloured stone around them, the cobbles underfoot, all of it seems to radiate the sun back at them. The perfume and aftershave from the people around her is heady – all that hot, damp skin. She loves being among them even as it's slightly overwhelming.

Others are beginning to have the same idea but they manage to get a table at the busiest place in the Piazza della Repubblica. The menus and prices are much the same everywhere, as are the huge square parasols that have been raised against the sun. Laura wonders if everyone is just copying each other, whether on other days another restaurant gets to be the one everyone crams into first.

Bastian takes the seat to her left and, as they study the menus and order the first bottle of wine, his knee bangs into hers again and again, not hard enough to rock the table, or hurt, so that it could plausibly be clumsiness, rather than something more deliberate. The denim of his jeans is rough against her bare leg.

She feels as though the ancient city is infecting her senses, sharpening them. When the wine comes and the waiter holds it up for their approval, the green glass turns opaque in the warm air as they watch. He brings a heaped ice bucket without being asked and the scrunching sound as he twists the bottle into it is delicious. She feels as though she can tune easily into every conversation around them, the Italian voices vying for her attention. And all the time Bastian is there, close enough that even when he's not quite touching her, she can still feel the intense heat of his leg.

Nick was initially awkward about the wine, saying he didn't want any and ordering himself a beer instead, but the same enchantment seems to be working on him now too. His beer finished, he pours Madison – who is drinking quickly again – the last glass of the wine and holds up the bottle at a passing waiter for another. Something has settled among them. The tension – and there have been individual tensions between all of them, except perhaps Madison and Nick – has dissipated into the hot afternoon.

They order like you're supposed to in Italy: *primi*, *secondi*, and *carne*. Even Madison goes along with it. The pasta course is the best: three large mushroom ravioli with truffle shaved on top.

'My God, I could eat like this for ever,' says Madison. 'Bast, please can we move here too?' She takes his hand and he squeezes her fingers. Laura realizes it's the first overtly affectionate gesture she's seen from him, though his leg is still touching hers.

Laura can't finish her *scallopine*, let alone manage dessert, but the rest of them do. She watches Madison eat her way determinedly through an enormous slab of tiramisu, cocoa powder sticking to her lip gloss, and thinks she loves her. She can't understand why she ever thought she was vapid, or cold.

'I don't feel guilty here,' says Madison, as she lays down her spoon. 'It's weird. It's like it doesn't count within the city walls or something.'

'What doesn't count?' says Nick, genuinely mystified.

'The calories,' says Laura. 'It's all right for you, you never put any weight on, despite being a pig.' As she says it, she knows it's not true, that since they moved to Italy he's developed a small paunch, but she loves everyone right now and wants to show them. Nick is smiling to himself, pleased. Such a small thing, like the parking, but he glows with it.

She's probably drunk but everything seems so easy here. It doesn't matter about the messages or that she likes it when Bastian touches her – it doesn't make any difference to her really liking his wife, or loving her own husband. Maybe the keys-in-the-bowl set had it right.

'Hey, Nick, I looked you up online this morning,' says Bastian. 'I had no idea you'd written so much. I loved that piece on Paradigm.'

Laura smiles into her glass as Nick replies, animated and sweetly boyish with the compliment. Another bottle arrives, some kind of dessert wine, the deep gold of honey. She didn't notice anyone order it. She's not sure whether it's the third or fourth.

'They were great,' Nick is saying. 'They had been put up in some soulless hotel on the M25 and they knew it was crappy, that back in the day they'd have been in the Dorchester, but they didn't care. They were just happy to be together.'

Bastian is nodding. 'That really came through. If some twenty-year-old had written it, it would have been patronizing, but you could tell you loved them.'

Nick is nodding. 'Yeah, exactly. When I first went in, I told them about some rare EP I'd hunted down in Our Price – it was this record-shop chain, long gone now . . .'

'I remember.'

'Anyway, as soon as I said that, I was in. They knew I

was a real fan. They were sharp, you know. Like you say, I think they'd expected the cool twenty-year-old to come along and make them feel like dinosaurs, but then they got me, and I was so obviously, embarrassingly excited. But it worked. It disarmed them. Jay even talked about the affair.'

'No way. And you didn't put that in?'

Nick sits back in his seat, grinning. 'It was off the record.'

Madison is smoothing her dress over her stomach, which is no longer flat. 'Look at this,' she says, grabbing Laura's hand and placing it there. It's slightly swollen with food. 'And I'm not even having a panic attack. I would like to walk some of it off, though. If I can stand up.'

When they've finished the last of the wine, they split the bill – Laura doesn't get involved in the good-humoured wrangling between Bastian and Nick over it – and begin a slow wander through the medieval streets. The sun is lower now, no longer beating down on their heads as it was before lunch, and the afternoon has turned mellow. She's a nice sort of inebriated, entirely relaxed without clumsiness. Her feet seem to float over the cobbles.

She stops at a bookshop, the volumes in the window dusty and sun-bleached. Without the weather, it would look sad but everything is gilded and made enchanting, like nothing has changed there in thirty years. A bookshop in a story, harbouring some magical secret within.

'You want to go in and have a look?' It's Bastian, his body casting her into cool shadow. She glances up the street and sees Madison and Nick in conversation, still walking slowly.

'OK,' she says, and he smiles and opens the door for

her, a small bell above it trilling. It closes behind them, and the hubbub of the street is shut off. The silence hums. She can suddenly hear herself breathe.

'Thank you for what you said to Nick before,' she says, running her finger along a shelf of art-history books, not taking in anything more than the name Raphael, which crops up again and again. He was born here, she remembers, but then the heat of Bastian's eyes on her makes the thought retreat again. 'About that band, I mean. You made his day.' In another place, on another day, she has a vague idea she would feel disloyal saying this, but she can't think why now.

'He's a great writer,' says Bastian. 'He shouldn't give it up.'

'I think he needed to, for a little while. He wasn't really getting anywhere. I think that's partly why he –' She stops. It still hurts. She has no idea why she's said it – why she's let that encroach on this golden day.

'Why he what?'

She shakes her head. 'Nothing.'

'Is that why you . . .?'

She turns to meet his eye in a way that she usually struggles to, the wine making her braver. 'Why I what?' She smiles to acknowledge that she's echoing him. They seem to be having a second conversation under the surface. 'Why we moved to Italy?' She shrugs and turns back to the books. 'We needed a new start. And here we are.'

Bastian is shaking his head.

'What?' she says.

'I don't get it.'

She laughs. 'We're talking in riddles here. You don't get what?'

'Nick is so lucky. Why would he ever look elsewhere if he had someone like you?'

She blushes, returns to the books. 'Nothing really happened. It was just a flirtation at work.'

He follows her along the bookshelves, away from Art and into History. *Arte. Storia.* History as story. Fictional, made-up. The name Castelfranco catches her eye and she pulls it out. It's a photographic history of the town. She flicks through it, sees the piazzas and churches she knows, all of it looking slightly wrong and out of scale: carriages instead of cars, men in hats and children without shoes.

Bastian looks over her shoulder as she turns the pages, her fingers fumbling a little when they stick. She can smell his cologne, woody and clean, and the more animal scent of his skin underneath.

'So how's that new start working out?' He says it softly.

She thinks she can feel his hand almost touching her, the heat of it hovering an inch from her waist. She summons her courage and moves into it. He turns her round to face him.

'*Come posso aiutarvi, signori?*'

The owner of the bookshop is just as she would have imagined: tiny, wizened, bespectacled. She goes to push away from Bastian but his hands hold her firmly in place, clamped around her waist.

The shopkeeper gestures at the book she's still holding. 'You like?' he says. 'You want?'

'*Quanto costa?*' she starts to ask, but Bastian is already

nodding, taking the book from her and handing it to the little man, who beams and beams.

'Oh, no, you can't,' she says, as she follows them to the counter.

'Looks like I already am,' Bastian says.

He opens the door for her on the way out too. She clutches her paper bag with the book inside. She'll have to say she bought it herself.

Madison and Nick are nowhere in sight. She might have been in the bookshop with Bastian for three minutes or three days. As they begin to walk slowly along, just about not touching, she feels the gaze of strangers passing over them, making the automatic judgements people do. It occurs to her that, like the bookshop owner, they will assume she and Bastian are together, that they're married. Her left thumb rubs the back of her wedding ring, a plain platinum band. She's fallen out of the habit of wearing her engagement ring here. It's antique and fiddly, and the stones are exposed at the back. She was forever cleaning it so they didn't cloud over.

She glances down. Bastian doesn't wear a ring. Some men don't, of course. Nick does. She pushes the observation away.

When a group of teenagers almost fall into them, oblivious to everything but themselves, Bastian moves in front, steering her out of their path. Wherever he touches her feels burnt afterwards. The sun has found a gap between the roofs and she blows her hair off her forehead, suddenly too warm.

'OK?' he says, as though there'd been some actual danger, and she nods, playing along, damsel-like. They face each other, unmoving, and a large tour party in matching T-shirts is forced to flow around them. She steps sideways to make room for an old man with a walking stick, taking Bastian's hand to move him with her, though it's hardly necessary. Bastian tightens his grip, pulling her towards him in the same moment.

'We should find the others,' she says, and moves out of his grasp, smiling to make it flirtatious rather than a rejection. She had let her hair down over lunch but now she fishes the plastic clip out of her bag to twist it up and off her damp neck. He watches her while she does it.

'Does that look all right?'

He reaches out and pulls loose a strand right at the back of her neck. Her hair there always goes into ringlets and he coils this one round his finger before letting it drop.

'There,' he says, and with the same finger draws a line straight down her spine.

'I remember,' she says, 'you doing that by the pool, at Ivan's.'

'You don't remember the rest? Shit, I'm hurt.'

She blinks, swallows. Her mind spins, combs for holes in her recollection. 'Oh. I didn't think . . . What did we . . .?'

He reaches out and strokes her cheek. 'So pretty when you're flustered. I'm kidding you.'

She colours. 'Oh. I . . .'

'I mean, it's not like I haven't thought about it.'

'You probably shouldn't say that.'

'Don't you like it?'

'No, the opposite. Too much.'

'It's driving me a little bit crazy actually, you under the same roof but no . . .' He tails off.

She would like him to pull her into one of the sunless alleys that run off the street they're on, narrow tributaries in deep shade, all grilles over dusty windows and iron bars that hold the old buildings up and apart as though separating drunkards. She can already feel the cool stone of the wall he'd push her against. Of course, she could be the one to lead him into the shadows. But even now, teetering on the edge, she's trying to hold on to some rules, some kind of plausible deniability. He has to be the one to do it.

They regard each other.

'This is a bit dangerous, isn't it?' she says.

'I like dangerous.'

'When I first saw you –' she begins, but he hushes her, smiling.

'Not now. Later.'

Nick and Madison haven't got far, which seems miraculous. When Nick looks up from a carousel of postcards and smiles, she feels a guilty rush of affection for him.

'Sorry. I stopped to look in a bookshop and then you'd gone,' she says, voice high and breathless.

'I was here,' he says simply. 'It's you two that disappeared. Madison's looking at bags.' He nods towards the shop opposite. Through the open door, she watches Madison turn to Bastian, who has already found her. She holds up a handbag, Schiaparelli pink, and he nods. His hands are in his pockets now. Laura can still feel the places where they touched her, the nerve endings still tingling with the contact.

The afternoon wears on, air thickening with the day's accumulating heat, swelling with it. They meander through the streets, up and down centuries-worn steps, stopping for *gelato*, debating whether they should go and see the Raphaels and the Titians at the Palazzo Ducale and deciding they can't really be bothered.

'What Philistines we are,' Laura says. 'But we can always come back. Do the cultural stuff then.'

'Oh, who cares about a load of old paintings anyway?' says Madison.

Nick laughs. 'I'm with you.'

Laura pokes him gently in the stomach. 'I care, actually. I like old paintings.'

'Well, you might,' he says, 'but most people just want to be able to say they've done stuff afterwards. That they've ticked that box.'

Laura opens her mouth to protest but is disinclined right now to disagree with anyone. It's probably true, and her objection to it some middle-class hardwiring she's barely even aware of. She feels sleepy and soporific, though she must have walked off the lunchtime wine by now. Madison had informed them a couple of streets back that they'd done more than thirteen thousand steps.

'Are you flagging?' says Nick, laying his hand on her shoulder. His face has taken on a strange cast under the rich glow of the late-afternoon sunlight. It's as though all the colours have been dialled up too high, turning them slightly sickly. Madison's shocking-pink bag, which she's already using, seems to pulse. 'Let's find the car. Is that OK with you two?' He turns to the Americans.

'Sure,' says Bastian. Though Nick has spoken, he says it to her.

Nick leads the way and they soon find themselves in much quieter streets. Some of them are too narrow for cars, the balconies jutting out above them so close that they're almost kissing. It's scruffier off the tourist trail, the walls graffitied and stained with trails of rust. A moped rounds a corner at speed and scatters them, Nick swearing over the wasp-whine of the engine, his voice echoing and bouncing. High above, the narrow slice of sky visible between the roofs has darkened.

'Surely it's not going to rain, is it?' she says. No one answers.

On the corner ahead there is a café in deep shade. There are no tables for foot-sore tourists outside. As they approach, three men exit the door, and there is a general impression of demonstrated wealth: sharp white shirts, expensive jeans, designer sunglasses. A car, black paintwork polished to a high shine, glides up to them.

'Hey, isn't that that Angelo guy?' says Bastian.

Before Laura can properly focus, the men shake hands and disperse, two of them into the back seat of the car, the third swallowed by the dark café once again. The car disappears silently round a corner.

'Are you sure?' says Nick. 'Why would he be out here?'

'Bigger fish than he seemed, maybe.' Bastian shrugs. 'It was definitely him.'

They set off again. Nick, at the front, is tense now, and she knows he's lost them in the warren of streets. He's never had a very good sense of direction. She's always made gentle fun of him for this, but she knows not to say anything now. Besides, she's still thinking about that strange sighting of Angelo, so out of context. A dark blot marring a golden day.

'I think we're too far to the south,' says Bastian. They've

stopped by a church covered with scaffolding, probably damaged by an earthquake.

'How do you even know what's south?' says Madison, laughing, her fingers entwining around his arm. She's the only one who doesn't seem to have noticed the change in mood.

Nick, face set, allows Bastian to lead them back towards the centre. They can only have been gone for twenty minutes but the atmosphere has shifted here, too. It's only just past six but the bustling streets now feel overrun. Music, amplified and pseudo-medieval, is coming from somewhere, and the crowds have grown louder to compensate.

'Let's stay,' says Madison, looking imploringly up at Bastian, 'have some more wine.' But he doesn't answer her, and as they move into single file to get through a solid clump of people watching a street performer, Laura finds herself between the couple. Under the cover of the crowd, Bastian's fingers finds hers, just for a moment, interlocking and then breaking apart again. Heat spreads through her.

When they finally turn into the street where the car is parked, Nick points it out as though he's been the one to find it. 'Here we are,' he says, but then stops dead. The wing mirror on the street side has been knocked off and is dangling by its wires. The car, already caked in dust and missing one of its hubcaps, now looks humiliatingly shabby. He lifts it back into position and fiddles for a while but when he lets go it inevitably falls again, knocking and twisting against the door.

'Great,' she says unhelpfully. 'I told you you should put them in.'

He rounds on her, suddenly fierce. 'No, you bloody didn't.'

Bastian lays a hand on his arm. 'I'll drive back, man. We can tape the mirror.'

Nick moves so Bastian's hand drops. 'No, I'll drive. It's my car.'

It takes ages to get out of the centre. Perhaps it's rush-hour, or everyone is trying to get closer to whatever is happening in the town. Laura has the sense again that they never quite understand what's going on, as though one hand is permanently tied behind their backs. They inch along streets nothing like the oldest lanes at the heart of the place, even the scruffy ones they'd ended up lost in. These are suburbs on the wrong side of the medieval gates, anonymously and generically modern: plate-glass shop fronts and purpose-built apartment blocks, all the lines hard and straight.

The sky breaks open as they join the *autostrada*. It's dry and then it isn't, rain suddenly pelting the windscreen. These abrupt about-turns in the weather always seem so Italian – dramatic and noisy – as though the people are forged of them. Inside the car it's silent, the conversation having faltered somewhere around Urbino's outskirts, the last bit of shine rubbed off the spell they'd all been under. The only sounds now are the frantic whirr of the wipers on the fastest setting and the roar of lorries as Nick overtakes.

Laura is sitting in the back behind Nick this time. Dread clutches her as he pulls out into the middle lane yet again. There are three enormous articulated lorries from the same haulage company in a row. Because they brought the car over from England and it's right-hand drive, the tops of the lorries' wheels are at eye-level on Laura's side as they pass, mere inches away, the spray too much for the wipers to cope with.

Around them, obscured by water now, the land is flat, and a buffeting wind has got up. Through the gap between the door and Nick's seat, she can see him having to grip the wheel tighter every time the wind shoves at the car. The high-sided lorries sway with it and, as they pass the second, some quirk of the air currents pushes at them even harder, making the car swerve towards the fast lane as if it's been kicked.

Nick slows down a little, and though there is relief in that, the overtaking of the third lorry feels interminable. Carefully, so she doesn't startle him, she reaches forward to touch his arm. It's an old wordless signal between them that she is afraid, that she needs him to do something to help her: slow down, usually, but in this case get past this last lorry and then stop overtaking.

When they had first got together, she had tried not to criticize, knowing how men could take it as a judgement on their driving, which only infuriated and made things so much worse. She had learnt to keep quiet in the past, but there had been a night, driving down the M3 to visit Nick's grandparents in Hampshire, when the combination of heavy rain and a hangover made her so anxious that she couldn't catch her breath. He'd asked her what was wrong, but she couldn't speak and the thought of him being distracted by her when he was still driving made it even worse: the panic rose until she thought it might take her head off. She'd just pointed at the road and hoped he understood. He had, pulling off at the next services. They'd parked there for an hour. He'd gone to buy her tea, loaded with sugar, and had stroked her hair.

Years later, just before the wedding, she and Lou had gone on holiday – a last girls' break before she tied the knot.

'Are you sure about this?' Lou had said one night, the only person who could have asked the question without Laura taking offence. 'About Nick?'

And when she'd nodded, she'd thought of that service station, the empty car park, dark and shining with rain, and Nick's hand on her hair.

Now, gently, she squeezes his arm. She has deliberately used her right arm so Bastian in the passenger seat won't see.

'What?' he snaps, and his tone makes her let go instantly. 'I'm trying to concentrate.'

She sits back in her seat and closes her eyes as they finally pass the double set of front wheels, but it's worse blind, and as she opens them again, she sees for real what her mind has been imagining, the vast bulk of the lorry swaying into their path, huge tyres straying over the white lines towards them.

'Nick!' she shrieks, before she can stop herself and he pulls to the left. Next to her, Madison grips the seat and Bastian in the front braces against his window as they veer into the fast lane. From behind them, someone sounds their horn, not a quick warning blast but a long blare, which makes Madison scream. Nick pulls right and puts his foot down at the same time, to get out in front of the lorry, which seems to have speeded up. The car rocks with the sudden changes of direction and Laura waits for them to completely lose control, to spin out in front of the lorry and be crushed by it. But then they are clear, back in the slow lane and out in front of the lorry, the car straightening. The rain abruptly eases, and up ahead an exit appears out of the spray, a wonderful green and white sign pointing the way.

'Pull off,' she says. 'Nick, pull off.'

He does, and in under a minute, like a miracle, they have come to a stop in the deserted car park of a builders' merchant. The rain has moved to the east, sweeping greyly over the hills, and the sun comes out.

Laura leans against the car, slowing her breathing. The tarmac dries as she watches it. She doesn't look at Nick and he doesn't come to her. Madison, silent for once, goes to Bastian and lays her head against his chest.

When they're ready to leave, the near-miss already retreating under the glowing benediction of the evening sun, Bastian gets in the driver's side without a word.

The WhatsApp message arrives just after eight: *Oi, we NEED to Skype and tonight! Stop bloody avoiding me.*

She rises from the table in the kitchen, where she and Nick have eaten cold leftovers in silence. They haven't talked through what happened on the *autostrada*. Bastian and Madison have gone out for a pizza and she'd thought that, once she and Nick were alone, they would go over it until it was just a story, an anecdote. But Nick has withdrawn into himself to the degree that she finds herself trying not to scrape her cutlery on the plate.

'I've got to Skype Lou,' she says. 'I completely forgot, what with . . .'

He nods without looking up.

She closes the snug door carefully behind her, then decides to take the laptop upstairs. The stone floors downstairs don't muffle sound.

Lou is eating cereal when she appears on the screen, her face in shadow because she's sitting in front of the window. The English sky behind her is blank with white cloud and Laura has a strange urge to cry.

'At fucking last,' says Lou. 'I've been trying to get hold of you for days. You've replied to about a tenth of my texts and no emails at all.' She stops, spoon hovering in mid-air, dripping milk. 'Hey, what's wrong, Chapman? Your little face looks all funny.'

Lou always uses Laura's maiden name, just as she did at university, though it annoys Nick. Now it makes Laura want to weep, a welling in her chest that she doesn't think she can swallow. Her eyes fill and she shakes her head.

'Shall I tell you what happened at work today?' Lou says, moving easily past Laura's inability to speak. 'That'll make you feel better about yourself.'

Laura laughs, though it comes out like a sob. 'It's just that we nearly had a crash on the *autostrada*,' she says. 'It was fine, it was just a near-miss, but it's shaken me.'

'Oh, love. Was it about half five, half six your time? I went all cold. I texted my mum to check she was still breathing but it must have been you.'

Laura smiles shakily. It's another of their old jokes, this, that Lou is vaguely psychic, though Laura knows that she secretly believes she is.

'Nick kept overtaking these lorries in the rain – biblical rain that came out of nowhere with all this spray. I really thought at one point we were . . . Anyway,' she shakes her head, unwilling to relive it after all, 'it's fine. Why are you eating cereal for dinner again?'

'I need to go shopping.'

'It was ever thus.'

'Yeah, well, it's all right for you in Italy, eating massive tomatoes from the market every day. Making your own pesto.' She pauses. 'Chapman, is it just what happened today? You seem a bit . . . wired. And I wasn't exaggerating before – you've been ridiculously elusive. You've lost weight too, you bastard. I can see your cheekbones.'

She switches on a light next to her laptop. It's out of shot but Laura knows exactly what it looks like: a squat plastic desk lamp that Lou stole from halls. A yearning to be in Lou's flat, wine in the fridge, the telly on in the background because Lou can't stand a quiet room, sweeps over her. 'I can actually see you now,' she says. 'I miss you.'

'Me too. But we'll come to that in a minute. First, I want you to tell me about your guests. As we've established, you've said fuck-all about them on WhatsApp and I need details. Are they a nightmare?' She gets up and shakes out another bowl of Coco Pops.

'You literally haven't changed since 1999,' says Laura.

'Stop avoiding my questions.'

'I'm not. They were with us today actually.'

'What – when you nearly snuffed it? How come?' Lou waits, spoon aloft again.

'We had a day out together in Urbino. Their idea.'

'That's weird. Isn't it? You four hanging out together. Is that normal?'

'They're our first guests. I don't know what normal is.

147

Maybe it's because it's only us and them. If there were more people staying . . .'

'So you must like them, then, if you're double-dating. Tell me what she's like. Madison.' Lou adopts her Chandler voice. 'Could that name *be* any more American? Is she massively high-maintenance? I bet *she* doesn't eat Coco Pops.'

'She's . . . she's not like I thought, actually. I like her. She is high-maintenance but she knows it so it's not annoying, somehow. She's really kind of frank and honest about it, about how she keeps herself thin to look good for men and stuff.'

Lou grimaces. 'How enlightened.'

'No, that's not . . . I can't explain. I thought she was really uptight. Actually, I thought she was going to be a total bitch who'd be straight on Tripadvisor moaning about thread counts. But she's not. She's fun. Kind of wild. We gatecrashed a party the other night. She made us go. We could hear this music in the valley, and we followed the sound until we found it and then just walked in and had a load of cocktails. She said that's what they do in LA.'

'How the hell did she persuade Nick into that?' It's a long-running assertion of Lou's that Nick is hopelessly square.

'He didn't approve at first. He thought it would be odd for us to be tagging along with our guests, getting drunk.'

'Well, it is odd.'

Laura shrugs. 'Anyway, he said we shouldn't but he was getting on my nerves doing his working-class shoulder-chip act so I said I was going and then he didn't want to

148

be left out. Plus he'd found this path that led to the house where we thought the party must be. He wanted to be the one to show us where it was.'

'Was he being competitive with Mr Madison? "Allow me to lead the way, ladies!"'

Laura laughs, slightly guiltily, and eyes the gap under the door.

'So, what's the husband like then? You've said nothing about him at all. You said before that he'd probably be really Muscle Beach. All protein powder and monosyllables.'

'Oh, he's fine. Pretty quiet.'

Lou plonks down her spoon. 'Christ, this is like getting blood out of a stone. You're going to have to give me a bit more than that. Is he fit?'

Laura gets up with the laptop and pushes the window wider with her free hand. She turns the screen round. 'Not being smug but look at that.'

The evening light is doing its celestial thing again. The rain has washed the sky clean, the entire valley clean, and the colours are brighter, richer than she's seen them.

'You're allowed to be smug. It's bloody glorious. God, I can't wait.'

Laura turns the laptop back. 'I was going to ask you about that. Have you booked your flights yet? You need to soon because the end of July, when the schools break up, gets really pricey.'

'Actually, I booked them at lunchtime. This is why I needed to talk to you.' She's smiling now, dark eyes shining in the lamp's glare.

'What do you mean?'

'I went on and the whole of July was ruinous but they

had a couple of seats left for an earlier date. So I went for that.'

'How much earlier?'

'Friday.' She pulls a face. 'Don't kill me.'

Laura stomach clutches. 'This Friday?'

'Oh God, you're fuming. Is it because of your guests? I promise I'll be as good as gold. I'll charm them, you know I will. People love me because I give everything away. And I won't swear if they're Christians. Not that they sound like Christians.'

Laura can't seem to arrange her face into a smile. 'It's just so . . . full-on with them here. I wasn't expecting you to . . . I thought it would be nice if we could go off on our own, have a little holiday here, like the old days.'

Lou is crestfallen. 'I didn't think of that. I just wanted to see you so much. Check you're really OK. It's been months and you've been weird lately. Shall I cancel them?'

'You can't. It's easyJet. They were probably forty quid.' Her voice is sharp and she sees Lou's face crumple slightly. 'Shit, sorry. It's been such a strange day. Of course I want you to come.'

Lou smiles tentatively. 'Really? You forgive me? I fly back on Monday. I could only get a couple of days off but I just couldn't resist. You need the practice anyway – you'll be full soon. And I can help. I make a mean martini, as you well know.'

Laura smiles, despite the tension already knotting inside her. 'Send me the details, then. I'll pick you up from the airport.'

'Yay! I'm so excited. And this way, I get to see the Yanks for myself, as you're not saying much.'

After the call, Laura goes back downstairs to put the laptop on to charge in the snug. As she pushes in the plug, the socket – new only a month ago – shifts, loose in the wall. She peers closer and sees the plaster has crumbled so that the screws have nothing to grip. She can see the bright plastic of a rawl plug.

She straightens, scattering the fall of plaster dust with her bare foot because she can't deal with that tonight. The socket is beneath the window, and because it's getting dark now, the lights bumping down the drive are obvious. She thinks for a second it's the Americans, returning from their pizza. But the headlights are wrong. There are four of them, two small round ones flanking the bigger ones.

As before, the car or whatever it is seems to stop the moment she spots it, as if whoever is driving can see her standing there, watching. She reaches out to snap off the light and waits, her skin goose-pimpling when she thinks the car is actually not stationary but inching forward, the incremental pace somehow more frightening than speed would be. But it's only her eyes straining in the dark.

She hurries through to the kitchen to get Nick but he's not there, the table uncleared, the little portable speaker still playing. When she gets back to the snug, the lights have gone.

Day 5

In the morning, a whirl of energy and peach perfume as she comes into the kitchen, Madison is ebullient again, kissing Laura twice in greeting. The previous night, when she and Bastian had returned from their pizza out, she had said she had a headache and gone to bed. Her eyes had looked red. This morning, brighter than Laura can remember seeing it, the shadow lines across the kitchen floor stark, it's as though the incident on the *autostrada* and whatever had happened during their dinner had never taken place.

'I messaged Ivan,' Madison announces, as Laura squeezes oranges, a tiny cut on her finger stinging. She puts it in her mouth, then takes it out again, suddenly self-conscious because Bastian has just come into the kitchen.

'I didn't know you had his number.'

'Oh, yes. He gave it to me, so we could arrange today.'

'Today?' Laura stops what she's doing.

'To go see him, swims in the pools and all. Don't you remember?'

'I remember him saying we should come but not that it was today.'

As Laura moves towards the fridge, Madison grabs her by the wrist. Her grip is strong; it almost hurts. 'You're coming with me. You have to. Besides, he wants you to. He mentioned you specially.'

'What's this?' says Nick, coming in, bleary-eyed. She'd let him sleep in after a series of nightmares. 'You should have got me up,' he murmurs, as she passes him.

'Laura and I are going to visit with Ivan,' says Madison. She eyes the plate of pastries Laura has arranged, then eats a single grape – feeling guilty, no doubt, about the two big meals yesterday. 'It's all arranged.'

'Oh, aren't the men invited?'

Madison laughs. 'Actually, I didn't ask. I thought it could be a girls' day. Anyway, Bast has work calls *again*.' She catches his look. 'Oh, I know you can't help it, baby.' She strokes his arm but he's gone back to his phone. She lets her hand drop.

'I don't have to go,' Laura says to Nick.

'Actually, you do.' Madison switches on her smile. 'I'm the guest, right?' She winks.

'OK, yeah, sure,' says Nick. 'I've got stuff to do round here. I'll have stuff to do round here till the end of time. You two go and enjoy yourselves.'

He smiles but there's a petulance behind it that Laura resents. She's been up for two hours already, and she was tired herself when the alarm went off, having been kept awake by him thrashing about restlessly all night. But there's a bitterer resentment in her, too. She can't stop thinking about how he was driving yesterday. He had been showing off, overtaking like that in the rain. He had been showing off in front of Bastian.

When the Americans have gone outside to sit down for breakfast, she turns to him. 'What things have you specifically got to do?'

'What?'

'You said you've got stuff to do round here. What in particular?'

'What's it to you, if you're going off to Ivan's?'

'Oh, don't be ridiculous. Angelo is coming back, isn't he?'

Nick flushes. He always does when he feels guilty. 'I haven't agreed to anything. He's bringing more men to have a proper look at Giuseppe's House and to do a formal quote. We don't have to go ahead.'

'Giuseppe's House? What's that got to do with the well?'

The flush is creeping down his neck. 'He asked about it last time. He says he knew the bloke who lived there. Nico, actually. Not Giuseppe.'

'There's still stuff we need to do to the main villa – to this house. We can't spend all our money on wells and outbuildings.'

'I thought we could rent Giuseppe's out as a self-contained unit. For people who want to self-cater. It would be easier for us.'

'But why didn't you say any of this to me? It's a good idea. But it's not just up to you. And, anyway, I don't like him.'

'Who, Angelo?'

'Yes, obviously Angelo. And his son. I bet they're dodgy too.'

Nick tuts unconvincingly.

'What was he doing in Urbino, then? You saw him. It was like a scene out of *The Sopranos*.'

'Bit of a stereotype, Laur.' He shakes his head.

'What about the lights?' she blurts.

'It's nothing. Wrong turns.'

'Funny you know what I'm talking about straight away,

though, isn't it? They were there again last night. They've unnerved you too, I know it.'

'Are you sure we're not just inviting ourselves over?' she says to Madison, as they set off down Nick's path. It looks different in the morning light: wider and less overgrown. Above them, the sky is flawlessly blue again. It's so bright that she's squinting in sunglasses.

When they reach Ivan's and find that he's alone, she's surprised and relieved, as though she'd half expected the party to have continued all this time, the garden still thronged with people. Somewhere in the near distance the guard dogs bark, just out of time with the music, which is coming from somewhere and everywhere, presumably thanks to some frighteningly expensive sound system with hidden speakers. It's not the languid hip-hop of before. This is more Ibiza chill-out.

Next to the topmost pool, in the shade from a huge square parasol like restaurants have, a tray of drinks is waiting.

'Oh, I love mimosas,' says Madison, when Ivan has kissed them both. 'They're mimosas, right?'

'It's a bit early, isn't it?' Laura finds herself saying.

'It's almost twelve,' says Ivan, smiling. 'But I have plain juice. Or mineral water?'

She ends up with a sparkling water, which is actually just what she wants after the walk in the sun. It comes with ice and a twist of lime, and she wonders if there's a maid somewhere, out of sight. She and Madison have taken a lounger each, a pristine white towel rolled at the foot of both. Ivan has gone inside to take a call, apologizing with a funny little bow as he went.

'Glad I made you come now?' says Madison. She's lying back, her broad-brimmed sunhat tipped so that her face is in shadow. She's halfway down her second cocktail. Her toenails – painted Chanel's Rouge Noir: Laura had seen the bottle in the en-suite – shine wetly in the sun.

The heat is liquefying a lot of the tension Laura didn't know she'd been holding. She still feels a little kick of anxiety whenever she thinks about the building work, but the after-effects of the *autostrada* seem to have evaporated into the perfect day.

'Where did you and Bast get to yesterday?' Madison says suddenly. She hasn't moved. As far as Laura can tell, behind the other woman's enormous sunglasses and the hat, she hasn't even opened her eyes.

'What do you mean?'

'When we got separated. Me and Nick were walking ahead and then we looked back and you two had just . . . gone. Nowhere to be seen.'

'Oh. Well, it was nothing. Just a bookshop that caught my eye. I went in and he waited for me. I like stuff like that – I'm a bit of a geek for old things.' She's talking too fast and makes herself stop. She wonders if this depiction of herself as some sexless bluestocking sounds as transparent to Madison as it feels.

She watches as the American reaches for her drink and Laura realizes she's holding her breath.

'That's what he said too. I guess you got your stories straight.'

'Oh, but that's what happened. It isn't a *story*. I just . . . I didn't . . .'

Madison laughs. 'Oh, my God, your face. I'm kidding!'

Laura lies back, gripping her water glass so hard that her fingers slip and squeak across the condensation.

'You're not his type anyway.'

'No?' She feels oddly furious now. *I hate her*, she thinks, even though she's also weak with relief.

'I mean that as a compliment.' Madison takes off her sunglasses and twists towards Laura. 'You're so good and kind of . . . pure.' She reaches out to tug on a lock of her hair. 'Look, you even blush. I don't think I've blushed since sixth grade.'

Laura doesn't know what to say. She resists putting her free hand to her cheek.

'I don't think Bast thought he'd end up with someone like me, the bold and brash girl from Texas. His family didn't either. When I met the parents, his mom said I wasn't what she expected. I think what she'd expected was a younger version of herself, you know? Petite and dark, never too loud. Ladylike manners. We had dinner in some stuck-up place where the waiters pretended they were French. She had this glazed smile on her face the whole time. His dad liked me, though.' She gets to her feet and picks up her empty glass. 'You wanna proper drink now?'

And Laura nods.

Ivan returns to the pool after his call but is soon on his feet again.

'I think it's going to be one of those days, if I'm not careful,' he says, as he retreats. 'Perhaps I'll turn it off after this one. What sort of host would I be otherwise? Ladies, please help yourselves to drinks.'

'Oh, don't worry, we will,' says Madison, raising her glass.

Laura drinks her first mimosa fast. She's thirsty and the sugary cocktail seems more quenching than the fizzy water had been. The alcohol seeps into her bones, loosening and softening her limbs even as her head remains clear. She adjusts the rake of the lounger – polished slatted teak on wheels, hundred of euros each, and she knows because she wanted something like it for Luna Rossa – and lies back. Around them, the cicadas buzz. The hot dry air is heavy with scent: jasmine and rosemary, undercut with the sharp holiday sting of chlorine.

'This place,' she says.

Madison turns to her, propping herself up on one elbow. 'Don't tell Ivan I said so, but you've got the better view.'

It's true. Their position, perched high on a steeper slope, is more dramatic, the valley not so much rolling away as it does here, but dropping dizzily.

'Bast said he might come by later. If he gets his calls done.'

Laura nods. An image comes to her: the two of them in the bookshop in Urbino, dust like smoke in a shaft of sunlight, his hand, brown and square, gripping a book shelf to block her way, just for a moment, his bare arm close enough for her to have put her mouth to it.

'You don't mind, do you?' Madison reaches out and tucks a strand of Laura's hair behind her ear. 'Would you rather it was just us girls?'

Laura shakes her head.

'These are pretty.' Madison pulls gently on Laura's narrow hoop earring. 'Did you get them here?'

A peculiar mix of guilt and shyness makes her reach for her drink and finish it. She springs up to mix something drier, less heady: an English gin and tonic. Ice cubes rasp together as she digs inside the silver bucket. 'Oh, I've had these for ever,' she says. 'And it's fine, if Bastian comes. Of course.'

'Maybe he could bring Nick with him.'

She grimaces before she can stop herself. Madison gives her a questioning look.

'Oh, he's just getting on my nerves, that's all. You know what it's like.'

'Honestly, not really. Bast and I, we argue. Of course we do. But he doesn't annoy me.'

Laura sits down. 'What – never? That sounds too good to be true.' She smiles to soften it.

Madison inspects her nails. One cuticle is slightly ragged and she bites off the loose skin. 'You don't get annoyed with someone unless you feel safe with them.'

'What?' She swivels round on the lounger. 'You don't feel safe with Bastian? Do you mean . . .?' Her heart thumps hard.

'Oh, I don't mean I feel *un*safe, like he hits me or something.' They both watch a tiny bead of blood rise on her finger. 'I mean safe like absolutely sure you've got them.'

'But of course you've got him. He's your husband.'

Madison pauses, seems to decide. 'Actually he's not.' She puts her finger in her mouth, sucks it.

'But I thought . . . And your ring.'

'I bought this.' She spins the big diamond, slightly loose on her long finger. 'With his money, obviously. I bought it from him for my birthday a few years back. People assume. I let them.'

'Oh. Well, it doesn't matter, does it? What difference does it really make, especially nowadays?'

'It made a difference to me, for years. That's why he refers to me as his wife sometimes. He thinks it keeps me sweet. Now? Maybe almost-wife is just fine.'

There's a lull in which Laura can't think what to say. Madison gets up and goes to the drinks table.

'Oh, sorry. I should have made you one.'

Madison turns. She's smiling again. There's steel behind it.

'You know how hard he pursued me when we met? I'd never known anything like it. I'd had boyfriends in high school, and at college, lots of them. I was one of those girls who was never without someone, you know? But it was always the same game: them acting keen and then turning cool, the usual bullshit. It wasn't like that with Bast.'

Though Laura has barely started the drink she made herself, Madison pours her another, much more gin than tonic. She goes to pick them up, then holds out her hands to Laura instead. 'Come on, let's dip our legs in the pool. I'm baking.'

Laura allows herself to be pulled up and they go to sit on the stone edge, side by side. The water is wonderfully cool. Their half-submerged calves look pale and distorted.

'So, tell me then, how you met him.'

Madison lifts one foot out of the water and ballet-arches

it. 'I had this shitty front-of-house job in a restaurant in Midtown.'

'So this was New York?'

'Yeah, LA came later. I hadn't been in the city that long. I greeted people, took them to their table, you know. Actually, I say people. It was men. The place was surrounded by offices. Finance mainly. Banks and corporate law.'

'And?'

'He came in one day. There was a bunch of them and they got pretty drunk. They were *loud*. We wanted to clear up for the evening service but they kept ordering wine. Expensive wine, too, but they were just throwing it back – it could have been any old shit. He was different, though. You noticed him because he was stiller than the rest. He was keeping up, but he wasn't weaving around on his way to the restroom, you know?'

'And he asked you out.'

'He gave me his card, said, "Call me tonight, when you get off." I said he didn't even know my name, and he said, "Tell me it later, when we talk." And I was about to tell him where to go because even though I liked him, thought he was gorgeous, I got asked out by three arrogant pricks on every shift. But then he smiled and said, "I really need you to call me. Promise you will." And he was looking at me with those brown eyes and, I don't know, it felt like he was already inside me.'

Laura's skin prickles, goosebumps rising on her arms.

Madison runs her fingers down the nearest one. 'See, look. You know exactly what I mean.'

Laura laughs, embarrassed, and rubs at her arm. 'I do know.' She thinks back, to when she did, before Nick. 'I've

162

talked about this with Lou. Most men don't pursue, not really. They do a little bit, at first, but they're always hedging their bets, keeping something back.'

'Exactly. I mean, the treat 'em mean thing, it works. But it makes you feel stupid too.'

'A bit desperate.'

'Yes! And who wants to feel like that? When a man you like says, "I want you," and keeps saying it, and watches you every moment, like he'll die if he stops – *that*'s what you want. And it's so rare. Bast pursued me. I mean like totally pursued me. I felt like I was being hunted down, in a good way.' She laughs. 'I'd never known anything like it. He made me feel amazing. I wanted him, but I also wanted me . . . I can't explain it.'

'No, I get it. I had it once too. You see yourself through their eyes, only you're suddenly about twenty times more special than you thought you were, than how you normally view yourself.'

'Yes, that's it. I felt like the most beautiful thing in New York.'

'Potent stuff.'

'God, yes. So, you see . . .' Briefly, she presses her lips to Laura's shoulder. They leave a slight sheen. 'But who was yours? Tell me.'

'Oh, someone years and years ago. At university. I can barely remember him.' She shifts with the lie, pumping her legs in the cool water, and thinks about what she might tell him about this conversation in an email later, though this reminds her that he owes her a reply, and that thought deadens her a little.

'How the hell can you have forgotten him?' Madison

shakes her head in mock-outrage. 'They're the ones you never forget.'

And, of course, she hasn't forgotten him. She never will. 'It's so long ago,' she says, because Madison is waiting for an answer. 'But you're right. I can remember exactly how he made me feel.'

By the time Ivan returns, Laura has finished both gins. She feels loose and comfortable in the shade of a parasol, just her legs in the sun, glistening with Madison's suntan oil.

'I can't believe you still use this stuff,' she'd said, turning over the bottle, its surface greasy, her fingerprints clear on the metallic label. 'Factor two!'

'I know, it's my worst vice,' said Madison, stretching her long lean arms up to the sky. 'But it smells so good.'

'Did you switch off your phone?' she says to Ivan now. She wags a finger at him and he shows that he's empty-handed. He's changed into a pair of beautifully pressed navy swimming shorts. With his towel over his shoulder and his side-parted hair, he looks like someone from the 1950s. His chest is hairless and narrow but strong.

'I'm so happy you came back to see me,' he says, drawing up a lounger so that he can be closer to them. 'I didn't know if you would.'

'Are you crazy?' says Madison. 'What with all the free drinks and multiple swimming pools?'

He looks down as he smiles and, despite the alcohol, Laura is still slightly embarrassed by Madison's brazenness.

'It's so kind of you to have us over,' she says, to make up for it. 'And for forgiving us for coming uninvited before. I wondered . . .' she pauses, then decides, thinking it might even make things easier '. . . would you like to

come over for dinner at the weekend? It won't be anything fancy – just the four of us and my friend . . .'

'What friend?' says Madison. 'Not Lou?'

She nods.

'Why didn't you say? I'd love to meet your BFF. You
mention her all the time. If you weren't with Nick, I'd
think you were in love with her.' She glances at Ivan.

'I only found out myself last night,' Laura says. 'Typical
Lou. She wasn't supposed to come until after you'd gone.
Are you sure you don't mind?'

'God, no. And, Ivan, you'll come, right?'

He inclines his head. 'Thank you. I would like that very
much.'

They chat about Ivan's business for a while, though
Laura is beginning to feel sleepy again, and can't really
absorb the particulars. Besides, Madison has comman-
deered the conversation, allowing her to retreat into the
background.

Movement in her peripheral vision makes her jerk up
just as she was wondering if it would be rude to sleep,
even as she was dozing off. A young woman in red shorts
and a white polo shirt, her dark hair pulled back in a
short ponytail, is approaching with a tray. So he does
have staff.

'*Buon giorno*,' she says lightly, and lowers the tray so they
can help themselves. It's crostini, like Laura had prepared
for Bastian and Madison's first night but these are works
of art, impeccably uniform, each fold of Parma ham the
same, each tip of asparagus at two o'clock.

'*Grazie*, Giulia.' Ivan gestures for her to leave the tray
and turns to Laura and Madison. 'I think we should have

some champagne to celebrate new friendships. What do you say?'

The phrase sounds odd, old-fashioned and mannered, and ironically makes his accent come through more strongly.

'I never say no to champagne,' says Madison. 'It's a life rule.'

Laura smiles. 'That would be lovely, thank you.'

He nods at Giulia, who turns smartly on her heel. They all watch her go. Laura has never understood why rich people want other people in their own home, however busy they are. She would be perpetually thanking them, and on her best behaviour. It would be like tidying up before the cleaner came, all the time.

'So, you didn't want to bring your husbands?' Ivan says, when Giulia has vanished into the house.

'Bastian might come along later,' says Madison. 'He's got work stuff to deal with. But Laura and I wanted to sneak off on our own, really.'

'And Nicholas?' Ivan smiles at Laura, his head on one side.

'He's got someone coming to quote for building work.' Recalling this, she's unable to keep the irritation from her voice.

'It's Angelo,' Madison says quickly, with a glance towards Ivan. 'They met here. Angelo's your friend, right?'

'I don't know if "friend" is the right word,' says Ivan.

'Is he . . . is he . . .' Laura can't think of anything but British colloquialisms she's not sure Ivan or Madison will understand. 'I was going to say above-board? I suppose he's very charming, but . . .'

'Angelo is important here,' says Ivan. He pauses as Giulia returns, her white-white tennis shoes silent on the granite. She's brought another tray, this time with three angular flutes and a bottle of Krug. She tears off the foil and uncorks it efficiently. As she pours each of them a glass, she holds the bottle properly, thumb pressed into the convex curve of the base.

Ivan waits until she's walking away before he resumes. 'Angelo knows everyone.'

'How did you get to know him?' says Madison. 'Did he do work for you here?'

'No, he didn't. I don't know how I know him. My partner – my ex-partner – probably introduced us. He liked men like Angelo.'

'And what exactly are men like Angelo?' Madison sits up straighter and widens her eyes theatrically at Laura. 'Don't tell me he's Mafia. We saw him yesterday in Urbino, coming out of some shady meeting.'

Ivan laughs. 'I did not say that. You did. What I mean is that Raoul liked that sort of charm in a man. Ostentatious. A little bit much. He was that sort of man himself, after all.'

'I don't think I like him,' says Laura, feeling as though it's safe to now. 'He *is* too much. It's as if there's something aggressive just underneath the charm.' She takes another sip of the champagne, which is perfect. 'He asked when I was going to have babies, that the house needed them. He pointed to his big gold watch.'

Ivan looks puzzled.

'Like your biological clock is ticking?' Madison shakes her head. 'What a dick.'

'But even if he hadn't said that, I don't think we need another well. We can't . . .' she stops, and then because of the alcohol says it anyway '. . . we can't afford that and a conversion.'

Madison sits back and blows a strand of hair off her forehead. 'Well, even if money was no object, who wants to spend it on a fucking *well*?' She rolls her eyes.

They all laugh. It's a talent of Madison's, this: to puncture the tension in the way she does. It makes you love her.

'So why is your husband seeing Angelo today, if you can't afford it?' says Ivan. 'It is easy for agreements to be assumed here.'

'I don't know,' she says. 'It's the way Nick is with cocky men like that. Men's men. He can't say no to them, or be his real self. It's as though if he goes along with them, he'll be one of them.' She can't quite explain what she means. 'He's always done it. He doesn't even like them, yet he wants their approval. He did it with the posh blokes where he worked, and at university before that. He thought the paper would be different because it was liberal but it wasn't.'

Ivan looks confused and it makes her laugh, the knot in her stomach at the thought of Angelo in her garden right now loosening a little. She finishes her champagne. Giulia, as if she's been watching from the shade of the house, is on her way back with the bottle held aloft.

'It's complicated,' she says, 'but, basically, they had money and he didn't. At university, there was a group of boys on the swimming team he tried to keep up with. They took the piss out of him for living at home, for having to get the bus to campus because he didn't have a car. He only told me that once, when he was extremely drunk.'

She holds up her glass for Giulia to refill and smiles at the others. 'Sorry. I don't know where all that came from. I've been thinking a lot about the old days lately, that's all.'

'Does he still know any of them?' says Ivan. 'Have they stayed friends?'

'God, no. They weren't real friends. People like that stick to their own in the end. They close ranks again. God, I sound like him.'

'You Brits are so weird with the class stuff.' Madison picks an asparagus spear off one of the crostini rounds and pops it into her mouth.

Laura smiles. 'But you have it too. Everywhere does. You said yourself the other night, about Bastian's family having money, the whole Upper East Side thing.'

'Yes, and didn't I pay for it?' She blinks, smile slipping, then turns to Ivan. 'So what's it like in . . . Where are you from anyway? We were wondering. I was hoping it was Russia.'

Ivan throws back his head and laughs. 'I am only a boring Czech, I'm afraid. Why did you want me to be Russian?'

'A real-life oligarch in the valley, who wouldn't want that?'

'Sorry to disappoint you. Do you know anything about my country?'

'Literally nothing. What can I say?' She shrugs. 'I'm an ignorant Yank.'

Laura sits up and her head spins, a slight delay between what she's seeing and what she can take in. 'I know something,' she says.

Ivan smiles. 'Just the one thing?'

'Dvořák,' she says triumphantly, though she slightly slurs the name. 'That's right, isn't it?'

'Very good.' He takes out his phone and scrolls. The dance music that's been playing so low that she'd tuned it out changes to classical. He turns it right up, and it seems to fill the valley, to be coming down from the sky.

Madison lies back and closes her eyes. 'I guess this is what heaven is like, if you're Catholic. Or Czech.'

Giulia is back. The sound of another cork being popped makes Laura and Madison jump, then laugh at the same time.

A couple of hours later Bastian shows up. A third bottle of champagne has been drunk and a fourth opened. When she sees him coming towards them over the grass, it's like she's been switched on, the woozy afternoon sharpening instantly into focus. The insects throb in the trees again. The pool filter sucks and gurgles.

'Baby, you came!' Madison is on her feet. She rushes towards him and stands on tiptoe to kiss him, her arms going round his neck. Through the loop of them Bastian meets Laura's eye and disentangles himself. She can't help it: the gesture makes her glow.

As they drink their way through the next bottle, Ivan switches back to the blissed-out dance music. Bastian pulls on his vape, its vanilla scent curling into the air.

'Has anyone got anything stronger?' says Madison. She winks at Laura.

'I stick to champagne,' says Ivan. 'But Giulia can make a call if you like.'

'Nah, don't worry.' Madison gets to her feet and

stretches exaggeratedly so that they all watch her. 'I just thought Bast might have got hold of something. He has his ways.'

Laura absorbs this, not knowing how she feels about it. She's always been so straight about drugs. Or, rather, she's never been offered them so has never had to make the decision. She'd smoked a bit of weed, obviously, and Lou and she once shared a pill at a festival, which didn't seem to do anything and was probably a dud. But she presumes Madison means coke, and there's something about that that she's always found a bit seedy, somehow.

'Read the room, Mads,' Bastian says. 'Why would you want to do that shit in a place like this?'

Madison's smile fades. 'OK, fine. Well, I'm going to swim, then. It's too damn hot. You coming in, Laura?'

While she hesitates, not sure she wants to, but feeling obliged to unite with Madison over this, Ivan stands. 'Please, all of you, enjoy the pool. Ask Giulia if you need anything at all. I have one more call I could not put off until tomorrow, so please excuse me for a small while.'

'We should skinny-dip,' says Madison, once he's gone. 'Or is that too much as well?' She shoots Bastian a funny little pout, half defiant, half sad, before diving in at the deep end. When she surfaces close to them, she holds her bikini top aloft, then throws it to the side, where it lands with a wet slap. It's impossible not to look at her breasts as her body rises out of the water, so firm and full on her almost bony frame that they're surely fake. Laura's wearing her sunglasses but she must have stilled, or in some other way betrayed the fact that she's looking, because Madison laughs.

'Worth every cent, weren't they, Bast?' She lifts and cups them, her eyes flicking from him to Laura, then dives back under the water. Laura swallows.

Bastian has moved his leg so his foot is close to hers, she doesn't know when. He shifts again so they're touching.

'Hey.' Madison has surfaced. Laura jerks her foot away. 'Are you coming in or am I going to have to come and get you?'

'Yes,' she says. 'Yes, good idea.' Her cheeks are hot, and she turns away her face so Madison won't tease her. Spotting her almost-full glass of champagne, she picks it up and downs it. Her stomach crawls and flips but it's not just nerves. She wonders if part of her is turned on.

'That's more like it,' says Madison. 'Now, jump.'

She does as she's told, feet first, closing her eyes and holding her nose like a schoolgirl. In fact, the whole situation makes her feel like a child pretending to be cool with the grown-ups. When she surfaces, Madison is close by. Coconut oil from her skin rainbows the water around her. Her eyes seem paler against her water-darkened hair, which streams down over her chest.

'You look like a mermaid,' she says, then glances away because it sounds so ridiculous.

Madison puts her arms around Laura's neck. Her skin is hot and slick, her breasts hard against Laura's. She pulls back slightly and Madison seems to let her go but then Laura feels her legs going round her waist. Madison lets her top half rise and float, her gravity-defying breasts now pointing skyward. Laura glances away and Madison, catching it, laughs.

'Take yours off,' she says.

'No.'

'We're all friends here.'

'I don't want to.' She reaches behind her and unhooks Madison's feet, but doesn't quite dare swim away.

A shadow blocks the sun. Bastian is standing at the edge, looking down at them.

'You ever slept with a woman, Laura?' Madison is close again. She runs a finger along the halterneck strap of Laura's bikini and then, so quickly it could have been accidental but wasn't, down and across her nipple, her long nail almost painful.

Laura shakes her head, not sure she'll be able to speak if she tries. Part of her wants to get out, but the rest of her can't move.

'You must have kissed a girl, though. Everyone did at college, for the boys.' She looks up at Bastian. 'You'd like us to kiss, wouldn't you? I know you think Laura's so pretty.' She winks at Laura. 'He told me, you know.'

She's right there before Laura can react, hands going around her waist to pull her close. Then her lips, soft and pillowy in a way so different from a man's, are on Laura's and moving, her tongue flicking into her mouth. Laura pulls away. She's breathing hard. She doesn't know what she wants to happen next.

Madison is looking at Bastian. 'Did you like that, baby?'

But he's bending down to scoop up her bikini top. He throws it at her. 'Put it back on. Can't you see you're embarrassing Laura?'

Madison's face falls so dramatically that it's almost

comical. Her blue eyes cloud over. Laura turns away, swims to the other end of the pool and clambers out. Her heart is beating fast.

Ivan is suddenly there, beaming at them. 'What have I missed?' he says.

They get back at about six, Madison heading straight for the villa, saying she wants to shower. It's the first thing she's said in a while. Bastian follows her but Laura hangs back in the garden, sitting down on the bench under the linden trees. She wants a moment to herself, to go over the day. The episode in the pool with Madison has already turned as weird as a dream, surreal and ungraspable.

She's only been there a few minutes when Bastian appears in front of her.

'Oh,' she says. 'I thought you'd gone inside.'

He shrugs. 'You want to walk a little?'

They wander across the lawn and into the shade of the olive grove. It's markedly cooler inside. The light is strange: diffuse and sallow, almost as though they're underwater. Insects and birds click and fuss around them, unseen.

She can't look at him, although she's hyper-conscious of his presence, an animal-like alertness that makes her skin sore, as if she's running a fever. And when she puts a hand to her forehead it does feel hot. So do her cheeks, though that's probably the day of drinking and the sun. She's hungry, she realizes, although she likes feeling empty, these days. It sharpens her. She doesn't want the cushioning and dulling that being full of food brings, not at the moment.

She reaches up to twist off an olive, which looks inviting

but is rock-hard. Bastian is over to her left, a good few feet away but, still, she thinks she can smell him. Not shower gel or aftershave. Him. She has always been a big believer in chemistry and pheromones. It has nothing to do with good looks. There are beautiful people who leave you cold, and odd-looking people you want to eat. She suppresses a smile because it's so like something Lou would say.

'What are you smirking about?'

She meets his eyes, softly dark as damsons in the muted light, and looks away again, like she's been singed.

'I was just thinking about chemistry, that's all,' she says, her voice too breathy on the last word. She wonders if he heard it – the giveaway that she isn't as brave as she's pretending to be.

He's turned to look at her squarely now. She reaches up for another olive and suddenly he's cleared the distance between them, his hand reaching up to take her wrist and pull it away. She can't meet his eyes now, so she concentrates on her own hand. He places his palm against hers, their hands splayed and pressed together, pulses to fingertips, though hers only reach the second joint of his.

With his other hand, he reaches out for a loose lock of her hair, tugging on it lightly. Then he pushes it over her shoulder and lets his fingers trail back over the skin where her shoulder bone juts. He presses his thumb into the rounded nub of it. It's so different when they're on their own. It's charged but it's also romantic. Not like in Ivan's pool.

'We shouldn't . . .' she begins.

'Shouldn't what?'

'Do this.'

'Do what?' He smiles, or maybe it's just a brief baring of teeth, which flash palely in the weird light.

'What was all that about, this afternoon? Before Ivan came back.' She forces herself to look him in the eye.

He shrugs again. 'Just Madison being Madison.'

'I found it . . . It was like a performance.'

'Yeah.' He sighs. 'It's part of her schtick. She likes to be the outrageous one. It makes things uncomfortable sometimes. It's not really me. I guess I'm more . . . I don't know, like, romantic or something.' He smiles and looks away, embarrassed.

'I didn't know if I was being boring.'

He shakes his head. 'It's all the fake stuff that gets boring.'

And then he is even closer, his mouth three inches from hers, and most of that is not distance but the difference in height. She knows her chin would fit perfectly into the crook of his neck. Time stretches and she swallows, bites her lip, resists the contradictory urges, which come upon her simultaneously – to step away or to fall into the kiss that is surely coming – to initiate one or the other because not doing anything is suddenly unbearable.

But he moves away, and she is left swaying. In that moment, she despises him. But then she sees Madison, just beyond the trees, hair up in a towel turban and squinting in full sunshine as she searches for something. Bastian, presumably. She hasn't noticed them yet, hidden in the watery gloom of the olive grove. Laura meets his eye, silently giving him permission to go. She is braver now they can't do anything, brave enough to give him the sort of smile that she knows he'll take as a promise.

She hears Madison greet him, the relief in her voice just to have found him, and she hates herself profoundly. That she's a woman's woman is one of the few parts of her identity she's never questioned. And yet she knows she'll do it again. *I can't resist him*, she thinks, but it's not true. There's always a choice. She could resist him. She just won't.

Day 6

Nick is out when Angelo's men turn up the next day. He's not in the house, though the car's still there. He's probably pottering in his bloody workshop, she thinks. She hurries across the terrace, doing her best to smile at Madison, who has been lying next to the pool since breakfast.

'Hey, are you looking for Nick?'

She stops dead. 'Have you seen him? Angelo's men have shown up again and it's his thing so he should be the one to deal with them.' She rolls her eyes, so it's more *silly Nick* than how she really feels.

'Yeah, he went past about twenty minutes ago. He was going for a hike.'

'A hike?'

'He had a little backpack and a bottle of water.' Madison shrugs. 'He was headed for the path.'

Laura inspects Madison surreptitiously through her sunglasses. Her skin is glistening with her coconut-scented oil. It's turning a shade of brick-brown so deep against the highlighted ends of her hair that it looks fake, like those girls on reality shows with their lip fillers and inch-long lashes. She thinks back to what happened at Ivan's and it makes her skin heat. Madison, though, seems completely normal.

'He didn't say anything to me about going for a walk. Typical. Thanks, though.'

She retraces her steps through the villa, bashing her hip on the sharp corner of the table because she's rushing. She's left the men out the front, on the drive, and is conscious of keeping them waiting even though she doesn't want them there.

When she left to look for Nick, there were three of them. They'd arrived in the cherry-red flatbed, Tommaso driving and two others squashed in next to him. There was no sign of Angelo. Now another van has pulled up: grubby white with rust on the wheel arches. Its two occupants have opened the back doors and are smoking in their shade. As she approaches, they turn and, for a horrible moment, she thinks one of them is the mechanic. She raises her hand against the sun: its almost-midday glare is suddenly angled right in her eyes. It's not him, thank God, but is surely a relation. He has the same arrangement of features, though in this man they're sketched in more crudely, and the same blue eyes, livid against his dark skin.

Her relief that it's not him is short-lived. Slowly, deliberately, so she can't miss it, he nudges the man next to him, whom she realizes she knows, from the work done on the pool. He must be employed by Angelo now. Something is muttered, which makes them laugh. The first flicks away his cigarette and, though it's still lit, he doesn't bother to stamp it out.

'*Signora.*' Tommaso comes forward. 'Your husband is not here?'

'No, he's not.' She doesn't smile. 'You'll have to deal with me.'

She's furious with Nick, and with these strangers who

have littered her drive, this obnoxious son of Angelo's, who thinks he has the right to look at her the way he is. He's smiling indulgently at her now, as though her obvious animosity is just a novel way of flirting with him. All this makes her assertive.

'Can I have a word?' she says, and walks backs towards the shade of the front door, assuming he'll follow.

'I don't know what Nick said to you when you were here before with your father, or yesterday, but we don't need another well.' She's speaking fast, not bothering to think of simple words to aid his comprehension.

'*Signora*, we know this land.' He smiles again, though it cools as she stares stonily back. 'My father, he understands it. His cousin owns the next property. The boundary there . . .' He waggles his hand, like a boat in choppy water.

'The boundary? What's that got to do with digging a new well?' Anxiety clutches at her. She'd hated the legal stuff from the outset: the meetings in rat-tat-tat Italian, the sense that nothing was entirely official and kosher. It always reminded her of those documentaries about people who sank all their savings into a Spanish villa only to find out the land was never theirs, that the government was going to bulldoze their retirement dream into the ground.

Tommaso blows out his breath, shrugs. 'It moves, yes? His land, your land, it's not sure. But he is family so . . .'

She swallows, mouth dry.

'It's not problem, *signora*. We are here now.'

'But Massimo –'

'Massimo is old. He forgets that English, German, they always want pool. As we say before, it's different with pool. So much water. Water is precious here, in summer. Like gold.' He rubs his fingers together, and she wants to go inside and shut the door in his face.

'So,' she says, forcing herself to speak calmly. 'What is this today then? Are you planning to start digging? Because I'm really not sure . . .'

He is already shaking his head and making soothing noises, his hands raised as though she's a skittish horse about to bolt.

'No, no, not today. For the well, we only look. Maybe we dig a little, to find the best place, but only a little. No, today we continue on the house. Giuseppe House, you say?'

'Hang on, you continue work? You haven't given us a quote yet.'

He starts to smile and stops when he sees her face. 'Nick and I, we agree everything. He doesn't tell you this? He doesn't tell you about the regulations? For the *terre* . . . For the earthquakes?'

'He . . . Look, I don't know what he's said to you, but we don't . . . We can't spend . . .'

He hushes her again and she wishes she had the nerve to slap down his hands. 'No more money today. The deposit is paid. Nick has done this. Don't worry, *signora*, there's nothing for you to do now. You can swim in your pool, have a drink, have a siesta. You don't worry about us. We do everything. We make safe. You don't know we're here.'

Before she can say anything else, he turns back to his men and barks an instruction, voice abruptly cold and flinty.

He looks back at her. 'Your car.' He gestures dismissively at it. It looks so shabby with its broken wing mirror. 'Is English.'

'Yes,' she says impatiently. 'We brought it over with us.'

He waggles his finger at her. 'You make Italian, *si*. You break the law here too.'

'What?' Panic grips her again.

He draws a rectangular box in the air. 'You have only sixty days to get changed or they can take it.'

He means the registration plates, she suddenly realizes. 'Is that true? We need Italian plates?'

His eyes narrow. 'Of course is true. And I think you are here longer. You should go to the *questura* soon, before someone tells.'

She knows that word. It's what the police headquarters for each district is called.

'Are *you* going to tell, then?' She's trying to be brave but the tremor in her voice is obvious.

He barks out a laugh, then places a finger over his lips. 'Not me, *signora*. But someone. Now, we look at the land?'

'You can come round the side.' She can't think what else to say. 'Follow me.'

As she leads them around the house, even as her anxious thoughts are trampling over each other, she's also conscious of her hips swinging, and the stretchy material of her sundress, the way it clings to her legs with static, which she always forgets until she wears it. It's a strange kind of relief to see Madison still lying prone by the pool, one oiled leg bent, the other stretched out, hipbones jutting sharply above her bikini briefs.

She lifts her head slightly as the men file past but she

doesn't sit up and draw herself in to hide her almost naked body, as Laura knows she herself would have done. The men look down at Madison, of course, one of them – the mechanic's brother or cousin or whatever he is – smirking quite openly. Madison stares him out, one eyebrow raised, until he looks away, and Laura wants to hug her for it.

'I suppose you know where . . .?' she begins, and Tommaso nods.

'We know this place,' he says again, and it makes her want to scream. 'We will be there when your husband comes back. You stay here, *signora*, with your friend. Is better like this.'

She lets them go and sits down heavily on the lounger next to Madison's.

'I thought you said you didn't need this damn well,' she says. She holds out her glass to Laura, who takes it clumsily, the ice cubes rattling.

'I'll fetch you another.' She starts to get to her feet.

Madison reaches out and pulls her down. 'No, silly. It's for you. You look hot, so drink, please. Tell me what's going on with those creeps. Something is. I get really bad vibes off them.'

'Oh, I don't bloody know. It's Nick. Like I said at Ivan's, he can't say no to things like this, to men like them. It's so typical that he's not here.'

'Do you want me to ask Bast to go talk to them, tell them to leave? He's inside working but I can get him. If Nick's agreed to anything he's not telling you about, it's better to get the full story. It's your place too.'

'No, it's fine. But thank you.' Something stops her confiding that Nick has already agreed to work being done on Giuseppe's House and apparently has handed over money for a deposit already. Embarrassment, she supposes, for admitting to not knowing anything about it. 'Besides, I want Nick to deal with it when he gets back from his walk. It's his problem, not mine, and certainly not yours.'

'Well, if Bastian can help with speaking Italian, let me know. We're your friends now, you know. Not just guests.' She squeezes Laura's hand. 'It's so weird but I kind of feel like I've known you for years.' She laughs. 'It's only been a week.'

Laura can't think what to say. She's afraid she might cry. Guilt in the face of Madison's kindness mixes queasily with her attraction to Bastian, and her fear of giving herself away. She bows her head, exhaustion coming over her like a wave. She'd slept only fitfully, drifting in and out of scenarios her conscious mind kept playing out: Madison half naked in the pool; the huge wheels of the lorry veering towards them; her and Bastian left undisturbed in the olive grove, how far they might have gone, what she would have let him do.

'Honey, you look like you need a nap.' Madison tucks a loose strand of Laura's hair behind her ear, and it's so like what Bastian had done the day before that she twists awkwardly away, standing and backing off until she makes herself stop, water slopping out of the glass she's still clutching.

Madison frowns. 'Hey, what's wrong? Are you sick?'

'I can't deal with all this,' she says, her voice breaking.

Madison gets to her feet in one easy movement and takes Laura's free hand, which she strokes. 'Those guys have really got to you. Go lie down. You'll feel better when you've had some sleep.'

'I can't leave you with them.' But she's only being polite now. In her mind, she's already lying prone in her bedroom, shutters closed. It will be cool and dim at this time of day.

'You can,' Madison is saying. 'Go. I'll make sure they don't do anything drastic.'

She does feel better after she's slept, which she does, deeply and dreamlessly. The jittery guilt has dissipated and seems almost alien to her now. Nothing even happened with him yet, she thinks, over and over as she showers, and puts on a clean dress. And yet. She regards herself in the full-length mirror, enjoying how the pale green dress that was a little bit tight only a month ago now moves easily over the swell of her hips and the jut of her ribcage, but still nips in to make her waist look neat and narrow. Her eyes have lost their shadows and she appears flushed and well: pretty.

She's been upstairs only a couple of hours but the nap has also pushed the earlier part of the day – Tommaso and his men, Madison by the pool – thoroughly into the past. To her, it feels like yesterday so it seems absurd that the builders might still be here. And yet they are: when she goes to the window she can see their vans parked on the drive. She heads for the other side of the house, for the Nun's Cell, so she can see out over the garden more easily, towards the pool and beyond to the outbuildings.

The lounger where Madison had been lying is now obscured by an open parasol. She notices Nick then, on the far side of the pool where, behind the balustrade, the land falls away. He's on his knees, leaning out precipitously over the water to reach for something: a bee or a butterfly, probably. She sees him smile and his lips move, and she realizes that Madison must still be there, for once in the shade. The little rucksack, emblazoned with the name of his old gym in London, is abandoned on the ground and his grey T-shirt is patched darkly with sweat. He's probably just got back. Time feels odd, elastic, as though she'd drifted into the future, but has now been tugged back for some significant reason.

A tiny noise or perhaps it's just a soundless shift in the air makes her swing round. It's Bastian. He stands framed in the doorway of the Spartan little room. Spartan except for her ceiling, gold-starred and Virgin Mary blue. His dark eyes scan round it, taking in the rickety rattan chair in the corner, the single bed, the plain wooden cross above the headboard – a relic she'd thought would somehow bring bad luck to remove.

Finally, he looks back at her. His gaze goes up and down and over her, quite unhurriedly. She lets him look, her heart speeding. He turns to close the door softly, silently. For a quite big man – not especially tall but well-built, his shoulders muscled to the degree that he's slightly top-heavy – he is light on his feet. Everything is done carefully, deliberately. It's impossible to imagine him stepping on a plug or stubbing his toe. A bubble of hysteria swells inside her at the thought but she makes herself breathe slowly until it subsides.

It feels different now to how it did among the olive trees, and in the bookshop. There's a palpable sense of purpose. As he moves towards her, she braces, gripping the windowsill behind her and feeling the same give in the old wood that she felt that first day in the master bedroom, when the Americans had just arrived. She had looked down on him as he looked up, those black eyes of his hidden by sunglasses, and she hadn't sensed anything. But had something undefined in her already known that this would happen, even then? Maybe.

She opens her mouth to say, as she did in the olive grove, that they shouldn't do this. It's not that she really thinks this – or, rather, she does think it, morally; she just knows that it won't make any difference. The reason she's about to say it is because she's so nervous she can't keep silent another second. But before she can, his mouth is on hers, and she has to stop herself smiling inside the kiss.

'I've missed you,' he says, breathing the words into her ear, sending arrows of heat through her. 'I've thought about nothing else all day.'

She thinks about what she could say – should say – about Nick and Madison, about trust and betrayal, but now he's touching her, fingers brushing her cheek and down her neck to her collarbone, then pushing into her hair at the back, bunching it in his hand and pulling it, not hard so it hurts, not quite, but so she has no choice except to look up at him.

He begins to kiss her again, and she tries to stay in her body and out of her head but the sensation of difference is so overwhelming that she can't help it. Everything is so *other* to what she's known for twenty years.

She has never cheated on Nick. Bastian's mouth is somehow wetter and hotter than his. And the concentrated strength of him, which is now pushing her so hard against the windowsill that the lowest two inches of her spine bloom with pain – that's completely different too.

Even as she's telling herself to be in the moment, she's up and out of herself and seeing them through the window as someone looking up from the garden might: Bastian's head bent to hers, their dark hair mingling and indistinguishable from that distance, her arms at her sides, braced to keep herself upright, palms splayed on the sill.

Ironically, it's this thought, the notion that someone (and who but Madison or Nick?) might be watching, that tips her into a place where she's feeling more than thinking. She shifts her position and it's only a slight movement but it opens herself up to him more. He senses it immediately, his hands moving out of her hair to grip her hips. His breathing changes. Low down inside her a beat quickens, everything around it loosening and falling away. He lifts her onto the shallow lip of the sill and her legs go round him. And then he stops.

'What?' Her voice is low, already rusty. 'What is it?'

He has stilled to listen, only his chest moving. 'Someone's come back inside.'

She hears it then. It has to be Nick in the kitchen: the slam of a cupboard door, the tap turned on full. He's directly beneath them, perhaps only eight, ten feet away from where she and Bastian are entwined, him hard against her even as her husband below them drinks a glass of cold water.

Day 7

'Do you want me to get Lou?' It's the next morning and Nick is eating scrambled eggs from the pan. They glisten, slightly underdone, and the anxious nausea that crawls up Laura's throat feels just like morning sickness.

'No, it's fine,' she says, swallowing the water in her mouth.

'Well, let me come with you, then. You haven't driven that far on your own here. The roads around the airport are really complicated.'

'Nick, it's fine. I'm not an imbecile. I've done that journey as many times as you, remember.'

'It's different when you're a passenger.' He clanks the hot pan down on the wooden worktop.

'Don't put that there,' she says. 'It'll mark it.'

'All right.' He shoves it into the sink. 'I'm only trying to help. Why are you in such a mood anyway? You've been banging on about how much you miss Lou since we got here.'

She presses her fingers to her temples. Last night in bed they'd argued about Angelo again and, because of Madison and Bastian, had had to do it at a low, repressed volume, which only made her more furious. She'd grabbed the iPad so that she could show Nick how little they had to spend on doing up Giuseppe's House, not noticing how still he went when he understood what she was doing.

'As I said before, I think it's a really good idea to have a self-catering place,' she said, as she punched in the pass-code for their online account for the second time. 'But we're going to have to wait till autumn, when we've had more bookings come in. God, this fucking thing is like Fort Knox.'

'Give it here.' He'd tried to wrest it off her, but seeing something odd in his face made her tug it back.

When the balance finally appeared on screen, the numbers looked so wrong they seemed to tilt and throb.

'Hang on, hang on,' she said, pressing the back button. 'Am I in the wrong account? Nick?' Her voice had risen, high and strained, and he shushed her, gesturing towards the closed door, the guests beyond it.

'Look, it's fine. We can do it. I've done the sums. We're about to get a load of bookings for August and September. The tourist season has got longer and longer here.' He was speaking fast. 'Everyone was going on about it in the chatroom I was in the other day. Childless couples coming here once the schools have gone back is huge now. Retirees too. September is as big as August.'

'Nick, where's the fucking money? They haven't done any work yet. What's going on?'

'Look, there are earthquake regulations, things they need to do before the real work begins. And there was also the pool.'

'What are you on about, the pool? Do you mean the well? I said I didn't want a fucking well.'

'Stop swearing at me. And keep your voice down.' He ran his hands through his hair. The skin of his neck was turning a livid red.

She flung the iPad down the bed and it hit the wooden end with a clunk. 'Tell me, Nick. It's my money too. Actually it's more my money than yours.'

'What's that supposed to mean?'

'Nothing.'

'You mean your parents gave us loads more than mine did. Than mine could afford. Sorry I'm not as privileged as you.'

'Oh, piss off, Nick. Anyone would think your family had worked down the pits. The point is, you should have checked with me. You know this. Now tell me what you meant.'

He breathed in and out through his nose in a show of calming down and she had to battle not to roll her eyes, or worse.

'I did mean the pool,' he said eventually. 'They did a good job, too.'

'But I don't get it. Those men who finished the pool were Massimo's men, weren't they?'

The red crept up into his cheeks, like a shaving rash. 'They work for Angelo.'

She shook her head, trying to understand, then remembered the builder she'd thought she recognized, laughing at her with the mechanic's relation. 'When did you even meet Angelo?'

Nick swallowed. 'A while back. In Castelfranco, just before we moved in. Do you remember when I went to watch Spurs in that UEFA match and you said you didn't want to come? You stayed behind at Nonna's place to read.'

'That long ago? Why didn't you tell me?'

'I didn't think you'd be that interested. Anyway, what does it matter whether it was Massimo or him? We needed someone to do the pool and Massimo was ill.'

'You told me his wife was ill.'

His eyes flicked from side to side. 'That's what I mean,' he said, after a lengthy pause.

'OK, so why didn't you tell me you knew Angelo after we crashed Ivan's party then? This is weird, Nick. There's something not right here.'

He didn't reply. A huge insect droned at the window, fat furry body and blurred wings. It banged heavily into the glass twice before veering away.

'It's fine,' he'd said eventually. 'I've got it under control.'

This morning she's too jittery to restart the argument. She'd slept predictably badly, the night spent alternately staring into the dark void of their bedroom and cycling through a series of anxiety dreams about having to sell the villa, or it simply falling down around their ears. Anger still simmers low inside her, but the greater part of her simply doesn't want to know, not today. She can't handle it with Lou coming as well. She wishes she could just go back to Urbino with Bastian, relive that day, at least until it turned.

'I'm not in a mood,' she says to Nick now. 'It's not about being in a *mood*.' She can't bear to look at him any longer. 'I'm just . . . Look, I need to go or I'll be late.'

He pauses, then steps towards her, kisses her forehead. He does it slightly too roughly, his own frustration and guilt breaking through the attempt at affection, and the force of it makes her step backwards.

'Take care, OK?' he says. 'I've taped up the wing-mirror so it's usable but you can't adjust it from inside any more.'

She nods, pulling her mouth into a tight smile. 'Thanks. See you in a few hours. Make sure you do cold drinks for the Americans about eleven.'

It's better once she's on the road. She'd forgotten in London, where they hadn't bothered having a car, how much she's always liked driving, how capable and grown-up it makes her feel. She opens the window six inches and the air is warm, even at speed. It smells of hot earth and sage and ozone from the Adriatic, out of sight to the east.

Passing through a village on the way to the *autostrada*, she stops on a whim at a bakery and buys two *cornetti*. Lou loves pastries. Biting into hers as she accelerates away, she realizes that beneath the low-level, nervy nausea she's had for a couple of days, she's actually starving. The sugar makes her feel almost immediately more together. *It's only Lou*, she says to herself. *She's on your side, always, whatever.*

She negotiates the tangle of roads close to the airport without incident. The whole journey, in fact, has been done on autopilot and she always drives best when she's not really thinking about it. She hasn't even needed to read the road signs properly, just keeping her eyes open for that symbol everyone everywhere understands, like a bird taking off at an impossible angle.

In the car park, her nerves fizz and she doesn't know how much of it is anticipation at seeing Lou (*What will she say? What will she say?*), and how much of it is the peculiar blend of fear and excitement airports always infect her with. She parks and checks her phone.

Just landed. I think we took a chunk out of the runway. You'd have hated it. The old boy next to me had his rosary out and

everyone clapped when we stopped. CAN'T WAIT TO SEE
YOU. Xxx

It's glaringly bright and echoey in Arrivals. Everything is shiny: cold steel and sheet glass and slippery tiles. It feels futuristic after Luna Rossa, like a different planet. Lou is first through the doors, pulling a tiny wheeled suitcase with one hand and waving manically with the other. When they hug, she smells as she always has, of apple shampoo and spearmint chewing gum.

'You are definitely skinnier,' she says, pulling back and inspecting Laura. 'And you weren't before. Back in April, you'd gone a bit . . .' She blows out her cheeks and Laura laughs.

'You promised me I didn't look puffy. I expressly asked you if I was getting a double chin and you swore blind I wasn't.'

'Obviously. What was I going to say, that you were turning into a bit of a porker? What kind of misery-guts wouldn't, in Italy? But now you're thinner than when you went. Thinner than you've been for years. What's going on, Chapman? Something is, I know.'

Laura takes the handle of the little case. 'Come on, I've only got twenty minutes on the car.'

'Well, fine,' says Lou, as she follows. 'I'll winkle it out of you. You know you're incapable of keeping anything from me.'

In the car, Lou polishes off her pastry before Laura has reversed out of the space. 'To be fair,' she says, licking her finger to pick up stray flakes, 'some of it is probably all those extra hormones leaving your system.'

'Oh, but don't forget Mr Cavendish said it only took two weeks for IVF drugs to do that,' she says.

'Mr bloody Cavendish. He always sounded like a twat to me. As if putting yourself in fake menopause and ramping it all up again so hard that your ovaries nearly explode takes a fortnight to sort out. Look, I wasn't having a go about you losing weight. You look amazing.' She squeezes Laura's hand on the gear stick.

'I feel good, actually. Like I haven't in years. It's like I've got my old self back.'

'I'm glad. You know I hate you being so far away, but if this is what it took then I'm glad. Although now you can come home.'

Laura laughs. 'Why don't you move out here?'

'Yeah, Nick would love that. Anyway, you know I couldn't be an expat, not even for you. I like the rain. I like moaning about the rain.'

They drive on. When they get to the smaller local roads, Lou winds down the window, falling uncharacteristically quiet as the breeze streams over her. To distract herself from her nerves, which had ebbed away as Lou chattered on but are now trickling back fast, Laura tries to see the landscape around her as Lou must, as she herself saw it just six months ago: the sheer painterly gorgeousness of it. But she can't. Her mind is already at the villa, the others noticing they're back, and getting to their feet to greet the new arrival.

In fact, no one does notice. Apparently no one hears the car pull up, or the front door slam behind them, thanks to one of the sudden gusts of wind that occasionally funnel up the valley to surprise. They don't hear Lou exclaiming loudly over everything, either: from the grand dimensions of the hall to the mint-green verdigris on the copper tap in the kitchen.

She'd imagined Nick coming out of the kitchen to greet Lou, wiping his hands on a tea-towel as his smile grew, because although the thought of her gets on his nerves, she always disarms him in real life. But he's nowhere to be seen.

It's Madison who discovers them first, suddenly appearing from the garden, empty glass in hand. She and Lou, catching sight of each other, both exclaim in an exaggerated, girlish way that Laura would ordinarily find funny.

'You must be Lou,' says Madison. 'Oh my God, I've heard so much about you.'

'All of it bad, I hope.'

'Oh, absolutely.'

They smile at each other and, though it's perfectly friendly, there's an edge Laura thinks she can detect. But perhaps she's looking for it.

'This is Madison,' she says. 'Our lovely guest.'

'And a friend now, too, remember.' Madison reaches out for Laura's hands, in that tactile way she has, pressing them between hers.

'Oh, yes, of course.' She's aware she's acting oddly, that she needs to say something more. She looks at Lou. 'We got really lucky with Madison and her other half. It's not like work at all.'

'And where is your hubby, Madison?' says Lou. Laura could kick her for using the word she'd made fun of. Lou's always done this, she suddenly remembers: a totally unnecessary proprietary instinct making her spiky with any new female friend of Laura's.

Madison doesn't seem to notice anything amiss. 'Oh, he's upstairs working.' She widens her eyes. 'LA is simply not functioning in his absence.'

Lou stares, then realizes it's a joke and bursts out laughing. The atmosphere thaws. 'Why don't we all have a drink?' she says. 'It's after midday, isn't it? I mean, it's only eleven at home but I've been up since God knows when so I think I deserve it.'

Madison points to the fridge. 'There's pink Prosecco. I bought it yesterday because it looked so delicious. Let's have it now.'

'Oh, but don't you want to save it for something special?' Laura feels as though she's operating at a hazy remove, like she's already drunk.

'Cheers, Chapman,' says Lou. 'Love you too.' She and Madison laugh.

When Laura stays rooted to the spot, Madison opens the cupboard and gets out three flutes. Lou goes to the fridge, eats a couple of olives from a bowl inside, and lifts out the Prosecco.

'Now *this* is what I was dreaming about on the Piccadilly Line,' she says, holding up the salmon-pink bottle with reverence.

Laura tries to smile but she's heard a door close upstairs. Her mind churns, calculating whether Bastian is wanting quiet for his call or coming downstairs to join them. White noise roars in her ears.

'Oh, here comes Bast,' Madison says. She goes back to

the cupboard. 'I guess we'll have to give him some too, dammit.'

As he walks into the kitchen, Laura watches Lou turn, a polite, expectant smile already painted on her face. She sees in slow motion the instant it freezes and falls. There's a pause, which seems interminable, then Bastian steps forward, puts out his hand.

'Hey, Lou. Good to see you. Welcome to paradise.'

'Baby, we're opening the pink Prosecco,' says Madison, heading for the garden. 'Guys, come out in the sun. I've got the glasses. Should we go find Nick?'

And then she's gone, leaving the three of them alone.

'My God,' says Lou. She looks from Bastian to Laura and back again. 'Sebastian Gallo. I haven't seen you since, what, 1999?'

He regards her thoughtfully. 'About that, I guess. You look great. Just the same.'

He smiles slowly, then heads out to join Madison, his fingers brushing Laura's arm quite deliberately as he passes her.

The moment he's gone, Lou rounds on her. Laura sees that she's not angry but truly shocked, her face pinched with it. 'What the actual fuck, Laura?' she says. 'No wonder you wouldn't say a word. Why didn't you tell me? Actually, no, I know the answer to that.'

It's this moment that Nick chooses to appear, and the way Lou goes to him for a hug – suddenly smiling again, and exclaiming at high volume how amazing everything is – tells Laura what she had known, really: that Lou won't betray her – never will betray her. It should make her feel better, but it doesn't. The sense that she's inches from disaster only grows.

She avoids being alone with Lou for as long as she can. And, actually, she's not sure that Lou isn't avoiding being alone with her, too. She certainly won't meet her eye over lunch under the pergola, which Nick has prepared without Laura asking him. Bastian and Madison have gone out so it's just the three of them.

Laura had been too distracted even to consider Lou's first meal with them, but Nick has gone to some trouble, disappearing at some unknown point to buy half a dozen varieties of the sort of oozing cheese Lou goes into raptures about. Despite the hot, panicky fog she's operating in, Laura is touched by this, whispering, 'Thank you,' in his ear and kissing the soft white skin just behind it. He glows with his success, and guilt makes her shrivel inside. Straightening, she finally catches Lou's eye. For the first time she can ever recall, her best friend glances away.

'Time I had the proper tour, I think,' says Lou, when they've finally finished. They have all lingered over the meal, presumably for different reasons. Laura had even suggested a *digestif* of sorts, though she didn't want it: Nick improvising with a generous slug of amaretto over crushed ice.

'Come on, then,' she says, getting to her feet. 'You haven't even been up to your room yet.'

They don't speak on the way upstairs and this silence is so unlike them that the soft veil of the lunchtime alcohol slips away.

She leads Lou to their second-best room, the only one with a balcony facing due west. By evening, the deepening sunset turns the light an astonishing pink so Laura has left the room unadorned to make the most of it, everything pure white, from the walls to the bed linen to the long gauzy curtains that brush the bare floorboards if there's a breeze.

'It's lovely,' says Lou. 'Thank you.' Her voice is stiff, formal.

Laura thinks of making an excuse to go back down, but she can't bear it like this. 'Lou –' she begins, and bursts into tears.

There's a tiny hesitation and then Lou's arms go round her. When the tears begin to subside, Laura lets herself be led to the bed. They sit down, side by side, facing the balcony doors. Above them there is a crack in the plaster Laura is certain wasn't there before, six inches high and pointing jaggedly towards the ceiling like a lightning bolt.

'So, did you plan this?' Lou says. 'Together, I mean. How long have you been back in touch?'

'I didn't know,' she says in a rush. 'I swear I didn't. When they arrived and I saw it was him, I nearly passed out.'

She can feel Lou's relief emanating from her, like a warm wave. 'Oh, babe, why didn't you say? So he's tracked you down and then just shown up? That's creepy as fuck. You need to get him out. Why hav–'

'No, wait. I *was* in touch with him already. I didn't know he would come here but we were messaging.'

Next to her, Lou seems to wilt.

'It was May when we started. It was just friendly at first. You know, how's life, what are you up to these days, all that kind of thing.' She stops. Lou is the only person she can confess this to. It's her one chance to be honest, and it feels suddenly crucial that she is. But she knows really that she's not just confessing to assuage the guilt about Nick. She also likes the idea that she has it in her to live dangerously like this – has it in her to shock.

'Actually, I suppose it was quite flirty from the outset. I contacted him first. I just did it one night. I crept downstairs when Nick was asleep.'

'But why?'

She casts around for a real answer. 'Lots of reasons, I think. I was angry. I was bored. I missed my old self. Nothing felt enough any more. And Italy ... Well, Italy didn't seem to be the solution after all.'

'So you thought you'd press the self-destruct button.'

'Maybe.'

'I told you moving to Italy wouldn't magically solve anything.'

'Yeah, well, I thought you were just saying that because you didn't want me to go.'

'I was, but it was true too. Surely you knew that, really? You were always the clever one when it came to analysing stuff.'

'Over-analysing.'

'Ha, yes.'

Lou puts her arm through Laura's and they sit quietly for a time. An oblong of sun is moving incrementally across their legs. It reminds her of sitting next to Madison by Ivan's pool. This is so much easier, though, despite the difficult conversation. Being with Lou is in many ways – the good ways – like being with herself.

'Do you hate me?' She knows the answer already but wants to hear it.

'No, I could never hate you. But I think you're being a complete idiot. I remember how you were after he went back to the States. Who finished your dissertation for you because you couldn't get out of bed?'

'I know, I know. You saved my life.'

'Well, maybe your degree. Have you slept with him?'

'No. I swear.'

Lou breathes out. 'Well, that's something. When do they leave?'

'Not for two more weeks.'

'Jesus. Come back to London with me on Monday.'

'You know I can't. What would I say to Nick? Besides . . .'

'Besides, you want to stay. Where he is. You've kissed him, presumably.'

Laura elects not to reply.

'Don't you remember?' Lou says. 'Don't you remember how he made you feel, what he did to you?'

'It's different now,' she says. 'Look, I haven't done anything irreparable. It was just a kiss. I won't do anything else now it's out of my system.' In this moment, she almost believes herself. 'I just felt like – like I needed it. Like I deserved it.'

Lou turns to her, brown hair red-lit in the sun. 'No one deserves him,' she says.

PART TWO

Day 8

She wakes at 2 a.m. exactly, her phone screen so bright when she rouses it that she has to shield her eyes. She has been dreaming about him, about Bastian, and it's the old dream she used to have at university after he went back to America: a party in a rambling house; an endless, futile search for him; the realization that he knows she'll be looking and doesn't care. Hardly the stuff of nightmares but bleak enough to cause her to wake feeling miserable.

LinkedIn had quickly become unwieldy when they'd first started writing to each other; they'd soon moved on to WhatsApp. Although it was easier on her phone, she regretted it. There was something more formal, more reverent, about the emails. They were longer, and more thoughtful, more like love letters. By comparison WhatsApp felt cheap. It wasn't just that, either. The immediacy of the short messages meant she was always expecting another. She checked her phone constantly, even when she knew it was the middle of the night in LA. 'What is it with you and that phone?' Nick said, more than a couple of times. 'Is Lou having another crisis?'

That he only suspected her of talking to her best friend helped with the guilt – not least because a horrible part of her wanted to rebel against his implicit trust in her – but the lack of let-up was beginning to unravel her. Instead of looking forward to a single, delicious email, she felt slighted when there wasn't a new message. Because of the time difference, she didn't even get a break at night. She checked every couple of hours, deliberately keeping the phone on the floor so the light didn't wake Nick. She grew to hate the 'last seen' feature, which told her when he'd last been on the app, evidently messaging someone other than her.

The whole thing was making her ill, she realized one day in late May. Outside, the garden was lush with new life. Nick had taken to going outside with his morning coffee, placing a chair at the edge of the olive grove, where he reckoned the view was most dramatic. He would sit there for half an hour each morning, just drinking it all in. He never took his phone. When she understood that she wouldn't be able to do that – that she would be restless and distracted without the ability to check hers, even for a few minutes – she knew it had to stop.

Let's go back to emails, she messaged him. *One a day each, and we actually talk about proper things, with paragraphs and whole thought processes.* He didn't reply to that for what felt like a long time. She'd spent the rest of the day in an ever-accelerating spin of anxiety and regret that she'd somehow offended him, that that was it and she'd heard the last of him. *You OK?* she'd eventually given in and sent, the possibility of him ending the torture with a reply irresistible. But that had also gone unanswered, though she could see he'd read it. *The two blue ticks of doom*, Lou had called them once, and she had laughed, not really understanding. She got it now. By the time she went up to bed, her whole body was leaden with the absurd and terrible grief of it.

But he'd written to her that night: a long email, which she had devoured in the dark of the snug, the pink and lemon dawn going unnoticed behind closed shutters. She'd got the new-mail notification on her phone but had deliberately waited till she got downstairs to the laptop to read it, and she stuck to this pattern until Bastian – and she *still* can't quite get her head around this – had arrived in person at Luna Rossa, the naked shock of it nearly rendering her unconscious.

Now, entirely awake in the smallest hours, she keeps to her own rule when the urge to read through their emails overcomes her, rising silently and tiptoeing downstairs. She doesn't think Nick has ever noticed her absence in the bed.

Tonight, in the snug, she sits down with the laptop but it's still attached to the wall by its cable and the movement wrenches it out. A green light flashes in the void behind the loose socket and plaster dust showers the tiles beneath. She wonders if she's fused the whole house but the worry of it – of the villa's soundness in general – is remote compared to him. As she opens the laptop, the faulty electrics are already retreating fast, out of her mind.

The document is large now, thousands of words carefully pasted in, as though she'd needed proof that she hadn't invented the whole thing. He'd sent her a brief one today, which she feels weird about, but will add to the collection anyway. *So now we get to sneak around under Lou's nose too.*

Seeking reassurance, or order, or something, she decides to read from the top.

I live in Italy now, in the Marche region. No one's ever heard of it but it's just north-east of Tuscany. It looks like Tuscany too, only with bigger hills and bigger earthquakes. We bought a villa with a beautiful name – Luna Rossa. Red Moon. It has the most incredible views across the valley. And actually it's not just a villa: there's land, lots of it, with olive groves, hazel and linden trees, and a collection of other buildings we don't know what to do with yet. In a way, it's more like a tiny village! I can go for a decent walk and not leave my own land. And after London, where everyone lives on top of each other, that's so strange. There, even houses worth millions have postage-stamp gardens and nowhere to park the car. Here, I wander round the villa and there's just so much space. All these empty rooms and every one belongs to me.

She remembers writing this one so vividly. How she'd deliberated about that single 'we'. *Obviously I'm married*, it said; a small prod to inspire regret. *Someone else wanted to be with me for ever.* And then the deliberate use of 'I' elsewhere, retreating back into the pretence that there were no barriers. A clear signal that she had remained her own person, rather than morphing into half of an impregnable unit.

In all of the messages, from the very start, she had been aware of walking a fine line, a tightrope strung high over a long drop. On one side, the depiction of an enviable life. Here I am, a success. I have sustained a grown-up, committed relationship. I am adored by a man with whom I have bought a piece of Italy. And on the other: I have never forgotten you. Take me.

She scrolls down the messages, away from the tentative early ones where she and Bastian took it in turns to present their biographies. *This is my life, what about yours?* She sees now that his are shorter, vaguer. He uses his to draw her out. Because Lou is there in the villa with her, she can't help reading the messages as her friend would, if Laura allowed her to.

With the spectre of Lou reading over her shoulder, the tone twists into something new and uncomfortable. She reads her own words, the spill of them, open and giving everything away, as she always did. And then his: opaque, almost closed. They would seem uninterested if it wasn't for all the questions. Questions that kept the conversation going and going until he arrived.

Since she walked into the garden holding a bottle of Aperol Spritz and saw him sitting there, time sticking and stuttering like an old VHS tape on pause, there have been hardly any. And while there's an obvious logic to that – why would they be writing to each other when they're under the same roof? – she knows it means something significant. It makes her uneasy in some indefinable way.

She skims the early ones again, hoping she's being overly critical, seeing the words through the prism of her own thoughts. But it's true. She hasn't lied, exactly. It's not that bald. She has exaggerated, though, in a hundred tiny ways that add up to something not quite true. Immersed in her emails, Luna Rossa rises, larger and grander than it could ever be. Their parcel of land – in many places steep and scrubby, basically unusable – rolls out, velvet green and abundant. *It's more like a tiny village!* The money they made from selling up in London is also abundant. There are hints that, instead of being chewed up voraciously by the villa, there is still plenty of it sloshing around.

She's almost boasting in the emails, and admitting that to herself now makes her cringe. Not only because she did it in the first place but because Bastian is now here, and must see the disparity.

There's something else too. When she's not talking about the villa, she's reminiscing about their time at university. She's always elevated the past to something she knows on one level it wasn't, even as she simultaneously believes it was – a kind of double-think in which the knowledge that you're wearing rose-tinted glasses doesn't stop everything looking rosy. Her diaries have been her accomplice in smoothing and polishing that time. Even now, making herself remember the bad parts, she sees herself prettily tear-stained and hollow-cheeked: misery cushioned in a silk-lined box. The stark grey depression Lou no doubt recalls, when she didn't bother washing her hair or getting dressed, is nowhere to be seen. Embarrassed, she closes the document.

She doesn't know why she does what she does next; her fingers on the trackpad seeming to move independently from her brain. She hasn't checked Madison's Instagram for weeks. It hasn't occurred to her to do so. Now, as the page loads agonizingly slowly, she feels vertiginous. In the corner of the room, something moves at floor-level, blacker than the shadows there. She registers dimly that it's probably a scorpion or a spider but then Madison's profile flashes up, and her eyes flick back to it, whatever is lurking forgotten.

There are seven new squares; seven posts about Italy. She can see this at a glance: the colours different from California, aged and softened. Ochre and umber and olive. She clicks on each in turn. As before, Bastian does not appear in any. But also as before, he is definitely the one behind the camera and this disturbs her to such a degree that she can't believe it hasn't until now.

Here is Madison stretched out on the stones next to the pool – *my* pool, she thinks, heart juddering. She's wearing a silver bikini Laura doesn't remember seeing and a transparent wrap that's been artfully pulled up around her waist. Her legs are impossibly long and slender, her ribcage raised out to push up her breasts. Her back is so arched that blue pool water is visible through the gap. She has turned her face to the camera and her dreamy half-smile is so intimate, so obviously for him, despite where she'll go on to post it, that Laura feels sick. She's never seen Madison quite like this: blurred and seemingly post-coital. *Fucked.*

She clicks on the next post. Urbino. Madison sitting at the restaurant table where they'd had that long, blissful lunch, everyone so effortlessly congenial, the sexual tension between her and Bastian almost tangible but not yet acted upon; comparatively innocent. She remembers this photo because Nick took it and Madison asked him to share it with her afterwards. He had Airdropped it to her instantly in that medieval city and they'd all remarked on how amazing it was that these things could be done, then laughed because it made them sound so past-it. She remembers that she had been in the photo, Nick telling them to get in closer. Her own phone is just in shot, where she'd had it out next to her wine glass. But she has gone, cropped out so it's all Madison.

She wants to stop looking, to shut the screen and

forget about it, shove out of her head as best she can these glimpses of Bastian as an established, official partner; someone else's. They make her so suddenly and corrosively jealous that she wants to lift the laptop over her head and throw it hard at the floor. But there's another shot attached to the Urbino post and she's already clicking on it. It's a selfie this time: Madison walking along, her phone angled up and on the diagonal in the way that people instinctively do now, perhaps because it enhances the cheekbones and sharpens the chin.

Urbino's fanned cobbles are behind her, and little groups of tourists snapped mid-sentence or slack-mouthed as they window-shop, none aware that they have been captured unflatteringly and put up online for ever. Off to one side in the foreground is an inch of hazy blue – it must be Nick's T-shirted shoulder.

Her brain makes the jump. It's the street the bookshop was on, and the leather-goods shop, though there is no sign of Madison's bright pink bag over her arm. It isn't yet bought.

She sees them then. Her and Bastian at the very furthest reaches of the shot, blurred but easily identified if you know who you're looking for. They're already dropping back, allowing the others to pull ahead. They have turned to each other and she remembers this moment precisely. It was the moment he nodded towards the bookshop and said, *You want to go in?* She sees now, pixellated as they are, that they're standing too close to each other. He is looking down at her and her face is tipped up to him; it looks like they're about to kiss. She imagines Madison pincering her fingers to make it bigger.

Now she shuts the laptop. She doesn't need to dissect the other posts forensically. She gets the gist with a glance: long fingers around a flute of salmon-pink Prosecco; an arty, sharp-lined shot of Ivan's black pool; a blazing sunset reflected in mirrored sunglasses.

The vertiginous feeling is back, Laura's thoughts tumbling through empty, lightless air. Madison has peeled off another layer of herself. This one has the capacity to be merciless, to reach out and take Laura's life from her. With those appropriated images of *her* pool, *her* view, the wine cooled in *her* fridge, it feels like she already has. She tells herself she's being paranoid, that this will look different in the morning, but there's no conviction in it. It feels hollow, naive, like she's being talked at by a well-meaning friend who doesn't get it.

She and Nick are in the kitchen, arguing under their breath. Outside, the afternoon hums with heat and cicadas. A line of ants marches past her bare feet, tiny centurions carrying ciabatta crumbs.

'Why did you do it, Nick?' she says. 'Why the hell did you invite Angelo tonight, knowing how I feel about this whole thing? It's bizarre. We've already rowed about it.'

'He basically invited himself.'

'He couldn't have invited himself to something he knew nothing about. So you must have said something. Why would you mention a dinner party to our builder? Were you showing off or something? *Oh, aren't we sophisticated up here at Luna Rossa!*'

Nick's lip curls. 'Don't be ridiculous. He already knew about it. Ivan must have said something to him. I'm telling you, he invited himself.'

She sighs, anger burning out abruptly and weariness taking its place. 'Have we even got enough food for an extra person?'

Nick concentrates on the chopping board where he's slicing fat cloves of garlic with great care. 'Two, actually. Angelo is bringing his girlfriend.'

'Wonderful. Are Tommaso and the rest of the men coming too?'

'I'll get more food. There'll be enough.' He stops, then seems to decide. 'Anyway, I'm the one doing it all. What difference does it make to you if we're six or eight?'

She opens her mouth to say that it makes a huge difference; that she doesn't want to be friends with the person they owe money to, have already given money to, who frightens her at some cellular level, who will take over and entirely alter the dynamic, which should have just been them, the Americans, Lou and the oddly soothing Ivan. But then Lou walks in and she decides not to.

'Everything all right?' Lou looks from one to the other.

'Laura is pissed off because Angelo's coming. But I've told her I'll take care of the food.'

'The creepy builder bloke? I'm not surprised. Who invited him?'

'Apparently he invited himself,' says Laura.

Nick rounds on her with a ferocity that makes her and Lou freeze. 'He did invite himself. How many fucking times?'

'Nick . . .' There's a warning in Lou's voice.

'This is none of your business, Lou,' he says. 'Please stay out of it.'

'Fine.' She walks back out to the garden.

'Don't speak to her like that. She's my best friend.'

He slams a dirty serving dish into the sink where it breaks neatly in two.

'God, Nick.' She rushes to the sink and holds up the pieces. 'You're being a total dick. I bought that in Florence.'

'How about you leave me to get on with things?' He's angry in a way she hasn't seen him in years, flushed and blank-eyed, his voice dropping dangerously low. 'Why don't you just go and find Bastian, see if he wants anything?'

'What's that supposed to mean?' She knows she should just walk away but something like excitement is coursing recklessly through her.

'Do you think I'm blind?' He turns to her, the small knife in his right hand. Pale parings of garlic cling to the blade. 'Do you think I haven't noticed the way you look at him? I sit there at mealtimes and watch you eat the food I've made while you gaze up at him through your fucking eyelashes.'

'Oh, that's right, it's all me. None of it's him.'

'Yeah, because that's what you should be worrying about right now. Whether he fancies you back.'

'He does watch me, though.' She remembers that the Americans are around somewhere, that Lou might be listening, and drops her voice. 'He's always watching me, brushing past me. If I'm looking at him, it's because I'm looking *back* at him. Because he makes me so self-conscious.'

Nick sneers, turns back to his chopping. 'You're absolutely loving it, is what you are. You think I don't notice things, that I'm oblivious, but I've been watching you. That secret little smile on your face. The way you're dressed.'

'What do you mean, the way I'm dressed?'

'Oh, nothing,' he says. 'Let's just leave it.'

'No, come on. I want to know what you're getting at.'

'OK. You look like you're going out all the time. You come down to breakfast and you've already got make-up on. You've done your hair.'

'So you'd rather I looked like shit around the place, in front of our guests? Is that what you're saying? Doesn't it occur to you that it might be nice for me to dress up a bit, to feel even slightly pretty after feeling so crap, so ugly, for so long?'

'Oh, Christ, this again.'

She's instantly enraged in a way she hasn't been since last December. They had been in the kitchen then, too, though it was London outside that time: rain running like mercury down black windows, the high, urgent note of a siren rising in the streets beyond. The same pure white energy pulses through her now. It makes her feel as if she could levitate above the tiles.

'Yes, this again, Nick,' she says. 'Sorry if you find it boring.'

'I don't. You know I don't. I know it was shit for you.'

'Which bit? The IVF, the miscarriages, or her?'

He doesn't move. His gaze is fixed on the chopping board, hand braced against the worktop. She doesn't move either. It's as though both of them are holding their breath. She knows him so well. He's deciding whether to say something that could be irreparable. And actually it's not just because she can, after twenty years together, virtually read his mind, it's because she's feeling the same urge. What would she say, if she was to open her hand and let the wind take everything?

Actually we've been emailing for months.

I've kissed him already.

Haven't you worked it out yet? Bastian is the one who'd broken me when we met. The one I wouldn't speak about, not even to tell you his name.

Don't you know, Nick, that you were only ever meant to be my rebound?

That she could say these things right now makes her shake. But then Nick turns to her. 'I'm sorry. I shouldn't have said that.' The words come out stiffly. 'Let's not talk about it any more. Someone's going to hear us.'

On one level, she wants him to know. A destructive part of her – or maybe it's just brave – wants to blow it all apart. She feels like it wouldn't take much, now, to tip her into doing just that.

Last Year

The Uber that has delivered Laura from the clinic drives away, leaving her alone in the gloom of the porch, scrabbling in her handbag for her keys. Finally, her fingers grasp cold metal. They had slipped down next to the small scan photograph.

The house feels different, smells different, even. It's as though she's been away from it for long weeks instead of two and a half hours. You're being stupid, she tells herself. You knew it was going to end like this. But she hadn't known, even as she had.

She opens the fridge, then shuts it again. The left salad drawer contains the medication that has to be kept chilled. There's some left over. Maybe she could give it back. It's worth so much money.

It starts raining as she goes upstairs. There's a pyramid-shaped skylight above the stairs to the loft extension where it always patters loudly. It's a sound she associates with feeling safe and warm in bed, Nick asleep beside her, the dull orange glow of the London night edging the curtains.

She goes right up to the loft room, which they're supposed to be moving into, but which still needs to be decorated, the tiny en-suite shower room fully plumbed in. Nick has been using it as an overspill for the mess he always seems to generate. There are boxes of old CDs he can't bear to throw out, folders of bank statements dating back to school and university days that he can't possibly need to keep, and a set of ugly free weights that roll and clink. Against one wall is a sofa-bed, still made up from his brother staying last weekend. She kicks off her shoes and gets in, twisting round to turn over the pillow. Underneath is Nick's iPad. He'd been looking for it last night, or was it the night before?

As she picks it up to shove it under the bed, it lights up. The screen is full of notifications, a tower of rectangular lozenges, all of them from 'J'. Only the first line of each message is visible, as a preview, but those previews are enough. On the skylight, as she reads each one and then again, the rain comes down harder, each drop a tiny blow.

She is sitting at the kitchen table when she hears the front door open. Her stomach lurches with a terrible excitement. She feels lit up with her own fury. In the bathroom mirror a few minutes ago, her colour had been high, her eyes fever-bright.

He doesn't look at her as he comes into the kitchen. When he empties his pockets into the long blue dish on the side as he always does – wallet, change, keys – he does it with less clatter than usual, his hand shaking slightly. He used to put his phone in there too. Or did he always keep it on him so she couldn't see messages coming in? She can't remember.

Neither of them has spoken yet and the silence is loud. She has a peculiar urge to laugh, or perhaps scream.

He darts towards the kettle as if unable to keep still any longer.

'Leave it.' Her voice is diamond-hard.

He freezes, then comes to sit down opposite her.

She doesn't want to see his expression, which will be frightened and sorry, like a little boy's, so she keeps her gaze trained on the dark whorls in the wood of the table, on the tiny crumbs caught in the deeper knots, remnants from breakfasts before all *this*. Though, actually, that's not right. They're not from before Nick was betraying her. He already was, had been for a while, presumably. She just didn't know it.

'What's this about, Laura? Your message was weird.'

She'd sent him a text, ignoring all his messages about the scan.

You should come home. I found your iPad in the loft.

'Laur?'

'You're a shit liar, Nick. If you didn't know what it was about, you wouldn't be looking like you are. Have you slept with her?'

He visibly jolts, then sits forward so abruptly that the chair legs slide and scrape on the floor. 'No, not even close. I promise.'

'What do you mean, not even close? You must have done something.'

'No, we actually haven't. We were put on this piece together and we just got on. We had this . . . connection.'

'Oh, well, that's a massive fucking comfort.'

He opens his hands, palms up, like a penitent. 'I swear it was just messages. Texts.'

'Endless messages. Hours and hours' worth. She said she wished she was with you, lying next to you. Do you think that's OK? Do you think it's fine because you didn't actually do it?'

'Not fine, no. Obviously. I know that. But it was just . . . talking, flirting. I never even kissed her.'

'My God. You don't think you've crossed the line, do you? Or you're trying to coerce me into thinking you haven't, that I'm overreacting. But you know this is cheating.'

'I'm not saying it wasn't wrong. But it wasn't like we were sneaking off to hotels. There's cheating and there's cheating.'

She gets up and goes to the fridge. She'd put a bottle of white in there an hour earlier, when she'd begun her vigil at the table, sitting in wait for him. The bottle frosts in the warm kitchen as she takes it out and pours. She's deliberately chosen one of the huge Waterford crystal glasses someone bought them when they got married. She sits again, catching his glance.

'I'm allowed it, remember? It doesn't matter now.'

He rubs his eyes. 'I'm sorry. I'm so sorry you came home from the scan to that –'

'What does J stand for?' She cuts across him.

'Does it make any difference?'

She stares him out.

'Jo. It's Jo.'

She drinks, puts the glass down carefully. 'You can't say you had a connection like it was something fucking *spiritual*, and then say in the next breath that it was just a flirtation. Which is it?'

His expression turns slightly implacable. 'I didn't touch her. We never did anything.'

'But you did. Are you really so disingenuous that you won't admit that? You spent hours writing messages to her, thinking about her, imagining you were with her, wishing you were. I'd honestly rather you'd just fucked her. Some drunken shag after work drinks would have been better.'

He won't meet her eye. 'We didn't do anything.'

'So you keep saying. Was it emails too? It must have been. Emails at work and texts for after-hours, yes? I want to read the emails. The other texts.'

His eyes flick from side to side, like a cornered animal's.

'Show me.'

'What's the point?'

'The point is, I want to see them. I'm your fucking wife. I've been injecting myself with hormones and feeling like shit and miscarrying your babies while you formed a *connection* at work with *Jo*. When I wasn't even sure about doing IVF in the first place. When it was you who was always cooing over toddlers in the park, not me. So show me all of it or get the fuck out of this house.'

They weren't really sexual. He had been truthful about that. They were romantic, though, and she thought that might be worse.

'What if we really do go to Italy?' he says, after she's read everything at the table while he watched, hands grasping his knees to stop them shaking. He looks defeated now under the kitchen spotlights, older by a decade than she's ever seen him, face sunken and eyes dull. 'I know I've been dragging my feet but, if we actually do it – sell up here, go out there for a few years – do you think you'll be able to forgive me?'

'I don't know,' she says honestly. 'Are you even sure you want me to forgive you? If I don't, you can have her instead. Have babies with her.'

'No, I want you.' His eyes fill with tears. 'It's always been you. It will always be you. She . . . I dunno. I think . . .' He rubs his face, hard. 'I guess I was flattered. It's no excuse. If you'll just let me prove to you . . .'

'You don't want to go. You've never wanted to leave England. You were just humouring me before, saying we might move out there one day so I'd carry on with the IVF.'

'I'd do it for you. For our marriage. In a heartbeat.'

She pours another glass of wine and walks out of the kitchen with it.

In the morning, he rings one of the estate agents that's always posting leaflets through the door and books a valuation. He speaks to his editor at the paper, says he won't be signing another six-month contract when the current one runs out. Laura assumes that he also, at some point, speaks to J, though she never asks.

Day 9

The light has almost gone, only a dim warmth hanging low in the western sky now, like a faraway war. The air from the open window at her back is, for the first time since early morning, cooler than the air inside. All day it's the house that provides relief from the heat, until it flips over at some point in the evening. Her dress scoops low under her shoulder-blades, and it's like the night is blowing softly on her. There was a fairy-tale she read as a child about the four winds competing for the love of a mortal girl. Was it the wild north wind who claimed her in the end? She can't remember.

Outside, under the pergola, she can hear the others speaking and laughing over each other quite clearly: garrulous, controlling Angelo with his smooth brown skull and silent sloe-eyed girlfriend; Ivan in his beautiful clothes, with his manicured hands; and of course Lou, Nick, Bastian and Madison, the latter's voice slightly louder than everyone else's, in keeping with the old cliché about Americans. Laura feels utterly separate from them, as though she's put on the kind of dreamy coming-of-age film for which she'd trawled Netflix before they left London. She'd watched everything filmed in Italy, however crap. *Stealing Beauty* had been her favourite, though it had made her feel old.

She doesn't feel old now. She feels twenty again.

The dinner party has been going surprisingly smoothly. As she'd hoped, Lou and Ivan have hit it off. She'd sat them together at one end of the table, deliberately putting Lou as far as possible from Bastian and Angelo. The builder – charm personified tonight – is up by Nick. She'd orchestrated all this carefully by writing out place names: gold ink on creamy deckle-edged card. Nick, noticing, had opened his mouth to protest his position, then closed it again.

They've all been at the table for some three hours now. She's grateful to Ivan for bringing half a case of excellent wine – much better than she and Nick could afford – because the number of empties piling up is verging on the obscene. She'd been in the kitchen opening yet another when Bastian came in from the garden, taking it from her and telling her to go to his room: his and Madison's.

Now, waiting for him, there's something she doesn't like about this high-handedness, even as it excites her. That he wants to be with her in the room where his wife – *almost-wife* – sleeps makes her question if this is as much about Madison and the illicit thrill of cheating on her as it is desire for Laura. But she doesn't want to think about that now. There'll be time enough afterwards to torture herself with it.

A tiny click makes her heart lurch. She watches as the door is pushed open and it seems like an age before he appears from behind it, almost comically slow. A nervous laugh rises in her chest and she knows, the thought as clear as cold water, that she'd let it out if it was Nick who had sneaked in to find her. They'd laugh about it together.

But she doesn't laugh now, even though the swell of hysteria inside her hasn't gone, and is only forced down so Bastian doesn't think she's ridiculously gauche.

He comes towards her but stops a few feet away. Under his gaze, which is always – *was* always – so intense, she can't keep still, unsteady hands going to her hair, smoothing it, twisting the ends into coils so they lie better.

'Why here?' she says, though she'd told herself she wouldn't.

'Because this room should be yours. If you were mine, if this place was ours, I wouldn't let anyone else have it.'

It's so much the perfect answer that she doesn't quite trust it.

Outside, someone drops something with a clatter and Angelo hoots, making her jump twice in quick succession. She bites down hard on her lower lip so she doesn't say anything, though it's hard not to launch into silly chatter, just to break the tension that seems loud in the room now that the sounds from the garden have subsided back into nothing.

'You don't really email me any more. I miss it.'

'But we're here, in the same place.'

'I know.' She drops her eyes, embarrassed, but he tips up her chin, forcing her to look at him.

'Did you prefer the messages to the real thing?'

'No, of course not,' though an irritating part of her brain wonders. '*No.*'

He strokes her cheek. 'It's driving me crazy, you being so close when I can't touch you. I see you there with Nick, his ring on your finger, and it makes me hate him.'

'It's not Nick's fault.' It's out before she can help it – even though another part of her likes what Bastian's saying: the naked jealousy of it, and the fact he's mentioned her wedding ring, despite never marrying Madison. She shifts from foot to foot, ashamed and thrilled.

'In another life, I'd like Nick,' says Bastian. 'He's a good guy. But in this one he has you, and that makes it hard for me to be in the same room as him.' His hand has moved from her cheek to the lobe of her ear. He tugs on her hoop earring. 'At least you're wearing these.'

'You remember.' She can't help smiling. *See?* she says in her head to Lou.

He nods as he begins to rub the sore muscles at the back of her neck with thumb and forefinger. 'Of course I remember. You're so tight here. Do you know, you've barely looked at me since Lou arrived? I always thought me and her got on, back then.'

'Did you?' She can't keep the surprise out of her voice. Lou had never liked him. A memory comes: she and Lou sharing a cigarette outside the library, the sky baggy with rain, people hurrying to get to their lectures before it split open. 'The trouble with a bloke like that,' said Lou, 'is that he's never going to love anyone as much as he loves himself.'

Bastian brings her back to the present, his thumb working its way down each of her vertebrae, circling hard. It's that slightly nauseating nerve pain again, and she resists the urge to move away.

He bends to kiss her collarbone, which makes her dissolve. 'Are you telling me that she never liked me?'

'You broke my heart, remember.'

'But before that?' He's pulled back for her answer.

She studies him, surprised he's missed a cue like that. It's the first time she's alluded to the end but he's more focused on Lou's twenty-year-old immunity to his charms.

'She thought you were up yourself. And it didn't help that you were friends with Theo and that lot. She always hated them, right from freshers' week.' It's an easy slide into the language of then.

'*Up myself*,' he says, smiling. 'I forgot that.' His hot hand is halfway down her back now, a notch below the line of her dress so that she can feel the pull on her shoulders as he stretches the fabric. It gives, and she understands that he's found the zip. The night's breath moves over the lower half of her back as he opens it to her waist. His mouth is on her collarbone again, the heat of it making her exposed back feel cold by contrast.

In one easy movement he lifts her onto the windowsill. It's too shallow to sit properly but the weight of him pins her there. His hand is on her thigh now, creeping under the hem of her dress and moving up the outside of her leg until he reaches her hip. His fingers find the ribbon tie. They're silly knickers she never wears, the ribbon bulky under close-fitting clothes, and a faff to tie and untie every time she needs the loo. She's embarrassed she wore them on the off-chance that he might see them, knowing he'd like them.

He finds the end of the ribbon and pulls. The satin knot slips apart immediately, and she knows the rest of the fabric is loose because she can't feel it any more. He was always so good at these things. He never fumbled, which in turn meant that she had never had to be ready to reassure, or pretend she was still in the mood when her body wasn't understood. Sex could so easily tip into the awkward, the ridiculous. But Bastian had always allowed her to remain outside her head more than anyone else.

He's kissing her neck now, even as his fingers are creeping inwards, over her hipbone, then down to the silky skin of her inside thigh.

'I loved it when you were there, you know. Standing there watching us. It turned me on.'

It takes her a beat to make sense of his words. Then she understands. 'You mean when you and Madison were in the shower?'

His breathing is louder in her ear now, more ragged. He's heavy up against her and it occurs to her for the first time that the half-open window is taking a lot of their weight. She glances down at the iron stay propping it open and sees that the old blunt-headed screws securing it to the frame have moved a little in the soft wood. She pictures herself falling backwards through the evening's violet air, thick with perfume and the day's heat but not dense enough to save her.

At the same moment she shifts forwards to get away from the drop, his fingers push inside her. It hurts and she can't help crying out. Not all of it is pain. Some of it is frustration because she's wanted this and she's angry with herself for breaking the spell, and angry with him for mentioning the shower.

He steps away from her and the traitorous knickers begin to slide down her leg. Furious, her fingers stupid with it, she hitches them up and reties the bow, pulling the ends tight enough to cut in and leave a mark. When she looks up at him his expression is oddly blank but then he reaches out to take her hand.

'I'm sorry I hurt you. I can't control myself around you, that's all. I –'

She shakes her head with impatience, stopping him mid-flow.

'Why did you do that? With the shower? Why did you want me to see you and her like that?'

He spreads his hands. 'I guess I wanted to make you jealous. I didn't know if I could get anywhere near you then. I hated thinking of you with Nick and –'

'Oh, me and Nick,' she interrupts. 'It hardly ever happens. It's like once every few months, if we put the effort in. I don't believe for a second it's like that with you and Madison.'

'But I heard you,' he says. He moves towards her again, takes her other hand, and places both of them around his waist. Then he combs through her hair with his fingers. She can feel them, hot against her scalp. She closes her eyes, feels herself begin to loosen again. 'I heard you with Nick the first night we were here,' he says, voice low and coaxing. 'Madison went out like a light but I couldn't sleep and it was hot in the bedroom, with the shutters closed. I wanted some air. I thought I'd go and sit in the garden, take it all in, think about how I was in the same place as you. I heard you when I was out in the hallway. That wasn't maintenance sex.'

'I pretended he was you.' She colours with the betrayal, which somehow seems worse than what she's already done. But then he's kissing her and she's just letting herself disappear into it when a noise on the landing – a creak from one of the old floorboards – makes them freeze. For a confused split-second, because of what he's just said, it's Bastian she pictures there, listening. But it can't be him.

'It's Nick,' she whispers urgently. Neither of them moves. It must be Nick. Who else would come upstairs now? Madison would have walked in, wouldn't she? It's her room. Laura's heart pounds in her ears as Bastian goes to the door and pulls it back. He disappears into the gloom and there's silence. She's about to follow when he re-appears, shaking his head.

'There's no one.'

She experiences a moment of profound relief before wondering if Nick had simply been too quick, retreating into the shadows he knows better than Bastian. Then a more disquieting thought displaces it: what if it actually *was* Madison? What if the reason she didn't just walk in was because she knew all about it, that this wasn't really about Laura and Bastian but some power game of titillation between him and Madison, with her the credulous, idiot pawn who thinks it might be *destiny*?

Day 10

The three women sit around the pool. Nick has told her to go and enjoy herself: he will take care of what needs doing in the kitchen. He's being polite but distant, not quite looking her in the eye. What seems like an extreme and deliberate civility – behaving towards her as though she was a guest he's known for only a few days – is unnerving. She feels as though she's about to step off some invisible ledge into thin air, her foot already out, weight shifting fatally.

She thinks back to what she heard last night, on the landing during the dinner party, as though she might be able to identify Nick's unique step if only she could play back the scene accurately enough. But she can't tell. She just can't.

Outside, with Lou and Madison, it's not much better. Nerves flitter inside her. Not like butterflies but moths, their bodies shedding dark dust. If it wasn't Nick, it must have been Madison. Or it might have been Lou, of course, and this is the least bad option but surely Lou would have said something by now and she hasn't.

It's not just last night. She can't tell how much the atmosphere is genuinely strained between her and everyone else, and how much is a generalized paranoia. Yesterday, she observed Lou and Madison getting on famously and it was ridiculous how jealous it made her. Although she wonders now if it was as much discomfort as jealousy, that Lou's enthusiasm for Madison is actually just a way of signalling disapproval because Laura is messing around with this other woman's husband.

Though Lou is only a few feet away, Laura is rocked by a wave of missing her, made worse by the knowledge that she's leaving later. Lou is self-conscious in her one-piece swimsuit, though she's doing a decent job of pretending she's not. Laura knows her too well, though. She's seen Lou's covert glances towards Madison's long, tanned legs, how she's pulled her sarong tight around her own, which are fleshy and winter-pale. All this makes Laura love her so much it hurts.

She puts a hand to her stomach, which is concave when she's lying down for the first time in years because she keeps forgetting to eat: the way Bastian looks at her has wrecked her appetite. It was the same back then, she remembers. Lou would buy her pizza in the refectory. *Eat, for God's sake! There's nothing left of you.* But she could only pick, her mind always on him, the thoughts spreading and expanding inside her until she was full.

Directly above them, the sun has burnt the sky white. She and Lou have raised their parasols against it but Madison has an amazing tolerance.

'How can you bear it?' Lou calls to her now. 'It's bloody roasting.'

'I'm a Southern girl,' says Madison, turning her head towards them, oversized sunglasses making her face sharp and elfin. 'This is nothing. It's ninety-five degrees in summer in Texas. Plus humidity.'

'I thought you were from New York.'

'No, that's Bast. He's the little rich boy from the big city. I'm more double-wide.'

Lou laughs. 'What does that mean?'

'Trailer trash. A double-wide is a big trailer. I'm exaggerating, but only a little. My daddy was a derrick-man on the oil rigs. It killed him, actually. In my last year of high school.'

'Oh, I'm sorry,' says Laura. 'I didn't know.'

Madison shrugs. 'No reason you would. Anyway, the point is that he was blue collar, through and through. Whereas Bast's dad would have owned the rig, you know? I married up.' She shoots a brief glance towards Laura, twists her ring. In Laura's sensitized mood, it feels like a challenge.

No one speaks for a while and, despite everything, the heat has made Laura soporific enough to sleep. She's just drifting away when Lou yawns noisily and sits up. 'It's interesting, isn't it, that none of us has kids? We're all about the same age, aren't we? How old are you, Madison?'

This is a question Laura hasn't dared ask.

'I thought you weren't supposed to ask a lady her age.'

Lou smiles. 'I'm not convinced there are any ladies here.'

There's a pause when Laura's stomach starts to tip but then Madison laughs.

'That's true. I'm forty-two. And, no, no kids.'

'You are in seriously good shape,' says Lou, and Laura can tell she means it. It's not just one of those things women say automatically: social grease. 'Didn't you want them? I think I do. Did? Sometimes. But it's hard to tell what's panic and what's actual wanting when you're single.'

'I never wanted them,' says Madison. 'My mom was one of six, my daddy one of five. I have a hundred cousins and three brothers I speak to once a year at Christmas. I think families are seriously overrated. And babies are seriously boring.'

'And Bastian felt the same?'

Laura tenses again. These are all questions she's wanted to ask herself but they still feel pointed, coming from Lou.

'God, yeah.' Madison sits up and twists her hair into a pleat, fastening it with a crystal-encrusted clip that bounces the sunlight like her ring does. 'You think Bast is the type to share attention with a kid?'

Lou smiles, first at Madison, then Laura. Laura knows she can't help it, that what Madison has said vindicates everything Lou's always tried to warn Laura about. The condescension of it makes her furious.

'I didn't really want them either,' she says. Lou turns to her in astonishment. 'Oh, I know you thought I did, with the miscarriages and everything.'

'You had miscarriages?' Madison leaps up. 'Oh, honey, I'm sorry about what I said. I shouldn't have been so flip.' She comes to sit on Laura's lounger, takes hold of Laura's hand and strokes it. Lou observes silently.

'No, please don't apologize. You couldn't possibly have known.'

Laura squeezes Madison's hand before letting it drop. She gets up and walks to where the shallow steps disappear into the water, wading in quickly because she knows the other two are watching her. The water is cool on her legs but shockingly cold when it hits her pelvis. She ducks underneath and swims to the far end, then back again. When she surfaces, Madison and Lou are still watching her. Lou's face has softened considerably.

Laura props herself a little out of the water with her elbows. Water runs off her to darken the pale stone. They're waiting respectfully for her to speak.

'I suppose I was never sure, that's all. Sometimes I thought it would be nice. I could picture a little boy in a duffel coat, running ahead of us in the park. He was never a baby, in my head. The idea of a baby terrified me. But I quite liked the idea of a five-year-old, you know? And then I couldn't get past ten weeks, so that became rather academic.'

Madison shakes her head. 'So you've been through all that, and then that prick Angelo comes into your house and tells you your clock is ticking. Wow, if I'd known that.' She's fierce, her face hard and beautiful, like it's been carved. It makes Laura glad and apprehensive at the same time. One of her first thoughts about Madison had been that she wouldn't want to cross her.

'Angelo said that? As in Angelo from last night?' Lou is outraged. 'What a wanker. I wish you'd told me, Chapman. I would have stuck my fork in his fucking crotch.'

'Yeah, and I would have held him while you did it,' says Madison. 'What the hell was Nick thinking anyway, letting him come? He's supposed to be on your side, isn't he?'

Laura pushes herself back under the water and swims to the other side, where she notices the astonishing view for the first time in days, as if it's new to her. She can't tell if her face is only wet from the pool water but she keeps looking at the valley until the urge to cry recedes. The view is even more like a landscape painting than usual.

The only sign it's real is the way it shimmers in the heat. And in the single car visible on the far side, smaller than the drowned wasp bobbing next to her. She follows its silent progress as it winds up the hill road, in and out of sight.

Most of her urge to cry is not even about the children thing. It's the building stress of what she's allowing to unfold, which she seems powerless to stop now it's in train. She wades back out and rejoins the other two as though the conversation about miscarriages had never happened. Somewhere a church bell is tolling, slightly flat. She wonders if it's a wedding or a funeral.

'So, I must say I feel a bit let down by the lack of handsome Italian men at last night's dinner,' says Lou.

Laura smiles her gratitude for the change of subject. She's not entirely sure she deserves it, just because she couldn't carry a baby to term.

'All you gave me was Ivan and sadly I am not his cup of tea. It's a terrible shame – he'd make me an excellent husband.'

'Are you dating back home?' Madison turns onto her hip.

Lou sighs theatrically. 'Yes. And it's a bloody nightmare. I don't know what the hell anyone did before dating apps, including me, but I loathe them.'

'Have you met any good ones? At least in the city – in London – you've got a big pool.'

'Yeah, you'd think. I've met loads of nice blokes. A few dickheads, but most are OK.'

'But you don't want OK.' Madison sits up, begins to apply more oil. The scent of coconut sweetens the air. 'No one wants *OK*.'

Lou reaches for the can of Coke that's been sweating on the ground next to her lounger and cracks it open. Laura doesn't know anyone else who still drinks the classic sugary one.

'It's the chemistry,' says Lou, after she's gulped some down. 'Or, rather, the lack of it. You message for a bit, and they seem great, and it doesn't matter how many times I do it, but I always think, Oh, now, *this* one. And then he walks into the pub and I know instantly that I'm not going to fancy him, however funny his messages are. So then I have to spend two hours with someone I know I'm never going to see again. It's not just the time either. It costs a fortune.'

'Two hours?' Madison pauses in her oiling. 'I'd just walk back out if I didn't like the look of the guy.'

Lou laughs. 'I could never do that. It's so brutal.'

'They'd get over it.'

'I wouldn't, if someone did that to me. I'd honestly throw myself in the Thames.'

'You have met a couple of decent ones, though, haven't you?' Laura says tentatively. She's still wary of Lou, which is such an unfamiliar feeling she doesn't quite know what to do with it.

'If by decent you mean passable-looking enough for me to sleep with them.'

Madison laughs. 'And not married, for bonus points.'

Laura stills, Lou's startled eyes darting straight to her.

'What?' Madison looks from Laura and back again to Lou. 'Did that happen to you?'

Lou hesitates for so long that Laura thinks she might keel over. 'Something like that,' she says, in the end. She fiddles with the ring pull of her can until she breaks it off, the *tink* of metal loud.

'You didn't know he was, though, right?' says Madison. 'It wasn't like you were on one of those sites where everyone's married and cheating, was it? Jeez, do you remember that Ashley Madison site? It was all over the news when they had their data hacked. Never have I hated my name so much.'

'Did you check it?' Lou's voice is soft.

There's a long pause. Then Madison laughs, and it's not her deep earthy one. This is brittle. 'Of course I fucking did.'

Laura wonders if she might actually be sick right there on the stones.

'I don't really get the cheating thing,' Lou says, when Madison doesn't elaborate. 'If you don't want to be faithful, then don't get married. Or, at least, be up-front with the person you're marrying. Tell them you're not sure you can do monogamy for ever.'

'Yes, because it's really that simple,' says Laura, the words out before she can stop them.

'I think it is,' says Madison. 'You're either loyal, or you're not. If you're not, own it. The trouble is, people are afraid to be alone. They think about when they're old and left with no one.'

Lou covers her ears.

Madison claps a hand over her mouth. 'Oh, I don't mean you. I don't mean single people out there being brave, looking for love in an honest way. You're not gonna be alone, girl. You're hot. And, never mind the men. You've got Laura, who I have to tell you has totally opened

242

my eyes to the whole sisterly solidarity thing. No, I'm talking about the cheats. They're the ones who'll end up on their own. You know, I'm many things. I can be loud. I drink too much. I'm vain. But I don't cheat.'

Laura concentrates on the ground.

'Hey, honey, you're not saying much.' Madison has raised her sunglasses to look directly at her. 'What did you mean? Why isn't it that simple?'

Laura stretches out her foot so it's beyond the shade line from the parasol. The stone is hot enough to burn but she leaves it there. 'Things change,' she says. 'Of course people don't go into marriage wanting or suspecting they might ever feel differently about that person. Most people have the best intentions. But you don't stay the same all your life, do you? Who you are, what you want. Ten, twenty years down the line, you can look at your other half and just not get them any more – not get what you ever saw in them.'

Madison pulls a face. 'I'm sure glad Nick isn't in on this conversation.'

'Yeah, and I hope this doesn't extend to friendships too,' says Lou. She's smiling grimly. 'I must be well past my use-by date.'

'Don't be ridiculous,' Laura says, too sharply. 'I'm talking about hypothetical long-term partners. Romantic, sexual. You wouldn't understand.'

'No, I guess not, poor perennial singleton that I am.' She gets to her feet. 'I'm going in for a bit. It's too hot for me out here.'

Laura finds Lou in her room, sitting at the dressing-table. The white walls that will turn rose as the day wears

243

on are still pure with midday light, brilliant against Lou's dark bob.

Laura can't think what to do. Should she go and put her arms around her? She can't seem to access her own instincts. She and Lou never fall out. It occurs to her that she's badly hung-over – and, as well as the paranoia, she's developed a headache that feels like a band tightening around her temples. She can't remember drinking any water today, only coffee.

'Sorry,' she says in the end. 'I didn't mean to patronize. You know I didn't. I've never been a *smug married*, God knows. I was just ready to have a panic attack out there.'

'Yeah, that was . . . uncomfortable.'

'Do you think she suspects?'

'Probably.' She sees Laura's expression and throws up her hands. 'What do you want me to say? She's as sharp as a tack.'

'I don't know what to say to *you*. You feel miles away.'

Lou sighs. 'I am, most of the time.'

'You know what I mean.' She hangs her head. She can feel tears coming again. Even as she thinks, *don't cry, don't cry*, they're already spilling over. Lou sees but doesn't move and this makes her cry harder. It probably seems manipulative but isn't.

'Don't get upset.' Lou's voice is flat.

'I'm sorry.' She sounds strangled. 'I don't know why I'm crying. I'm all over the place.'

'Where did you go last night?' Lou's gaze is fixed on the view.

The urge to sob abruptly abates. Laura swipes at the

tears on her face with the heels of her hands. 'What do you mean?'

'At dinner. When we had a break before pudding. You went into the kitchen and didn't come out.'

'I did.' She shakes her head, like a guilty child.

'Not for ages. Bastian went inside *to the bathroom*,' she does inverted commas in the air, rolling her eyes, 'and was mysteriously gone for ages too.' She meets Laura's eye squarely for the first time that day. 'Have you let him fuck you yet?'

The words make Laura flinch. She takes a sharp breath. 'No. No, I haven't, but . . .'

'What?'

'I – I thought someone was there . . . I mean, we thought we heard . . .'

'Oh, you nearly got caught? I guess that's always a risk if you mess around in the same house as your husband and your lover's wife.'

'She's not actually his wife.'

'What?'

Laura shakes her head. 'Never mind. Look, I know it's wrong. We've been through this. But I need to know who it was. If it wasn't you, it must have been Nick or Madison. No one else would come upstairs, would they? Did anyone else leave the table?'

'I can't remember. I was hammered.'

'Nick's being weird, but we're always pissed off with each other, these days. But then Madison . . . If it wasn't her, then how on earth did we end up talking about . . .'

'If it was Madison, you're screwed,' Lou cuts across her. 'As it were.'

Fresh anxiety surges up inside her, hot and caustic.

'I know you like her,' Lou says. 'I do too, actually, and to my own surprise. But under all that touchy-feely La-La Land shit, I think she's a stone-cold bitch. You heard her out there. I think you need to be really careful. Much more careful than you're being. If we were in Texas, I'd be worrying about whether she had a gun.'

Laura chokes out a laugh.

'I'm not even joking,' says Lou. 'You need to stop this before something happens.'

Something happens.

Something will happen.

She senses it again, just as she had early that morning with Bastian in the kitchen. It was only a week ago. It seems unbelievable.

She realizes Lou is looking at her, waiting for some sort of response. And so, because she loves her and doesn't want her to worry, she nods, as though she'll genuinely consider her best friend's warning. She won't, though. She's too far gone. It feels like it's out of her hands. And, despite the tears and panic, there's a strange kind of liberation in that.

The hours until Lou's departure drain away steadily until, quite suddenly, the two of them are in the car again.

'Did you check in online?' she says, when the silence between them begins to feel louder than the engine.

'Yes, you asked me that already.'

'Right. What time do you land?'

Lou sighs. 'Half eight.'

'Not too late, then. For work, I mean. Tomorrow.'

'Yeah.'

It's not until they're on the *autostrada* that Lou speaks again. 'Look, I know you don't want to hear this but I need to say it.'

Laura braces.

'I love you and I think you're making a mistake. I don't care if you split up with Nick. He's a lovely man but I never thought he was enough for you. So this is not about me being resistant to change or weird about divorce because my own parents split up.'

'No, I never thought –'

'Let me finish.' She touches Laura's hand on the steering wheel, just briefly. 'This is not about me, is what I'm trying to say. That you kept all this from me. I just feel like you've had a shit few years and he's made you feel sexy again so suddenly you're going to press that self-destruct button and fuck everything else. Which is fine – I mean, honestly I'd be on board with that if I thought you wouldn't get hurt. If all you were going to do was shag the bloody mechanic. But it's not. It's *him*. Sebastian. He destroyed you back then. I don't know what you've done with those memories, whether you've repressed them, or tidied them up, or what. But he did. He's bad news.'

Laura presses down on the brake because while Lou was speaking their speed had crept up to ninety. She has no memory of driving the last few miles. 'That was twenty years ago,' she says eventually. 'I'm not the same person I was then. He's not the same either. We're adults now.'

'Why did he come here, and without telling you? Have you asked him?'

Laura moves into the outside lane but slightly over-steers. Lou grabs the underside of her seat as they swerve away from the barrier.

'Laura. Have you?'

Sweat inches down her spine. She's asked herself the same question, so many times, especially in the early hours. Most nights she's taken to waking just after two, unable to get back to sleep until the birds start up and lull her back to sleep.

'I guess he wanted to see me.'

'He simply couldn't keep away.'

'Piss off, Lou.' It comes out more exhausted than anything.

'I just want to know what the endgame is here. You two getting together, with Madison and Nick given their marching orders? There are consequences to all this and you're not thinking about them. You don't want to. And, actually, do you know what? I don't think you'd even want to be with him, not really. I think deep down you know what he's like, that no one could ever be as important to him as he is to himself, that he's utterly unreliable, and spoilt, and do you know what else? He's not cool.'

'What?'

Lou is worked up now. She looks like she does when she's tipsy, arguing with someone about politics in the pub, her chin thrust out, her finger jabbing. It's endearing until it's directed at you.

'He's not. He's like a shell. There's no substance to him. I've always thought this, from the first moment I met him at uni.'

'If only we all had your powers of perception.'

Lou ignores her. 'I remember it so clearly. We were in the Vic and he was with those dicks from the hockey team, or was it lacrosse? They'd just got back from bloody Loughborough or somewhere, one of those sporty places, but they'd beaten them and they were all congratulating each other. And he came in and they were all clapping him on the shoulder. Do you remember they called him Al, as in Al Pacino, and thought it was so witty?'

'It was as in Capone, actually.'

Lou snorts. 'God, they were stupid, most of them. But, anyway, I could kind of see why they thought he was exotic. Why you did too. He was so slippery. You knew certain things about him that seemed really glam – that he was basically the only American on campus, that he always had money, that he'd got into Yale, blah-blah. He was perfect romantic fodder for that bloody diary of yours because there wasn't anything solid about him. He was like a fucking ghost. You could merrily fill in the blanks yourself.

'Do you remember, you were always obsessed with this idea of meeting the great love of your life at university? You were always going on about this statistic, that seventy per cent of people met their other half at uni or whatever.'

'I wasn't always going on about it.'

'You were. We'd go to the Lemmy and you'd be scanning the queue for the bar and I'd think, For fuck's sake, she's scouting for The One again.'

From nowhere, Laura bursts out laughing. Lou turns to her in total astonishment and then starts laughing herself. Within seconds, they're hysterical, Laura wiping away tears so she can see the road.

'Pull over, pull over!' Lou shrieks. 'We're going to die.

You're going to kill us. Although at least it would save Madison a job.'

They dissolve into a fresh fit of giggles. Laura isn't sure now whether she's crying as well as laughing. She feels as though she's over-brimming, emotion spilling over and in danger of drowning her. The sign for the airport looms up and she wrenches the wheel to the right. The blaring horn of a van behind them makes them both scream. Lou winds down the window and sticks her arm out, middle finger raised. Her hair whips into her face, sticking to her lips. The driver of the van toots his approval.

'Italians are great,' says Lou, wiping her eyes. 'Maybe I should move here.'

'If you do, I promise I won't have sex with Bastian.'

Beside her, Lou stills.

'I'm joking, I'm joking.'

'You're not, though. I absolutely know you're going to. It has an air of total inevitability about it.'

Neither of them says anything for a while. The land is boring here, rolled out flat and dotted with scrappy farms. Everything suddenly looks unsettlingly foreign: the rust-red pylons and petrol-station chains, the high crash barrier painted black and white, dinked and scraped so many times. They'd have replaced it in England.

She thinks about what Lou said to her before: *Come back with me*. Right now, she wishes she could. If she had her passport, she thinks she would. She usually carries it – force of habit from the early days when it was always being demanded as ID for opening bank accounts and the rest of it – but not today. She'd swapped bags when they all went to Urbino, so she looked smart for Madison. Ironic, really.

'You don't need to come in,' Lou says, as they turn off for Departures. *Partenze.* To part.

The tears that threatened when they were laughing swell behind her eyes again. 'Are you sure?' she says, though what she really wants to do is insist, ignore Lou, find a parking space and see her off anyway.

'Yeah, honestly. No point you paying. I'll go straight through, have a glass of wine, buy myself a massive Toblerone, the usual.'

Laura pulls up where other cars are dropping off relatives, where boots are open and trolleys are being fetched. She watches two tiny old ladies clasping each other, an old-fashioned tan leather suitcase on the pavement beside them. Both are holding white handkerchiefs. She can't tell if they're sisters or friends of many decades. She wonders what they regret.

'I should have stopped at that bakery,' she says, as Lou opens the door.

'What?' She twists round.

'I should have got you another pastry.'

'I told you, I'll get something in there. Don't worry.' Lou's voice is gentler now.

Laura gets out but Lou has already lifted her case from the boot.

'Right, then.' They hover a metre apart.

'Please don't hate me,' Laura blurts. 'The last few years have been so hard. This is the first time I've felt like me in so long. The first time I've felt alive.'

Lou sighs. 'If you don't love Nick any more, if you want to leave him, you know I'm here for you. You can sleep on my sofa-bed till the end of time. It's not the affair thing. I know I shouldn't say it because I do like Nick, but he was fucking useless when you were doing the IVF, even though he was the one who'd pushed for it in the first place, and I could have cheerfully strangled him when he was flirting with that woman at work, if only you'd let me. If we're having a confessional, then I'll tell you that I never thought he was right for you. He never lit you up. I think you know that too, in your heart of hearts. So, if you want to move on with someone else, I'm behind you, totally. But not with *him*. I'll say it again: he's really bad news. He always was.'

'You say this but I don't know what you mean. Yes, I was heartbroken when he went back to the States, but he was always going to go back. It was nothing unexpected.'

'I know you kept ringing him at the end. To be honest, I know you wrote him letters too. I saw one once, before you posted it. I'm sorry I read it but I was so worried about you. You asked him in it why he never replied to anything.'

'He warned me he'd do that. He said it was the only way to get through it.'

'Did he? Have you just made that up? I don't think you know any more what happened and what you've come up with in your head to transform it into something better than it was.'

'You make me sound totally pathetic. I'm not sure that's the best tactic if you're trying to turn me off him.' Her voice has become brittle, although it's actually to ward off tears again.

Lou's face hardens in response. She pulls up the handle of her little suitcase, yanking at it when it sticks. 'You shouldn't bloody need turning off him. Christ, you're the most determined romantic I've ever known. I bet you dug out the old diaries when all this started up, didn't you? Looking for proof that you and him were always destined to be together. But no doubt it's conveniently slipped your mind that you didn't write anything for weeks after you and he broke up, when it all went to shit. I said at the time that you should, that it might be cathartic, but you refused, said, "Why would I want to remember this?" I thought that was fair enough. But I'm telling you now, for the record – for your ridiculously one-sided record – that he's not a nice guy.'

Laura wants to cover her ears. She shifts from foot to foot because her instinct to flee, to get back into the car and drive away from what Lou might be about to say, is so strong.

'I've got this crystal-clear memory of us going up to him and the others in a club one night,' Lou continues. 'And you tapped him on the shoulder and he looked round and saw it was you but he was talking to someone else. He just put his hand out, like *Stop*, while he finished the conversation. You stood there waiting behind him, this fixed smile on your face, for about six minutes.'

'And this is your *evidence*? That he was a bit of a dick in a club twenty years ago? Who wasn't?'

Lou is shaking her head. 'No, no. I'm not talking about that night. That sort of thing was par for the course with him.'

'So what, then?' She jangles and squeezes the car keys, pressing the sharp edges into her palm.

'Are you actually serious?' Lou is fierce now, her cheeks flushed. When she pushes her fringe off her forehead, her hand trembles. 'Look, I didn't want to bring this up – you were always so funny about it – but I know you remember that night at Theo's house when it was his birthday. I know you made me promise at the time that we wouldn't talk about it again, but I didn't think you'd buried it so deep that you could pretend it never happened.'

Laura can't seem to get her breath. 'Look,' she manages to push out. 'Please just leave it. It's all so long ago.' She intends to sound impatient, almost bored, but it comes out desperate.

Lou is squinting into the sun. 'I just wish I'd stayed. I tried to make up for it afterwards, but I've never really forgiven myself. I didn't even tell you I was going home.' Her voice is barely audible over the roar of the *autostrada*, strangers shouting goodbye, a plane coming in to land.

'We were all drunk that night. Everyone was.'

'Oh, so you do remember, then?'

She adjusts her sandal strap to avoid meeting Lou's eye. 'I just think you're being a bit OTT about it. You always had such a chip on your shoulder about Bastian's lot. You never really gave him a chance once you knew he had money. That whole working-class-hero thing, like Nick does, though at least he actually is. Unlike you, with your violin lessons and your place at grammar school. Like your mum wasn't deputy head there.' She tells herself Lou deserves it.

'Yes, because this is really about me and my hang-ups. You're lying to yourself, Laura.' She looks like she might cry, suddenly, all her ferocity melted away. 'I'm really worried about you.'

'Well, don't be. I don't need it.'

Three short blasts of a horn make them turn. It's a taxi,

and Laura realizes she's parked in a rank, that all the other cars are cabs too. She holds up a finger.

'I should go,' says Lou, shortly.

'I'm sorry,' she begins. 'I just . . . Do you remember that evening we were up on the roof? It was the most amazing sunset.'

Lou sighs. 'Not really. You mean in the third-year house?'

'You must remember.' There's a pleading note in her voice. 'I told you we had to remember, because it was this real moment. It was like *the* moment; this weird kind of epiphany that we were at the beginning of everything. Like the threshold of our lives, or something.'

'OK, maybe. It rings a bell.'

'I felt so alive. I want that again.'

'But you can't go back. None of us can. Most of us wouldn't want to. I hate to say it, Laura, and I'm saying it with love, but you need to grow up.'

The taxi driver hits his horn again.

'You'd better move.' Lou nods towards the car. 'We'll talk tonight, OK? I'll Skype you when I get home.'

They pause. Laura's face is hot. She feels breathless and she doesn't know if it's from hurt or fury or humiliation. They're slightly too far apart to hug without one of them going towards the other and she's glad of it. Lou doesn't move towards her either. Laura knows they won't speak tonight.

After Lou has disappeared through the automatic doors, Laura doesn't get straight back on the road. She drives to the quietest corner of the short-stay car park and allows herself to cry for five minutes, timing it on the dashboard clock so she has to stop. Afterwards, she tells herself that Lou has no right to judge her, that she's been a crap friend and that perhaps they've finally outgrown each other. But none of it rings true. What she actually feels is abandoned.

The drive back towards the villa is done entirely on automatic pilot. She only notices where she is when the exit for Castelfranco jogs her brain. Suddenly reluctant to face the others, eyes still red, the urge to cry not yet entirely suppressed, she decides to drive into the town, maybe have a coffee. They could do with a few supplies anyway, and perhaps saving Nick that job later will smooth things over with him.

It's blessedly empty in the central piazza, though preparations have begun for the annual *festa*: workmen disgorging metal poles from the back of a van in the far corner, speakers already mounted on streetlamps. It's just past three and the sun is intense. It perches on the rooftops like a searchlight, giving the whole place a stunned air. The market stalls have been cleared away for the day and only a few tables are occupied outside the café. One patron, sitting alone, stands out from the ageing locals with his pale jacket and Panama hat. Ivan. She hovers, deciding whether to pretend she hasn't seen him, but then he waves. As she makes her way over, she realizes she's glad he spotted her before she could run. There's something undemanding about him, calming.

'Hello, there,' he says, in his quaint way. *Old sport*. 'You look a little lost.'

She smiles, senses that it must look unconvincing, thinks of Lou and finds herself on the verge of tears again. Some of this is her usual monthly hormones, she knows, but some of it is also a kind of grief.

'Oh dear,' says Ivan, getting to his feet. She knows he's going to produce a perfectly laundered handkerchief before he brings it out and hands it to her.

'Ignore me, I'm being ridiculous.' She laughs shakily and swipes at her eyes as Ivan beckons over the sullen waitress.

'What would you like to drink?' he says. 'Will we have Prosecco?' When he smiles he looks like a boy.

'I shouldn't.'

'But would you like to?'

She nods and he speaks to the girl in swift Italian.

'I can only have one, though, I'm afraid. I'm driving.' She sinks into the chair, forces her tense shoulders down. 'I don't want to end up like whoever was driving the Alfa that went off the side of the road.'

'Ah, yes. That's been there for a long time. Raoul used to say that it was like art, that it represented the corruption Italy can't seem to free itself from. He talked for a time of having it brought to the garden, so we could dangle it off something there, like an installation.' His eyes dance as she laughs. 'Fortunately it wasn't to be. It's not still there because the police can't be bothered to remove it. It remains as a warning. Or so rumour has it.'

'A warning?'

'From one family to another. Some labyrinthine vendetta no one can remember the origins of. *Two households, both alike in dignity in fair Castelfranco*. Or perhaps not.'

'But surely if there's some sort of feud that's even more reason for the police to take it away.'

'Not if someone high up in the police is a member of

the same family.' Seeing her expression, he raises his eyebrows with a smile.

The waitress reappears and he takes the bottle from her to pour it himself. She stalks away.

'She always spills it,' he said confidingly. 'I think she does it on purpose. She doesn't like foreigners.'

'Like strangers.'

'Yes.' He lifts his glass. 'Here's to new friends, no longer strangers.'

They clink, and she feels herself start to let go for the first time that day. The Prosecco is good: perfectly cold and dry. Her arms, resting on the table, feel cool where they touch the metal and hot where the sun hits them. She closes her eyes. 'I've just come from the airport.'

'Your friend has gone, then? I liked her. She was great fun.'

'Yes. I'll miss her. Although . . .'

Ivan doesn't say anything when she tails off and it's quiet between them for a time. It's unusual to feel so comfortable with someone so recently met.

'I already miss her,' she says eventually. 'And I've missed her every day since we moved here. But I'm also relieved she's gone. She was making me worry about some things, and I can't quite cope with it at the moment. I've got enough on my plate with the guests.'

Ivan nods. 'Perhaps when you have more guests, you will by necessity keep them at arm's length. That will be easier, less . . . consuming. When I met you and Madison, I thought you were close friends. I thought you had all known each other for years.'

'I didn't think I'd like Madison,' she says, without intending to, 'but I do.'

'I like her too. I thought when I came to dinner, How lovely these women are! But then I always like women so much. If only I could want them too.'

She laughs. 'That's what Lou and I always say. Men have a lot to answer for.'

'They do. *We* do.' He tops up her glass. 'Leave the car, if you like. Giulia is coming to collect me in a while. We can drop you off. But only if you want to, of course.'

She nods, smiles. 'I really would. Thank you.'

'It was an interesting combination of people the other night,' he says, after a time. 'I was surprised to see Angelo there. I suppose Nick asked him.'

'Oh.' She sits up a little straighter. 'He said *you* did. Well, more or less. Something about you already having dinner with Angelo? Nick wasn't very clear. And then, of course, the girlfriend had to come too. I don't think she uttered a word all night.'

Ivan takes off his horn-rimmed glasses and begins to polish them on his shirt. 'Angelo is not my friend, as I think I said before. But it pays to get on with him. It makes things easier round here. We were talking about the car that went off the road . . .'

The Prosecco has already begun to loosen Laura, but this cuts through the pleasant haze. 'Angelo's family are involved in the vendetta?'

'Do you know, I think half of it is made up for the likes of outsiders like us, who have watched the *Godfather* films too many times. But his is certainly a big, important family in these parts. They have . . . What is the phrase? . . . fingers in every pie.' He points to the men erecting some sort of stage from the poles. 'They work for Angelo, for instance.'

She sits up a little straighter.

'As long as you stay on the right side of him, he's fine. How have you found his work? He's pressuring me to use him for some of my own projects – I am undoing the worst of Raoul's excesses, as I told you – but I'm not sure yet whether to give in to him.'

'Oh, he hasn't really done much yet, just a bit of paving around the pool when our original builder couldn't finish the job. I've actually been clashing with Nick about it, though. He's paid for more work that I didn't even know about. It infuriates me that Nick is incapable of being assertive with men like Angelo. It's not like we owe him a favour or something, so why not just say no?'

Ivan is frowning at his glass.

'Sorry, I'm going on. It's just that . . .' She pauses, then says it anyway. 'Well, we don't have bottomless savings. If we're going to spend what money we do have, I want it to be on things for the guests – stuff that might actually earn us some more money back, not a *well*.'

'No, I wasn't . . . You're not *going on*.' He tests out the idiom. 'It's just that I thought Angelo had quite a lot of work planned for you already.'

'Oh.' Laura doesn't know what to say. Incomprehension tightens her chest. 'But he can't have. I mean . . .' She tails off.

Ivan turns up his hands. 'Perhaps I'm mistaken.' He sips his Prosecco, then seems to decide. 'But, actually, I'm quite certain I'm not. Angelo himself mentioned work he had coming up at Luna Rossa months ago.'

Laura's chest tightens even more. She makes herself

breathe out slowly. When Ivan holds up the Prosecco bottle, she nods gratefully.

She stands on the drive for long minutes after Giulia and Ivan have dropped her off and driven away. It's early evening now, and the shadows have stretched out. The one cast by the cypress stretches almost to the wall where the gap used to be, a long finger pointing: a reminder to be wary.

She doesn't need a reminder.

The house, rose-gold in the rich light, looks as much part of the permanent landscape as the rocks and olive trees. From this angle, the Americans' car just beyond her peripheral vision, it could be abandoned, albeit in a picturesque way. One of the roof tiles has slipped and looks like a crooked tooth.

It strikes her that if they were to leave tomorrow Luna Rossa would be just like Giuseppe's House. People would wander through the rooms and make up stories about what might have happened to make the last occupants flee. She thinks about Giuseppe – actually Nico, the Italian for 'Nick', it suddenly occurs to her – and wonders if he's dead. She thinks about the vendetta.

Nick is in the kitchen, chopping herbs. The kitchen is full of their vivid scent and his fingertips are green. He turns as she puts down her bag but says nothing. It makes her feel like walking straight back out of the house and down the Roman path until she reaches Ivan's. She knows she would be welcome there. Giulia would show her to a guest bedroom. The sheets would be pressed and cool.

The soft hum of expensive air-conditioning would lull her into a dreamless sleep.

'I was beginning to think something had happened to you,' he says eventually.

'I texted and said I'd bumped into Ivan.'

'That was ages ago. Did you drive over the limit?'

'No, I got a lift. I left the car in town.' She thinks about getting into the conversation they need to have, and feels another wave of exhaustion. 'Do you want a hand?'

'No, thanks.'

'Come on, let me.' She opens the dishwasher and pulls out the top drawer, clean glasses tinkling.

'Leave it, will you? I'm doing it.'

'Nick, let me help. Don't be such a martyr.' It's out before she can help it.

He puts the knife down, wipes his hands very precisely on a tea-towel and turns to face her, his mouth a thin line. 'How drunk are you?'

'I'm a bit tipsy. I had a few glasses of Prosecco in the piazza. I felt like I needed them.'

'Yeah, and why's that?' He folds his arms.

She meets his eye. Maybe it's the alcohol still moving around her blood, or maybe it's Nick being so prissy, but she doesn't feel like running away now. 'Look, I know you're angry with me because I'm back late, and because you think I'm not pulling my weight here –'

'There's a bit more to it than that,' he cuts in.

'Go on, then, spit it out. Let's do this.'

Bastian appears in the doorway. Neither of them had heard his approach.

'Hey, you're back,' he says to Laura. He smiles at her as

though Nick isn't even there. It seems glaringly obvious there's something between them.

'Give us a minute, will you, mate?' Nick's voice is cold. There is so much hostility in that last word that Laura wonders what she's let herself in for.

'You OK, Laura?' Bastian hasn't acknowledged Nick. He's still looking at her.

She glances instinctively towards her husband. His arms are still folded but his fists are clenched now.

'Yes, I'm fine,' she says hurriedly, resisting the urge to usher Bastian out. 'Absolutely fine. Dinner will be about an hour.' She has no idea if this is true but she's desperate to get rid of him before Nick blows. He hardly ever loses his temper but when he does it's dramatic. 'I'll call you and Madison then, OK?'

Bastian nods and leaves, thank God.

'It's a fucking joke,' says Nick, when they're alone again.

'What is?'

'The way he looks at you, like he's already had you.'

'Nick –'

'Oh, don't act the innocent. You fucking love it.'

She hates it when he sneers like this. She knows it's because he's hurt and needing reassurance, but it inspires the opposite reaction in her at the worst possible moment. 'Please don't be like this.'

'Like what?'

'So aggressive. We need to talk properly.'

'About *him*?' He swallows as he waits for her answer. They're as scared as each other, only about different things.

'No, not him.' She makes herself meet his eye. 'Don't be ridiculous. It's something Ivan said. About Angelo.'

Nick turns back to the chopping board but he doesn't pick up the knife. He's tense, waiting to find out what she knows, what she's found out. It feels as though the ground beneath her is beginning to open, revealing a sinkhole that's been there the whole time.

She moves to the counter so she can see his face. 'Ivan seems to be under the impression that Angelo has been involved here for ages. That it was his men working on the pool from the start, rather than Massimo's. You said to me before that it was just a bit of finishing off. Was that a lie?' Something else occurs to her. 'Was Massimo's wife really ill or did you make that up because you'd met Angelo in the bar and given him all the work instead?' She can imagine this scenario: Nick wanting to impress, show he had money to spend, that he was in charge of this big ambitious project. It reminds her of her own email to Bastian.

Nick has never been a good liar. He looks like a child caught out, guilt-racked and miserable. Now, he looks guiltier than she would have expected, and this sobers her up.

Something else comes to her. She has let everything with Bastian and Lou and the rest of it distract her.

'Nick, look at me.'

He does, but only briefly. His face is pallid where it was red before.

'Tommaso said something weird to me last week. About the boundary.'

She watches her husband shift about on the spot as if he'd run if he could. Instead, he yanks open the fridge, gets out a beer and drinks half of it in one go.

'Nick, you're frightening me. I told you last year that I couldn't deal with you keeping things from me again.'

He puts down the bottle with a heavy clink. The beer starts to fizz out and he has to clamp his mouth to it. The scene feels like a bad joke.

'It's OK,' he says. 'I've sorted it now. There was a bit of an issue but it's fine. It wasn't so much a boundary thing, although there was an element of that because . . .' He tails off.

'Hang on, what? You're not making any sense. Start at the beginning.'

'Are you sure you want to do this now? I really need to get this dinner started. You said it would be an hour.'

'Forget dinner. They can wait.'

She leads him outside so they can't be overheard. Nick is clutching his beer. She wishes she had one too, but she wants a clear head. Any traces of the Prosecco haze seem to have gone.

They sit on the ends of two loungers next to the pool, both of them facing the view.

There's silence between them for a while and then, after a long sigh, Nick begins to speak.

'You loved this place immediately. You fell in love with it. We were both pissed off with driving around getting lost and you looked so exhausted. I was worried about you and the . . .'

'The pregnancy.' Not a baby.

'Yes. Then we got here and you lit up. You looked like your old self. And I remembered that, after the pregnancy didn't work out, and you found . . . the messages, I thought, At least I can make sure she gets the villa. That's in my control. I felt like I owed you that, after all you'd been through – all I'd put you through.'

She considers reaching out to him, telling him that he didn't owe her, that they'd made a joint decision about the IVF, that his near-miss with the woman at work is almost forgiven, but she doesn't move. Instead her gaze stays fixed on the view: her beloved view. It's almost entirely in shadow now, taking on its mysterious night-time guise. Only a small area on the uppermost slopes is still bathed in golden light.

'Is this even ours?' she says.

His head snaps round. 'What do you mean?'

'This. The view. Luna Rossa. Could it be taken away?' She thinks again about those Spanish retirement dreams, the bulldozers and the wrecking balls.

'Of course it's ours. What do you mean by that?' Irritation has crept back into his voice, but again she knows that it's not quite what it seems – that his impatience is masking panic.

'You're scared, Nick. And I don't really know why so I suppose my mind is going to worst-case scenarios. You know I hate to be surprised. Please will you just tell me properly about Angelo? None of what you've said quite adds up. It makes me think about all those times you went off to see the *notaio* and told me to stay behind because you knew I found the legal stuff stressful.'

'Look, none of this is to do with that. The Angelo stuff is completely separate. Luna Rossa is ours. I've got all the paperwork. Legally it all had to be translated into English because my Italian wasn't up to it. Do you remember?'

She nods. 'OK. So, Angelo, then.'

He lets out a long sigh. 'I did meet Angelo in a bar, like I said. He seemed to know who I was, but I guess not many Brits buy houses round here. We're not in Tuscany. He started off friendly, said he knew Luna Rossa well, that he'd played up here as a boy because his uncle, or maybe it was great-uncle, lived here, had a farm round here.'

'Where?'

'I'm not quite sure. He wasn't clear. The point is, the farmhouse has gone. It collapsed in an earthquake in the seventies. Or it was so badly damaged it had to be pulled down. I couldn't quite understand but I think there was a landslide so maybe it was unstable. Anyway, he also said the boundaries were different then – that Giuseppe's House and the store behind it belonged to the uncle. We were sitting up at the bar, I remember it really clearly, and I could hardly hear him over the football commentary and the espresso machine going and everyone shouting at each other, you know how they do.

'He took my beer glass and his coffee cup and made this map. My glass for Luna Rossa, his cup for Giuseppe's House. Then he drew this wobbly line in sugar with his finger for the boundary. It didn't make any logical sense. The olive grove was Luna Rossa's, for instance, but the buildings by it were not. The thing is, the uncle or who-ever he was had a son. Angelo referred to him as his cousin. *Cugino*. This was Nico.'

'But surely this must have come up when the purchase was going through. If it didn't, then Angelo is lying, or he's wrong. The lawyer or the *notaio* would have flagged it.' She sounds surer than she feels.

Nick runs his hands through his hair. 'It was flagged.'

'*What?*'

'It came up, towards the end. I didn't tell you because,

well, because of what I said before. I didn't think you needed to know unless it was going to be a big problem, like a deal-breaking kind of problem. And it wasn't. There were loads of little complications that had to be ironed out. I didn't tell you about all of them, because I didn't see the point in worrying you. I wanted to take that off you.'

'But this doesn't sound like a little complication.'

'Well, that's how they made it seem.'

'So are the buildings ours or not?'

'They're as good as ours. They will be.'

'Will be? Nick, I don't understand.' She feels sick and dizzy, the paving stones shifting, like plates deep in the earth.

'There's a ten-year rule here. Nico inherited the land from his father. The main house had gone by then but he lived for a while in what we call Giuseppe's House. Then he left town, the house stood abandoned, and forty-plus years later, we turned up wanting to buy. It was assumed, I honestly think in good faith by the agent, that the buildings belonged to Luna Rossa. The previous owner never did anything with them but it sounds as though she let Signor Ricci assume they were hers. Maybe she thought they were. And because there was no other house up here, it made sense.'

'But they weren't hers?'

'No. Or probably not. The thing is, Nico is almost certainly dead. He was well into his thirties when he left and hasn't been heard of since. Even Angelo assumes he's dead. Either from some ancient vendetta thing Angelo probably made up, or of old age. And if he isn't dead, he's stayed away for nearly half a century. Why would he come back now?

'Anyway, to get round the ownership thing, there's a law here – that's the ten-year thing. If Nico doesn't claim his part of the land in ten years – nine and a half now – then it's definitely ours. But to all intents and purposes it is anyway. He's not coming back.'

She makes herself breathe out slowly. Perhaps it isn't so bad. 'Right, so let me get this straight. The worst case is that, by some miracle, he shows up, moves back into Giuseppe's House and we can't convert it into guest accommodation. Is that right? Because that would be really annoying but it wouldn't affect Luna Rossa. We'd still have all this.' She gestures around at the view, the cloud-canopied pine, the brand-new pool.

Nick pauses. 'Well, strictly speaking, no. But it won't come to that. It just won't.'

She studies his face. It's taken on a waxen cast now that the sun has dropped below the horizon. Just as the garden has been drained of colour as night creeps over it, so has Nick.

'Everyone kept going on about the outbuildings as though that was all that mattered. Like you just have, I assumed this contested boundary was down by them somewhere. It wasn't until Angelo drew that map on the counter that I got really worried. So I went back to the *notaio* – this must have been in late April. It was all there in the documents, an actual map with a red line showing what belonged to whom, but no one had shown me before. When I said this, he said I never asked. I dunno, maybe they made it all about the buildings because land is cheap here, and because it's too rocky to farm. They're used to the views – they don't see them as we do.' He finishes his beer and puts the bottle down clumsily. It rolls under the lounger.

'So where's the line?'

He twists round, grimly determined now, and points to the place they eat dinner every night. 'It goes right through the middle of the pergola. From there back to the house is Luna Rossa's. So are the drive and the olives either side of it. Everything between the house and the road, basically.'

'But this side?' Her hands are clammy. 'Right here, where we're sitting?'

He shakes his head. 'We'd still have an acre or so. I mean, it's not going to happen anyway, but we would.'

'By the road? Or if we dig up a load of eight-hundred-year-old olive trees? I don't think we'd even be allowed to do that, would we? So basically we have a house and a drive and that's it. And presumably if Nico did decide to come back, we've built him a lovely pool for free.'

She thinks about getting angry with Nick for keeping all this back from her, but she hasn't got the headspace for it. Or the energy. They sit on in silence, her mind reeling. A small part of her brain wonders vaguely what Madison and Bastian are doing, if they've been down to the kitchen and found dinner half prepared but the place deserted, like the *Mary Celeste*. Her thought processes are sluggish but slowly, slowly, something else comes into grim focus.

'If Nico is dead, doesn't his property go to his family? Can't they claim instead?'

'Maybe, if he was definitely dead. But there has to be

proof. And there isn't. He's assumed to be alive unless there's evidence saying otherwise.'

'But we have to worry about him either turning up, or turning up dead, for the next ten years.'

He looks like he might refute this but then hangs his head. 'Yeah, basically.' He goes to reach for her hand, but doesn't quite have the nerve. 'And that's where Angelo came in. He says his family have been looking for Nico all this time, that his loss has been a terrible thing for the family because they can't grieve for him properly. He hinted at the bar that they were getting close to finding out what happened to him. He said something about Sicily, about going there himself to talk to people who might have known Nico.'

Everything grinds into place with a shriek. 'And he said that if you sacked Massimo and gave him all our building work he'd maybe let the boundary thing go.'

'Something like that.'

'But there's a possibility that he won't let it go, and we will have given him thousands of euros to convert a house, dig a pool and a brand-new well, all of which he can then take ownership of. He's a fucking genius.'

'He seemed like a good guy. I think he probably still is, really. We talked about a *quid pro quo* and we were laughing about it because it was Latin and . . .' He catches her look. 'It was just going to be the pool and maybe the conversion, much further down the line. But then they came back and said about the well, and the earthquake regulations stuff.' He puts his head into his hands.

A movement off to the side makes them jump. It's Madison, wobbling slightly on high heels in the gloom as she makes her way across the garden. Laura hadn't noticed how much the dark has thickened around them. The lit pool glows out of it, like a slab of blue ice. Beyond it, the valley is now a black void.

'We'll talk more later,' she says grimly, as she rises to greet their guest.

Day 11

Laura wakes from a dreamless sleep to find Nick gone from the bed. One of the shutters is half open, admitting a bar of sunlight that has warmed the sheet where his indentation is still visible. Her phone tells her it's after eight so he must have let her sleep in. She feels the usual stab of irritable guilt until she remembers the conversation from last night. Adrenalin surges through her at the thought of losing half of their land. And not just the land but the pool, the out-buildings and the view – which could be built in front of.

She dresses quickly, not bothering to check her reflection, Bastian's desire not a concern today. At the window, she sees that Angelo's men are already here. As well as the cherry-red flat bed and the scruffy white van there is a larger black one she hasn't seen before. It squats menacingly in the drive. How many more men are in Angelo's employ? They seem to be multiplying.

She rushes out into the hallway and almost collides with Bastian.

'Hey, slow down,' he says, his hands coming up to grip her shoulders. They feel hot. 'What's the rush?'

She glances behind him towards the open door of his and Madison's bedroom.

'She's outside doing sun salutations.' He smiles at her with a raised eyebrow, encouraging complicity, but she has zero inclination today to make fun of Madison's regimes.

His smile twists into something sulkier. He runs one finger down the bare inside of her arm and though it feels good – so good that she briefly closes her eyes – she makes herself step away.

'What's wrong with you?' He closes the gap between them again.

'The builders are back.'

He shrugs. 'That a problem?'

She does not want to tell Bastian about this. She remembers those breezy emails about the extent of their land and what they were going to do with it, and nausea sloshes in her stomach.

'I just don't want them here.' It comes out curtly. She thinks to soften it by making a joke about him, her *guest*, not being inconvenienced, but she's too afraid of being asked for a refund. The numbers in her and Nick's bank account are sobering. Shaming, too.

He pauses, and she realizes he's deciding how to react. He's planning his next few moves. She'd forgotten he did this, like so much else she's chosen not to remember. He takes hold of her hands and, in her strange state of detachment, she thinks, *Oh, so charm it is*. It might have been coldness or petulance. She has experienced both from him in the past. Internally, she curses Lou for making her think like this.

He laces his fingers through hers and backs her into the wall. She lets him kiss her, but he must sense her detachment because he stops. He doesn't move away, though, and she feels pinioned against the cold white plaster. It emphasizes the great heat of him.

'Come on,' he says. 'Let me take your mind off it.'

Nick could come up at any minute. Feasibly he could even be in one of the other bedrooms, watching them right now through a crack in the door. She still hasn't worked out who caught them, or almost caught them, on the night of the dinner party. Her eyes dart around the hall.

Bastian is kissing her again, his tongue in her mouth. It feels large and muscular and she has to resist the urge to turn away her face. This instinct not to offend an aroused man, where does it come from? Is it to protect their feelings or yourself from their fury if you reject them? She has no idea.

His hands move to her waist, then up and under her vest top. He strokes her sides before going up, as she knew he would, to her breasts. He kneads them in the way men do, and that's never really done anything for her. His breathing changes, and she shuts her eyes, passive. One of his hands moves down, palm flat against her belly, knuckles catching on the waistband of her shorts and then he's past it and cupping her, his fingers pressing against the cotton of her underwear, and finally she starts to feel something, a slow pulse that speeds and sharpens at the thought of those fingers pushing into her.

He stops so suddenly that she sways where she stands, just like in the olive grove, only this time with her legs awkwardly splayed.

'Forget it, then,' he says, expression shuttered. 'If you're not into it.'

It's so ingrained in her to soothe his feelings that she puts a hand to his cheek, ready to apologize and kiss him. That's all it would take – all he wants – to get back to where they were. She still feels hot at the core of herself:

she does want him. But the numbers spin again in her head and she lets her hand drop.

He pulls his phone out, makes a show of checking something. 'I'm going outside to swim,' he says, without looking up from the screen. 'So the room's free.'

He's halfway down the stairs when she works out what he means. The room is free for her to tidy it. Temper and humiliation flare, twin flames spreading through her, even as another part of her wants to chase after him and make it all right between them.

In the kitchen, dirty breakfast plates are piled next to the sink. The three-hundred-euro copper tap she bought in a fit of madness has been dismantled, its parts laid out on the work surface, like a dissection kit. Next to it is a garish plastic bottle of what must be limescale remover. Something else broken.

She goes to the fridge and takes out a glass bottle of fizzy mineral water, drinking straight from it, a tiny act of rebellion against what or who she's not sure. Outside, sounds of industry are slicing into the still morning. From the shade of the pergola where she can't easily be seen, she watches Bastian and Madison by the pool. He is sitting between her legs so she can apply suntan lotion to his back. His tattoo winds down between his shoulder-blades, black and sinuous. She's not sure whether she thinks it's sexy or tacky – he didn't have it back then. No boy she knew then had a tattoo. Now everyone seems to have one.

His head snaps up at the shriek of a drill and Madison begins to massage the place where his neck meets muscle, pushing her thumbs hard into it. Quickly, not wanting them to see her, she crosses the grass and ducks into the cool interior of the olive grove.

When she reaches the outbuildings she hangs back to count the men. There are eight today. Of the three who must have come in the black van, two are the men who cemented the paving around the pool. She saw one last time, but now the other is here too. If it hadn't been for Nick's confession, she would have assumed that both once worked for Massimo but were now employed by Angelo. In fact, they had obviously worked for Angelo all along. They're a little older than the rest and she finds this oddly reassuring. Still, when they turn at her approach and she nods a greeting, there is no obvious recognition on their part, though she had taken them drinks and complimented their work for three days in May. They simply stare back at her. The third man, whom she has never seen, looks like a more grizzled version of Angelo. Another relation, then.

Nick is among them, looking like a different species. He is the tallest there but somehow the least substantial, his rounded shoulders apologetic. The sweat darkening his T-shirt seems to convey not manliness but fear. She suspects the men despise him and he's aware of this. He hasn't noticed her yet, too deep in conversation with Tommaso. She watches her husband nodding earnestly, one hand ruffling his hair, like an actor's hammy interpretation of anxiety. He's obviously been doing this for some time because it's sticking up all over his head. It gives him the look of a helpless boy again: one who's just been woken from a bad dream.

When he spots her, he looks so relieved that a concentrated bolt of fear strikes her. He's kept all this from her so carefully for months, presumably because he thought he could handle it. If her presence is now a comfort he must know he's entirely lost control.

She hasn't been to this part of the property for a while and she sees now that they are making rapid progress. The cliché of foreign builders who dawdle, who can't be rushed, falls to dust. Giuseppe's House has been gutted. The orange wood panelling has been torn out and lies in split and shattered piles in the dirt, the unvarnished parts like pale, exposed wounds. She steps inside and it looks twice the size. Hollowed out and taken back to pale plaster, it's probably the same sort of square-footage as their London place had been. She feels as though she's gained something she didn't even know she had, only for it to be snatched away immediately.

'Good, *si*?' It's the builder related to the mechanic. He's come in behind her. He looks her up and down, so swiftly she could hardly rebuke him for it. She wants to go further in, see what else they've done, but not with him watching her.

When she gets outside, Nick has gone. So has Tommaso.

The other men glance up as she comes into the clearing. They're taking a break, perching on the stone steps that run up the outside of the store, and on a couple of rickety old chairs brought out from inside Giuseppe's. There are plastic water bottles and cans of beer. One is eating a sandwich: puffy focaccia in a paper bag turning transparent with oil. He watches her expressionlessly as he chews.

Overhead a large bird circles on the thermals. Its cries bounce around the valley and off the windowless end wall of the store. She thinks it's probably some sort of raptor but she doesn't know what, though she squints hard at it, hand shielding her eyes against the midday sun. When she looks down, the men are watching her. They're oddly quiet.

'Where did they go?' she says, gesturing to the space Nick and Tommaso had occupied. '*Dove sono andati . . .?*'

A couple shrug. Another parrots her '*dove sono andati*', adding a couple of words she doesn't know. She swings round, some sixth sense prickling the back of her neck, and finds the one from inside has followed her out and is standing too close. Though she tries to stifle it, she jumps. Someone laughs.

He's carrying a beaten-up stool that was in Giuseppe's kitchen and sits down on it, reaching into his back pocket and bringing out a squashed pack of cigarettes. He holds it out to her.

She shakes her head. '*No, grazie.*'

'*Lei non le vuole le tue sigarette sporche, Carlo.*' This from another of the men. More laughter.

Carlo must be his name. And *sporche* – she knows that. She'd overheard a mother saying it in the market to her little girl, who was picking things up off the ground. Laura had looked it up in the pocket dictionary she keeps in her handbag. It means 'dirty'. Are they saying she doesn't want his dirty cigarettes or something worse, something to do with her, or perhaps even to do with the mechanic and her?

With Carlo on the stool behind her she is surrounded. *Just walk away*, a voice in her head tells her, but something keeps her rooted to the spot. It's partly stubbornness, an urge to show she won't be intimidated, that she's braver than her husband, but some of it is more animalistic: an instinct that if she moves, they'll move. Her legs feel simultaneously weak and heavy in the way they do at a great height – at the top of a skyscraper or the edge of a cliff.

'You want beer?' She swings round. It's the man who must be related to Angelo. He gestures to a plastic bag on the ground in the shade. Another half-dozen cans are inside.

She hesitates, her thoughts muddled. Would it be better to say yes, to be polite? Or would that send the wrong signal?

'*Alle donne inglesi piace ubriacarsi, no?*'

'*La birra l'avrebbe resa più simpatica.*'

They laugh, and Carlo gets up off his stool to saunter over to the bag. He picks up a can, turns to her and makes as if to throw it to her. She lifts her hands to shield her face but he doesn't let it go. More laughter ensues and her face burns. He comes towards her, opens the can with grubby fingers and holds it out to her, but when she shakes her head, he pulls it back. While the others laugh again, he remains unsmiling as he holds her gaze. He's so close she can see the broken veins in his eyes. He holds it out once more and she reaches for it this time, even though she wills herself not to. She gets her fingers around it and, though she doesn't even want it, they tussle a little for it. When he abruptly lets go, she stumbles backwards and it comes to her then what he's done. It's just like when she and his mechanic cousin or brother fought over her keys.

'Hey! Get the fuck away from her.'

His voice is not so much loud as hard, like steel.

Everyone freezes. Bastian walks into the circle. His feet and chest are bare. The sun glances off the muscles of his oiled shoulders. His brown feet, planted solidly, are pale with dust. The loose stones don't seem to bother him. He hasn't glanced at her yet. He's looking unhurriedly at each of the men but saves Carlo for last. He walks up to him, putting himself between the Italian and Laura. She can smell his hot skin: coconut, salt and chlorine.

'I said, get the fuck away from her. *Vai a farti fottere.*'

Carlo backs off, spits in the earth. But he won't meet Bastian's eye. He's not going to challenge him.

'What's going on? *Scusi? Scusi? Signore?*'

Tommaso bustles towards them. He doesn't look at or address Laura, though she is apparently his employer. Not that she cares about that in this moment. Nor does she care about the earlier exchange between her and Bastian. She's just happy he's here. Her knees feel like they're about to give way.

Bastian takes hold of her elbows and studies her closely. 'You OK? Did they do anything to you?'

She shakes her head.

Tommaso is trying to get Bastian's attention and reaches out to touch his arm. Bastian whips round. 'Don't fucking touch me, man.'

Tommaso steps back, hands raised in surrender.

'Your men have been intimidating her, not treating her with respect.'

'Respect?' Tommaso, recovering, laughs at this. Laura cringes.

'Yes, respect.' Bastian steps towards him and Tommaso

backs away again. 'I think you're done here. You should get out.'

'Oh, no, *signor*. We are not done. There is an agreement here. You ask Nick.' He acknowledges Laura for the first time, giving her a look that's something between a sneer and a smirk.

'You need to leave,' says Bastian.

Tommaso glances at his watch, shrugs. 'OK. Today, we leave. But we come back tomorrow, with my father. You ask Nick, *signor*. He will explain, if *she*,' he flicks his head towards Laura, 'does not understand. Nick understands.'

They leave, though the clearing still thrums with tension. She feels as though even if the boundary business can be resolved, this part of the property won't ever feel benign to her, a toxic gas colouring the air for ever.

Bastian's hands are still cupping her elbows, as if he's the only thing holding her up. His brown eyes as they watch her are steady.

'What is a "*cornuto*"?' she asks.

'Did one of them say that to you?'

'I think it was that. I went into the house, to look, and when I came out Nick and Tommaso had just . . . gone.'

Bastian raises his eyebrows and she knows what this means. *Yeah, where the hell is Nick?* It's not like she's not thinking it herself.

She takes a breath. 'So, I asked where they'd gone and one of them said that, kind of muttered it, and they were laughing.'

Bastian sighs. 'Well, it's pretty insulting, especially in the south.' He sees her face. 'Not about you, though. About Nick. It means "cuckold".'

1999

The two of you have been at a ball. It's the sort of university that hosts a lot of these, at least one a term. You're wearing a short, strappy dress you've put on in desperation because you've worn everything else recently. It was cheap, less than twenty quid. That probably shows. Made of bright white Lycra, it stretches tight over your body, scooping down low at the front and riding high up your thighs. Lou had said it looked shit with bra straps showing and your strapless one is so ridiculously uncomfortable, with its three-hook fastening and sticky silicone band, which pulls at your tender flesh, and the half-moon under-wiring which leaves welts on your highest ribs. Just before you got into the cab, feeling invincible on vodka punch, you'd pulled it off, gone without.

But once you got there, you remembered that that kind of physical discomfort was better than feeling self-conscious all night. It was only just after Easter but much of the ball was being held outside – there were dodgems, waltzers and a bucking bronco set up next to the Great Hall. It had been sleeting on and off all day, like it sometimes does in April, a mean little trick played just when spring's progress seemed irreversible. The boys kept making comments about glass-cutters and, mysteriously, Rachel – until you worked out that they meant Rachel from *Friends*, whose nipples always showed. Obviously this was a compliment, but it was still embarrassing.

Anyway, at some point you don't care any more, and then the evening does that thing that always happens when you're properly drunk: time spinning and knotting into something meaningless, so that five hours seem to pass in five minutes and then it's over and you're stumbling along in your heels behind this boy who's ignored you all night, who might have kissed someone else when he was inside and you were out, screaming on the waltzers with Lou.

But at some point he put his dinner jacket round your shoulders and you cling to this, like your fingers clutch the lapels to stop it slipping off. Because it's so unexpectedly gentlemanly. You save it up like a jewel to take out and hold up to the light if anyone says anything tomorrow about that other girl he was supposedly with.

It's raining now, hard, and the streetlights reflect dismally out of potholes filling with water. You get to a crossroads and pause while he continues without you, not noticing you've stopped. The left road would take you back to your own house. Straight ahead, still a couple of miles away, is his. There are no cabs tonight.

You pat yourself, ludicrously, because of course there are no pockets in your stupid slip dress. Literally no one ever carries a handbag. Your mum is always saying it's daft and what on earth do you do with your things, but usually you're in black boot-cut trousers like every other girl wears to everything, and although they ride low and cling, there's always at least a small pocket: enough for a lipstick, a door key and the university's version of a credit card, which you can load up and use at the campus bars.

You try to turn your mind to where you could have put

your key, your card, but it's so sluggish. All you can process clearly is that your feet are killing you, wet and slipping in five-inch heels, your entire weight held up by two thin plastic straps lashed across your toes.

'What are you doing?' He's finally noticed you aren't still tottering along behind him. He holds out his hands in a what-the-fuck gesture. 'Come on, I'm getting wet.'

'Do you think I should just go home?' you call. 'I don't know where my stuff is. My key.'

'You won't be able to get in, then,' he says logically.

'Why can't we go to my house? It's nearer.'

'I don't want to.'

'Would you rather be on your own?'

He shrugs, then turns again, starts walking away. 'Do what you want,' he says, over his shoulder.

You take off the heels and the pavement is slick and freezing through your tights but they're already ruined and you're already cold and wet and, besides, it hurts way less.

'Wait,' you shout. 'I want to come with you.'

His room smells surprisingly nice. You've been in the kitchen here, once, but never upstairs. It smells of outdoor things: ocean and ozone. The duvet when he pushes you back on it must be clean on that day. It's still stiff from being dried on a radiator. You stow this fact in the same place as the lent dinner jacket: evidence of civility; an understanding of how women should be treated, and proof that maybe he actually planned to bring you back here. Evidence that he's decided you're one kind of woman and not the other.

Even though you like him so much that it makes you

feel almost insane some days, you really just want to go to sleep now you're in the dark, on a bed, out of the rain and off your feet. As soon as you close your eyes, you can feel yourself drift away, a soft black tide pulling you towards nothing.

'Come on,' he says. 'Help me out here.' He's already peeled off your sopping, laddered tights and your underwear. Your feet must look dirty and you curl your toes, ashamed. He pushes you back and eases your dress up round your waist. You reach down to try to cover yourself. Now your eyes are adjusting you see that dawn is coming. The rectangle of light behind his white blind seems to grow more distinct by the moment, like someone dialling up the contrast. Your white dress glows against the dark duvet.

He eventually wrestles the dress off over your head, pushing your arms up when the straps get tangled. When you're naked he puts his mouth straight to one of your breasts while the hand that's not propping him up roams over your stomach and round to your buttocks, squeezing and squeezing the flesh until you wonder if he thinks you're fat.

'You're fucking freezing,' he says, stopping for a moment, and you put your own hand where his just was, to see if it feels horrible. You pull the discarded dress back over yourself.

'I'm so drunk,' you say. 'I feel sick.'

'No, you don't,' he says, and pulls the dress off you again, throwing it to the floor. Something clinks as it lands and you realize it's your key. You remember now how you'd tucked it into the lining just under your breast, safe.

'I don't want to,' you say.

He pauses. 'Oh yeah, I heard you do this.'

'What?' Your eyes snap open. But then you get it: of course people have talked. It's bullshit that only women gossip. Men are worse. You imagine what has been said: that you had been seeing this boy last term, and another before that, in second year, and hadn't slept with either of them.

You aren't a virgin, it isn't that. You'd got that out of the way in the sixth form. You hadn't wanted to go to university saddled with not having done it, and had been surprised by how many people hadn't when you got here. With both of those boys you'd been seeing, you just hadn't liked them enough – hadn't wanted them so much that you couldn't resist. You'd started to wonder if there was something missing in you until *him*. But it wasn't just about desire anyway. It was the fear of getting a reputation if you did give in, especially if you were just pulling on nights out. Of course, it was different if a boy took you out for dinner, if he took you home for the weekend to meet his parents.

'Come on,' he says again, but he seems a long way off now. His silhouette, his movements, are hard to comprehend until you work out that he's torn open the foil square of a condom and is putting it on. When he slides back down on top of you, elbows clamping either side of your shoulders as he starts to kiss you again, hard, you can smell the rubber on his fingers. You hate that smell.

'Can we wait?' you say. 'I really feel shit.'

'No,' he says. 'You're being a prick-tease.' He prises your legs open wider, pokes around with his fingers to work out where he needs to push. You're dry there, you're certain. You register embarrassment about this more than fear at what's he about to do. Because you've wanted him, haven't you? You've thought about how much you want to sleep with him, so this, while not how you'd imagined it, not at all, is basically OK.

But instinct rears up in you anyway, and you reach down to put your hand between him and you. He's nudging hard at you now beneath the slightly tacky, dusty texture of the condom that you can hardly bear to touch. You wonder if you've got the energy to give him a blow job instead, to make up for refusing full sex. But even as you consider this, he's pushed away your hand and hard into you in one determined motion, and you're sucking in your breath because, even through the drink, it burns.

Afterwards, you decide it didn't really happen. The next morning, hung-over, his housemates playing *Goldeneye* downstairs and his mood softer, you do it again. It doesn't hurt much this time; you're actually turned on. You decide to make this your first time with him. You tuck the previous night away for good.

Day 11 continued

'Thank you,' she says. 'My actual hero.'

Bastian has led her into Giuseppe's House, picking up one of the chairs the men had brought out, so that she can sit down. It's a relief to be away from the sun, which was beginning to feel brutal out in the clearing, where the outbuildings conspire to reflect and intensify it.

It's a relief to sit. She turns her face towards the window. Someone did a bad job of putting it in once upon a time but the view, blurred but still visible through cobwebs and dust smears, is spectacular. Out there, much further away now, the huge bird wheels on the thermals rising out of the valley's bowl.

'I think that might be a golden eagle,' she says. 'It was right above us when the men . . . Before you came.'

Her shakiness has almost gone now, or has at least been replaced by a different sort of tension. She watches Bastian move around the room. He's ostensibly looking at what the men's work has revealed and what still remains, hanging on in a few dated fragments, but she suspects he's unable to keep still, and is walking off excess adrenalin and testosterone.

He must feel her eyes on him because he stops and turns. They hold each other's gaze for what seems like a long time. Normally she'd glance away, made shy by the intensity of his attention, but the episode with the men, which is already passing into something surreal in her mind, provides some detachment.

She goes to him, placing her hands flat on his chest. Briefly, the thought rises – traitorous brain – that she's only doing this to pay a debt, to say thank you. *To the victor the spoils.* She starts kissing him to dismiss it. He kisses her back, enthusiastic, and she realizes that she's never taken physical charge with him. How different it might have been back then if she'd been more like this. All the power she might have wielded.

It moves quickly. It's as though he knows she's not going to stop him. The thought of Nick coming back to find her floats into her head so she takes Bastian's hand and leads him upstairs. When she turns to smile at him, the ghost of her and Nick that first time shimmers in the air, but all it takes is remembering those messages between him and J on the iPad, the rain hammering on the skylight, London darkening around her, and it begins to recede. Then she thinks about how Nick has made them and Luna Rossa vulnerable to Angelo, and it's gone.

The men's destruction hasn't yet reached the larger of the two bedrooms. It remains suspended in a time earlier than the rest of the house's seventies additions, as though Giuseppe (because he's still Giuseppe to her) had left his mother's room untouched out of sentimentality and the kind of deep and holy respect men only pay to their mamas, as though they've never had sex at all.

They lie down on the bed and the pink bedspread exhales dust under their weight. The mattress sags dramatically in the middle, pinning them together. It makes her laugh but he remains serious, his face intent as he climbs on top of her and begins kissing her in the tender spot behind her ear and down her neck. Over his shoulder, a small plaster statue of the Virgin Mary watches them from a little shelf high up on the wall.

They don't take off their clothes, or not many of them. She likes this: the urgency of it, the need to get to the point. She doesn't actually want much foreplay and she's already wet anyway. She knows that without checking, from the way she feels there, that heavy ache, the low-down pulse. And even if she hadn't been sure, it would be confirmed by the way he groans when he puts his hand into her knickers and opens her up.

'Take them off,' she says, and she means her underwear but he stands to remove his shorts, the mattress protesting and shifting, tipping him side-to-side like they're in a bed-sized boat. He doesn't take his eyes off her and she looks right back at him, not breaking the contact that feels almost physical as she takes off her knickers herself, dropping them to the floor.

She thinks he'll push inside her immediately but he doesn't. She lifts her hips but he holds himself slightly above her as they kiss. She reaches down to guide him in, but he takes her wrist and pins it above her head.

'Do you want me to fuck you?'

'Yes,' she breathes.

'Say it then.'

'I want you to fuck me.'

'Again.'

'I want you to fuck me.'

His full weight is on her now and she can feel him right up against her, almost inside her. But still he waits.

'Please,' she says, and it's almost a sob. She can feel him smile into her neck but she's too far gone to care whether she should mind.

Nick is in the kitchen, as he always seems to be these days. He's gutting an enormous fish. She hovers behind him as he works, eating olives and shifting from foot to foot. She's showered, scrubbing herself clean of Bastian until the hot water ran out. The ends of her hair drip on the tiles and coldly down her back as she tries to think of something to say.

When Nick turns, suddenly aware of her presence, she doesn't meet his eye but catches the end of his quizzical expression before he returns to the fish. He can't understand why she hasn't sought him out yet, to grill him about the builders, and what he was discussing so intensely with Tommaso.

'So they cleared off early today,' he says, head bent to the chopping board. The fish's scales have lost their rainbow iridescence. The skin looks more like dull metal than something organic. 'It was weird, actually. They just went without a word.'

'You put the tap back together,' she says.

He pauses at the jump in conversation and then nods. 'Yeah. Managed to get it working.'

'Well done. Was it just limescale, then?'

'No, that was weird too. I didn't really do anything. I just had a fiddle with it, put it back together and it was fine. Maybe it's haunted.'

They laugh carefully. Tears smart in her eyes. They are edging so carefully around each other. But she knows what Nick is worried about. He on the other hand doesn't know why she's being so cautious. He can't possibly have an inkling about what she did this afternoon, or he wouldn't be looking round at her as he is now, so hopeful that they might be OK tonight. He must have folded away his suspicions about Bastian for now, having decided the boundary issue takes precedence. Like so many men, he's always been good at this, Nick: the compartmentalization of life. He's always been genuinely able to stop thinking about one thing if something else needed his attention more.

'Is that just for us?' She gestures towards the fish. She doesn't want it. She doesn't feel like eating anything Italian. She wants beans on toast in front of the telly in London. A sob threatens, but she manages to swallow it. She hears Lou, whose voice has been unusually – though perhaps predictably – quiet since she left. *This is what I was trying to warn you about.*

Nick is considering the fish. His finger scratches at a mosquito bite and she remembers how, not that long ago, they had competed to see how many they could squash against the bedroom wall when they forgot to close the shutters after dusk: dozens gathered there, to lie in wait for their hot human skin. Some of those little black smears are still there. The bite, just under his ear, is a red, swollen lump. He invariably reacts badly and it's always felt like a tiny rebuke because she made him come to Italy when he is so patently made for England.

'Nick?'

'Oh, sorry. No, the Americans aren't going out now. So we're eating together. Luckily I had this in the freezer. Only took about forty minutes to defrost outside in the shade. I don't know why they changed their minds. Madison didn't say.'

Her stomach pitches and tips. 'Oh, right. That's a pain. I was hoping for a quiet night.'

'You not feeling well? You've been upstairs for ages.'

'Yes, sorry. Bad period, you know.'

'Did you take anything? There's some soluble paracetamol in my bedside table. I got Mum to send me a load. It works quicker. I couldn't find any in the chemist here.'

'I'll go and have a look. Thanks.'

She walks out before he notices that she's crying, unable to hold back any longer. Lovely Nick, so kind even when he's stressed, even when she's . . . The financial stuff doesn't rouse any anger in her right now. All she can see is what he tried to tell her: that everything he did was for her, that keeping it secret was just protectiveness. Because finally he'd been able to shield her from something after being so incapable of protecting her from all the fertility shit, from their own faulty bodies.

'Dinner will be in about forty,' he calls after her. 'Do you mind doing the table?'

'Sure,' she manages to say.

She goes into the snug, opens her laptop. No emails. She hadn't expected one, really. It's become a reflex to check. There's nothing from Lou either. She thinks about Skyping her but dismisses the thought almost immediately. What would she say?

Between her legs she still feels swollen and slightly raw.

But even now, tears itching her cheeks as they dry, her body betrays her, sparking into life at the thought of what she did – what *they* did – only a few hours ago.

Does Madison know, and is this why she and Bastian aren't going out? Laura tries to think objectively about this. She is certain about very little, but she feels pretty sure that Madison isn't the type to hold back. There would be screaming and things thrown, surely. But there has been nothing. She hasn't seen the other woman all day. In fact, she's hardly seen her since before Lou left, after that awkward conversation about infidelity by the pool. Laura has done this on purpose; feeling guilty in a way she didn't before she and Bastian did anything. It hasn't been enough to stop her but, still, she's missed Madison.

Would she undo it if she could, winding back time to when Bastian saw off the builders, thanking him and removing herself from temptation? Or, even better, not going down to the outbuildings at all?

She knows she wouldn't. She knows, if she gets the opportunity, she'll do it again.

The change in the weather is instant. One moment, she's laying the table under the pergola, the garden around her as still and warm as a room with the windows closed. The next, the leaves of the vines that twist around the pergola's struts are rustling in earnest. The corners of the tablecloth are lifted by invisible fingers, and the pressed linen begins to slap at the wood. Metal tinkles against china as the cloth ripples under the cutlery.

She strikes the match she's just got out the box – one of the long cook's matches she always uses to light her table candles, like a ritual in church – and it's snuffed out immediately.

She abandons the table and goes to the balustrade by the pool to watch the sky darken. In the distance, thunder is beginning to rumble, like a low warning growl in the back of a big dog's throat. Way off at the other end of the valley, towards the mountains, whose peaks are visible on a clear day, a silver-blue curtain has fallen. It's already raining there.

'I guess the gods are pissed about something.'

She spins round, hand flat to her chest in shock. Madison is just a few feet away. She's wearing a plain white dress and her feet are bare. Her long hair whips and snaps in the wind.

'Yes, I don't think we'll be eating outside, after all,' she manages to say.

They clear the table together, restacking the tray Laura brought out only five minutes earlier, in an entirely different day. The wind has begun to whine around the pergola now. It rattles the vine leaves harder, exposing their pale undersides, the two greens strobing. Rose petals fall around them, like heavy pink tears. Laura would laugh at the Italian melodrama of it if she could, if her nerves weren't stretched so tightly that it feels as though the wind could make her shatter.

'You're trembling,' says Madison. She lays her left hand on Laura's as if to still it. Hers is larger and bonier, the veins more prominent. The big diamond has twisted round so that it sits coldly between them, pressing hard into Laura's finger, just above her own wedding band. She pulls away, pretending not to notice Madison watching her as she grabs the tablecloth and gathers it into a ball, though she's only just ironed it.

'Give it here,' says Madison, taking it off her and folding it deftly.

'Thanks.' She lifts the laden tray and heads back towards the house with it. The thunder rolls, a little nearer now.

'What's going on?'

In the kitchen, Nick has put on his portable speaker, which is playing Oasis. They had intended to wire up the whole villa with Sonos but balked at the cost. Oasis always reminds her of the first year at university, when it felt like every single boy in halls was playing 'Wonderwall' on repeat.

'We can't eat outside,' she says. 'There's going to be a storm. The wind's already up and rain is heading this way. I'll set up in the dining room.'

He pauses the music just as the thunder sounds again. It's still a low roll but it's definitely getting closer. They haven't had a proper storm yet, not the kind they've been told about – the sort invariably described as biblical, which tears down trees, strips roofs and takes out power lines.

'Have we ever even eaten in the dining room?' says Nick, just as Madison comes in with the tablecloth. 'I hope I haven't left it in a mess.' He's switched to his jovial tone.

He has left it in a mess. She simply piles up the detritus from various small-scale projects in the corner of the room. Tiny screws and picture pins roll around. At least he'd put newspaper on the table, which is actually quite beautiful, with elegant carved legs and a smooth patina from years of careful polishing by an unknown hand.

She always thinks of the pergola as an outdoor room, particularly once the cobalt night sky has been turned black by candlelight. But once the table is recreated in the underused dining room, the main light turned off so only tea-lights blaze, there is an intensity of atmosphere that you would never get outside. Without the constant clicking of the cicadas, the fussing of birds in the trees, it's unnervingly silent and ominous.

Nick comes in with a huge platter of sliced plum tomatoes, deeply red and unctuous. Torn-up mozzarella – the best kind – and basil leaves are scattered over them.

'It's like the flag,' she says, and he looks confused, then gets it, laughs.

'It's a Caprese salad. But, yeah, I guess it's like the flag. No olive oil, you'll note.' He drops his voice. 'Madison said she wants oil on the side from now on. She thinks she's *gaining weight*.' He raises his eyebrows.

'Can you bring your speaker in? It's too quiet in here.'

'It just died. I've put it on charge.'

At that moment, the Americans walk in. Without meaning to, she locks eyes with Bastian. The look he gives her is so intensely intimate that she can't believe Nick and Madison don't protest, outraged. He might as well just stand there and admit what they did together earlier.

Madison looks up from pulling the tablecloth straight, one eyebrow raised. A roll of thunder rattles the window. 'Storm's a-comin',' she says.

But the storm doesn't come. Not during dinner, anyway. Instead it grumbled on in the distance, like a warning that it would be only a matter of time. And while it had been tense and stilted in the dining room, the explosion Laura had been expecting hadn't quite gone off inside either. Madison had done most of the talking and Laura couldn't read her mood. One minute she was brittle and too-bright, picking at her food. The next she'd lapsed into a woozy, Southern drawl that made her seem like she'd taken Valium. Maybe she was just drunk. They'd got through four bottles of wine and Madison had barely eaten a thing. Maybe the moments when her focus sharpened again to a point had required enormous effort.

After Nick's hastily assembled pudding of figs, *gelato* and crushed amaretti biscuits, they drift outside, as if giving in to the weather's petulant demands for attention. The odd shaft of golden light punctures the leaden sky, and the combination has the weird effect of turning up the colour elsewhere. The green baize of the valley floor is lurid. The turquoise pool hurts her eyes.

Madison has the idea of moving the modular garden furniture to the pool terrace so it looks out over the view. It's made of that light woven plastic that looks like rattan and they transport it easily. It looks perfect there when it's all set up. Laura doesn't know why she and Nick didn't think of it themselves.

'Is it getting closer or what?' says Bastian, as a low roll moves languidly around the valley, as if it can't quite muster the requisite energy to tip into a proper storm. The rain has moved away but Laura thinks the thunder might be getting louder now, just a little. Nick has gone inside to make drinks. Madison has asked for a Pornstar Martini.

When he returns, he's carrying all the cocktail-making kit on a tray.

'You're in luck, Madison. I found a pomegranate at the bottom of the bowl. I thought all the fruit had been used up in your smoothies.'

If she notices the mild dig, she doesn't react.

'I decided to bring the bar outside, so I could watch the weather come in,' he continues, one hand clutching a bottle of Passoã, the other fiddling with his phone. 'I didn't want to miss anything being stuck inside.'

He picks up something from the tray. It's the little wireless speaker.

'Fully charged.' He throws it to Laura without warning and slightly too hard. She almost misses it, scooping it up two inches from the ground. As she holds it aloft to make the point and Bastian claps, the first ghostly strains of Portishead wind into the air, the bass vibrating into her hand. That's what Nick had been doing on his phone: finding the right music. He turns up the volume and the sound is surprisingly powerful, the bass solid, holding its own against the low-down reverberation of the thunder. She wants to see his face but he's at the balustrade, elbows resting on the rail, staring across the valley. *Dummy* is their album. Lots of couples have a song but she and Nick had this whole album. During the summer they'd got together, they'd played it on repeat in his tiny bedroom at home. Aside from the pub, she can't remember them being anywhere else, though surely they'd gone to her house sometimes.

Nick had smoked roll-ups then – it went along with the whole skater-boy vibe he was trying to cultivate – and his room always smelt of tobacco and toast. His parents liked Laura: they always smiled indulgently when they answered the door to let her in, and as she went sheepishly upstairs to find him. She was his first proper girlfriend and they were so relieved they didn't even care about the smoking.

After Bastian, Nick's room was a nest perched high out of harm's way. When he had a shift at the pub, which was more often than her because he needed the money in a way she didn't, she would curl up on his childhood bed and sleep. The music would insinuate itself into her dreams, languid and eerie but eventually, by association, comforting.

It's not comforting now.

'Who's this?' Bastian has refused a cocktail and is drinking Peroni from the bottle. Madison has drawn her long legs underneath her and twisted round to face him. She holds her cocktail in one hand, and strokes Bastian with the other. Every so often, he shoots her a quick glance. It's a signal to stop, but she doesn't.

'It's Portishead,' says Nick.

'Weird name.'

'It's a place. Near Bristol, where the band came from.'

Bastian nods. 'Right.' He lifts his free hand and Laura thinks he's going to bat Madison's away but he doesn't. He lays it carefully back on his leg.

'I discovered them quite late,' says Nick. 'At uni. This had come out a few years earlier. There was this whole trip-hop scene. Bleak as fuck, most of it, but in a good way. You must know Massive Attack?'

He won't, Laura thinks. Bastian never really listened to music. It had taken her by surprise when he seemed to know about the band Nick had interviewed for the paper, the band they'd talked about in Urbino. She thinks back to his student room, the monochrome space she used to think smelt like a Hamptons beach-house would, but was probably just supermarket fabric softener. He had an expensive sound system, presumably shipped over at great cost, but she can't remember it ever being turned on.

'Don't think so,' he says now, shrugging. He finishes his beer, reaches over and takes another from the ice-bucket Nick brought out on the tray. Madison hands over the opener and Bastian prises off the top, letting it drop to the ground and spin under the sofa.

'Ah, they were huge,' says Nick. He's back on his phone and Laura knows what he's going to play. 'Teardrop'.

'Oh, wait,' says Bastian. 'I know this. I've seen these guys play live.' He looks at Laura, his head on one side as he considers. 'Yeah, I saw them at college.'

Nick raises an eyebrow. 'Really? I didn't know they toured over there.'

Bastian takes a long drink of his beer while Laura holds her breath. 'No, this was in England,' he says eventually, apparently having made up his mind. 'I did a couple of semesters over there. It was like an exchange programme.'

'You went to England during college?' Madison pauses in her stroking. 'You never told me.'

He shrugs. 'It was only a few months.'

'Where were you, in London or something?'

'Exeter.'

Laura freezes. She can't quite believe he's said it. When her brain catches up with itself, a dozen thoughts scramble over each other. Did she ever tell Madison exactly where she went to university? Madison's blank, alcohol-blurred expression reassures her that if she did then

Madison has forgotten. But what about Nick? *Nick*. Her heart trips.

'It's this sleepy little town,' Bastian is saying. 'I'd never heard of it till I went.'

'It's a city actually,' says Nick, slowly. 'Because of the cathedral.'

He's looking at the ground. His skin, which he hates because it always gives away his feelings, is reddening. Or was it already like that, its colour high from the alcohol? She's not sure.

'Oh, yeah, the cathedral.' Bastian laughs. 'That's why all the clubs had to close so early. Some old law or something. I never got it. Why does a cathedral care what time you go home?'

Nick's foot taps fast, out of time to the music. He is still intent on the ground. Laura knows he's figuring things out. Or he already has and is now trying to contain his conclusions.

She never told him Bastian's name. 'I don't want to talk about him,' she'd said, early on, when Nick was trying to get out of her what had happened with this American ex who had ruined her final term – who had almost caused her to fail her degree. 'Do you understand? I *can't* talk about him.' She was lying on Nick's bed, looking at the ceiling. He was propped on his side, studying her profile. He loved her already, she knew. They both knew he liked her more than she liked him, and that she was going to be hung up on this other boy for a while. They both knew he was happy to wait.

Pushing himself up on one elbow, he had kissed her forehead. 'Well, whatever his name was, he was a bloody idiot. Let's just agree he never existed.'

Laura knows she must speak, must say something right now, if there's any hope of saving this. *You were at Exeter, Bastian? That's so weird! Exeter is where I went. When were you there?*

She says nothing. Her mind races but she can't seem to force herself to speak. She might only make it worse.

'When were you there, Bastian?'

Nick has asked the question for her. His tone is odd, artificially light, and she wonders whether he's enquiring or confirming.

'Ninety-nine,' Bastian says. 'Easy to remember. Everywhere played that Prince song on loop.'

Madison suddenly sits up straighter. 'Wait – isn't Exeter where you went to college, Laura?'

She recalls their conversation in the piazza, Madison admitting she'd looked Laura up, just as she had Madison. If only Nick were not here, this could just be a coincidence.

'Yes, that's right,' she manages to say. 'Well remembered.'

'So?' Madison's gaze is locked on Bastian. 'Were you there together at the same time? Am I missing something here?'

'No,' she says, before Bastian can be any more reckless. 'We must have just missed.' She catches Nick's shake of the head and cringes.

'This is so weird,' says Madison. She still hasn't taken her eyes off Bastian. 'It's like I don't even know you.' She slaps his knee, and though her body language is playful and she's smiling, she does it with enough force that it's a sharp crack on the close air. 'I bet you broke some hearts while you were there, didn't you?'

Bastian laughs. They show each other their white American teeth. It couldn't be called smiling. He reaches for a lock of Madison's long hair and tugs at it, hard enough to jerk her head.

'You know me better than anyone,' he says. 'And I told you about England. You just never listen.'

Madison begins to run her long nails down the leg she hit, where there's now a red mark. 'No,' she says. 'It's you who never listens.'

Laura can't watch them any more. It's excruciating. But in glancing away she catches Nick's eye. He's finally looked up from the ground. She realizes that in twenty years together neither of them has ever done anything unforgivable. Not even J was that, however much it had hurt. That she, Laura, might be the one to bring down the walls of their marriage makes her dizzy.

'Hey, Nick,' says Madison. She's finally taken her eyes off Bastian. 'Throw me your phone. I want to play something.'

She seems to take a long time scrolling. Bastian sips at his beer almost constantly. When he tips it up and there's none left, he seems thrown before reaching for another. He's sitting with one arm stretched along the back of the sofa, like on the first day, only this time it points away from Madison. Where before he seemed utterly at ease, and likely would be in any situation you cared to drop him into, his position seems contrived now, his muscles bunched and tense. She wants to pull him aside and ask him why he said that about Exeter, but she knows the answer. In many ways, Bastian is like a child. He doesn't think much in terms of consequences.

The speaker sits on the low table next to the sweating ice-bucket. The little light flashes, showing it's still connected and waiting for the next song. Laura watches Madison's long fingers, her ring dull in the bruised light, until she finally finds what she's been searching for. She looks up and the two women's eyes meet properly for the first time in hours, maybe all day, just as the first notes of the song play. Nick, the music geek, who has gone to stand again at the balustrade, turns with a strange smile for Madison within two bars. Laura is only a beat behind him in recognizing it. 'Jolene' by Dolly Parton. A good old Southern girl, just like Madison.

Gooseflesh rises on her arms because she really *knows* this song. Whatever else she might have guessed, Madison couldn't possibly know that 'Jolene' was one of her and Lou's classics. They would play it when they got home from a disappointing night out, singing along with their mouths full of Marmite toast or pizza or chicken kebab, hamming up the drawl.

'Some people think Dolly is just this kitsch pair of tits,' Lou had slurred one time, 'but she's actually a fucking genius. "Jolene" is fucking genius. She doesn't go to her man to beg him to stay, she goes to the *other woman*. And although she's saying, ooh, I can't compete with you, with your eyes of emerald green and all that, you know there's so much more to it. You know she's really saying, "Come on, girl, you know you can do so much better than him. He's an idiot but he's my idiot so don't make me fucking *shoot* you."'

The wind wrenches Laura out of the memory. They've all noticed it because it's impossible not to. It must have quietened right down, a withdrawal only evident now it's back with such renewed force.

Nick turns off the speaker and the wind seems to rise again in response. It buffets around the contours of the land, shoving and jostling, flexing its muscles. On the narrow terrace where Nick takes his morning espresso, the aluminium folding chair he keeps there is picked up and flung down, landing on the edge. They watch it tumble over to the garden below, apparently in slow-motion, landing with a clatter.

Laura looks up to the sky and it's a hundred shades of silver and blue and dirt. The first flash of lightning makes them all jump, even Madison, whose attendance on Bastian has been laser-focused. She begins to count aloud, her accent as strongly Southern as Laura has heard it, the *four* as round as it's long. When the thunder comes, at six, the loudest yet, she hugs her knees to her chest, a small smile on her lips. Laura would have had her down as a screamer in a storm, but it's like she's woken up.

When Madison looks back at her, Laura finds she can't look away. Madison keeps staring, her head on one side, her hair blowing Medusa-like round her head. The lightning flashes at the same time as a tile is plucked from the roof by the wind to smash on the ground where the sofa was before they moved it. Madison begins to count again, her eyes never leaving Laura's, only getting to five this time before the thunder booms.

It's Nick who saves her – Nick, who has finally worked out who Bastian is, even if he doesn't know the rest of it yet.

'OK, enough,' he says. 'We need to go inside before

one of us is electrocuted.' He starts to pile the tray with glasses and empty bottles. Laura stands on shaky legs to gather the sofa's throws and rugs into her arms, their bulky softness a sensory comfort she wants to hide in.

Still, she can't help stealing glances towards Madison. The American woman has finally stopped staring at her, and has gone to stand where Nick had been. Her hands grip the balustrade as she looks out over the valley, the lean musculature of her arms making her look like a statue. Not one of those flesh-padded statues you see everywhere in Italy, but a kind of warrior goddess.

Bastian is watching Madison too, though as ever his expression is somewhere between inscrutable and entirely closed.

'Hey, Mads,' he says, and she turns. It must only be a second – half a second – before she smiles the smile Laura knows from her Instagram page, but for that instant, her blue eyes are utterly cold. If the song hadn't been enough of a clue, this would confirm it. She knows something. She might know everything.

The lightning flashes again and, this time, the thunder is only a second or two behind it. Three of them jolt in shock: it's the first proper clap, a sound she can never reconcile to the mere expansion of air. This sounds like sheet metal dropped from an enormous height. Only Madison appears unmoved.

'Come *on*,' says Nick. Laura marvels as he dares to nudge Madison's arm, to gesture with his head for her to follow him and his tray towards the villa. But she does, leaving Laura and Bastian trailing after, Bastian carrying nothing but his half-drunk beer. When he puts a hand out to touch her back, running a finger down her spine, she rounds on him.

'Are you fucking insane? I think she knows. Nick too. Or he's worked out who you are anyway, even if not the rest. Don't you get that?'

He shrugs, drinks from his beer. He's stopped walking so she has too, without meaning to. Nick and Madison have disappeared inside the villa.

'Why did you say that about Exeter?' she says. 'What are you trying to do?'

He shrugs again, making her want to slap him. She can't read him at all. He might be angry or stressed or entirely at ease. His surface is smooth and opaque, like Ivan's dark pools.

'Christ, aren't you worried what she's going to do? She's probably conferring with Nick about it right now.'

'She'll calm down,' he says, as the first drops of rain fall. It's just a few at first, fat splashes that spot the pale stones, but then it seems to switch instantaneously into a proper deluge. She and the heap of blankets are soaked immediately. It comes down so hard that it hisses.

She turns to run towards the villa and something small and hard hits her scalp, right where she parts her hair. She looks up, for an unhinged second expecting to see Madison there above her on the balcony, arm still raised from launching a stone at Laura's head. But then the stones are everywhere, and the phrase 'a hail of bullets' means something for the first time. The tiny and not-so-tiny spheres of ice bounce off every available surface. They begin to fill the pool. The violence of those thunderclaps makes more sense now.

And she understands something else too, then, about what he's just said. *She'll calm down.* He's done this before.

Madison is just going up to bed when Laura gets inside. She catches sight of the American's white dress through the banisters as she disappears up the stairs.

Nick is loading the dishwasher in the kitchen and she thinks of asking him if Madison said anything before she went but doesn't dare. As Bastian passes by on his way in from the garden, Nick pauses very deliberately in his clearing up. Bastian, who had looked as though he was gearing up to say something, simply puts his empty bottle down on the side.

'I think I'll go up too,' he says.

'Yeah, you do that,' says Nick.

Bastian leaves without another word, tracking wet footprints as he goes.

After he's gone, she and Nick stand in silence. Then he turns on the tap and begins washing up the cocktail glasses with great care. If it wasn't for his still-flushed cheeks, she would believe him utterly absorbed in the task.

She's just reaching towards him when the lights go out with a bang. An enormous crack of thunder follows immediately afterwards.

'Shit,' he mutters. She can hear him rooting around in cupboards. 'Where are all those candles you buy when we need them?'

The tall tapers she and Madison brought in earlier are lying in the corner next to the toaster but the matches take longer to find. She's just convinced herself that she left them outside when Nick cries out in triumph, the rattle and rasp as he opens the box and lights a candle a disproportionately comforting sound.

They go up to bed, tacitly agreeing to leave the kitchen till morning. The power isn't coming on anytime soon, though the worst of the storm has passed, the gaps between the thunder and lightning widening as they brush their teeth and undress in the almost-dark. She knows she ought to take Madison and Bastian some candles but nothing could entreat her to knock on their door. Just say something, she thinks. Let's get this over with. But Nick remains silent.

The sheets feel cool when they slide between them, and very slightly damp. Except for the last of the wind beyond the thick walls, the house seems quieter than usual. Perhaps it's because the electrics are dead, a hum too low to notice until it's off.

She lies there, listening but hearing nothing, waiting, trying to breathe evenly. It occurs to her that if Nick falls asleep now it actually makes it easier for her. *It's not like you were even that bothered*, she'll be able to level at him tomorrow. *You just went straight to sleep.*

But then, just as she's sure he's not going to say anything, that he's dropped off, he speaks.

'Just tell me one thing,' he says, words tight. 'Did you know? That it was him who was coming?'

'No, no.' The words rush out of her. There's so little she can deny, if he dares to ask the questions, but she can honestly deny this. 'When I saw him –'

'OK,' he cuts across her, voice cold, in a way she's never heard before. 'That's all. I need to sleep now.'

And he does, in the way that men seem able to, as

though they have the facility to simply flick a switch in their minds. She turns over, towards the window. Anxiety has left her entirely wakeful. She needs to try to sift through the last fifteen or so hours, come to terms with them, but it feels impossible. Too much has happened.

She watches the sky clear slowly through the open shutters. When the room grows stuffy at about three, she gets up to open the window they'd closed so it didn't bang. Somewhere out in the becalmed garden a nightingale has begun to sing. The stars come on just after four. She lies on her side watching them flicker, eyes stinging with exhaustion.

Day 12

She must eventually fall asleep because Nick has to wake her in the morning, shaking her arm in a way that's almost rough.

'There's been some damage outside.' He points to the window facing the drive. She goes over to look, expecting more slipped roof tiles, maybe a felled olive tree. But it's neither: it's the wall. There's a car's width gap in it just as there had been when they'd arrived. For a foolish moment, she wonders if she might have dreamt the last months, if she's been gifted another chance. But then she peers again and sees it's not the same. It's wider for a start, and it looks rawer, too, as though the hole has been punched through it very recently, which of course it has. Someone must have done it when the storm was at full throttle, or else in the night, once they were all in bed.

'What do you think happened?' She turns back to Nick.

He shakes his head. Under his freckles and sunburn, he looks grey.

'It was them, wasn't it?'

'I don't know.'

'Really? Nick, come on. You really think it could be anyone else, when we're half a mile from a road that sees twenty cars a day?'

Her voice has risen and he glances towards the door to hush her.

'What have you got us into with them?'

'Well, maybe you should talk to Bastian about why they're angry.' He rounds on her eagerly, a less frightening enemy. 'I had just sorted out the next tranche of payment with Tommaso yesterday and suddenly they're leaving. Angelo texted last night.'

She waits, afraid to speak, not only because of the trouble they might be in, but because she's in danger of saying something irretrievable.

'He's furious. He said his son and the men had been insulted. He said that –'

'Nick, stop.' Something in her tone or her face makes him close his mouth. 'The only person who was insulted was me.' She battles to keep her voice low and level. 'But you wouldn't know that because you'd gone off and left me to fend for myself with a load of macho misogynists.'

Nick blanches. 'Did they do something to you?'

'Not really. They scared me, but nothing happened because –'

'Because Bastian rode in on his white charger.' The injured outrage is back.

'Yes, because, of course, that's the burning issue here.'

While Nick stands there so pale, her face is growing hotter. She puts her hands to her cheeks to cool them. She can't believe he hasn't guessed what happened between her and Bastian afterwards. Nick has known her for twenty years. They've been reading each other for half their lives. He hasn't got it, though. She knows he hasn't. Madison is a different matter.

'Look, I was actually pretty terrified,' she says. 'They were being really unpleasant, saying things in Italian and laughing. They'd surrounded me. I don't know if they would have actually *done* anything, but the point is, it felt like they could, and that if they did, I wouldn't be able to stop it. Don't you understand how that might be quite traumatic? All Bastian did was tell them to go and they absolutely deserved it.'

'And what did Bastian deserve?'

'*What?*'

'Oh, forget it. I can't deal with this now. I've got to make an egg-white fucking omelette for Madison. You know we're going to Ivan's before the *festa*?'

The medieval festival in Castelfranco. It starts tonight. She'd completely forgotten about it.

'Madison must have bloody arranged it,' says Nick, pulling open the door so forcefully that it bounces back at him. 'We're all going there for drinks apparently. Six sharp. So you'd better have your game-face on by then.'

Going down to breakfast she experiences something like stage-fright. Her hands are ice-cold and clammy and her mouth is dry. But when she forces out a strangled 'Good morning,' to Madison, who is eating alone under the pergola, the American looks up from her plate with the blinding full-wattage smile Laura hasn't seen in a while.

'Hey, hon. Have you *seen* the sky this morning? It's like that damn storm never happened at all.'

Laura looks up and sees she's right: the storm has washed it clean. Way off down the valley, where the shroud of rain hung yesterday, the Apennines are visible again.

She glances back at Madison and it's just like when she looked at Bastian last night. There's a split-second when the other woman's expression is entirely blank and cold, her eyes navy blue and narrowed, but then it passes and the smile is back and Laura hopes her overwrought brain imagined it.

'Bastian is sleeping in after a bad night,' says Madison.

Laura watches her cut neatly into her omelette, load her fork, put the knife down, move the fork to her right hand. The whole laborious operation is strangely absorbing.

'Oh dear,' she says, when she realizes she's supposed to say something.

'Yeah, poor baby. He's got a lot of work stress at the moment. Nothing's going right for him.'

'That's such a shame, when you're on holiday.' It's like they're strangers, her voice weirdly robotic. She feels like she's watching herself perform from above.

When Madison doesn't say anything else, she casts around for a topic unrelated to him. Distantly, she registers that the vines and roses have survived the wind and rain, though they've lost many of their leaves.

'Someone swept up here.'

'Must have been your saintly husband first thing,' says Madison, sweetly. 'You look like you didn't sleep too good either.'

She attempts a smile. 'I'll be all right. Nick said you're going to Ivan's for drinks tonight before the festival. Is that right?'

'What's all this *you*? We're all going. Ivan asked specially after you when we spoke on the phone. Quite the little fan club you've got going here. What's your secret, Laura?'

There's a beat of silence.

'So, can I get you anything else?' She's so desperate to

leave the pergola that she's fidgeting around like an awkward teen. She puts her hands behind her back so Madison can't see them shaking.

'Hey, hey.' Madison pushes away her plate and stretches out her hand. 'You're as jumpy as a cricket this morning. Come here.'

Laura shuffles forward. Ashamed of how clammy it must be, she offers up one of her hands. Madison takes it, turns it over and strokes the palm. One of her nails is short and, without polish, down to the quick. Laura understands the rest are fake.

'Such pretty little hands,' says Madison. 'Like a child's. Now, look at me.'

Laura does. She manages to keep her gaze steady but she can't help swallowing.

'You need to go eat something,' says Madison. Her face is a picture of concern. It looks real enough. 'Go eat something and tell Nick this omelette is the best I've ever had. OK?'

Laura nods and walks away. It takes everything she has not to break into a run.

She stays inside for the rest of the day, dusting and scrubbing and polishing without stopping: a myriad of small punishments meted out to herself, one after another. It's probably the most perfectly beautiful day they've had since moving to Italy, but she doesn't deserve to be out in it.

By five, she's ready to go to Ivan's. Her expression in the dressing-table mirror is sombre, her outfit sober. She's wearing a deep blue dress with a modest neckline and a

317

full skirt she's been meaning to chop three inches off. She's glad she didn't now. She wants the coverage.

The only jewellery she's wearing is her wedding ring. While she waits to go downstairs, she works the plain platinum band up and down from the back with her thumb. It's looser than it's ever been. She must have lost more weight. The band of untanned skin beneath it is starkly white.

Finally Nick calls her name from downstairs. He must have got ready ages ago; she hasn't seen him for hours, hasn't seen any of them. The stage-fright feeling is back. As she stands, the room shunts down and up, her vision slipping like a faulty lift. She puts out a hand to the dressing-table to steady herself while the snow of low blood sugar makes her briefly blind, like the hail filling the pool the previous evening. Despite Madison's instruction she's eaten nothing all day but a couple of stale slices of ciabatta. She tells herself it'll pass soon. Everything will pass soon.

They're waiting for her in the hall. She takes the stairs slowly, mindful of more dizziness but also because she's acutely self-consciousness. Halfway down, she dares to look at them and stops short. They're all in medieval costume, Nick too. Madison is impossibly slender in a long belted dress the colour of wine. Her hair is gathered into a complicated plaited bun and crowned with a black velvet circlet wound round with gold brocade. Bastian, who is watching her intently, looks unnervingly Italian in a dark blue tunic, completely at home in the clothes of his ancestors. It's like that costume ball scene in *Rebecca* turned on its head.

Only Nick looks awkward, his ochre costume clashing with his pink skin. He can't meet her eye.

'Where's your costume, honey?' Madison has surely contrived this and yet she seems genuinely perplexed.

Laura grips the banister rail, tears prickling behind her eyes. 'I didn't know we were dressing up.'

Madison looks at Nick, who shrugs. 'I thought you were sorting yourself out,' he says, glancing in Laura's general direction, then away. It's such an obvious lie that no one can think of anything to say. Madison goes to the bottom of the stairs. Her fingers go to her hair and start pulling out pins. She lifts off the circlet and holds it up.

'Come here. You can have this.'

They stand together at the mirror in the hall, Madison's hands on Laura's shoulders. The surface of the old glass is wavery in the evening light that streams in through the open front door. It turns them soft-edged and faded, like a painting. A portrait of two sisters who look nothing alike. Behind her, Madison is half a head taller.

'There,' she says, when the circlet is secure on top of Laura's head, her loose hair arranged in dark waves over her shoulders. 'I doubt it's historically accurate but it works. You look like a little Madonna.'

It's not until Giulia is showing them out into Ivan's garden that it occurs to Laura that Angelo might be here. She hangs back, letting the others go through the doors first, putting off any confirmation that he is. Bastian, misreading this, slows his step. He is darkly beautiful in his navy blue and silver tunic but she can't bear to look at him.

'Baby, what's wrong?' He breathes the words into her

ear and her traitorous body responds. He smells of heat and summer. 'I haven't seen you all day. We need to talk, make plans.'

'Not now,' she says. 'Please,' she adds, because she's not sure how up to resistance she is. She'd thought about the *festa* earlier this week; how they might lose the others in the crowd; the dark corners they might find to be alone in. But things have changed now. Madison knows something, maybe all of it. Nick knows who Bastian is. It's all coming apart at the seams, just as Lou had feared.

At least Angelo is nowhere to be seen. Ivan rises to greet them, kissing Madison on both cheeks but pulling Laura into an embrace. She adores him but wishes he hadn't. It's only an acknowledgement of their shared confidences the other afternoon but it must look to Madison like favouritism and that's the last thing Laura wants demonstrated by another man, even one who definitely doesn't desire her.

They sit in a loose ring on the terrace while Giulia pours each of them a glass of champagne. Apart from the murmured *grazie*s and *prego*s as she goes round, no one speaks. Ivan cocks his head to the side like an alert bird and Laura knows he's picked up on the strained atmosphere. He catches her eye and shakes his head imperceptibly, asking her silently what's going on, but she glances away, pretending not to have seen.

'So, you must tell me how you found the storm,' he says eventually. His tone is easy, betraying no sign that he's noticed anything amiss. 'I'm afraid I lost one of the garden sculptures to it. The wind knocked it over and it broke cleanly in two. It was one of Raoul's favourites.' His eyes sparkle and Laura smiles despite herself.

Madison laughs. 'What a tragedy,' she says. 'I guess that's saved you a job.'

Giulia tops up her glass, which is already half empty. Laura's hardly touched hers and decides there and then not to have more than this single drink. It might be the only thing she can control tonight.

'I have to tell you, guys, I've seen much worse back at home,' Madison is saying. 'Not LA, I mean home-home. The South. I remember as a kid, it would just get hotter and hotter until you felt like something heavy was pressing down on you. It made people crazy. We'd all be praying for it to just *break* already. But then, when it did, it really did. One minute it was silent, and I mean silent because the birds and insects always knew it was coming and they'd be waiting for it just like we were, and then the next, the sky just cracked open. That's what it sounded like – like God had reached down and snapped the whole sky in two.'

Ivan is smiling. 'I got caught in a storm in Louisiana once. I'll never forget it. But I promise you, we got off lightly last night. They often do much more damage. In August, when the temperature is hotter to begin with, the thunderheads are huge. You see them coming down the valley from the mountains, like mountains themselves. Sometimes they ring the church bells as a warning and, like you say, everything else is silent. You can imagine how it sounds.'

'Like the end of the world.' Laura doesn't mean to say the words aloud. They all turn to her.

Ivan smiles again. 'Exactly like the end of the world.' He holds out his arm for them to inspect. 'See, even talking about it gives me the gooseflesh.'

Laura rubs at her own arms. Bastian is watching her, she knows. She always knows. She keeps her gaze trained on Ivan, or on her own hand gripping the champagne flute. She thinks how much she had relished Bastian's eyes on her before, how she had preened in a hundred tiny ways – turning her face to its most flattering angle, tucking her hair behind her ear to show off her neck, playing with a chain around it so he imagined his mouth there. She thinks of what Madison said about her childlike hands and wonders if it's a lucky guess – an *unlucky* guess – because Bastian had once said he loved how small and neat they were.

Ivan is addressing Bastian now, and Laura realizes he's trying to help her, forcing Bastian to look at someone else.

'And how are you enjoying Italy, Bastian?' he's saying. 'You must have Italian blood, surely. You look like you've just stepped out of a Raphael in that costume.'

'It's beautiful,' he says, his eyes flicking from Ivan and back to Laura. 'Everything I could have hoped for.'

Her cheeks burn. She hates him a little in that moment.

Madison squeezes his knee, forcing him to look towards her. 'Poor Bast has had a lot of work stuff to deal with, which is a shame. They won't leave you alone, will they, baby?' She holds her glass up to the hovering Giulia for more champagne.

Bastian's jaw tightens. 'It's OK. I've closed on a couple of deals today.'

It sounds like a lie but Madison turns to him, eyes wide. 'Oh, you didn't tell me. That's amazing, honey. Oh my God, I'm so relieved.' She turns to Ivan. 'I'm sure Bast won't mind me saying that it's been pretty rough lately. We weren't sure we could even afford to come out here, you know.'

Bastian stills.

'Yeah, I mean it's always brutal in Hollywood.' Madison shakes her head sorrowfully. 'You clash with the wrong person and suddenly you're out in the cold. And, you know, it's an expensive place to live. We run a coupla cars, there's gym memberships, club memberships, the spa, entertaining clients at the best places –'

'They don't need to hear all this,' Bastian interrupts. 'Why don't you let someone else speak for a while?'

His tone is so cold and so final that Laura's head snaps up in surprise when Madison continues.

'Oh, baby, we're among friends here. They don't mind, do you, guys?'

Nick shakes his head. 'Not at all. You can tell us any-thing.' Though he's trying to suppress it, he's a whisker away from smiling.

'Aw, thanks, Nick,' says Madison, blowing him a kiss. 'I feel like this is a safe space for us, and it's just not healthy to bottle stuff up, you know? The thing is, it's been real hard for Bast because he grew up so privileged. So I guess there's, like, *shame* in him not having money any more. For me, it's normal. Most of the time I was growing up, we never had a dime. My daddy was terrible with money. He drank or lost at poker everything he earned. If we needed shoes or whatever, my mom had to steal it off him when he was asleep. When he was killed at work she found out he'd let the life insurance lapse. You don't forget a lesson like that, you know?'

Despite herself, despite the awfulness of everything, Laura can't take her eyes off Madison now. Maybe it's the drink – the American woman is on her fourth glass – but actually the alcohol seems to be sharpening, not blurring, her. Her accent is changing again, though, and Laura wonders what it means. A loss of inhibitions or something more deliberate? The cadences have altered, like they did in the storm, the vowels stretching out, like a cat on hot stone.

Laura understands in a lurching rush: it's a trap, the languid Southern drawl employed to disguise the ferocity of the attack. Madison is limbering up. She's going to take Bastian apart. Laura can only assume that she'll be next.

The few tourists in Castelfranco without costumes stand out like emergency flares. It is they who are self-conscious, rather than those decked out like extras in their richly coloured tabards and hose and girdled gowns. Laura catches the eye of another outsider, a portly man in a Nike swoosh T-shirt. He shoots her a grimace of solidarity. This *festa* is not putting on a show for visitors, like some places do: it still belongs to the town. As the locals she passes openly stare, she has never felt more out of place. She even knows the Italian for this, having felt it from the start in one way or another: *fuori posto*.

Still, they are a sight to behold en masse: gorgeous in their scarlet, gold and green plumage. Of course, there are plenty of small incongruities once the eye is tuned in: nail varnish, wristwatches, sunglasses, the ubiquitous mobile phones and iPads held high over heads to capture the scene.

The air is full of the smells of meat and burnt sugar. Food stalls line one side of the piazza. None of them have eaten – it was too early before so they'd planned to get something here. But much of it, on closer inspection, is offal: brains and liver and sweetbreads. Nausea and hunger war inside Laura. Nick, who seems hyper and oddly elated, says he's up for it and orders something dark and shining in a rough-textured bread roll. Madison squeals as he bites into it and the filling bulges out, a piece of it landing wetly near his feet. It looks like liver or maybe kidney. Laura's stomach tips.

Ivan leads them towards one of the lanes that form the old town's arteries. It's much darker here. What felt like a Disney approximation of medieval in the last gilded spill of evening light is starting to feel real as the sun falls away below the roof lines. It's only now that it's truly possible to imagine they've hurtled back in time. The faces looming out of the shadowy lane are the same as those she's seen in frescos, as though the surface of the gene pool has lain undisturbed for five hundred years.

She stops to watch a craftsman who is shaving down a buttery leather belt in long, graceful strokes. She can smell it, tar and tobacco and a tinge of rot. The movement is mesmerizing and she lingers. When she looks up, there's no sign of the others. They've been absorbed into the throng. She stands on tiptoe but all she can see over the dark heads are the red tunics so many are wearing. It strikes her for the first time that no one is wearing bright blue like her, even though she thinks of it as such an Italian shade: *azzurro*, the same colour as the Adriatic waters to the east.

She hurries along in the direction they'd been heading. There is a balcony from where they're going to watch the parade that opens the three-day festival; Ivan knows the contessa who owns it and the enormous apartment it belongs to. After a while, she sees she's too far back from the piazza the balcony must look over. She stops and looks this way and that, an island in the river of scarlet and crimson that flows past, thick and clotted. Hands brush her hips and hair and bare arms, but it's never quite brazen enough for her to protest.

She sets off again, back towards the piazza. Music has struck up now. Drums thud and reverberate through the cobbles under her thin-soled sandals. Although she's drunk very little, she's beginning to feel peculiar, detached and jittery at the same time, a note of dread sawing away in the background, off-key.

When she stops, unsure of her direction again, a woman with tilted almond eyes turns to look her up and down. The phalanx of young men surrounding her do the same. The woman has sky-high cheekbones, the skin stretched over them the colour of old-gold with its dash of dull green. In her arms is one of those miniature Italian greyhounds, pin-boned and tiny, its taupe pelt gleaming. Laura can't place why the sight of them seems so familiar until she remembers the Da Vinci painting of a woman holding an ermine.

She's still transfixed by the woman, the way the crowd parts respectfully around her, when someone's hands clamp around her waist. She tries to twist away but she's already being pulled into a lightless alleyway she hadn't even noticed, one of her sandals coming half off as she's hauled over the cobbles.

With an enormous effort, she wrenches herself round,

ready to claw with her fingernails, to bring her knee up to his crotch. She knows she's going to be faced with Carlo, she knows it.

But it's not Carlo. It's Bastian. The nap of his dark tunic gleams like the greyhound's coat in the light from the alley's single streetlamp. His hands cup her face. 'Baby, you're shaking.'

'You just abducted me off the street.' She pushes his hands off her.

'Hey, I didn't want the others to notice.'

'Where did you all go anyway? I lost you.'

'Madison dragged Ivan into one of the shops. We turned round and you'd gone. Nick went off to look and I said I would too. I guess I chose the right way.' He gets hold of her wrist and pulls her to him with little effort, though she tries to resist. 'Hey, you're sexy when you're mad.'

He walks her backwards into the arched doorway of an old apartment building, dark as a cave. As he crowds her up against the row of bells to kiss her, an old man with a walking stick comes out. Noticing them, he lifts a shaking hand and she thinks he's going to cross himself but he places it flat to his chest. '*Amore!*' he cries, smiling, as he moves stiffly out into the alleyway and towards the crowd that flows on past, like a swollen river.

Bastian catches the door before it closes. He pulls her into a communal hallway, chill and dimly lit. The marble underfoot slaps against her sandals. It smells complicated: of stale coffee and old dust heated on light-bulbs and turned fishy.

'Come here,' he says, pushing her against the wall. It's

cold through the thin cotton of her dress and she shivers. He thinks it's the effect he's having and starts to kiss her again, his hands beginning to roam, going round her waist and lifting her off the ground. She feels small and delicate held there, feet dangling. He lets her slide slowly through his hands so she's draped over him, her arms round his neck, and she's finally kissing him back when the light snaps off without warning.

'I need to see you,' he mutters, pulling away to push the big round switch. It comes on, humming and clicking as though resentful of the disturbance, and she realizes it's counting down. She thinks she might welcome a permanent pitch-dark. She still wants him, of course. She suspects she always will. She's pictured this exact scenario and it turned her on. But now it's happening, everything else is beginning to intrude. She keeps seeing Madison in the mirror behind her; feeling her long fingers, cool and careful as they adjusted the headband, diminishing her own costume so Laura might feel less foolish.

'We shouldn't be doing this,' she says, turning her mouth away from his, and it's such a cliché of infidelity that she's ashamed, and obscurely grateful for the mean wattage of the hallway's light.

'What?'

'You heard me.'

'Come on.' He reaches down to get his hand up and under the long skirt of her dress. The sheer amount of fabric makes him clumsy and he swears under his breath as the light goes out again. The plunge into darkness and attendant loss of sight makes his hand seem larger, rougher, the skin of her inner thighs more tender.

'No, Bastian.' She pushes his hand away, though it's still inside her dress. 'Stop.'

He pushes her harder into the wall, her legs forced wider open. She plucks at his hand through layers of cotton, the volume of which is now making it difficult for her rather than him. But he's already there, his fingers pushing hard into her, a ragged nail catching her. She cries out and he rubs hard at her, as though that might turn things around.

'Get off me,' she says, and this time he seems to hear her. He pants into her bare shoulder, the hand inside her dress now resting hotly against her hip. She extricates herself carefully and he lets her go. She presses the light switch. He looks jaundiced in the paltry light. It seems to highlight every line.

'I shouldn't have to tell you twice.'

'I thought you wanted it.'

'I thought I did, but then I didn't.'

She wants to ask him what Madison was saying at Ivan's about money – their lack of it – but she wants to leave more. He lets her go. She steps out into the alley and the sound of the crowd meets her like a wave. The door clicks behind her and though she's torn, wanting to make it OK with him, wanting to lose herself as she had yesterday, she forces herself to walk away without looking back.

She's not expecting to find the others. She assumes they're on the contessa's balcony, wherever that is. She finds she doesn't really care. Perhaps Madison's sharp eyes will pick her blue dress out of the crowd. *A little Madonna.* She can't hear it without thinking of its opposite, and wonders if that was exactly what Madison was getting at.

She weaves through the crowd. The atmosphere is more raucous than it was. Eyes have glazed and faces are shiny with sweat above the heavy costumes. In the crush at the centre of the piazza, it must be close to a hundred degrees. She's being carried along rather than choosing a direction.

The fountain looms up ahead, the crowd parting to move around it. She manages to push her way towards it and find a tiny section of stone lip to sit on. Kicking off her sandals, she rests her bare feet on the cobbles but they're sticky with beer and wine and thrown fruit, as well as radiating the day's absorbed heat. It's then that she notices him, sitting in the shadows beneath the stone arches on one of the gelateria's red plastic chairs. It's another fight to get to him.

'Nick.'

He looks up and she sees he's been hit, hard. One eye is closed and already swollen, and there's blood crusted around his nose. There's a circle of vomit next to the chair, his horrible sandwich barely digested before it came back up.

'Oh God.' Tucking her skirts under her, she kneels at his feet and lifts his head to inspect him properly. He doesn't seem to have the energy to hold it up. Blood and sick-stained napkins are crushed inside one fist. As she looks into his good eye, a tear spills over it.

'I've fucked everything,' he says, only just audible.

'What happened to you? Was it them?'

He takes a shuddering breath. 'I dunno. Probably. They had masks on.'

'Masks?'

'Animal masks.'

'Jesus.'

'Yeah.' He shifts and winces, holds his ribs. She carefully lifts his stained tunic. Livid bruises are already rising on his pale skin, from his sternum right round his side.

'God, Nick. We need to go to the *carabinieri*.'

'They took my wallet.'

She shakes her head, not understanding.

'They'll say I was mugged. They'll say it happens to tourists sometimes, if they're unlucky. Nothing personal, nothing they can do, et cetera.'

She can't think of anything to say. She takes the hand clutching the napkins and sees the knuckles are grazed. Very gently, she kisses them.

He lets out a sob.

'Oh, I'm sorry, did I hurt you?' She flushes at the double meaning but he's shaking his head.

'It's not that.'

'What, then?'

'There's something else I need to tell you.'

She waits, holding herself carefully. Somewhere, someone is playing a lute or something similarly absurd and it's completely out of tune. She wishes with all her might that they were back at Luna Rossa. The thought of being stuck in this heaving square while their beloved villa sits empty clutches at her heart. She has a vision of getting back to it to find their possessions in a pile on the drive. Or worse. Her mind conjures up the bulldozers and wrecking balls again. Someone dousing the place in petrol before throwing a lit match.

'Tell me,' she says. 'Just tell me. We're losing the villa, aren't we?'

He looks up. 'No. Not yet. Maybe not at all.'

'What, then?'

He hangs his head and she resists the urge to shake him.

'I took out a loan.'

Her mind reels. 'A loan?'

'To buy the villa. For the work we needed to do.'

'What – like a mortgage? But we paid cash. That was the whole point. We could be mortgage-free.'

'They put the price up.'

'Who? The vendor?' She'd met the old woman from Milan who'd sold them Luna Rossa only once, on the day they signed for ownership.

'Yeah, her. It's really normal here. Do you remember what Signor Ricci said about it? That as soon as you register any interest, the price goes up, that it's artificially low before?' He looks at her desperately.

'Yes, I do. And the price did go up. And we found the extra twenty thousand.'

'It went up again. And again, actually.'

'And you didn't tell me.'

'It was for the same reason. It all happened at once, really. That and the boundary thing.'

'So you just kept on doubling-down?'

He puts his head into his hands and sucks in his breath as he knocks his battered eye. 'You needed that villa. I owed you it.'

She remembers thinking the very same thing that first day. *You owe me this, Nick.*

'So we have no money left, we're going to need to pay God knows how much for the building work, we may not own all the land we bought, and we've also got a mortgage to pay off.'

'*You* keep saying mortgage. I couldn't get one. We didn't have any salaries to get a mortgage.'

'Oh, shit. You mean an actual loan.' The last piece clunks mercilessly into place. 'From Angelo.'

He nods, face down to the filthy cobbles, fingers digging hard into his scalp.

She decides they will get a cab back to Luna Rossa. Finding one requires a long walk, away from the old town's confusion of narrow streets, which have been closed off for the *festa*, towards the kind of light industrial edges that no one ever thinks to prettify. Where the centre felt oppressive, off-kilter, the newer parts of Castelfranco are simply bleak. In many ways, they could be in some soulless suburb in England – tarmac under fluorescent light looks much the same anywhere. But the air is far too hot for home, the wind too warm. It smells a little of drains.

'Don't you think we should have found Madison and Bastian and told them we were going?'

Nick is more anxious than she's ever seen him. He has been asking her questions like this since they left the square, like a child seeking reassurance. She thinks she could probably persuade him to do anything in his current mood – pack up the bare bones of their possessions and simply drive away, for instance – but perversely this makes her want to stay and face things head-on. For now, anger is crowding out most of the fear.

It's pitch-dark on the road the taxi driver takes. It's not the way they normally go and her stomach lurches at the thought that he's recognized them. Saying nothing to Nick, she studies the man's profile, his stubby fingers tapping the steering wheel in time to a song in his head. A plastic saint swings beneath the rear-view mirror as they skirt another bend in the road.

She imagines him coming to an abrupt stop, forcing them out in front of the car, headlights pinning them there, insects swarming thickly in the twin beams. Then the roar of another engine and a cherry-red flatbed pulling up in a storm of dust. She shoves away the image and squeezes Nick's hand. Somewhere she's furious with him, of course she is, but for now her anger is trained exclusively on Angelo.

The driver, who has ignored them since they set off, half turns, saying something neither of them catches. She glances at Nick to see if he understood but he shakes his head at her, his good eye wide as another wave of anxiety visibly washes over him.

'*Scusi?*' she says, leaning forward and breathing in sweat and cologne. '*Può ripetere?*'

'*Scossa,*' he says slowly, enunciating the two syllables as if she and Nick are particularly slow, which here, she knows, they are. *Sco-ssa*. Then, as if he can't resist it, as if he can't tolerate their inability to understand his language at normal speed, he rattles off another couple of sentences, the usual machine-gun rat-tat-tat, his right hand leaving the wheel to emphasize each word with pinched fingers. *Scossa*, she hears again. Also *stasera*. She knows that one. It means tonight.

Something clicks in her brain.

'*Scossa*,' she repeats, leaning forward again. The driver's gold chain glints. '*Terremoto?*'

His face splits into a grin. He smacks the dashboard. '*Sì! Sì! Terremoto.*' He turns serious again. '*Sei o sette scosse stasera, nelle montagne. Piccole. Ma domani . . .*' He grimaces.

She replays the words slowly in her head and, to her surprise, she understands them all.

'What's he saying?' Nick's fingers as he clutches hers are slippery. His injured eye is almost closed now.

'There have been some earth tremors, in the mountains. Just little ones, but he said something about tomorrow.'

She grips the back of the driver's seat. '*Domani*,' she begins, '*più forte? Scossa* or *terremoto?*'

Più forte. Stronger.

The driver briefly takes both hands off the wheel to shrug and turn his palms up – the universal sign for not knowing – and they swerve slightly before he rights them.

She sits back. *Terremoto* means earthquake. Literally *earth movement*. Tremors are pretty common here, close to where the Eurasian and African plates grind up against each other. There was a cluster of small ones back in April, which they slept through and only found out about afterwards. This had unnerved Laura at the time, but an actual, proper earthquake? The notion of one striking at any moment is so terrifying it's actually impossible to absorb.

Nick pulls at her hand. 'So?'

'Nothing,' she says. 'It's fine.'

He seems to accept this. She feels him relax, and it perturbs her again how entirely he seems to have ceded responsibility to her. Briefly, she wonders what Bastian would do in the same situation, but this is another thought better tucked out of sight, no help to anyone right now.

The road has been climbing for a while and she suddenly sees where they are. It's only a minute or so to the turn-off for Luna Rossa. Somehow, they've approached it from the opposite direction, but she doesn't care why or how. Relief courses through her, instinctive and animalistic – because, of course, it changes nothing. Despite Nick's so-called mugging, they were probably safer in town, among the crowds.

She tells the driver where to turn and they begin to bump down the drive. The olive trees are dense enough that the villa isn't visible at night until you're almost at the clearing. But tonight you can spot it almost immediately, light blazing from every window. Flickering through the dark trees, the black velvet of the valley at its back, it seems to hover in mid-air, like an alien craft.

'They weren't on when we left, were they?' says Nick, voice strangled.

She doesn't bother answering.

Scrabbling in her purse for the fare, she struggles to add up the coins and creased notes. In the end, she simply piles it all into the driver's hands. He shakes his head. Not enough.

She turns to Nick. 'Right, go in. There's a twenty in my green bag by the bed. Inside pocket.'

At the front door, he hesitates and turns back, but she gestures impatiently for him to go in. There's no one here now: the only car parked on the drive is theirs – the Americans' hire car left at Ivan's – and she can't picture Angelo's henchmen bothering to come here in the dark on foot.

Besides, in her heightened state she can sense the villa's emptiness.

It's dead quiet once the low throb of the taxi's engine has been absorbed by the night. Even the birds and cicadas are silent and she wonders vaguely if that's something to do with the tremors. Some half-recalled fact about animals fleeing from this kind of thing well ahead of time, able to hear a warning to which humans have long grown deaf.

She and Nick sit opposite each other in the kitchen, elbows on the table. She's wrapped a picnic ice-pack in a tea-towel, which he's holding gingerly to his eye. He's forgotten the beer he got out of the fridge. It sweats into the wooden tabletop. She thinks about drinking it herself but she's not convinced she could swallow anything. Except for the illuminated strip set into the extractor fan, the house is dark around them. She'd gone round and turned all the lights off with her knuckle, not wanting to touch with her fingertip where a stranger's had so recently been. She refuses to think much more about this – it's too disturbing.

'I need to tell you something,' she says now.

'I don't want to know.'

'Nick, I have to.'

'No. You don't. I can't handle it. Not on top of everything else.' He reaches for the beer and drinks it in one. Going back to the fridge, he hesitates, then gets a bottle of vodka out of the freezer.

'Want one?'

'No, and I don't think you should have one either. You're probably concussed.'

'Probably.' He sloshes a large measure into a tumbler and drinks half of it.

'Nick. At least have some tonic or something.'

'Nah,' he says, and laughs. It sounds manic, and totally devoid of humour. 'I'll take my Dutch courage neat.' He holds up his glass to her in a toast and downs the rest.

She doesn't understand him at all. She would want to know everything. She knows her imagination would come up with something much worse than the reality. But Nick is not her. Just as Nick would rather be kept in the dark, she would never have taken money from someone like Angelo. Remembering it makes her harden.

She watches him pour another huge measure of vodka and hardens a little bit more. If Angelo's men were to come back tonight, he couldn't hope to defend them. He's a fool, she thinks, though it's a horrible thought, and God knows she's hardly blameless herself. The money stuff, though. That's all on Nick. *I married a fool.*

By the time she hears another engine outside, he is on his third large vodka. He is already determinedly drunk, face bright red and the closed-up eye a livid, shining purple. She stands, tensed, as the front door opens and closes, but she can hear the high pitch of a woman's voice and realizes it's only Madison and Bastian.

Only.

But it's better than the men. She's afraid of what Madison might say or do to her over Bastian, and she's also afraid that Bastian will punish her for her rejection of him at the *festa*, but just having them back in the house makes her shoulders drop a little.

Madison clacks into the kitchen on her tall heels. Her

arrangement of plaits is falling down, loose strands of damp hair around her face. Her colour is up in the way that Nick's is and Laura supposes that she's as drunk as him.

'Hey, guys!' Her voice is a shock in the kitchen that has been so quiet. 'Where the hell did you get to? You never even came to the palazzo at all.' She slurs *palazzo*.

'These shoes have been killing me.' She kicks them off, stumbling into a cupboard as she does. 'And this dress is so fucking hot. Hey, are we doing shots? I wanna do shots.'

She pulls out the chair next to Nick's, the wood scraping on the tiles, then notices his face.

'Oh shit! What happened to you?'

He grins, good eye glassy. 'Got mugged, didn't I?'

'Oh my God, did you go to the police? You need to go to the police.'

Her voice is grating. Laura wishes they would both go to bed. Nick is almost asleep anyway, his head drooping three inches from the table as he tries to listen to Madison, who's taken his hand in hers.

'We told the police,' Laura says. 'They're coming tomorrow to take a full statement. That's where we went. Then we got a cab home.'

The lie comes easily.

'Right, come on, Nick,' she says, before Madison can say anything else. 'You need to go to bed.' She reaches for the vodka bottle to return it to the freezer but Madison's hand grabs it, one of her long nails spiking Laura's hand.

'Did I get you?' She laughs. 'Sorry, honey. But I want vodka too.'

339

Laura opens her hand. 'Of course.' She fetches Madison a glass and puts it down on the table, slightly too hard.

Nick is a dead weight when she tries to lift him out of the chair. He's very nearly unconscious. She could do with Bastian's help but doesn't dare ask where he is. He must have gone straight upstairs.

Nick reaching back blearily for his glass infuriates her enough to find the strength to wrestle him to his feet and out of the door. In the hall, without an audience, he takes a little of his own weight, and this enables her to get him up the stairs. In their bedroom, she rolls him into the recovery position in case he's sick. Before she leaves the room, she puts on one of the bedside lights so he can find his way if he wakes. She studies his unconscious form for a moment but, besides anger and deep irritation, she can't really muster any feelings for him at all.

It's as she's coming down the stairs that it happens. Her feet are bare on the worn-smooth stone, which feels so solid but suddenly shifts under her. It's only brief and even as it's happening, her brain working fast, she thinks it's her – another low-blood-pressure episode. But then a framed picture at the bottom of the stairs slides vertically down the wall to land upright on the bottom step. It hesitates for a moment before falling on its face, glass smashing.

She rushes into the kitchen.

'Did you feel that?'

'Feel what?' Madison looks up from her vodka.

'A tremor. An earth tremor. They've had them up in the mountains tonight.'

Madison shrugs and Laura wants to slap the drunkenness out of her. She can't cope with her and Nick being like this when at any moment Angelo might show up, or the earth might open and swallow them all.

'Where's Bastian?'

Madison looks round sharply, eyes narrowed and navy blue in the low light. 'Why'd you wanna know?'

'Because if there's going to be a proper earthquake tonight we need a plan. I need to know where all of us are. The electricity could go out like it did in the storm. We might need to, I don't know, shelter somewhere.'

She glances around at Luna Rossa's old walls. Surely they've witnessed scores of tremors in their time, and survived them all. But she knows there are things you're supposed to do in an earthquake and she can't quite remember, all her knowledge rooted in Hollywood disaster films. You don't go outside in case something falls on you, she thinks, but surely that wouldn't apply here. This is not the city. All she can clearly picture is Japanese children crouching under their school desks while a siren blares.

'Let's go find him, then.' Madison gets to her feet, swaying as she does. Everything about her seems hopelessly inebriated until she grabs hold of Laura's arm. Her fingers grip so hard that Laura knows she'll be left with fingermark bruises.

'He wouldn't speak to me on the way home, you know,' she says indistinctly, as they climb the stairs together. 'Giulia drove us. Ivan was in front and we were in back and he didn't say a damn word the whole time. He was like it at the palazzo too. He went off to find you and when he came back he was mad. When Bast is really mad he goes, like, silent. What d'you do to him, girl?'

She takes a risk. 'Nothing. I didn't see him. I found Nick in the square and he told me he'd been mugged. Then we had to find a cab.'

'What about the police?'

They pause on the last step together.

'After that,' she says.

Bastian is on his phone when Madison pushes open the bedroom door with a bang. He lifts a finger to stop her speaking. Laura hangs back on the landing. His voice is too low for her to catch what he's saying and she counts backwards in her head. It must be afternoon in LA. A work call, then. A memory comes, so box-fresh she must have deliberately withheld it from herself, like the diary entries she is beginning to understand she manipulated for her future self. She is sitting at the top of the stairs at Bastian's student house and he is below her, on the phone to someone back home. He's talking in the same soft, not-quite-discernible tones while she waits forlornly.

She'd asked afterwards who it was. 'Just someone from home,' he said and, when she asked who, smirked. 'Why?' he said. 'You won't know her.'

He only makes her – and Madison – wait a few minutes this time.

'Was that news about one of your big deals, baby?' Madison has begun to unwind her hair, which she does so deftly that Laura wonders if she's quite as drunk as she's made out.

Bastian meets Laura's eye. She knows the look he gives her of old: a bolt of concentrated desire that is capable of turning her physically weak. She makes herself look away.

'Did you feel the tremor just now?' she says, voice not quite steady.

He shrugs, smiles. 'I live in California.'

'Well, there have been others in the mountains tonight, and they're saying there's a chance of a bigger one at some point. I thought I should warn you.'

Madison starts to unzip her long velvet gown. It gets stuck at the waist seam and she gestures impatiently for Laura to help her. She fumbles as her fingers touch the hot, smooth skin of Madison's lower back but then it's free. Madison steps out of it, letting it puddle on the floor. Entirely unselfconscious in a sheer black bra and tiny thong, she stretches out on the bed, back arching, toes pointed. It's no more flesh than she's shown off by the pool but it feels different here, the three of them together in the bedroom. The charged air sparks.

'So,' she says, to the ceiling. 'Are you going to tell me, then?'

Laura's stomach turns over.

'About these deals, I mean.' She laughs, turning her head towards Laura. 'What did you think?'

When she says nothing, Madison sits up and pats the bed next to her.

Laura retreats a couple of steps towards the door before she can help herself.

'Hey, where you going, girl?'

'Nowhere.' She sees the stool by the dressing-table and pulls it out. It's strewn with Madison's clothes and she pauses, unsure what to do. She'd really like to leave.

'Just throw them on the floor,' says Madison. Her eyes glitter, and Laura wonders again whether it's real intoxication or a decent performance of it. She obeys, though, and sits. The legs of the old stool move under her slightly as she does, like teeth loose in their gums.

'Did I ever tell you how me and Bastian met?' says Madison. She throws the question over her shoulder at him but he is apparently engrossed in his phone again, and ignores her. His stance by the window is tense, though: shoulders squared, the hand not holding his phone curled into a fist. It's obvious he's listening.

Laura tries to smile, friable with nerves. 'Yes, you did. You were working at a restaurant and he came in and asked you out.'

'Is that what I said?' Madison tips her head back to laugh, showing her long throat. 'It was actually a strip club. I was a dancer. He couldn't take his eyes off me.'

Bastian mutters something Laura doesn't catch.

'Oh, I – I see,' she stutters. 'Well . . .'

Madison laughs again, louder this time, higher-pitched. 'I'm kidding! Oh, my God, your face. Trying so hard not to look horrified. But wait a minute, do you think I look like the kind of girl who works in a place like that? Did you think it was like *Flashdance*? That Bast came in one night and saw gold in the trash?'

Her voice is suddenly so fierce and hard in the room that Laura rears instinctively back. The stool rolls and groans under her.

'No, no, I didn't . . . I just . . .'

Madison puts her head on one side, baby-pouts. 'Aw, I know. I'm only teasing. You're a sweetheart really.'

She twists round so her legs are crossed, like one of her Instagram yoga pictures.

'The thing with Bast is that, at the beginning, when it's all new, he loves you so hard that you can't see straight. You know what they call it? Love-bombing.' She glances towards him. 'And that's exactly what it feels like. You don't know what's hit you. It knocks you right off your feet.'

He's not even pretending to look at his phone now. His eyes flick between Madison and Laura. His dark eyes in the low light are impossible to read, but he's smiling again. It's a lazy smile. No, not lazy. *Sated* – as if what Madison is saying is filling him up.

'You told me about how he pursued you,' Laura says, slightly nauseous at her daring – she's aiming this at Bastian too. 'We were talking about how rare it is, for men to do that properly.'

'That's right.' Madison smiles at both of them. 'It's basically irresistible. And you had it too, once, didn't you, Laura? You said it was for ever ago, that you couldn't really remember him, only the feeling. Though I didn't believe that was true then, and I definitely don't now.'

Laura says nothing. What can she say, looking up at Madison from the bottom of the trap she's just fallen into?

'The thing is,' says Madison, once the silence has yawned wide enough, 'the thing that's not so fun is when it stops. I swear, it's like the fucking sun's gone out. You go from feeling like God's gift to absolute zero. Like you've just disappeared. I used to follow you round the apartment, Bast, do you remember? Like a kid or a puppy.

Please speak to me! Please tell me what I did wrong!' She crawls to the other end of the bed and kneels up to wave in his face. 'I'm right here! Can't you see me any more? Please love me again!' The little-girl voice makes Laura go cold.

Madison sits back, adjusts the pillows behind her. 'So that was, you know, *shit*. I, like, mourned the loss of the old Bast for months. I told myself I'd leave. I made this big decision: if he doesn't want me any more, I'm not going to stick around. I'm not going to live off scraps. But when I finally packed my bags, he wouldn't let me go. He sat me down, said we were a good team. What he meant was that I was good at charming his boss and his clients when we went out for dinner. Just the right amount of flirting. I looked good on his arm. I looked *great*.'

Bastian watches her while she talks and it's the most engrossed Laura has seen him in his almost-wife since they arrived. Madison feels it too. She shimmers under the glare of his attention. She holds herself differently against the pillows: shoulders back and breasts raised, abs taut and legs long and lean down the mattress. She might sound wearily cynical but it's clear there's still no better drug for her than him, rapt like the old days, his eyes drinking her in, eating her up.

'So, we struck a deal, didn't we, baby? He knew that my weak spot – my *other* weak spot – was money. Growing up poor is one thing. But when it looks like you might just stay poor for ever, that the whole American Dream rags-to-riches shit might not happen for you, and then someone comes along and pulls you out of it, you'll do anything to stay there. It was one thing making this grand speech about not compromising, saying that if he didn't love me completely then I was gone. It was another to actually pick up and go. I wasn't sure I could do it. He knew I couldn't. The alternative was to go back to the kind of hole I'd been renting, where it always stank of other people's cooking, where you could never get the toilet bowl clean, whatever you put down it.'

She holds out the hand with the diamond ring and the lights of it scatter across the ceiling.

'So we made a deal. Bast was still good at deals back then, weren't you, baby? But so was I. The very next day I went out and bought this ring. He'd earn the money and I would look after everything else. I'd also let him do what he wanted. He'd mess around, sure, but he'd always come back to me. He'd always provide. And it wasn't like there was no love. We were always good in bed, weren't we?'

But Bastian is looking at Laura now. 'That's enough,' he says, eyes flicking to Madison for a split second.

'Well, is it, though?' She cocks her head again, considering. 'I don't know about that. I think Laura should know what our agreement was and how you've been breaking the terms of it all over the place.' She smiles at Laura. 'I don't mean him fucking you.' She waits a beat while Laura sucks in her breath. 'I mean the money. There's nothing coming in, hasn't been for a while. There are no deals, are there, Bast? You're not doing deals on these calls, are you? You're running through every contact in your cell and begging.'

Bastian steps towards the bed and Laura instinctively stands, sure he's going to hit Madison. She, to her credit, or something like it, doesn't so much as flinch.

But he doesn't hit her. He looks down at her and laughs instead, and it's just as empty as hers was. 'Fuck you,' he says easily. 'There's plenty of money coming. Fact is, I'm bored of you. I can see now that there's nothing left. It's been over for years.'

Laura winces. She remembers with a clutch of her heart his ability to turn completely cold. She'd once explained to Lou that it was just the way he coped with difficult feelings. That he had to shut down or he'd go to pieces. Lou had merely looked embarrassed.

Madison is regarding Bastian with a raised eyebrow. 'Let me guess,' she says slowly, turning back to Laura. 'He's never felt a connection like this. He was too young and scared to appreciate it back then but he's not afraid any more. Did he tell you that you're one of the Great Ones? What is it again, Bast? "You're only allowed three great women in your lifetime. They come along like the great fighters, every ten years, and I know you're one of them"?'

She laughs. 'He said it, didn't he? Was it this time or back in the past? You know, it's actually a line out of a movie. *A Bronx Tale*. You seen it? It's a coming-of-age story. Italian-American kids running through fire hydrants in the sixties. You know the kind of thing. Robert de Niro was probably in it, maybe playing a priest, or was that *Sleepers*? Anyway, Bast loves that movie. Did you notice how much he loves the schmaltz when you were together? Why are heartless men always so sentimental? It's fucked up. My daddy was just the same. Beating my mom one minute and crying over his Dean Martin records the next.'

Her accent has slipped and stretched. *Ma daaaddy*.

'He probably does think he loves you,' she says, accent sharpening again. Though she's still talking to Laura, her eyes are back on Bastian. 'In as much as a man like him can. Didn't stop him from looking in every real-estate agent's window in town the other day, trying to work out how much this place might be worth.'

1999

You're at a house party for Theo's twenty-first. This is more unusual than it sounds. Hardly anyone throws parties in their actual house, though you had assumed – mainly from novels – that you would be going to them all the time. Theo's house is not one of those way out in the country, but it is large and laughably grand for a student let. His father bought it cash for his son and his friends to live in while they're here. It's in a quiet residential area well away from the narrow streets of Victorian terraces where most of the students rent. You imagine the neighbours are very unhappy.

The house is accidentally minimalist. That is to say that it's basically empty. In your little house, which you share with Lou and two other girls, there are pictures and photo collages and even a yucca plant. Bastian has come round precisely twice, and on both occasions he commented on this. 'It's like a proper place,' he said, and what he meant was that it felt like a home.

In Theo's house, where the countryside gang spends most of their time because living ten miles out is actually a massive fucking hassle, there is nothing that is not essential. A huge telly, a sofa, a PlayStation, two ugly armchairs that recline, like Joey and Chandler's, and a glass coffee-table that will be shattered somewhere between the stripper leaving and you being coaxed into the empty bedroom of a housemate who is away for the weekend, sailing.

But that's a few hours away yet. There is a banner in the sitting room that's not usually there. Someone has stuck it with gaffer tape to the high picture rail. It has Greek symbols daubed on it in black marker pen, and you remember that Theo decided to celebrate at home because he wanted a frat party. Bastian has been advising him and someone has managed to track down those red plastic beer cups you always see in American college movies.

The boys – that hardcore of public-school boys for whom Bastian is the exotic mascot – are wearing matching rugby shirts with the same Greek letters embroidered on the breast, and their nicknames on the back. Hip-hop is being played at deafening volume, and when someone's girlfriend tries to change it, she's brayed at.

You find the stripper's performance viscerally awful. You've never seen one in real life before. Of course she's older than in the films. She has a deeply normal body, English-pale, veined and moly. She looks like a mum. She probably is. The whole thing – every single thing about it – is excruciating. How dead-eyed she is as she performs. How dead-eyed Theo is as she lifts his hands to her large, loose breasts. He is performing for the boys who paid for her just as much as the stripper is.

'This is painful,' says Lou, in your ear. You turn to her and see she can't quite focus. Her eyes slide. When she blinks, it takes slightly too long.

'You're hammered,' you say.

'Something's got to get me through. Can we go soon? I love you, babe, but I really hate these people.'

You search the room for Bastian. In your peripheral vision, the stripper sprays squirty cream on her chest and grabs Theo's head, pulling it into her cleavage. The whole room crows their approval as she meets their gaze. Is she bored? Is she cringing? Someone says, loudly, 'Jesus, she's so fucking rough,' and you know she must have heard. You try to imagine what it must be like to do this job in a university town, pushing forty. How she must despise you all.

At some vague juncture, Lou disappears. You assume she's left you to it and you don't blame her. You hate it here too, if you're being absolutely honest. The difference is Bastian. Because of him, you can't leave. If someone queried this, you would explain that, as his girlfriend, he would be offended if you abandoned his friend's twenty-first. Of course, it's also because you don't really trust him. But, weirdly, it's not just that you need to keep an eye on him and what he gets up to. It's the other way round, too. You suspect that if you aren't right there in his line of vision, you'll fall cleanly out of his thoughts.

You spend an hour or maybe it's two in the kitchen with the boys who circle the edges of the core group, like penguins never allowed their turn in the warmth of the huddle. They're doing shots of tequila, knuckles and worktop sticky with salt and lemon. One boy saws at a greenish lemon with a blunt knife, so ostentatiously drunk and clumsy that he's probably stone-cold sober.

Someone has thrown up and has clearly tried but failed to wash it all out of the weave of his jumper, the mingled stink of vomit and damp dog making you cover your nose. But, still, when they beckon you over to join in, you do. You have this weird conviction that if his friends approve of you, even the try-hard ones, your stock will rise. And if they want you, and there is one who always stares at you through disarmingly long eyelashes, then even better.

By the time you go back through to the living room, the numbers have thinned. The hired disco ball tracks dismally over the ruined carpet and shattered coffee-table. From the kitchen you'd heard it break: the crash and the cheers that followed. Proof of a great party. No one cares that it will cost money to buy a new one because there is always more money. And if anyone did care they would keep it quiet, for fear of showing themselves up to be . . . what? A pov? A chav? Hopelessly bourgeois? You're never quite sure.

The cleverer rich kids read Bret Easton Ellis's *Absolute Zero* and think it's genius because it's about the New York equivalents of themselves. All that cash and coke and still not happy! *Poor babies*, says Lou, chucking her copy at the wall. She's got this gruff northern accent she puts on, usually to horrify Sloaney boys who've sidled over to chat her up. *What a load of soft shite. Bloody idiots don't know they're born.*

The thought of Lou makes you smile. For a moment, you picture yourself simply walking out. It would take about thirty-five minutes to get home and yet again you're wearing stupid heels but it would probably be quite nice, the evening warm, this part of town quiet enough to hear the foxes and wood pigeons and the susurration of the M5 in the distance.

Maybe you would have done it but then Bastian is there,

one arm looped round your head to cover both your eyes, the other round your waist and dragging you backwards. You breathe in the Dior aftershave you bought him at great cost from the department store in town and pretend to struggle as he pulls you up the narrow servants' stairs at the very back of the sprawling house, where no one else is.

The door shuts at the same instant the arms release you but as you turn to face him his mouth is already on yours, his hand kneading your left breast hard, which hurts because your period is due in four days.

'Bastian, hang on,' you say into his mouth, which is somehow both wet and slack, and bone-hard at the same time.

He doesn't answer but his fingers are at the waistband of your black trousers, fumbling for the button. It's stiff and you can't quite bring yourself to help him but anyway they're so low on your hips that he gives up and starts tugging them down without undoing them.

'I said hang *on*,' you say, irritation creeping into your voice because this is so far from how you want it, and whatever else is difficult about being with Bastian, at least he's usually good at this stuff. 'You're going to rip them.'

But he continues as though you haven't spoken, breathing so hard into your neck that it's wet there. His hand continues to push down the narrow gap between the tight, still-zipped trousers and your flesh.

You turn your head away from his mouth as he starts to kiss you again. Your eyes have adjusted by now and it's then that you notice the dark bulk of a figure in front of the window. Your whole body jolts with the shock of it.

'There's someone in here,' you say, voice pitched high with alarm.

The shadow laughs and the sound of it makes you freeze. Not just in the sense of going still but going cold, too. You know that laugh. It's Bastian's.

You shove hard at the person pressing against you and the 'Fuck's sake,' as he loses his balance and crashes to the floor is unmistakably English. And not just English but lazy-mouthed, public-school English. Theo.

You scrabble for the light switch, hand frantically patting along the wall, but you can't find it. And then Bastian is there instead, his hands reaching for yours, and then moving up to stroke your hair. He reaches down to turn on a desk lamp.

'Hey, hey,' he says, 'calm down.' You watch his pupils contract. 'He's just drunk. It's his birthday.'

'What the fuck, Bastian?' You're whispering for some reason. 'He was all over me and you just stood there and watched.'

'Baby, it's his birthday. It was only a kiss.'

'No, it wasn't. He was forcing his hand down . . .' You stop. 'Did you plan this? Did you tell him he could have me?'

He puts his head on one side, mouth turning up into a little smirk. 'Come on, you said you were up for it.'

'*What?*'

'We talked about it. I know you remember. It was in my room that time. You said you'd be up for a threesome but it would have to be two guys, not you and another girl.'

You open your mouth to speak but a sob threatens to

come out instead. You close it again as Bastian leads you over to the bed.

'Here, sit down next to me.'

You allow yourself to be pulled down beside him. You desperately want things to be OK again. He holds your hand between his. They're warm. One of his thumbs rubs at yours.

Theo has got to his feet. He comes to sit on your other side.

'Sorry, Laura. I'm so fucking drunk.'

He starts laughing and Bastian joins in.

'Don't you remember talking about it?' Bastian says, when Theo has quietened down.

'Yeah, but . . .'

'You said there was a night back at home when you were kissing these two different guys, going from one to the other, and it was a turn-on because they both wanted you.'

You think back to this. You'd been lying on Bastian's bed and you were feeling in charge for once. You'd told him this story, which was partly true, though you'd made it sound way sexier than it was, when in fact it was only your sixth-form leavers' ball and everyone was totally drunk and kissing anything that moved. It had been friendly, really, a kind of mutual affection for these people you'd known since you were eleven and might not see again, once all of you were scattered, like seeds, across the country. There had been very little that was sexual in it.

Not like this, now. The two boys sitting either side of you are actually men. Bastian's hand is on your thigh and Theo has peeled down the narrow strap of your vest top to kiss your shoulder.

'Isn't she amazing?' says Bastian. 'I told her, she's one of the Great Ones. I knew as soon as I saw her.'

'Yeah.' Theo's mouth is still on her, and the word vibrates through her.

'Kiss him for me,' Bastian murmurs, into your ear. 'It'll get me hard to watch you.'

'Don't you mind?' you say, too late realizing that it sounds like this is the only thing stopping you.

'Sure I would, if I wasn't here, if you were with some stranger, but this is different. This is you doing something for me.'

He begins kissing you properly, and it's so different – so much better – than with Theo, that your body half responds. You twist round towards him and away from Theo, in an attempt to shut out the latter. You're hoping he'll get bored and give up, stumble back out into the remnants of his own party.

But he doesn't. He gets his hands under the hem of your top at the back and pushes it up. You wriggle away but he's trying to lift it over your head, and Bastian is holding up your arms to help. You don't know why you let them other than some bleary sense that it's so much easier than telling them to stop. Anyway, maybe you like it. Or maybe you will soon. Maybe you should like it.

'You're so cool, Laura,' Theo is saying. His breath is hot on the back of your neck. Bastian's tongue is in your mouth. 'I said so, to Seb, when he first pulled you. I said you were kind of naturally sexy and cool. Like, not a slag but not up-tight either.'

He reaches round for your hand and puts it on his crotch. 'See what you've done to me.'

Bastian's hand is in your underwear now. Somehow he has undone the stubborn button and the zip of your trousers without you realizing.

'You're really wet,' he says, though you're pretty sure you're not.

As the two of them crawl over you with their hands and mouths, you ask yourself again whether you're aroused. You honestly don't know. You can't separate any of the strands out. There's the straightforward turned-on that men seem to feel so easily, and then there's the arousal that's at a remove and which comes from the power of your effect on someone else. And then there's the turned-on you tell yourself to be because it means you're uninhibited and sophisticated. Perhaps you're all of them. Or none.

You're all lying down now and, for some reason, you start thinking about the boy whose duvet it is. Theo will tell him about this when he gets back from his weekend away. *Mate. You might want to wash your bedding.* They will laugh.

Your total conviction that Theo will do this makes you sit up. You don't feel drunk but you've had so much tequila and vodka over the course of the evening that you must be.

'Hey, what now?' Bastian says, and the impatient catch in his voice is just what you need to scoot to the end of the bed and stand up. Your bra is still looped over your shoulders though Theo has managed to undo the fastening. Bastian, so much more adept, has taken off your trousers and your knickers and you grab them now, pulling them back on.

'OK, fine, be boring then,' he says, voice expression-less. You don't reply. Theo, judging by his breathing, is close to passing out.

Now that you're preparing to leave, you're deft and definite about it. As you dress, you're working things out, assessing the damage. You let them take your clothes off while they kept theirs on. You let both of them put their fingers inside you. On the plus side, you didn't let them have full sex with you. You pushed Theo's head away when he tried to go down on you. It's not too bad.

It's only as you look around for the door, disoriented in the unfamiliar room, that you notice the red light. It's only a tiny detail among everything else that's whirring and circling in your head. A stand-by light from a stereo or a TV, you assume, in as much as you think about it at all.

In fact, you're not far off. It's a video camera, which Theo bought on a whim for eight hundred pounds, in order to film his birthday party.

You never see the footage. 'There wasn't much to see anyway', says Lou, who had gone round to Theo's and, after watching it, had destroyed it, pulling out the spool of film with a hair-grip until it was a two-metre-long tangle of torn plastic yarn on Theo's living-room floor. 'There was hardly any light so it was really grainy.'

'Do you promise?'

'I promise. You could barely even tell it was you.'

'What if there are copies?'

'Then I'll do this to them, too,' she says. She reaches into her pocket and pulls out the ball of tape, holds it towards you. 'But there aren't any. Theo swore to me. I said if I heard even a sniff of a rumour about a copy I would go to the police. He's too fucking stupid to know that the police couldn't do anything.'

'Because I let them, you mean.'

Lou shrugs. 'It's not your fault. It's Sebastian's fault.'

'What about Theo?'

'Theo's a dick, but Sebastian is supposed to be your boyfriend.'

'I told him I was OK with it.'

'Did you? At the time, or hypothetically, before you realized he'd actually put you in that position without asking if it was OK?'

'He goes back to New York on Friday.'

'Yes, and thank fuck for that.'

'It wasn't that bad, really. They were just drunk and messing about. We were all wasted.'

'So why can't you bring yourself to leave the house, then?'

When Lou goes up to campus for lectures that you should be attending too, you go to the phone in the hall and dial Bastian's number. It rings and rings.

You fish out your diary from under the bed, find a biro. You write the date, underline it and pause. You sit like that for a long time. When you put it back, the page is still blank but for the date. Why would you want to write any of that down? Why would anyone?

Day 12 continued

Laura stands. She needs air. There doesn't seem to be enough of it inside the bedroom. She stumbles down the stairs, Madison calling after her. She doesn't stop.

At the unlit pool, she grips the balustrade to lean out over the dark valley. And it really is dark, except for the odd farmhouse. She wonders who else is out there, staring into the black and wondering how the night will unfold: false alarm or something cataclysmic.

She turns sharply at a sound behind her. It's Bastian. Perhaps he thought she meant him to follow her. Perhaps she did. She has no idea.

'Did you see the lights down there?' With the villa behind him, he's no more than a silhouette. A firefly glow makes her startle until she smells cigarette smoke. Mingling with the night air, the combination still reminds her of university, fondly and painfully at once.

'What happened to your vape?'

'I wanted the real thing.'

She shivers, wraps her arms round herself. 'Anyway, what lights?'

'In Giuseppe's House. Isn't that what you call it? Where we . . .' He laughs softly.

She goes over to the far end of the pool to peer through the trees. He's right. There are lights on. She didn't even know the electricity was still working there.

There's never been any reason to go there at night. She shivers again.

'Hey, why so worried? The builders must have left them on, that's all.'

She shakes her head.

'Do you want to go and check it out?' His cigarette glows again.

She glances back towards the villa.

'Madison's asleep,' he says. 'Passed out cold.'

She hesitates. Obviously she should go back inside the villa, away from him. She steps towards him, intending to carry on past, and stops instead. 'What she said, about looking at house prices . . .'

'That's bullshit. I was just daydreaming about getting a place here myself. Window-shopping, like people do when they're in a beautiful place and don't want to leave.'

At that moment, the ground shudders, just a couple of times. She reaches out to grip the balustrade, like she's on the deck of a ship caught in unpredictable waters. The movement starts again and she cries out in fright, a wounded-animal sound. This time it's longer and some-how louder, though she doesn't really know what *it* is. The earth tearing, presumably, miles down. It stops again and she discovers she's holding her breath.

Bastian, whose arms had gone out for balance, moves towards her.

She holds up a trembling hand to halt him. 'Just . . . Can I have a cigarette?'

It goes straight to her head so she sits down heavily on the ground. It tastes more unpleasant than she remembers and she stubs it out. Nick always hated her smoking, complaining about the smell when she got home from a night out with Lou.

After a few minutes with no more tremors, she pulls herself up and turns towards the outbuildings again.

'What if someone is still down there?' she says. It's more for something to say than any conviction that anyone is hanging around.

'Well, if they are, you've got me.'

He catches hold of her wrist. Unhurriedly, as if he knows she won't pull away, he lowers his head to the soft skin where her neck dips into her collarbone and holds his mouth there. His arms go around her. 'We have so much to discuss,' he breathes into her. 'About what happens next.'

Her insides tense: from nerves and adrenalin, mainly, but also from an awful, detached kind of glee. Here, at last, is proof that she was right about their specialness all along. *You can't fight destiny.* Inside her head, Lou scoffs.

The door to Giuseppe's stands open, but maybe it did anyway, because of the building work. The lit-up clearing between the outbuildings feels eerie: big oblongs of shadow and light falling at strange angles. She's never seen it like this. It looks like a village abandoned in an emergency. Bastian goes inside and returns almost immediately.

'Come look at this.'

'What is it?' Her voice is shaky, her mind going to bodies and blood and horses' heads.

'Hey, it's just some graffiti.' He takes her hands in his. 'You think I'd let anything bad happen to you?'

'I . . .'

She feels odd. She's felt like it all night about him, an

365

instinct to pull away countered immediately by another part of her brain. *But you wanted this, didn't you? You always wanted it. And now you've almost got it.*

She lets him lead her inside. The words are daubed in black paint, the letters cramped and tilted backwards.

STRANIERI USCIRE

Strangers out

'It doesn't mean anything,' he says. 'Just some local kids looking for something to be angry about.'

She stares at him, but of course he doesn't know the half of what Nick has got them into. 'I don't know what to do,' she says simply. 'Everything's such a mess.'

'It won't be, soon. Madison and I have been over for a long time. I think you and Nick have been too. You know this is right.'

She shakes her head. 'No, no. You don't understand.'

'I do. I always understood you. We've always understood each other.'

'Are you going to say the thing about the Great Ones again now?' It's out before she can bite it back.

For a split-second, before he looks hurt, his eyes narrow. 'Madison is bitter because she's so proud. But you heard her. She only ever wanted me for the attention and money I gave her. It's our time now. You and me.'

'Is it?'

'Don't you want it to be? I know you want it to be.'

She looks at him properly. Someone has removed the waxy orange lampshade from the overhead light and he appears older under the bare bulb. It doesn't make her any less attracted to him. She thinks, in fact, that he's more beautiful now than he was at twenty-one. Already she feels a kind of grief and it's not because they're never going to end up together. It's because this man standing in front of her is a different person altogether from the one she'd dreamt of. The realization makes her feel leaden. Foolish, too. He'd always given her so little that her imagination had been forced to fill in the gaps.

'What exactly do you have planned for us?' she says.

He moves eagerly towards her, oblivious to her tone, which is weary, hearing only the words.

'I've had enough of the US,' he says, speaking fast. 'It's been an incredible experience for me, discovering my roots. I want to stay here, with you.'

It's as if Nick doesn't exist.

'We were going to go to Tuscany once. Do you remember?' she says. 'I'd read about the Palio and you said you'd take me to Siena to see it.'

He covers it straight away, but she spots the irritation that she's halted him mid-flow.

'We can go to Siena whenever you like,' he says. 'Sell this place and get somewhere there.'

'That's why I always had this thing about Italy,' she says, as though he hasn't spoken. 'People always asked me, when Nick and I were selling up, *Why there? Why not France? You'd be so much nearer home.* And sometimes I would say it was the food, and other times I would say I'd been dreaming of Italy since I was a little girl.' She looks at him. 'But it was because of you. Because of what happened with us at the end.'

'I don't get it.' He shakes his head. He's struggling to quash his annoyance now, jaw set, nostrils flared.

'No, you wouldn't. To be fair, I've only just worked it out myself. I think I felt like if we'd made it on that holiday after my finals then everything would have been OK. It was like a sliding-doors thing. Another me went travelling with you that summer and had the perfect time. It made the rest of it OK.'

He shakes his head again, more insistently this time. 'That was for ever ago. We need to think about now. Right now.'

'Why did you come here? What was really in it for you?'

'No one ever made me happy like you did back then. No one ever got me like you did. Like you do. We're soulmates, Laura. I know you understand that. You're just scared right now.' He steps forward. Barefooted as she is, he looms over her.

She swallows. 'Was there anything about me you wanted? I mean, specifically me, as opposed to how great I was for your ego?'

He frowns. 'What do you mean?'

'Never mind. Do you remember I wrote a diary back then?' She tries to keep her voice neutral.

He smiles, nods. It probably feels like safer ground. 'Yeah. You wouldn't let me near it.'

'You read it once, though. You turned up when I was late back from campus and waited in my room. You knew where I hid it and you read it, even though you knew it was private.'

'How do you even remember this shit? I can hardly remember anything from back then.'

'Yet you remember enough to know that we were soul-mates. I was mortified when I realized you'd read it. I mean, so embarrassed that I wanted to die. It was all about how much I worshipped you. How insane the whole thing made me.' Her hand goes to her stomach, still nauseated by the twenty-year-old memory. 'I thought you'd run a mile.'

'But I didn't, did I?'

'Not then, no.'

He sighs, looks sad. She fights the urge to go to him, to touch him. Her fingertips tingle with wanting it. She could be with him at last. She could leave Nick and Bastian would leave Madison. The possibility glitters darkly in her mind. She wonders how long it would be good for. A year? Six months? Maybe no time at all if she told him what was going on with the villa.

She forces herself to step away from him. 'You didn't think it was too much. For you, Bastian, nothing would ever be too much.' Her voice has turned steely. She can feel her blood rushing in her ears, egging her on. 'Just like nothing is ever enough. It made you feel amazing. When it comes to adoring you, I'm the best you ever had. That's why you're here. The big house in Italy, now you've run out of money, is just a bonus.'

Bastian is about to say something when the ground beneath them shudders again. Debris from the renovation, the tools left behind by Angelo's men, all of it rattles. It's the strongest one yet. Interminable seconds pass and then it stops.

She doesn't notice Bastian's approach. He's suddenly inches away, reaching out to cup her face in his hands. She doesn't pull away, too frightened by the tremor to move.

He lifts her chin and kisses her on the mouth. 'You were always too clever for your own good. So much going round this head of yours.' He presses his thumbs into her temples, slightly too hard.

'Didn't . . . Haven't you been listening to what I've been saying?'

'You need to think less and feel more now.' He kisses her roughly, his tooth catching on her lip for a moment.

It's still good. Good enough to make her dizzy. But she pulls away again, makes herself walk to the other end of the room. He lets out an impatient noise, which she ignores. When she turns, his foot is tapping the floor, his jaw is tight again.

'I never wrote any of the bad stuff down in those diaries,' she says. 'I was ashamed to admit I was putting up with it.'

'Why are you being like this?' He tries to modulate his voice, but she knows him well enough to hear the anger creeping in. 'Why are you trying to ruin this?'

'One of the things I didn't write down was that night at Theo's. His twenty-first. It was themed like a frat party, I guess in your honour. Do you remember what happened with him and you and me? Do you remember the video camera?'

'This is bullshit. I came all this way –'

'I didn't ask you to,' she interrupts. 'I didn't ask for any of this.'

'Yes, you did. You were bored out of your mind before I came back into your life.' He sees her face. 'You deserve more, is what I'm saying. You deserve the best.'

'And that's you, is it?'

His jaw tightens again. 'Well, it's not Nick, is it?'

'Nick's a good man.'

He sneers. 'But you don't want him. You want me.'

'I don't know if I do. Not the real you, whoever that is. I made up the person I wanted. Lou tried to tell me.'

'Fuck Lou.'

She flinches but doesn't look away.

'I came here for you,' he says, coming towards her. 'I've just destroyed my relationship and, what, you don't want me now?' His voice rises and his hands curl into fists. She automatically steps backwards, stumbling slightly over some loose rubble. Her female instincts scream inside her: apologize, smooth, make it OK again. She forces herself not to. Her legs feel like they might give way.

'I didn't ask you to come,' she manages to say again. 'And now I want you to go.'

As she says it, the room begins to move again, more violently this time. There's noise but, as before, it's so integral to the shaking that it's indescribable, pitched somewhere beyond normal hearing. Then it stops. Silence comes down like a blanket.

She finds she's half crouched, hands out for balance. It's fundamentally terrifying, this proof that the ground is not *terra firma* after all. When she's afraid on a plane, she loves coming in to land even though she knows it's the most dangerous part. She just wants to leave behind the uncertainty of thin air. Now it's the other way round: she wishes she could be lifted up and away from the treacherous ground.

Bastian is eyeing the ceiling, where a fine shower of plaster dust is raining down from one corner where it seems to be sagging. It suddenly occurs to her that she can leave, that she must leave before it starts up again and the whole lot comes down on top of them.

She straightens up but then Bastian closes the gap between them and grabs her by the elbow, holding her fast.

'Wait a minute.'

She tries to wrench her arm back but he's too strong. A vein stands out on his biceps, winding up and over the tight swell of it.

'What are you doing?' Her voice shakes. 'We need to get out of here.'

'I haven't finished talking to you yet.' His expression is set hard. 'You need to hear what I have to say.'

'Are you insane? That ceiling could come down. There could be another tremor in a minute.'

'I want us to talk upstairs. I want to remind you what we've got together.'

The room begins to move again. A shrieking sound makes her cry out. It's coming from the fabric of the building. It stops again – the movement and the noise – but the fall of plaster from the ceiling has become a steady stream. The bulge in the ceiling has swelled and spread.

'Bastian.' She fights to keep her voice low and calm. 'We need to leave. Now.'

'Not until you've heard me out.' He pulls her towards the stairs and she sees that they've been partly wrenched from their moorings. They creak horribly as he pulls her up them.

He's gone mad, she thinks. He's lost it.

What Madison had said tonight about their financial

situation is frightening her. Money stuff – debt, fear of losing everything – makes men do crazy things. Look at Nick. But where Nick despairs, Bastian is angry, profoundly outraged that he should be humiliated and thwarted.

They're halfway up the stairs when a voice rings out.

'Stop there.'

Bastian swings round, Laura stumbling down a step as he half takes her with him. Madison is in denim cut-offs and a worn grey T-shirt, her hair scraped back into a high ponytail. She looks beautiful. Laura is half-surprised there's no raised gun.

'Where are you going?'

'Where does it look like?' he sneers.

'Maybe it's me, but I don't think she wants to go.'

'Why don't *you* go? No one wants you here.'

'Yeah? Laura seems kinda relieved.'

If she was ever that drunk, Madison seems completely sober now.

'You thought I passed out,' she says to Bastian, as though she's overheard this thought. 'But I was just biding my time. I wanted to see what you'd do.'

'Oh, but we –' Laura breaks in. 'I mean I wouldn't have done. It was just once.' She stops.

Madison waves a hand. 'I don't mean that, or not just that. I mean I wanted to hear what he said to you, how he explained away the money stuff. What did he say? How'd he get you down here?'

'The lights were on. They were all on in the villa too, when we got back.' She swallows. 'Angelo's men have been trying to scare us.'

'What?' Bastian's grip on her arm loosens slightly and she shakes it free.

'Nick owes them money,' says Laura. 'There's a boundary issue. That would probably go away if we had the money. But we haven't. We're almost out.'

There's a silence and then Madison starts laughing. 'Shit, I *knew* Nick was in over his head. So basically everyone's broke except me.'

Bastian stills. 'You? What the fuck's so special about you?'

Madison smiles. 'You got me to do the money stuff because I was real good at it, remember? You made fun of me for being so careful, for my little filing cabinet in the basement, but that was because you've never known what it is to have nothing. I've looked after all of it for years. The mortgage, the cars, insurance, everything.'

'So you got the house insured. Who gives a shit? I'm not talking about the bills. I'm talking about the investments I told you to make.'

She seems to consider, eyes glittering. 'It's a good job I didn't make them, then, isn't it?'

'What? What about that project Jeff wanted me in on, and the start-up thing? What about . . .' He grinds to a halt. He's so alert Laura can feel it vibrating off him. 'You're not smart enough, Madison.'

'No? You sure about that?' Madison puts her head on one side. Her shining ponytail swings. She laughs and looks at Laura. 'When I was a kid, my mom had this old tin box hidden under the sink. She'd put loose change in it, the odd dollar bill, anything she could squirrel away. Only I knew about it. The men of the house didn't lower themselves to looking in kitchen cupboards anyway. Every couple months when I was little, when we still got on, she and I would go for a sundae together, just the two of us.'

Bastian makes a dismissive sound. 'Here we go again with the hillbilly shit. What the fuck has your *poor downtrodden momma* got to do with anything?'

Madison smiles. 'And you think I'm the dumb one. I'm saying I've been doing the same as her, all along, but I haven't been wasting it on sundaes. That filing cabinet you've never bothered looking in is my little tin box under the sink. Those investments you told me to make were bullshit. I saved the money instead. I made my own investments. Everything's safe as houses. I've even got you insured, baby. If some eighteen-wheeler takes you out on the freeway, I get three mil. And you consented to all this, by the way. Never read any of the forms I put in front of you, just signed your name.'

Bastian's face clears. 'So we have more than we thought? What about the second mortgage? Did that even happen?'

'Oh no, we got that. Well, you did. Anyway, when you're careful, it all adds up, you know. The only real loss is the money you got when you turned twenty-five. You blew that all by yourself – nothing I could do about it.'

He goes down a step, towards Madison. He's forgotten Laura. 'What do you mean, *you did*?'

'I mean, the second mortgage is in your name. I kept the cash. At first, anyway. Then I bought a seafront apartment in Malibu. I've been renting it out to this nice couple with a baby. But it's mine. If I need it.'

Bastian's expression turns weirdly fixed, manic. As he

shifts his weight to go down the rest of the stairs towards Madison, another tremor begins. He's the least clumsy person Laura's ever known, but he stumbles hard into the wall to which the staircase is no longer entirely joined, his feet going from under him. His head smacks into the plaster with a thud.

She hesitates but, as his eyes flicker open and he grimaces from the knock, another shudder beneath them spurs her into moving. She half trips past him, down the stairs towards Madison, where she stops, breathing hard. The two women face each other.

'Go,' says Madison. 'Get out of here before the whole thing comes down. I'll deal with him.'

'Madison, I'm – I'm so . . .'

'For God's sake, go.'

Laura is in the dead-centre of the clearing when it begins properly. No *scossa* this time, but a full-blown *terremoto*.

First there's a sharp jolt, like someone has thrown the brakes on the world. Then the shaking starts and this time it doesn't stop. The noise it generates is much louder this time, and it's more like how you'd expect the splitting open of the earth to sound: a guttural roar, or a gigantic wave as it breaks, except this one keeps on breaking.

Later, she learns it lasted just seventeen seconds. But this is enough for the structure of Giuseppe's House to fail. The chimney tumbles into the roof, which comes down through the top floor's ceiling, a huge supporting oak beam with it. This slams down into the staircase, causing it to collapse.

Of course, this is what will be pieced together afterwards. All Laura knows in the moment is that the lights in

Giuseppe's go out, the noise is deafening, the ground roils and undulates like water, and she can do nothing but crouch into a ball, making herself as tiny as possible until it's all over.

When it does stop, she grabs a handful of her skirt to cover her mouth and nose from the dust. It hammers down, not only dust but rubble. She covers her head with her arms until it's over. Slowly, slowly, as the dust literally settles, the moon comes on and, by its cool, miraculous light, she sees that Giuseppe's is no longer standing. Or at least the top half isn't. Where the upper storey was, there is nothing but air.

She stands and sways, dazed. Her head feels odd until she realizes that it's heavier than usual from the sheer amount of dust caked in her hair. She takes a cautious step, as though navigating cracked ice, but the ground holds firm. For now.

She turns to what's left of Giuseppe's. Bastian and Madison are still inside. She hesitates, torn. To the villa where Nick was sleeping, or to where she knows help will be needed. A cry decides her. She only just catches it, the sound faint. She has no idea which of them it might be.

The rubble gets larger as she gets closer to the ruined building. It's mingled with broken window glass and she treads carefully so she doesn't slice open her feet. The cry comes again. It sounds more female now.

'Madison?'

As she gets closer and the moonlight grows stronger, the atmosphere clearing further, she can see that the ground floor is not as comprehensively destroyed as she thought. The stonework around the door might have

gone but the window lintel has held. She has a sudden recollection of watching the golden eagle through its smeary
glass. That glass has now gone but for one long shard
somehow still clinging to the old putty. She covers her
hand with her skirt and knocks it clear, then clambers up
and over the sill, praying it holds, praying the pressure in
the earth far below has dissipated enough.

'Madison? Bastian?' She doesn't dare shout – the structure around her feels too fragile for that.

And then a glint of something bright. It catches the
moonlight for half a second, like the flash from a distant
lighthouse glimpsed at sea. It's gone then, but she goes
towards where it was. It shines briefly again and the dirt
around it moves. She realizes it's Madison's ring at the
same moment she takes in a patch of grey T-shirt and a
coil of hair, like a powdered wig.

She reaches for the ring and finds the hand. It's warm
and she squeezes it, feeling the faintest response. 'I'm
here,' she says. 'Madison? Come on, you need to get up.'

A low moan somewhere further into the gloom, where
the moonlight hasn't reached, makes her wheel round.

'Bastian. Bastian, can you hear me?'

She needs him to make another sound so she can follow it. Behind her, Madison screams in pain as she comes
to. When Laura turns, she is twisting on the floor, clutching her shoulder.

'Is it broken?'

Madison is apparently unable to speak. Her breathing is
shallow. Even through her coating of dust, she is ashen.
She grips her shoulder, closes her eyes. Her lips move as
she counts her out-breath.

Bastian moans again. Madison is in pain but not in danger so Laura moves gingerly towards him, through the matchstick remains of the staircase. Beams and spindles and planks lie piled up at odd angles. If it wasn't for the open sky, the stone floor under her feet, she wouldn't know which way was up. She sees him then, under a confusion of broken wood, like a giant's kindling. He blinks at her from the gloom of the small void he's trapped in, his long eyelashes thick and pale with dust.

'Can you move?'

He gathers himself, then pushes up hard, straining to lift the wood off his back. It shifts a little and she braces for a catastrophic collapse. It doesn't happen, but he's still stuck. She begins to lift the smaller pieces she's strong enough to move, one by one. There is so much debris, not just wood but chunks of plaster and broken furniture, even the statue of the Virgin Mary that was in the bedroom, now missing her head.

She feels like she's working against the clock. No doubt she is. Even if there's not another earthquake coming, there'll surely be aftershocks. Bastian pushes up again, bellowing with the strain of it, and the pile shifts a little more. There's one huge beam he won't be able to move, that he's lucky didn't kill him outright. Even with her help, there won't be any moving it, but if there's enough time, they can probably make a gap he can squeeze through.

But there's not enough time. The vibrations begin again, not with a jolt but a slow shake, which builds. She hopes to God this is a good thing, that this means it *is* an aftershock and not a new earthquake that will dwarf the one before. Even as she's thinking this, the far wall, at the back of the house, begins to sway, rippling in a way that a solid wall cannot possibly survive. It collapses inwards with a mighty crack that sends a new layer of dust up and over them.

She and Madison scream as it comes down. Bastian is too intent on freeing himself. He begins to scrabble at the stuff trapping him as the shaking continues. Laura, like him, knows with absolute certainty that the other walls will follow suit.

'Laura. Laura, please.'

She turns. It's Madison. She's lying on her back in the rubble, trembling hard with shock. 'It's dislocated. I can't get it back in,' she mutters, through gritted teeth. With an almighty effort, she rolls onto her front and tries to crawl towards the door but she can't seem to get to her feet or lever herself past the bigger pieces of rubble because of the pain she's in.

An old friend of Laura's had had a shoulder that dislocated. She can still remember seeing him on the school football pitch once, rolling in agony like Madison. She'd seen exactly how the coach had got it back in. She goes over to Madison with purpose, pulling her onto her back. Holding her tightly by the wrist, she lifts Madison's arm, ignoring her screams, until it reaches ninety degrees. It clunks home, the force and the internal tearing making Laura retch. Madison, though, instantly calms. It's in.

Around them, the shaking continues as if it will never stop. She rushes back over to where Bastian is still trapped and resumes her efforts, trying to move the biggest pieces of wood while he pushes from within. He bellows with frustration.

She stops. She knows to her marrow there is no time left.

She has to choose.

When the shaking and the roaring finally stop, she picks herself up and looks around. She sheds dust as she does, like she's made of it. Her ears ring. To her surprise, the world is still there. Behind her, most of the outbuildings remain standing, more or less. As the earth settles and the moonlight begins to filter through again, their silhouettes still approximate buildings, though Giuseppe's is now entirely lost, reduced to rubble.

'Come on,' she says, putting out her hand. 'Get up. It's over for now.'

They stumble uphill towards the villa. She expects to see it fallen, or at least mortally wounded: a foot-wide crack fissuring straight through the old stucco. There is fallen masonry and the line of the roof looks wrong, like an old mouth without its false teeth, but it's basically OK. Luna Rossa is still standing.

A figure stands before it, shaken but unharmed. Nick. He looks at the two of them in turn. 'Bastian,' he says. 'Where's Bastian?'

Laura can't speak and only shakes her head, but Madison can.

'He's gone,' she says.

Day 13

Somehow she sleeps. It's fitful – aftershocks and dreams of Bastian jerking her out of it – but when she wakes the sun is high, blazing on as if nothing has happened.

The sheets are gritty with dust and tiny stones, and her body is bruised and grazed all over. Three fingernails are broken off below the quick, queasily sensitive when she rubs at the skin there. *Bastian is dead.* The truth hits her again and she has to lie very still so she doesn't throw up.

Nick is in the kitchen when she makes it downstairs, drinking coffee at the table, and it's just like so many other mornings, except that the contents of the cupboards are smashed, the ceiling plaster cracked and *Bastian is dead*.

She goes to her husband and curls into his lap. His black eye is livid in the bright light, the exact colour and shine of a new aubergine.

'I've spoken to the police,' he says. 'Well, I tried. I'm not sure how much detail was understood. They thought this house had collapsed at first, but I think they got it eventually – that it was another building on the land, and that only one person was inside. They're sending an ambulance to collect . . .' He tails off. 'I was thinking I should ring the American authorities, maybe. Like the consulate or whatever.'

'Yes.'

'Laur, what are we going to do after this?'

'About Angelo?'

'About us.'

She buries her head in his chest, smells his smell.

'We'll always be friends,' he says, into her dusty hair. 'I'll always love you.'

She nods, biting down on her lip so she doesn't cry. He's right about this, though. About them. She knows he is. She can't speak so she squeezes his hand. He squeezes back.

They sit quietly for a while.

It's Nick who breaks the silence. 'I'm going to sort the money stuff out for you, OK?'

'No, not just for me. For you, too.'

'Yeah, but it's you I need to . . .'

'Nick,' she says, to stop him. Because they're entwined, she feels him go still. 'Part of the reason we've ended up here is because you were always trying to make it up to me. For the baby stuff, for the messages with Jo. You've got to stop now. I'm not saying this to be cruel but it's made it worse. In a weird way, you've made it all my fault.'

'How have I?'

'Because it's like everything you've done for the last couple of years was to make me happy, or to protect me, or be forgiven by me. It's cast me as this person who is so difficult to please that I've driven you to making all these ridiculous decisions behind my back. That none of the Angelo stuff would ever have happened if I'd just been more reasonable.' She pulls away from him to see his expression.

He looks crushed. 'That isn't how I thought of it at all.'

'No, but that's how it makes me feel.'

He shakes his head. 'I just wanted everything to be perfect for you.'

'And how's that panning out so far?'

There's a beat and then, thankfully, he smiles. 'Yeah, actually really amazingly. I've surpassed all expectations in my astute handling of this.'

They laugh, then fall quiet simultaneously. She knows he's remembered about Bastian too. Not just that he's dead, which still feels unreal and perhaps always will, but what she did with him.

'I had a call from Tommaso just before you came down,' he says, after a long moment.

'Oh, Christ. What did he say?'

'I didn't pick up. I couldn't face it. He left a voicemail.'

Something in Nick's tone makes her swivel round in his lap to look at him properly.

'And?'

'I think he'd heard about Bastian.'

'Already?'

'It was maybe half an hour after I spoke to the police. We know he and Angelo have connections.'

Her heart has started to beat hard. 'Tell me what he said.'

'It wasn't so much what he said. It was how he sounded, which was totally unlike the arrogant little shit he is. It took me a minute but then I got it. He was nervous. Really nervous. He said that, because of the earthquake, they'll have to postpone the rest of their work here. He apologized, twice. Then he said something about regulations. I couldn't really make it out, it was so garbled.'

'Regulations?'

'Yeah, as in earthquake regulations. You know they're pretty hot on it here. He told me weeks ago that we had to pay for Giuseppe's to be retrofitted so it complied. They had supposedly done that already, though I couldn't see that they'd done anything structural. I was trying to talk to him about it the other day, when Bastian told them to leave. When I left you on your own with the men. Anyway, we definitely paid for the work. I've got the bloody bill.'

'But if they didn't do it properly then that's . . . that's manslaughter, isn't it?'

Nick shrugs. 'Maybe. It should be. But I don't think we'll hear from them again.'

'Does this mean the boundary issue has basically gone away?'

He crosses his fingers.

'So it wouldn't be a huge complication if we sold up?'

'No.' He shrugs. 'If we wanted to sell up.'

'Don't we have to, if we're . . .?'

He smiles sadly. 'We could share it, maybe. Not live in it together, obviously. But keep it. Get someone to run it for us as a rental, maybe. I've grown more attached to it than I thought I would.'

'I don't know, Nick.'

'No. Maybe you're right. As usual.'

They both look down at the floor. She knows, like her, he's trying not to cry.

She pushes out a laugh, though it sounds more like a sob. 'Maybe Madison could buy us out. She's a wealthy woman now.'

Nick looks up. 'What do you mean? I thought Bastian . . .'

'Madison took things into her own hands years ago. Saved money he'd told her to invest, bought her own apartment on the quiet. There was life insurance, too. A lot of it.'

'God.'

'Yes. Not her mother's daughter after all.' She glances up at the ceiling. 'How is she, by the way? Have you seen her?'

'She's asleep, I guess. I didn't want to disturb her.'

'I should go up. She's still lost her husband.' She uses the term deliberately.

As she stands, her balance feels off and she sways on the tiles, heart clutching in fright. But it's not another aftershock. Nick is still staring into his empty coffee cup. It's just her balance's memory of the pitching earth, as after a day on a boat, the shifting sea felt long after dry land has been reached.

At the foot of the stairs she pauses at the mirror. Her reflection is deathly pale and she's not sure how much is dust and how much is shock. When was it she stood there, Madison half a head taller behind her, fixing the velvet headband into place? That it wasn't weeks or days ago, but only last night, is impossible to absorb.

She knocks before she goes in. She can picture Madison so clearly on the bed – grey T-shirt torn, bruised legs hugged to her chest, open eyes blank with shock – that it takes Laura whole seconds to understand that she's not there.

The bed is neat. It looks unslept in. In a square of sun that hurts to look at are two items. A note and a diamond ring. Laura picks up the ring first, sliding it on over her wedding band. It's too big and the stone swings with its own weight, bouncing sparks across the room. She picks up the note. Madison's handwriting is surprisingly elegant and old-fashioned. There's only a single line.

Maybe I should have hidden it under the sink for you.

An enigma to the end, Laura isn't sure how Madison intended either the note or the strange and unexpected gift of the diamond. On the one hand, the ring represents the relationship Laura helped destroy. On the other, it's a windfall that releases her – and Nick – from a significant amount of debt. Freedom and guilt in a fragment of cut and polished carbon. She squeezes her hand into a fist, the stone's edges sharp against her soft palm.

Treading carefully, mindful of possible instability, she steps out onto the wrought-iron balcony that she never really got to enjoy, shading her eyes against the fierce sun. The valley looks unchanged at this distance. Seemingly benign and eternal, there is no sign of yesterday's violence in the natural landscape. It's only in the few buildings that dot the far slope that damage is visible, if you look closely enough: tumbled walls and sunken roofs.

It's still beautiful, of course. But she understands that it's also indifferent, to her and everyone else. She remembers how, when they first came here, the place had seemed to call to her. *Aspetta, signora! Wait!* Now she knows it doesn't care whether she's here or not and, though that should make her feel sad or alone, there's something liberating about it. Heavy obligation has lifted away. So has the past.

She turns to look at the pale pitted lane Madison must have left by, alone in the big hire car in the early hours of the morning. Laura knows she'll never see her again. It's brutal to think it but Bastian's death has opened up new possibilities for both of them. Apprehension sparks inside her but there's more hope than fear. She knows it'll be her turn soon: driving away with the window down, hot air streaming in, dust rising in her wake.

Acknowledgements

Summer Fever began as a story about a marriage going wrong but ended up being as much about female friendship and solidarity, which is why I've dedicated it to the women in my life. With that in mind, I must first thank my brilliant editor Jillian Taylor, who always understands what I'm trying to do, and always makes it better. Huge thanks, too, to Grace Long, Sophie Shaw, Jen Harlow, Beatrix McIntyre, copyeditor-extraordinaire Hazel Orme, and fellow MJ writer Costanza Casati – who was kind enough to check my terrible Italian. Thank you also to my wonderful, endlessly empathetic agent, Becky Ritchie at AM Heath.

I'm always saying how grateful I am for my writer friends, and how they've been the best thing about being published, but it bears repeating. Thank you to Hayley Hoskins, Amanda Reynolds, Rosie Walsh, Emylia Hall, Emma Stonex, Katie Fforde, Katherine Webb, Jenny Ashcroft, Cesca Major, Sarra Manning, Iona Grey, Lucy Foley, Hannah Richell, Jo Harkin, Dany Atkinson, Kate Thompson, and all the amazing Swans and Stroud/Cheltenham writers. Big love also to The Novelry gang, particularly the inimitable Louise Dean, who helped me get a first draft of this book written in three short months. Lastly, a special mention for my best pal and bookish sister, Claire McGlasson. What would I have done without you last year?

Huge thanks and love to my family, whose unwavering support I so appreciate. Mum, Steve, Joan, Sarah, John, Sophie, James and of course Jasmine. And not forgetting my lovely dad, of course, who we lost in early 2021. He was so proud of me for getting published. Dad, you're much missed. Big love also to my non-book friends, many of whom have been in my life for more than half of it now: Bruna Magor, Darren Loftus, Chris Spellman (see?), Jade and Josh Bell, Des Yankson, Tim Ovenden, Dwy and Rod Owen, Helen Hockenhull, the Keohanes, the Chapmans and the Laceys.

Author's Note

I haven't made explicit in the story exactly when it's set but Laura's age makes it 2019, just before the pandemic hit. I've also taken the liberty of entirely ignoring Brexit, which I can't imagine many readers will mind, whatever they voted. Please excuse any errors on the finer points of Italian property law, land ownership and earthquake regulations – they are all my own. Perhaps it's also worth pointing out that my depiction of Exeter University is fictional, and not drawn from my own experiences there, although I think there are many details my fellow graduates might recognize . . .

WANT MORE
SUN-DRENCHED SUSPENSE?

DISCOVER THE MUST-HAVE
RICHARD & JUDY PICK

READ ON FOR AN EXCERPT…

We follow the slower, narrower D roads after Lyon, sunlight slanting through long lines of poplars. I'd forgotten the meticulous commitment to signposting every minor village and hamlet, not just when you enter but when you leave too, the name slashed through with red. The countryside around us feels endless after London: age-softened farmhouses and the occasional shuttered restaurant marooned at the margins of vast fields. I glance over at you, drinking it all in. It must be so exotic to you, yet it's where you spent your first four years.

The sun climbs as we drive, the car growing steadily hotter. You fiddle with the radio, snorting with derision at the terrible French pop songs but stopping when you find a station playing Edith Piaf. I wind down the window and, in the first blast of air, I smell the past. It's indescribable. The closest I can get to it is hot stone, lavender and a distant note of something like panic.

Half a mile from the house, we almost get lost, which seems absurd given that I've lived more of my life in this part of the world than any other. A petrol station has appeared on a corner once occupied by a peach stall we used to stop at, and this throws me enough to miss first the turn and then the sign. It's only when we're suddenly in the heart of the old village – the dappled shade of the plane trees, the café's round silver tables and the dusty awning of the *boulangerie* all utterly unchanged – that I realize where we are.

I turn the car around with a screech, not yet ready to be seen by anyone who might know me, and soon we're bumping down the dirt road to La Rêverie.

Quite abruptly, more quickly than is comfortable, we reach the rutted track that winds down to the ramshackle barn where logs for winter fires were stored, along with the rusting rollers and ancient farm tools my father pointlessly hoarded. I don't look at it, driving round to the front of the house instead.

I turn off the engine. You're silent next to me. I reach out to tuck a loose strand of hair behind your ear: English mouse and a little ragged at the ends because you're always trying to grow it longer. You've made me promise you can have it streaked when you turn sixteen. *I want it blonder*, you've been saying all spring. *Not this nothingy colour.*

'Mum, I don't think I remember this,' you say now, your voice high and young. 'I thought I did, when we turned off, but . . .'

'It might come back,' I say, hoping it won't, that everything from that time has been permanently erased. You were so young when we left, and I tell myself, as I have so many times, that that's why you've apparently forgotten everything.

We get out and the ticking under the car's bonnet echoes the cicadas that fill the bushes around us. Their cries will get faster and more frenzied as the day wears on, the sun steadily climbing, the temperature rising. '*Écoute, chérie. Écoute les cigales*,' my mother used to say when I was little, in a bid to stop me running outside and getting overheated. *They'll tell you if it's too hot to go out today.* I'd forgotten that.

The house is exactly as a foreigner would picture a *maison de maître* in the South of France: thick grey stone and a steeply pitched roof, tall symmetrical windows concealed by mauve-blue shutters, the paint powdery with age and the ferocity of the sun. The garden that surrounds it is walled at the front and topped with railings. I push back the metal gate, whose letter box still bears my maiden name in faded letters, and it swings in easily, as if used every day.

Inside, the bougainvillaea spills over the grass and the lavender bushes have gone woody and sparse, but it isn't as unkempt as I imagined a garden abandoned for a decade would be. It still looks like the place I remember. Weeds grow up through the path to the door, but the dense column of cypress that casts one side of the house into deep shadow always needed cutting back, even in my earliest memories. I glance up at the furthest bedroom window, the one most obscured by the cypress's deep shade, and see that one of the shutters has slipped its hinges.

By my side, you crackle with something: anticipation, mostly, but also a little fear. Perhaps you've caught it from me.

'Was that her room?' you ask.

I look sharply at you. 'That's right. Do you remember?'

'Just a guess.'

You look at it hungrily then, as if the braver part of you wants to believe someone is up there now, watching you through the gaps in the shutters. The cicadas have stopped, and the silence is unnerving. Then, in miraculous unison, they start up again, even louder than before, and I stride determinedly towards the front door, fumbling in my bag for the key, knowing that if I don't go in right now, I might drag you back to the car and drive straight home.

The church-cool air of the darkened hallway smells of mingled damp and smoke from the recent fire. Beneath them, faint but bone-deep familiar, I can just discern La Rêverie's older scents: beeswax, butter-softened garlic and my mother's olive soap.

I'm so struck by this that it takes me a while to notice that your breathing has changed. I scrabble in the inside pocket of my handbag, praying that the inhaler I carry from habit rather than necessity is still there. At last my hand closes around plastic. I pull it out and shake it.

You're fine after a couple of puffs, though your hands are already beginning to shake – a side-effect of the drug seeping into your muscles.

'Okay now, darling?'

You nod, just once.

'It must be all the dust and damp,' I say, and you nod again, though both of us know that your asthma is triggered by stress and not by allergies.

While you're unpacking, I wander around the house, methodically opening each door, except the one I'm not yet ready for. The shutters scream as I push them back, revealing fat black flies in sinister piles on the windowsills. As the light floods in, dust swarms.

Last of all, I steel myself to go and look at the fire damage. I know it's in the scullery off the kitchen – *la souillarde* – a small space housing little more than a sink, draining board and a couple of curtain-fronted cupboards that remains dark and cool however stifling it gets outside.

Its window is no bigger than a sheet of paper, with chicken wire instead of glass in the frame.

Though the smells of fresh damage are strong when I open the door, it's not as bad as I've been imagining since I received the letter. Two of the whitewashed walls are now marbled with black. In places, the marks are as high as my head. It's hard to tell what is scorched and what is mould, the evidence mingling darkly. But whatever happened here, water must swiftly have followed fire. Otherwise the whole house would have gone up.

As evening begins to thicken around the house, you ask if we can go and eat in the village. We walk the ten minutes in, the tarmac soft under our feet, legs shiny with insect repellent in preparation for the evening's emerging mosquitoes. The sun has already dipped behind the hills by the time we sit down at a table outside a pizzeria that wasn't here before. We're overlooking the tree-shaded patch of earth where the old men always played *boules* in their caps and braces, and doubtless still do, though they're not out for the evening yet.

You ask me to ask the waitress for a Coke, too shy to try speaking in French, and I order a beer instead of my usual wine. When it comes, so cold that droplets of condensation have formed on the glass, I gulp it down like water and gesture for a second.

I catch your disapproving look and smile. 'I saw that, my little puritan. It's not like I've got to drive.'

'It must be strange being back,' you say cautiously, when you've finished your food. You're swirling a plastic stirrer around your Coke glass.

I nod, though the second beer has made it less so.

'Do you miss it now that you're here?'

I look up, surprised at your perceptiveness. On leaving for London when you were four, I bundled everything into a deep drawer marked 'France' and slammed it shut, forgetting there was so much to love about home.

'I'm sorry I've kept you from the house for so long. You were born here too. It's as much yours as mine.'

You glow. 'It is?'

I smile and squeeze your hand.

'Mum, are you sure there's no way of keeping the house? It's such an amazing place. We could come here every summer. We could.'

I bat away a moth as it dances close to my eyes. 'It's impossible, *chérie*. I would need to buy out your aunt Camille and I can't afford it. You know what she's like.'

You frown, pulling your hand away, and for a split second you remind me of your sister. 'I don't think you'd do it even if you did have the money.' And then, as if you've heard my thoughts. 'It's because of her, isn't it?'

I dig my fingernails into the table edge. 'Emma, do you have any idea how hard it is for me to be back here?' The alcohol makes the words sharp and I regret them immediately. 'Look, let's not argue. I'm sorry I didn't bring you before, but we're here now, aren't we?'

You don't reply but after a while you nudge my hand in apology. Quite suddenly, I want to cry.

The walk back from the village is dark. No, not dark: pitch-black. The stars have been blotted out so thoroughly by clouds that it takes until we reach the turn-off before I can distinguish the shadowed bulk of the hills from the sky.

Despite the lack of visible moon, La Rêverie seems to stand in its own dim pool of light as we approach. Or perhaps it's just our eyes, still adjusting to the countryside after years of London's perpetually thrumming glow. It looks bigger by night, a monster of a house rising out of its dark moat of garden. I don't look at the windows as we go up the path, keeping my head down, pretending to hunt in my bag for the key I'm already clutching.

Earlier in the afternoon, I had shaken out my mother's soft old linen, only a little musty, and made us up a bed each: the creaking mahogany double Greg and I once shared, which was my parents' before us, and one of the narrow twins in the bedroom next to it for you. Your old room has only its small cot-bed and I don't want you in there anyway.

'I remember this,' you exclaim, in the room that's been a spare my whole life, pointing to the faded blue *toile de Jouy* wallpaper, which, in one corner, has begun to peel. 'I used to sit on the floor and make up stories about the people.' You go closer, tracing a finger across the men in stockings, the ladies with their pompadours and fans. 'I remember them.'

I wake at exactly three in the morning, the dimly glowing hands of my travel clock a perfect L. Downstairs, at the very edge of my hearing, I hear the ormolu clock in the salon as it chimes the hour. The bright, metallic ting is a sound older than memory to me, one that marked a benign passage through all the nights of my childhood, and I turn over, comforted. I'm just slipping into a dream of my mother winding it when I sit up, the bed groaning with the suddenness of the movement. I haven't wound the clock.

The next morning I find you at the bottom of the terrace steps, barefoot in the long grass. I shade my eyes against the startling glare of the sun, my head tight from lack of sleep.

'I found the swimming pool,' you call up to me, full of glee. 'I didn't know there was one. It's so cool.'

You don't remember it from before. I try to smile: this is a good thing.

'Perhaps we can see about filling it, if the pump's still working,' I make myself say. You're a strong swimmer; I've made sure of that. I paid for years of lessons at an over-chlorinated municipal pool near our flat in London.

You look at me oddly. 'It's already filled.'

I know it was emptied ten years ago, when we left for good. Neither Camille nor I have touched it since.

But of course you're right. The water glimmers mysteriously through the row of parasol pines my conservative father planted in the fifties for the sake of his daughters' modesty. It isn't the blinding turquoise of resort swimming pools but deep, darkling jade. On overcast days I always thought it looked like green ink.

I kneel at the edge and dip my hand in. Hardly yet warmed by the sun, the water runs like chilled silk through my fingers. There are only a few leaves and insects floating on the surface, clustered at the far end. Someone has cleared it recently.

I wonder if Olivier Lagarde arranged it. Perhaps he wound the clock in the salon too. I have the strangest sense that these things are simply the house welcoming us back. And perhaps trying to keep us here.

I glance at my bare wrist. 'What time is it?'

'About half ten, I think.'

I get to my feet. 'I have to meet the solicitor at eleven, in the village.'

'I'm staying here.'

I pause. 'I thought you wanted to go to the hypermarket. You'll have to come with me if you do. I'm going there on the way back.'

You grumble as we walk to the house but I know you don't mind, really. You've never been the sort to put up much of a fight. My lovely biddable girl.

Only one other table is occupied at the café in the village – a couple, Dutch most likely: all long legs and hiking equipment.

'Darling, why don't you go and look in the *tabac* over there?' I hand you a crisp ten-franc note. 'Buy some postcards. The solicitor and I will be speaking in French.'

You blink, slightly stung, but go anyway, just as the waiter arrives.

Olivier Lagarde turns up just as you disappear into the shop across the square. He's much handsomer than I'd expected from my dim memory of his father. It's already hot and he's rolled up the sleeves of his shirt, his arms burnished against blinding white cotton and the chrome of his watch. His grip when he shakes my hand is firm and warm. As he sits down, the Dutch woman's eyes rake over him and I feel a little jolt that she might assume we're together.

'*Madame Winters, thank you for meeting me today.*' He smiles easily, appreciatively, his eyes intent when I meet them.

'*Please, call me Sylvie,*' I say, looking away first. '*And it's Durand again, actually. I'm divorced.*'

'*Bien sûr. Sylvie, then. You've seen the damage now, I gather, and that it's really quite superficial. I hope that was clear in my letter. I didn't want to worry you unduly. You were lucky, though. It could have been . . .*' He spreads his hands. There's no need to say how it might have turned out.

'*Do the police know who did it?*'

He shrugs. '*Kids with nothing to do, who else? It happens all the time in the countryside. Especially when people know a house is standing empty.*'

'*Have they arrested anyone?*'

He shakes his head. '*To them it's a small thing. They couldn't find any signs of forced entry. I'm sorry, Mada— Sylvie, but they weren't very interested. One of them said it was probably the Gattaz boys.*'

I nod. It's a name I haven't thought of since childhood. That and the French that comes so effortlessly is both liberating and rooting. No, confining. I wonder if this is how it's going to be: the inexorable descent into the past; the years in England flickering and fading at the horizon.

I take a sip of my coffee: tiny, bitter and delicious. '*I don't remember you. From growing up round here, I mean.*'

'*No, I went to school in Avignon. Stayed with my aunt during the week. My father insisted, but look how it turned out.*' He smiles wryly. '*I ended up here anyway.*'

'*Monsieur Lagarde,*' I begin.

'*Please, if I'm to call you Sylvie, you must call me Olivier.*' He smiles again, as though we've shared something intimate.

It occurs to me that he might be flirting but I'm so rusty I can't be sure.

'*D'accord,*' I say, inclining my head. '*Olivier. I said to you on the phone that it might be time we sold La Rêverie. We've been putting it off, my sister and I, and I'm not sure why any more. Maybe what happened is a sign that we should get on with it.*'

'*I can help you sell, if that's what you want. I can put you in touch with someone at Century 21. Martine. She's good. But you should know that it's a sluggish market. The old Pelletier farm has been empty for two years now.*'

He catches the waiter's eye, then looks back at me. '*Stay for another?*'

I find myself nodding and he holds up two fingers.

'*It's the best time of year for the tourists, at least,*' he continues easily. '*There's a chance someone like them*' – he nods at the couple in walking gear – '*might decide they want their own piece of France. Five good-sized bedrooms, a big garden with a pool: it would make an excellent holiday home for a family. Though we're slightly off the beaten track here, of course. Now, if it was an hour closer to the coast things would be easier . . . I said the same thing to your sister when we spoke.*'

The sun has moved so it's beating down on my head. I shift slightly towards Olivier to escape its glare and knock against the table. He puts out a hand to steady it.

'*Désolée,*' I murmur, aware of the heat rising in my cheeks.

Absurdly, I find myself wondering whom he would judge to be the more attractive of Camille and me. Your aunt was the archetypal Parisienne even before she was one. She always looked down on the ageing housewives in the village for their thickened waists and badly dyed hair. I hadn't seen her without an immaculately made-up face since she was eighteen. I run my hand through my own unbrushed hair, then make myself stop.

Across the square, you sidle out of the *tabac* and stop to turn a carousel of postcards.

'*May I say, Sylvie?*'

I wait, hoping he isn't going to say what I think he is.

He looks uncertain for the first time. '*I just wanted to say how sorry I was for your . . . loss. I hope you don't mind me saying this, but after what's happened at the house, I felt it would be strange not to.*'

This is why I hadn't wanted to see anyone who knew me from before. Though it feels like Olivier is coming from a place of genuine concern, I know what people in this village are like. Always hungry for more gossip, they're perfectly capable of filling in any gaps with speculation and guesswork. I wonder what they came up with about us, which rumours persisted, and firmed up over time into hard truth.

'*Thank you, it's kind of you to say so,*' I say. '*Though . . .*' I pause '. . . *I would prefer you not to mention anything about it in front of my daughter. In front of Emma. She doesn't know everything about . . . what happened here. About the fire – the old fire.*'

He nods and we finish our coffee in silence. I'm glad when you come sauntering over, hair shining in the sun, a paper bag in one hand and a chocolate ice-cream in the other.

'It's not even midday,' I exclaim in English. Olivier laughs, probably grateful the tension has been broken. I smile at him and, just like that, the awkwardness melts away. I can't help it, I like him.

'I love it here,' you say, eyes bright and imploring. 'I hope the house stuff takes ages.'

Olivier grins at you. '*Pas de problème, Mademoiselle.*' He switches to heavily accented English. 'In France, these things always do.'

Drained by the sheer size of the *hypermarché*, the two of us are lying prone next to the pool by two o'clock. The sun is fierce, like a physical weight pressing down, its effect almost like a sickness. I know I need to get on with things but my limbs have turned watery. I feel as if my hope to leave by the end of the week is spooling away, out of reach.

I drag over the only working parasol so it covers you and pull my own lounger into the dappled shade of the oleander tree. When I shut my eyes, patches of brightness bloom pale red through the lids. I'm just drifting into sleep when I hear screaming. I leap up and towards you without conscious thought, heart galloping, but you haven't moved. You're still sleeping, the headphones clamped over your head continuing to buzz.

I must have imagined it, teetering on the brink of dreams. I lie down again but can't settle, the echo of that phantom noise still reverberating in the heavy air. I recognize that scream. It's the same voice that murmured in my ear as I drove south. A girlish voice, melodic but threaded through with steel.

I go back to the house and find my eyes drawn to the *souillarde* door. Behind it, the cold tiles under my bare feet are a shock after the sultry garden. The air is like wading through river water, my arms goose-pimpling as I inspect the mould again, as if I might find clues written in its patterns.

I'm sure it's got worse overnight, the black marks beginning to spread around the small window like a dark, blurred-leaf creeper. I bought a spray that should bleach it away but I don't want to be in here. There's a prickling at the back of my neck, the kind that says you're no longer alone, though I know I am.

I'm just pulling the door shut behind me when I catch movement through the window. It's so brief that it's not even a shape, more a shift in the pattern of light out there by the barn.

An old gate is tucked into the overgrown hedge at the side of the lawn. It's rusted shut when I get to it, white paint blistered, and it screeches as I wrench it open. It doesn't look like anyone's used it since we left, which should be reassuring but isn't. It only adds to the dreamlike strangeness I can't shake, of a place simultaneously abandoned and alive, like pockets of heat and cold in the sea.

The patch of earth between the house and the barn is palpably hotter and drier than the garden. I don't go into the barn. I already know what the damage looks like in there.

I shade my eyes to check the path snaking away towards the drive. There are no footprints but, further away, something has raised a cloud of ochre dust. Out on the main road, the wasp drone of a moped engine fades out of hearing. Once the air clears, everything is still, baking in the afternoon glare. The only movement is the heat shimmer that warps the distant blue hills.

He just wanted a decent book to read ...

Not too much to ask, is it? It was in 1935 when Allen Lane, Managing Director of Bodley Head Publishers, stood on a platform at Exeter railway station looking for something good to read on his journey back to London. His choice was limited to popular magazines and poor-quality paperbacks – the same choice faced every day by the vast majority of readers, few of whom could afford hardbacks. Lane's disappointment and subsequent anger at the range of books generally available led him to found a company – and change the world.

'We believed in the existence in this country of a vast reading public for intelligent books at a low price, and staked everything on it'
Sir Allen Lane, 1902–1970, founder of Penguin Books

The quality paperback had arrived – and not just in bookshops. Lane was adamant that his Penguins should appear in chain stores and tobacconists, and should cost no more than a packet of cigarettes.

Reading habits (and cigarette prices) have changed since 1935, but Penguin still believes in publishing the best books for everybody to enjoy. We still believe that good design costs no more than bad design, and we still believe that quality books published passionately and responsibly make the world a better place.

So wherever you see the little bird – whether it's on a piece of prize-winning literary fiction or a celebrity autobiography, political tour de force or historical masterpiece, a serial-killer thriller, reference book, world classic or a piece of pure escapism – you can bet that it represents the very best that the genre has to offer.

Whatever you like to read – trust Penguin.